Too Wilde to Wed

BY ELOISA JAMES

BORN TO BE WILDE

TOO WILDE TO WED

WILDE IN LOVE

SEVEN MINUTES IN HEAVEN

A GENTLEMAN NEVER
TELLS (a novella)

MY AMERICAN DUCHESS

FOUR NIGHTS WITH
THE DUKE

THREE WEEKS WITH
LADY X

ONCE UPON A TOWER

AS YOU WISH

WITH THIS KISS
(a novella in three parts)

SEDUCED BY A PIRATE
(a novella)

THE UGLY DUCHESS

THE DUKE IS MINE

WINNING THE
WALLFLOWER (a novella)

A FOOL AGAIN (a novella)

WHEN BEAUTY TAMED
THE BEAST

STORMING THE CASTLE
(a novella)

A KISS AT MIDNIGHT

A DUKE OF HER OWN

THIS DUCHESS OF MINE

WHEN THE DUKE RETURNS

DUCHESS BY NIGHT

AN AFFAIR BEFORE
CHRISTMAS

DESPERATE DUCHESSES

PLEASURE FOR PLEASURE

THE TAMING OF THE DUKE

KISS ME, ANNABEL

MUCH ADO ABOUT YOU

YOUR WICKED WAYS

A WILD PURSUIT

FOOL FOR LOVE

DUCHESS IN LOVE

BY ELOISA JAMES

Too Wilde
to Wed

The Wildes of Lindow Castle

Eloisa James

HarperLuxe™ is a trademark of HarperCollins Publishers.

An Imprint of HarperCollinsPublishers

HarperCollins books may be purchased for educational, business, or sales promotional use. For information, please e-mail the Special Markets Department at SPsales@harpercollins.com.

FIRST HARPERLUXE EDITION

ISBN: 978-0-06-291242-8

HarperLuxe™ is a trademark of HarperCollins Publishers.

Library of Congress Cataloging-in-Publication Data is available upon request.

19 20 21 22 23   ID/LSC   10 9 8 7 6 5 4 3 2 1

This book is dedicated to my husband, Alessandro, because the simple joy of knowing he is mine underlies every happy line I write.

Acknowledgments

My books are like small children; they take a whole village to get them to a literate state. I want to offer my deep gratitude to my village: my editor, Carrie Feron; my agent, Kim Witherspoon; my Web site designers, Wax Creative; and my personal team: Kim Castillo, Anne Connell, Franzeca Drouin, and Sharlene Moore. While writing about North's experiences in America, I exchanged many e-mails with the Revolutionary War expert Jim Piecuch; my great thanks for his kind attention to my questions.

Lord Hon, Baron of Houston, Renfrewshire (Scotland), dances three times with Diana during a ball, incurring North's jealousy, because Dr. Johnny Hon was kind enough to bid energetically in a charity auction benefiting my daughter's public high school in New York City. When I offered a "character" to the auction,

I never imagined I might be given a real lord to depict in *Too Wilde to Wed*. Thank you, Dr. Hon!

People in many departments of HarperCollins, from Art to Marketing to PR, have done a wonderful job of getting this book into readers' hands: my heartfelt thanks goes to each of you.

Finally, a group of dear friends (and one teenage daughter) have read parts of this book, improving it immeasurably: my fervent thanks to Rachel Crafts, Lisa Kleypas, Linda Francis Lee, Cecile Rousseau, Meg Tilly, and Anna Vettori.

Too Wilde to Wed

Preface

Lindow Castle, Cheshire
County Seat of the Duke of Lindow
July 6, 1778
Betrothal party for Lord Roland Wilde and
Miss Diana Belgrave

Lord Roland Northbridge Wilde—known to his friends and family as North—had been taught at his governess's knee that a gentleman defines himself by his respectful and decorous manner toward the fair sex. He did not ask indelicate questions, nor engage in boorish behavior.

Even, or perhaps especially, if the lady was his fiancée.

It never occurred to North that he might be tempted to behave otherwise. As a future duke, he considered it beneath his dignity to kneel while asking Miss Diana Belgrave for the honor of her hand in marriage, but he donned a coat that had been praised by the king himself. The ring he slid on her finger had belonged to his grandmother, the late Duchess of Lindow.

He bent to kiss her cheek, registering how much he admired light gray eyes ringed with dark blue. She misunderstood, turned her head, and soft lips touched his.

That was the moment he grasped that civilized manners are no more than a thin veneer over the inner man. He found himself in the grip of a ferocious wish to engage in ungentlemanly behavior.

In the next weeks, he told himself over and over that an honorable man does not tempt his bride. Lord knew his older brother Horatius—who should have been standing in his shoes—wouldn't have succumbed to an undignified impulse.

Horatius had probably never had them.

Perhaps it was a good thing that North kept finding himself on the other side of the room from his fiancée. His father's house party at Lindow Castle—in honor of their betrothal—offered all too many opportunities to kiss in corners, or worse. He had the impression that his brother Alaric had abandoned all propriety in his pursuit of Miss Willa Ffynche.

Yet Diana never approached him, or sought him out.

She often made excuses and fled the room. Alaric had asked North outright whether his fiancée liked him.

Liked him?

North didn't think about whether people *liked* him. He was going to be a duke. It was irrelevant.

Now the question nagged at him.

He couldn't remember when he last heard Diana laugh, even though her joyful laughter was what first caught his attention. She didn't look like a young lady celebrating a betrothal. She didn't look as if she had captured the best prospect on the marriage mart.

She looked miserable.

At the moment his fiancée was staring out the window of the drawing room, her arms tightly wound about her middle. As he watched, she raised her hand and—whisked away a tear?

He made his way between his father's guests, thinking hard. It was too late to dissolve the betrothal. Besides, his gut-deep feeling that he wanted her had not eased.

Still, they had to talk.

Two minutes later, he ushered her into the library. When she looked up at him inquiringly, he registered that violet smudges lay under her eyes.

"Shall we sit?" he asked, but it wasn't really a question.

Diana sat, hands folded in her lap, and regarded him

mutely. She was an extraordinarily well-behaved young lady.

As a future duchess should be, he told himself.

His uneasiness growing stronger, he chose his words carefully. "Are you entirely happy with our upcoming wedding, Diana?" He almost said, "Miss Belgrave."

She returned his gaze for a moment before she looked down at her hands. "Certainly," she murmured.

Bloody hell. Alaric was right; she didn't like him. This match was a mistake.

But he still wanted her. And he was all too used to getting what he wanted. Perhaps she was merely shy. Perhaps . . .

Discarding the question of gentlemanly conduct, he tilted up her chin and lowered his mouth to hers.

For a second, they were frozen in place, like lovers in a painting. Her lips parted in surprise, and he couldn't help himself, coaxing her lips wider as he tasted her.

Her tongue met his, curious . . . innocent. He deepened the kiss, and her arms rose and curled around his neck. She made an inarticulate, sweet sound that hit him like a blow.

If he didn't stop now, he would ease her backward and kiss her until she moaned again and again, until she abandoned all propriety. Cried into his mouth, begged him for more.

Making an iron effort, he pulled back before he could lose control. Diana was staring at him, beautiful eyes wide, mouth open.

"You will be a marvelous duchess," North whispered, his voice deep and low.

For a moment he saw pleasure in her eyes, a surprised delight. But another emotion—sorrow? guilt?—followed just as quickly. She pulled away and jumped to her feet.

Before he could stand, Diana bobbed a curtsy and said that she needed to visit the ladies' retiring room to pin up her hem.

That was the last time he saw her.

She jilted him without a note, his ring left carelessly on her dressing table, along with her other jewelry. She took only a hatbox with her on the public stagecoach.

North traveled to London, but discovered Diana's mother knew nothing of her flight. He searched for months, and finally, on the eve of his regiment's leaving for America, he found her. Diana answered the door of a small cottage, far from London.

Sunlight loved her, he thought numbly. It lit the perfect cream of her cheek, the shadow cast by her fringe of eyelashes. Diana stared up at him in shock, a simple bonnet framing her face. Deluded fool that he was, he found himself memorizing every detail so that he could take it with him into war.

He could have sworn that she was happy to see him, if astounded to see him in uniform. Perhaps they could make this work. He could find out what made her flee, and fix it.

Then a cry sounded from behind her, high and young, full of tears. A baby, on the verge of wailing.

A child who couldn't be his.

Diana's eyes met his. "I'm sorry, North," she whispered. "I'm so sorry."

Frost settled deep in his bones, though perhaps he should have felt the chill in his chest. His world shifted.

Without another word, he turned and strode away, swung himself up onto his horse, and spurred it to a gallop.

The dust rose up to meet him and he welcomed it. An officer—and a gentleman—blinked his eyes to rid them of grit.

Never a tear.

Beatrix's Babble
By Subscription Only
March 12, 1780

Young ladies swooning over the infamous adventurer and author, Lord Wilde, may not realize that his older brother, Lord Roland, now rivals him in infamy. Beatrix has learned that the future duke's exploits on the American continent were many and of the sort that would make a proper woman faint dead away!

Matrons among us will remember that Lord Roland's engagement was abruptly broken off nearly two years ago . . . when the lady in question fled her own betrothal party. In a truly shocking turn of events, Beatrix has heard on the best authority that the lady has returned to Lindow Castle with a child in tow, and is now working as a governess! It is not a leap of intellect to assume that Lord Roland is in for quite a surprise when he returns from quelling the rebellion in the colonies.

Generally speaking, Beatrix prefers to not sully the ears of young ladies with stories such as these, but she feels it is important to note that mothers should take care: This particular Wilde is, by any estimation, Too Wilde to Wed!

Chapter One

Lindow Castle
May 15, 1780

Diana Belgrave rarely thought about the days when she'd been the pampered heiress who had taken London by storm and stolen the heart of a future duke. When she did, she found herself shaking her head.

She had been so impossibly young, willing to do anything to satisfy her ambitious mother—a feat that, with the benefit of hindsight, Diana knew to be impossible. Perhaps that was the definition of maturity: recognizing that pleasing everyone was not possible.

In the long run, she wouldn't have pleased her fiancé North (or, more formally, Lord Roland) either, or so she told herself when she was feeling guilty. After all, he hadn't actually proposed to *her*, to Diana. He had offered his hand to a quiet and biddable young lady, a role her mother forced her to play.

The flicker of desire she used to catch in his eyes? It wasn't for her, but for her mother's creation, that docile creature in towering, bejeweled wigs.

She had a distinct feeling that North had never liked the way he felt about her; his desire for her made him irritable, as if it diminished his power. As if it meant she possessed some part of him, and the future Duke of Lindow was used to being the absolute monarch of his world.

Just imagine how angry he would have become on learning that the woman he'd chosen as his consort wasn't really that woman at all.

With a sigh, Diana pulled herself back into the present. Once upon a time, she had been a future mistress of Lindow Castle; now she was a servant in it. More importantly, she'd been an unhappy young lady, but she was a very happy governess. Perhaps not a *good* governess, but she liked the work.

Most of the time.

Bending over, she scooped up her two-year-old charge, Lady Artemisia Wilde, and propped her on one hip. Then she turned to the three-year-old seated on the floor, drawing designs in mashed turnip. "Godfrey, do you need to use the chamber pot?"

Her nephew, Godfrey Belgrave, shook his head, which was lucky because at that moment Diana saw the chamber pot was lying on its side on the hearth rather than neatly hidden behind its screen.

Hopefully, it had been empty.

She smelled of turnip, and she was desperate for a cup of strong milky tea. But the tea was cold, and the last of the milk was dripping off the nursery table, joining the mash.

The housekeeper would shriek if she saw the children's dining room before Diana had a chance to clean it. Mrs. Mousekin never ceased to be stunned by the disarray that seemed to follow Diana and the children everywhere, but at this point, the housekeeper's outrage was mostly a habit.

Or so Diana liked to tell herself.

She couldn't seem to combine basic hygiene with a happy day for two toddlers.

"DeeDee." Artie sighed, pushing her fat little fingers into Diana's bun and pulling out a lock of hair, which made the entire coil fall down Diana's neck. It took a lot of energy to hurl food around the room, and Artie had woken well before dawn, so it was time for a nap. The child stuck the hair in her mouth and drowsily put her head on Diana's shoulder.

Diana took a deep, steadying breath as a wave of exhaustion bore down on her. It wasn't merely the long day, but the unnerving sense of doom hanging over her head.

North was home.

Those three words kept echoing in her ears. Her former fiancé had returned from the war in the colonies.

She had known he was on the way; she had sobbed with pure relief half the night after the duke announced his son was selling out. It meant she wasn't responsible for killing a future duke. As far as she could tell, their broken engagement had precipitated his decision to buy a commission. If he had died . . .

Well, he hadn't died.

She could move on from terror to guilt for all the other things she'd done to his life, most of which he didn't even know about yet.

In the last few minutes, two footmen had made excuses to run up to the nursery and warn Diana of the arrival of North—or Lord Roland, as she ought to call him now. Everyone in the household knew that the duke had ordered that no letters mention Diana; he hadn't wanted his son distracted by domestic matters in time of war.

To put it another way, everyone knew that North's supposed bastard was in the household—except North.

Perhaps no one would tell him she was here. After all, Artie's parents, the duke and duchess, were in London, and Lady Knowe, the duke's twin sister, rarely visited the nursery . . .

No.

If no one else, Boodle, his valet, would reveal the news. Boodle viewed North as an extension of his own consequence, so any slur on his master's reputation—and a bastard definitely qualified—was a personal insult.

Boodle must be in transports at His Lordship's return. After North left for the war, Boodle had served the duke, North's father, but he had found His Grace's complete lack of interest in his own appearance galling. Now that the duke's wildly fashionable heir had returned, Boodle would once again reign supreme over all other gentlemen's gentlemen—at least, after the knotty problem of North's by-blow was resolved.

During their betrothal, North had been starchily respectful. He had never laughed, belched, nor told a joke. He didn't get angry either. He kept a tight rein on his emotions. Perhaps laughter was too spontaneous for a duke's heir. Or perhaps he had no sense of humor.

No matter how calm his nature, any man would be explosively furious to learn that he—or perhaps even worse, his father—had been housing a child under false pretenses.

Diana straightened her shoulders, steeling herself. She was no longer the compliant girl she'd been. She was a strong and independent woman, who received a wage that she herself had earned.

She had many things she longed to say to North, and no matter how enraged he was—rightfully enraged—she meant to get them out. She refused to waste all the nights she'd been unable to sleep, anguishing over what she had done to him. Even if he kicked her out of the house tonight, she was going to apologize first.

"Gird your loins and do it properly," her grandfather would have told her.

Godfrey made his way over and grabbed her skirts with a sticky hand. He was not an attractive boy, being possessed of knobby knees, angular cheekbones, and rust-colored hair.

But he was *hers*, no matter what he looked like. Diana was still trying to understand how she could take one glance at a scrawny, wailing baby and know instantly that she would do anything—sacrifice anything—to keep him safe.

"Time for baths," she told the children. Halfway down the corridor, she paused to adjust Artie's weight on her hip. "Sweetheart, please don't drool on my neck. Godfrey, could you walk faster?"

She could have groaned at her own foolishness, because one only had to ask Godfrey to do something to incite him to its opposite. Sure enough, the little boy fell to his knees and scuttled back down the corridor toward the dining room.

"Godfrey!" she called, struggling to keep her tone even. He became naughtier if people shouted at him.

"I'll go," Artemisia said, spitting out Diana's hair and wriggling. "I'll get Free," which was what she called Godfrey. Godfrey didn't call his playmate anything because—at well over three years old—he still hadn't said a word.

As Diana put Artie on the floor, she heard footsteps creaking on the bare wooden stairs leading to the nursery wing. Panic raced through her veins.

No.

Her former fiancé wore high heels, she reminded herself. High heels. Striped stockings with clocks. Tawny silk coats. The type of wig that obliged its wearer to mince across the floor or risk it falling from a great height. He was dandified, proper, and boring.

North had been as much Boodle's creation as she had been her mother's.

A man rounded the corner; her heart thumped once and settled. It wasn't North, but the castle butler, Prism.

To her chagrin, Diana discovered that she had flattened herself against the wall, as if expecting the sheriff. She dropped into a jerky curtsy. "Good afternoon, Prism—" She coughed. "Mr. Prism."

The first few weeks she was in the nursery, she had made mistakes like that all the time—the result of having been raised a lady and hired as a servant. But she hadn't made one in well over a year.

Mr. Prism was tall and distinguished. To Diana, he appeared to be a gentleman, but Prism wouldn't agree. Hierarchy and blood were all-important to him; it didn't matter a whit that he had better manners than most lords. It had offended his sensibilities when a lady who had visited the castle as the guest of honor returned as a servant.

"Miss Belgrave." He didn't bow, but an invisible bow hovered around his waist.

"May I be of service?" Diana inquired. As a pampered young heiress, she'd always felt uncomfortable around servants, who never overlooked the fortune her grandfather made as a grocer. Now that she *was* a servant, she found most of them endlessly kind. Prism, for one, regularly ignored her mishaps in the nursery.

At that moment, she heard the tinkling clash of a handful of cutlery bouncing—or so she guessed—off the fire screen in the dining room.

Prism flinched. Everyone in the castle was familiar with Godfrey's naughty temperament. The servants loved comparing North's childhood pranks to Godfrey's.

That always made Diana feel guilty, since the two had nothing in common except childish misbehavior. She was so tired of the fib that had brought her to the nursery that it would almost be a relief to leave the castle—if only the idea of leaving Artie wasn't so agonizing.

Diana had seen Artie's first tooth and her first step. She'd stayed awake for three nights when Artie fell ill with a lung complaint; the duchess arrived from London to find her youngest daughter sitting up and asking for cake.

Another handful of cutlery clashed into the iron fireplace screen. In a powerful display of butlerian nerves, Prism managed to ignore it.

"Miss Belgrave, I wish to inform you that Lord Roland has arrived home and is currently with his valet, changing from his traveling costume. One would hope that Mr. Boodle will allow Lady Knowe to impart important information concerning the family."

From his disdainful air, Prism had no more faith in Boodle's discretion than Diana had.

Still, Diana felt a wash of relief, because now she had time to drink a cup of tea and rehearse what to say to North. It would take Boodle three hours at a minimum to wrestle his master into the luxurious garments of a future duke.

Boodle couldn't wait to dazzle the household once again with his valeting skills; he wouldn't allow his master to leave the bedchamber until North shone like a prize pig.

In Diana's humble opinion.

Whether in London or the castle, her former fiancé had always been impeccably attired—and that wasn't to mention the times she'd been almost certain he was wearing lip paint. No man's lips were that deep rose color.

She folded her hands at her waist, the way her own governess used to. "Thank you very much for the warning, Mr. Prism."

"Inasmuch as Lord Roland does not know that you and Master Godfrey are in the household, he may be surprised," the butler said, in a powerful understatement. "I wish to reassure you that His Lordship is a consummate gentleman, who will receive the news with equanimity."

Diana could attest to that, since at times she had felt as if she were engaged to a pasteboard version of an English nobleman . . . if pasteboard could bend at the waist and mimic all the airs and graces of a courtier. North was a gentleman through and through, and his emotions would be as muted as his clothing was extravagant.

They both turned their heads at the sound of someone quickly mounting the stairs to the nursery suite. Diana's heart jolted into a sickening rhythm against her ribs.

No three hours' respite.

No tea.

Prism was not a butler who would welcome being a witness to an uncomfortable encounter. "I shall speak to Mabel about her absence at morning prayers," he said, heading for the nursery dining room.

He was about to discover that the nursemaid had missed more than prayers, but Diana didn't say a word. The butler's horrified, "*Miss Belgrave!*" overlapped with North's arrival at the top of the stairs. Diana didn't respond to Prism, or allow herself to step back against the comforting wall. Instead, she kept her eyes fixed on her former fiancé.

North had changed. His face was leaner and more

angular, with weary crinkles at the corners of his eyes, making him look older than his twenty-nine years.

Surprising enough, he didn't appear to be angry. But he always had a face that expressed little emotion, thanks to a strong jaw, high cheekbones, and the effortless nobility that made him look as if he were posing for a portrait.

A portrait of a duke, naturally.

As he strode toward her, his boots clipped the floor. Boodle hadn't had time to transform his master into a future duke; North was still dressed for travel, his black riding frock splashed with mud.

He stopped in front of her. If anything, he seemed faintly amused.

"The last time we saw each other here, you were headed for the ladies' retiring room," he observed. "That must have been one of the longest visits in the history of the castle."

"I should never have left without breaking our betrothal in person, or at least writing you a letter," Diana said, words she had longed to say for almost two years tumbling out of her mouth. "I'm so sorry, North. I'm just so *sorry*. I behaved terribly, and—"

She broke off as Prism reemerged from the dining room, his cheeks drawn as tight as those of a boy sucking lemons. "Lord Roland," he said, bowing. Turning to Diana, "Where is Mabel?"

"In the dairy," Diana said. "She'll return soon, Mr. Prism."

"*Mr.* Prism?" North repeated. His eyebrows locked together.

Boodle must have told him she was employed as a servant; did he think that Diana could continue to address the butler the way a lady might? What was proper for a guest was insolence in a servant.

"I shall send Mabel back to her post," Prism said, ignoring North and fading toward the stairs as only a butler could do.

Diana turned back to North, trying to decide if she should move on to the subject of Godfrey, or repeat how apologetic she was to have jilted him in such a public fashion.

"Who is Mabel?" North asked.

"She's the nursery maid. I'm the governess," Diana explained. "I'm really more of a nanny, but Lady Knowe was kind enough to give me the title. Mabel has fallen in love and is often absent from her post." She hesitated, and added, "I apologize again for the graceless way I ended our betrothal."

He didn't shrug, but his expression made it clear

that he couldn't have been more uninterested. It was ancient history to him; she was the one who couldn't forget her bad behavior.

"Diana," North said, "what are you doing in my home?" A hint of ironic humor lurked in his eyes, but mostly, he just seemed tired.

That look he used to give her? The one that promised secret delights?

Gone without a trace.

Of course, it was gone. She wanted it to be gone.

"I might add that my valet is under the impression that I fathered your child," he said, his voice even.

"There wouldn't have been time for that," she blurted out. "Not between all those lectures you gave me about the duties of a duchess."

With an inward groan, she added that sentence to the list of stupid things she had instantly regretted saying. Some days the list grew hardly at all. Others . . . Well, other days she embarrassed herself fifty times before bedtime.

Genuine surprise crossed North's face. Of course, he believed she was the meek creature whom her mother had tailored to a nobleman's specifications.

"I shouldn't have said that," she added quickly. "I seem to have forgotten the rules of being a lady, let alone a future duchess. Servants tend to be much more direct. More to the point, I didn't bring it up as a defense for my behavior."

"I was trying to ease your entry into the peerage," North said. He didn't raise an eyebrow, but somehow he managed to give his words a sardonic air without moving a muscle. "I apologize if I made you uncomfortable, or bored you."

"Imagine, you almost married a woman whose heart belongs in the servants' hall," Diana said, offering him a tentative smile. "You should be on your knees thanking me for running away."

"As I recall, I didn't kneel when I proposed to you," North remarked. "I think we both agree that we are better unmarried, at least to each other."

He was right, so it was absurd that his comment stung. It wasn't what he said as much as the indifferent look in his eye. Whatever affection he had felt for her was gone.

She had behaved appallingly. Not worth his . . . his affection, if that's what it had been.

His earlier sentence sank in, and she said with a little gasp, "You didn't tell Boodle the truth?"

"I am a gentleman, Diana. I judged it best to inquire about your intentions as regards my supposed son."

As she stared at him, a crash sounded from the dining room—and this time, it wasn't knives and forks, but china. Experience told her that Godfrey had managed to crawl onto the table and was now throwing plates over the side.

She turned and raced down the corridor. Artie might be in the path of shattered dishes, and the housekeeper had been threatening to deduct breakage from her wages.

Behind her, North barked, "Diana!"

Skidding into the room, she found Godfrey sitting in the middle of the table, Artie beside him, wrestling over a plate. Diana felt another stab of panic at the idea of separating them. Artie was Godfrey's tie to the world, the only person who really understood him.

"DeeDee," Artie shouted, dropping her side of the plate and waving her hands in the air. "Free is throwing things again."

Godfrey threw the plate into the wall at the precise moment North arrived at her shoulder.

Diana swept Godfrey off the table and put him on the floor, crouching before him. It was hard to ignore North's presence behind her, but she had learned that Godfrey only listened to her directly after he was disobedient. A delayed reprimand was the same as approval.

"Darling," she said, holding his eyes, "you must not break plates. It is very naughty, and it makes Mrs. Mousekin angry at both of us."

North had stepped up to the table. "You must be Artemisia," she heard. "I'm your oldest brother. We haven't met since you were a newborn."

"My name's Artie," his sister informed him.

Diana focused on Godfrey's face. He never spoke, but she was certain that he thought deeply. She had the idea that he might be smarter than the average child.

"Please promise me that you won't throw any more plates off the table or at a wall?" She had to be very specific when reprimanding her nephew.

Godfrey's limpid blue eyes were as sweet as an angel's as he planted a squishy kiss on her cheek. Her arms wrapped around him for a moment, and she set him free.

Artie swung her legs over the edge of the table. "Down." She lifted her arms to North.

The courtier Diana remembered, the man who wore violet-colored silk embroidered with silver thread, would have avoided a sticky child.

"She's a Wilde, all right," North muttered. He picked up Artie with no sign of distaste.

As he put her down, Mabel ran through the door. "You needn't have tattled on me to Prism—" Her voice choked. "Forgive me, my lord. I didn't know you were here." She curtsied, head bent.

"Are you responsible for the condition of this room?" North asked her.

Diana followed his gaze and saw that yellow liquid had soaked into the hearth rug from the overturned chamber pot. No wonder Prism had been so anguished. "No," she said quickly. "Mabel is not in charge of the children's manners; I am. So if you are going to scold, you should address me."

"Take the children elsewhere," he said to Mabel. Diana had forgotten his utter assurance. North ruled his world and every person in it, except his father and stepmother.

Another reason to be happy their marriage hadn't taken place, she reminded herself. She had always dreaded the moment when her fiancé discovered that subservience didn't come naturally to her.

"Certainly, my lord," Mabel murmured, adding in a dulcet tone that Artie and Godfrey rarely heard, "Come along, my dears."

North watched them leave the room before turning back to Diana. "My sister is sucking her thumb," he stated, clearly appalled. "She did not greet me properly. I'm not sure she knew *how* to greet me. Are you really her governess?"

Diana choked back a wayward giggle. It made odd sense that she saw strong emotion on his face only when it came to deficient etiquette. "Didn't Boodle inform you of my position?"

"My valet told me you were living in the castle along with a son of mine, and I could find you in the nursery. It did not occur to me that a woman who was to be my duchess might be employed among the domestics," he said, adding dryly, "I was preoccupied by the miracle of my fatherhood."

Diana's heart started thudding so hard that her chest hurt, but it would be too revealing if she rubbed it. "There is nothing shameful about having employment," she managed. "It's a good deal more respectable than spending one's life drifting around a parlor."

At the same moment she realized that military service to His Majesty's army was scarcely drifting around a parlor, he apparently decided that her remark was beneath his notice.

"*You* are the castle governess? Where are my other siblings?" North asked, glancing around as if his brothers and sisters might jump out of a corner at any moment.

"Viola, Betsy, and Joan are in London with Her Grace, as the Season is in full swing. Before you say anything, I have been an *excellent* governess to the girls, on those occasions when they were home from their seminary."

"What about the boys? Are you telling me that you are fit to tutor them in Latin?"

Diana certainly was not, since her mother had actively avoided teaching her anything other than ladylike skills; Mrs. Belgrave had been certain that lords preferred ignorance so they could tutor their wives. Frankly, North's repeated efforts to instruct her on the strictures of polite society had proved her mother's point, though it wouldn't be politic to point it out.

"Spartacus and Erik are at Eton and in no need of tutoring," she said, leaving it at that.

"Diana, allow me to ask you once again: What are you doing here? You left me, which was certainly your prerogative. Whether owing to my sermonizing on the duties of a duchess or not, we have had no child together."

Diana swallowed hard. Her second impulsive decision had come home to roost. "Lady Knowe came to see me shortly after you left for war."

His frown deepened. "She neglected to mention that visit in her letters."

"She found me desperate," Diana said, clutching her hands together so hard that her knuckles turned white. "My mother had thrown us out, and I had almost no money. Lady Knowe assumed the child was yours and shamefully, I allowed her to believe it. I am deeply sorry for that."

She searched his face. He still showed no signs of

rage, but he didn't appear forgiving either. Forgiveness was not something one could ask for, she reminded herself. She had learned that lesson from her mother.

"I have taken no support from your family," she said, a hint of pride entering her voice—because she *was* proud of being employed. It was about the only thing she was proud of. "The castle was in need of a nanny, so I took the position. It was your aunt's idea to hire me as a governess."

"Why?"

"A governess is one of the upper servants," Diana explained. "Lady Knowe thought it would be easier for the household to accept my presence, as governesses are often ladies. She was also being generous, as a governess earns a larger wage."

There was a moment's silence. Then, "I would imagine there are those who have concluded that I forced my fiancée into a menial position so she could support my bastard."

"That is true, I'm afraid, but it never occurred to me, nor to Lady Knowe," Diana said, with complete sincerity. Her hands were visibly shaking so she wound her fingers together. "I have regretted that rash decision so many times since then. I would have left and found another position, but Artie . . ." Her voice trailed off. "I love your sister. I didn't want to leave her."

Not leaving the castle had been a grotesquely selfish decision, in retrospect. "I didn't do anything with malice," she added, with a little gasp. "I promise you that."

"I know."

She'd underestimated him when they were betrothed. North lived by an ethical code of conduct—a gentleman's, if you will—that meant he would never be unkind. He weighed every decision for good or ill before making it. She threw herself into hot water and hurt people along the way.

"I'm so *sorry*," she said again.

"You've made that point."

"I feel like a condemned prisoner desperate to express remorse."

"Do I feature as the executioner, or the judge? Will your head be chopped off with a sword, like one of King Henry VIII's wives, or will you be sent to the gallows, like a thieving servant?"

"You have every right to play the executioner, North. I've treated you reprehensibly. Horribly."

Chapter Two

I f North had ever bothered to inventory the worst days of his life—he hadn't—he would have ranked the day his older brother Horatius died at the very bottom. The battle of Stony Point and Diana's flight from their betrothal party would have vied for second-last.

Those three awful events were bad enough.

But this day was likely to join their ranks. He had forced himself to stop thinking about Diana, and it gave him a sense of vertigo to see her now. When they'd first met, she'd reminded him of an exquisite porcelain statue of a French lady-in-waiting, her face whitened with rice powder, her lips tinted crimson, a patch worn high on one cheek.

Now she was wearing a muslin cap tilted to one side, and bundles of thick, dark red hair fell down her back. *Red* hair?

In view of her penchant for powdered wigs, he had had no idea her hair was red. Her eyelashes matched her hair, and her cheeks had a rosy glow. She looked messy and delicious, as if she had just climbed from bed.

The thought made him recoil.

More importantly than her hair color, he didn't remember her saying much during their betrothal. She certainly hadn't responded with more than murmured agreement to his attempts to ease her into the life of a future duchess. But now she couldn't stop talking. She had a way of going at a subject sideways, but she was being very clear about her apologies.

He didn't need or want them, but her earnestness was soothing. It had galled him that the woman he had chosen to be his duchess didn't have the courtesy to inform him in person that she was breaking their engagement.

"It was very wrong of me to allow your family to believe that you fathered my child." Diana was wringing her hands, and her cheeks had turned from rosy to red.

Indeed.

In his heart of hearts, he resented being jilted far more than discovering that his father had been supporting his supposed bastard.

"Where is the boy's father?" he inquired.

"He's dead," she said, coloring even more. "But he—"

"I don't want to know," North stated. The boy had clearly been born before they met. It only made sense that the father had died. North could not imagine a man who had garnered Diana's affections not keeping her.

The way she had concealed the child from him, from all society, bamboozling him into a proposal, sent a flare of anger down his spine—that instantly flickered and died. After his experiences in the war, who cared what she had done?

Not he.

She had probably done him a favor by drawing him into a scandal. It would hold off the marriage-minded mamas. He didn't intend to seek a wife until the event was forced onto him by the need for an heir. He might even allow the title to descend through Alaric's line.

"Does my stepmother know that Artemisia displays all the elegance of a grocer's daughter?" he asked, deciding to lead the conversation toward the reality that Diana would have to leave the castle. He couldn't have his former fiancée working in his father's household. It wouldn't *do*, as his own governess would have said.

"You must be very angry at me to refer to my grandfather," Diana said, her eyes fixed on his. "You are one of very few people in polite society who never found reason to chide me for the audacity of having a grocer for a grandfather."

"I apologize if you thought I was referring to your grandfather. I used the common phrase without thinking."

"Why should the world consider a grocer more impolite than a cobbler?" she said with a rueful smile. "But so it is."

North was rarely dumbfounded, but he found himself silenced by Diana's smile, by her self-possession, by how different she was from the girl he'd pledged to marry. He couldn't even remember what question he had asked her: Somehow they had ended up in a different place. Circuitous conversation was apparently a characteristic of hers.

"I am not ashamed of my grandfather." Diana wrinkled her nose, a charming gesture. "Frankly, before I became a governess, I would have been appalled by Artie as well. That's why children are confined to a nursery, you know. So that no one grasps how uncivilized they are. Or has to endure their company, more to the point."

He did remember her smile. The first time he saw Diana, he had strolled into a ballroom and watched an unknown young lady say something that made the fellow she was talking to fall about laughing.

Diana had laughed along with him, the kind of unrestrained laughter that most ladies stifle before a sound passes their lips. North had registered that she was exquisite, with a heart-shaped face and a trim figure. But that wasn't the important part. Her lips looked as if their natural curve was a smile.

From that moment, he had wanted her with a burning, intense focus that he had experienced only a few times. While trying to stay alive on a battlefield, for example.

"As for Artie's manners, I'm afraid that she has the concentration of a canary and the temper of an irritated bull," Diana said. "I did teach her to curtsy, but her legs are too plump to bend correctly."

"Your description would cover all my father's children at that age," North observed.

Diana clasped her hands behind her back and looked him straight in the eyes. "I haven't slept for many a night thinking how dishonest I have been to you, your family, and the household, all of whom have been nothing but kind to me."

North was conscious that he didn't like the way she referred to him, as if he were an elderly uncle, perhaps. A kindly parishioner. "What's done is done," he said. "But now——"

"This is why I never come to the nursery!" His aunt,

Lady Knowe, appeared in the doorway, hand on her heart, glancing around the room. "Is that a chamber pot on its side? Yes, it is," she answered herself. "And is that one of my beloved nephews, returned from dangerous shores and not come to pay me his respects? Why, yes, it is!"

North grinned and strode over to gather his aunt into a hug. Lady Knowe was tall and broad-shouldered, with an unfortunate resemblance to her twin brother, the duke. Those who loved her boisterous kindness didn't give a fig about her noble nose. "I meant to change out of my traveling dirt before greeting you, Aunt Knowe."

She put her hands on his cheeks and looked him in the eyes. "Are you sound in limb and mind, my dear?"

"Yes," he said, keeping it short, because he hadn't lost a limb, but he'd lost something. Not his mind; at least not entirely. His ability to sleep was gone. His enjoyment of food and women.

His aunt's hands fell from his face. "It's a fruitless war, and I'm confounded that the asses in Parliament can't see it. Your father has done his best to persuade them, but to no avail."

North had made his feelings clear to the Ministry when he sold out. But the fools he spoke to hadn't spent time in the colonies. They didn't understand how committed to freedom American soldiers were, nor how wily their general was. Far away from the blood and smoke of battle, a herd of asses—to borrow his aunt's word—arranged and rearranged regiments with all the concern of boys playing with tin soldiers.

"At least you're out of it," his aunt said, wrinkling her nose. "Diana, my dear, what is that appalling odor?"

"I apologize, my lady," Diana said, dropping into a deep curtsy.

Before he thought about it, North reached out and pulled her upright. "Stop."

She turned a little pink. "I am a member of the household."

"No, you are not," he stated. While he was at it, he plucked off the large muslin cap that belonged belowstairs, not on a lady's head. "Whether or not you have spent an inordinate amount of time in the nursery, you will not address my aunt—or Prism, for that matter—as if you were a servant."

"I *am* a servant."

At the same moment, Lady Knowe said, "She's as stubborn as a mule, North. You won't have any more luck than I did."

North frowned at Diana. "I refuse to allow my fian—my *former* fiancée to become part of the household."

"I already am," Diana said. "Everyone is used to it."

"That's not quite true," Lady Knowe put in. "If you haven't yet heard Boodle's thoughts on the subject, North, you will."

"You cannot remain in this position," he said, pointing out the obvious.

An expression passed Diana's eyes so quickly that he couldn't read it. "I agree. And I'm sorry."

What was that, the seventh time she'd apologized? He had the feeling she would happily keep repeating it all day.

"I do believe that Diana worries she broke your heart, North," his aunt said, her eyes twinkling.

"Allow me to reassure you; I doubt I have that capacity," he said, adding wryly, "My consequence was dented, which was probably beneficial for my character."

"Undoubtedly," his aunt said, chuckling.

Surprising him again, Diana laughed as well. "I lost any consequence I had the day I donned that cap, and I truly believe it's been good for my soul. I just wish that I had been honest about Godfrey."

North was trying to decide whether Godfrey was the man with whom Diana consorted, or the boy she hadn't introduced him to, when his aunt changed the subject.

"This room is a disgrace," she announced. "North, I should like you to escort me to my chamber, after which you must change out of your travel-stained clothing. I haven't seen you so disheveled since Alaric tipped you into the horse trough." She turned to Diana. "He was wearing the family suit of armor, the one that lurks quietly in a corner of the entrance hall."

"I'm impressed," Diana said to North. "It looks as if it'd be very difficult to walk in."

"More so now that its joints have rusted," his aunt said. "I shall ask Prism to send up a maid immediately, Diana. My nephew is immaculate compared to the hearth rug."

"Thank you," Diana said, dropping a curtsy. "I curtsied to Lady Knowe when I was a visitor to the castle," she said, in response to North's scowl.

"I begged Diana to join me as my guest," his aunt chimed in, "but she refused. Come along, North. The two of you must stop quarreling, because it's only in melodramas that a duke falls in love with a governess." She managed to appear amused, mischievous, and satisfied, all at once. "I shall expect you to join us for supper, Diana."

Diana opened her mouth, clearly to protest, but his aunt held up her hand. "We need to make plans for your welfare. No important conversations should be conducted in a room as malodorous as this one. Moreover, when there is rough ground to be covered, a glass of wine does not go amiss."

North bowed.

Diana might call herself a governess if she wished, but he had never bowed to a domestic before. He made his bow a trifle deeper than it might have been, to make a point.

"Well, this is a pretty business," his aunt said, when they were out in the corridor. "I find you crossing swords in the nursery with my favorite member of the household. There are dark circles around your eyes. You've managed to become alarmingly muscled and gaunt at the same time."

"Nonsense," North said, pushing away an image of the maggoty rations his soldiers were allotted in America. "What does Prism make of Diana's presence?"

"Prism's great gift as a butler is to know what the family wants before they do," his aunt said. "Diana refused to dine with me until Prism convinced her that I would take the children to Bath out of pure loneliness, leaving her behind. As if *I* would go anywhere with babes in tow!"

"I am surprised that my father agreed to employ Diana. Surely you didn't believe the boy is mine."

"Of course not, darling. I presented it to the duke as a *fait accompli*," his aunt said, gripping his arm as they began descending the stairs. Lady Knowe was fond of heeled slippers that made steep wooden staircases like this one somewhat perilous.

North was torn between aggravation at the situation, and frustration at himself for feeling even the slightest attraction to Diana. "How on earth did you learn of her situation?"

"I know you. Something had happened just before you left the country, and Diana was the obvious answer."

North's mother had died when he was too young to remember, but Aunt Knowe had always been in the castle. "It took me months to find Diana, as Mrs. Belgrave refused to tell me her address. How did you manage it?"

"I barged straight into the woman's sitting room and threatened to eviscerate her," his aunt said cheerfully. "An utterly repellent creature, I might add. She had the audacity to inform me that her daughter had stolen a fortune in emeralds."

"Prism returned Diana's jewels and clothing to her mother," North said, remembering his incredulity when Prism gave him back his betrothal ring.

"Diana is no thief. When I found the poor girl, she

had scarcely a ha'penny to her name. I actually had someone investigate Mr. Belgrave's will to make certain that her mother hadn't stolen Diana's inheritance."

"Mrs. Belgrave disowned her?" An uneasy memory of the shabby little house in which he found Diana came back to him.

"Her foolish father left only a proviso directing his wife to dowry their daughters," Lady Knowe said, nodding. "From what I hear, the woman is racketing around town, allowing herself to be courted by fortune hunters, no doubt draped in the very jewels she accused Diana of stealing."

North assumed that Diana had chosen a poor man over him. But her lover had died before North had met her, in light of the fact that her child was three or four years old. "Bloody hell," he said, his voice grating. "I rode away and left her there."

"Understandably," Aunt Knowe said, patting his arm. "I had to bully her dreadfully before she would agree to return to the castle. In the end, Diana came only on the condition that she be employed. Unfortunately, neither of us envisioned the outrage that would result."

North shrugged. "It's not as if the Wildes are unfamiliar with scandal."

"I shall miss her," his aunt said, pausing at the bottom of the nursery steps. "She was such a gloomy creature when you first brought her here that I wondered at your judgment, but now she can keep me laughing all evening. At least, on those occasions when I convince her to dine with me."

His aunt sounded lonely, to North's surprise. He always envisioned Aunt Knowe buzzing happily around a castle full of guests.

"Have my father and stepmother been spending most of their time in London?"

"The House of Lords, and the war," she said with a sigh. "In addition, dear Ophelia has to find husbands for the girls. Betsy is in the process of taking London by storm and yet she turns her nose up at every offer. Ophelia misses Artie terribly."

"Why doesn't she simply take Artie to London?"

"I never took *you* to London as a boy, did I? Children don't thrive in coal dust. Your father's second duchess took Joan to London, and the poor babe developed a bronchial complaint within the week."

"Why would she have taken Joan to London? I don't remember ever seeing that particular duchess in the nursery."

His father's second duchess had been fertile—giving

him four children in six years—and adulterous. She'd run away with a Prussian count shortly after Joan was born, and Parliament had granted the duke a divorce with unheard-of speed.

"Joan is the youngest, and has a Slavic appearance," his aunt said bluntly. "I suspect her mother meant to take her abroad, but Joan was lucky enough to get a cough and begin wailing night and day, so she was dispatched back to the castle."

"That's appalling," North said, taken aback. It would have been devastating for all of them if Joan had been taken from their family.

"Your father would have gone after her," Aunt Knowe said. "He would never have allowed one of his daughters to be taken off to the continent by a mother who couldn't remember the child's name from one moment to the next."

"Yet Joan is not his child?" North asked, not certain how they got on to the subject.

"What I am saying is that child rearing has nothing to do with blood. My brother is Joan's father, and that's all there is to it."

"I see."

They had reached the door of his aunt's bedchamber; her hand tightened on his arm and fell away. "Poor Boodle pined like a heartbroken milkmaid while you were gone. It's time to allow the man to have his way with you."

North groaned. He'd managed very well in the army without a valet. "I'm surprised he didn't leave for another position."

"Your father needed a valet, and of course, Boodle enjoyed the consequence of serving a duke. But you are his masterpiece," his aunt told him. "The moment we had news of your imminent return, he found another valet for your father. In his mind, you hired him to take you to the heights of fashion, and he dreams of future glory."

"This is not going to end well," North said.

"He's hoarded a collection of prints of French courtiers and broods over them like a hen with golden eggs," his aunt said. "I shall expect to see you glittering from head to foot in a few hours."

When North didn't answer, she chuckled. "What was it that my father used to say? Ah, yes: 'Distance lends enchantment.' I think he was talking about the company of women, but it applies to valets and their masters as well. Poor Boodle, he's forgotten what a stubborn mule you can be."

"'No man is a hero to his valet,'" North said wryly, capping her proverb with his own. "He'll remember shortly, if he's forgotten."

Lady Knowe pushed open the door to her bedchamber and paused. "I forgot to ask! I assume you saw your father and Ophelia before you left London?"

"Only briefly," North said. He had planned to spend time in London, but the city's raucous noise threatened what little sleep he got these days. "They will bring the family as soon as they're able."

His aunt's shrewd eyes searched his face, no doubt grasping his inability to stay in London for more than a few hours.

All she said was, "Until they arrive, we will take our meals in the small dining room."

He bowed, but she kissed him in lieu of a curtsy, and held him for longer than etiquette demanded. "I'm glad that you're home, dear," she said in a rough voice. "We missed you so much."

North's bedchamber was in a different wing. Lindow Castle had begun as a medieval fortress, but various dukes had made their mark by adding a tower here, or a wing there . . . Now it was an eccentric hodgepodge of a building.

As a boy, he had spent years designing and redesigning a light and airy country mansion, with bathing chambers and dressing rooms attached to bedchambers, and a nursery wing at the top of a steep staircase. With architectural ambitions in mind, he had given the money he inherited from his mother to his boyhood friend Parth Sterling, who had tripled it in value.

He had the money to build another castle, if he wanted.

But at twenty-three he had become the duke's heir, and someday this castle would be his. The most he could do would be to add a turret to a structure that already had three too many, in his opinion. He pushed open the door to his bedchamber with more force than needed.

"There you are, my lord!" Boodle cried. His valet was a tall, thin man, powdered and plucked and be-wigged. He stood beside a bath of steaming water scented with bergamot. Shaving tools were arranged on a length of toweling.

A mustard-yellow coat embroidered with bunches of cherries and a pair of matching breeches were lovingly laid out on the bed. The waistcoat was cream silk dotted with cherry twill, and the shirt's lace-ruffled cuffs would graze his knuckles. Three pressed neckcloths awaited, in case the first attempts were not entirely satisfactory.

North paused in the door, rubbing his chin. His stubbly chin.

"Come, come, my lord!" Boodle exclaimed, waving his hands in the air. "We have no time to waste. Lady

Knowe will become tetchy if the meal is delayed more than a couple of hours, and I have the challenge of a lifetime in front of me."

He was vibrating with the excitement of a man facing a heated battle.

North was not.

Chapter Three

Diana soothed Mabel's aggrieved feelings, played with the children, fed them supper . . . and all the time her fingers trembled as if she were an aspen tree in a storm. When the children were in bed, she retired to her private chamber, a luxury for which she'd never been more grateful.

Mabel was a terrible gossip, and responding to her prying questions with dignity had taken a terrific act of will. Once alone, Diana sank onto her bed and stared at the wall.

Something about North's face bothered her. In plain fact, he had been no more than an acquaintance when they were betrothed; a ring hadn't made them friends. They had scarcely spoken to each other. Still, he didn't seem—she couldn't quite put her finger on it, though she kept going round and round.

Something had changed. Lady Knowe had seen it too; her eyes had lingered on North's face. He'd lost weight, but that wasn't it. His face was more spare, more grim. Yet his natural expression had always been severe.

It wasn't her concern, Diana reminded herself. She had to make plans to leave, perhaps in the next day or two. The thought of leaving Artie made Diana drop her head in her hands—not just because the idea broke her heart, but for Godfrey.

Her grandfather would have told her that all good things must come to an end. A jolly, plain-spoken man, he had watched with astonishment his daughter's efforts to shove her children up the social ladder.

Even thinking of her grandfather's whiskery kindness made her feel better. He would have understood why she had returned to Lindow Castle. Any port in a storm, he would have said.

The thought made her calmer, and her fingers stopped trembling. The storm had passed. She had saved money from her salary. And now she knew how to work hard. That was a blessing. Prism would give her a reference, as would Lady Knowe.

She stood up and began unpinning her apron. Lady Knowe maintained a large correspondence, so perhaps she knew someone with a position open. Diana could be a companion to an elderly lady, for example.

Or she could work in a shop.

She could picture herself behind a counter selling lacy fripperies. Taking off her gown and washing at the basin, she imagined herself in Hinshcliffe & Croft in Covent Garden, presiding over the best muslins, painted nankeens, and dotted chintzes.

Her mother had always overseen her wardrobe, but along the way Diana had silently formed opinions about how a lady ought to dress. In her estimation, her wigs had been too high, her jewels too shiny, her spangles too glittering.

She would be good at advising young ladies; she could steer them away from the anxious mistakes her mother had made. Put them in dresses that would flatter a young lady, rather than demand to be praised in their own right.

That thought led directly to her own plight. She had exactly three gowns to choose from, none of which was flattering.

Thinking of the indifferent look in North's eyes during her feverish apologies, she longed for one of the magnificent dresses she used to wear. Preferably one that made the most of her bosom.

Her choice was between three plain, black gowns. Diana had been in mourning for her sister Rose when her mother threw her out, so she hadn't protested on being informed that she could not take the exquisite confections in which she debuted.

Only later had she realized that she could have sold them. She had been close to her last shilling when Lady Knowe found her.

Like elderly crows, all three gowns showed signs of wear. With a sigh, she chose the least dingy. She hadn't a drop of powder to cover her disreputably colored hair, or the spray of freckles over her nose.

Her mother had shuddered over Diana's hair—and decided to marry her to a Scotsman, who would presumably be less repulsed—but it was her freckles that were the bane of Mrs. Belgrave's existence. At one point Diana's entire nose had peeled after her mother applied yet another poultice designed to whiten skin. The freckles were still there a week later. After that, Diana grew to be an expert in the art of applying white paint followed by clouds of rice powder.

It didn't matter what she wore tonight, because the spray of freckles over her nose was about as easy to overlook as a leopard's spots. North would take one glance and recognize how lucky he was to have escaped the marriage.

She owned only one piece of jewelry, a locket with a miniature of her sister's face tucked inside. To most

people, Rose's smile would seem improbably sweet—
and yet the miniature had been accurate.

Rose had been far prettier than Diana, socially
graceful, lovable in every way. Mrs. Belgrave hadn't
needed to point out that she'd lost the worthier
daughter.

With the skill of long practice, Diana banished
her mother's complaints from her head and kissed
Rose's nose.

She slipped the locket inside her bodice and set
off downstairs.

While stripping off his clothing, North kept thinking about the fact that Diana was in the castle. In the
months after he went to war, still raw from being jilted,
he had imagined encountering the bastard who had
got her with child and knocking him down the stairs.

War had an uncomfortable way of stripping away a
gentlemanly mask, and soon enough he graduated to
dreams of killing the debaucher with his bare hands.

But that man was dead, and Diana had been thrown
out by her mother, two circumstances that he hadn't
imagined. Thank God Aunt Knowe had found her.

The thought of Diana's hardship made him restless,
and he stepped into the tub, sat down, and picked up a

ball of soap that smelled strongly of flowers and pine-apple.

"I'd prefer plain soap," he said to Boodle, holding it up.

His valet gaped at him. "That scent is specially blended for you, my lord. Chosen after four hours in the perfumery."

"You spent those hours, not I," North reminded him.

"As soon as His Grace reported that you were returning to England, I spent days, not hours, refreshing your perfumed goods and *accountrement*." Boodle waved his thin fingers toward the dressing table, covered with glass bottles and boxes of patches. "Your scent is guaranteed to be sold to no one other than yourself for a period of ten years!"

"Plain soap," North repeated.

He tossed the wet ball of soap in the air, and Boodle managed to catch it. He raised the soap to his nose and took a sniff. "Exquisite! Magnificent! Everyone agreed that the Marquess of Saltersley will smell better than—"

"If you recall, Boodle, I do not use that title," North observed, an edge to his voice. His brother Horatius had been the marquess, and while North had no choice about taking on the dukedom, he had refused the courtesy title. "Fetch another soap, if you please."

Boodle scuttled into the corridor, muttering to himself.

Lying back in the tub, North forced himself to face the truth: He still wanted Diana. Perhaps he wanted her even more than he had when they were betrothed. If he started kissing her now, the way he had at their betrothal party, he wasn't sure he would stop.

It was an unpleasant discovery. It made no sense that he found her more sensual when wearing a drab servant's dress and a tired muslin cap.

Likely his desire was a natural response to her intrinsic beauty, indicating nothing more important than the fact he was alive and male.

Boodle came back with a ball of soap that smelled of honey. Good enough. North began scrubbing off the dirt of the trip from London to Cheshire, made in three days instead of five.

It was to win Diana that he had first hired Boodle, who had tutored him about patches, powder, and wigs. His valet's handiwork had transformed North into a fashionable dandy, a perfect consort to Miss Belgrave in every detail except his refusal to wear face paint. He had dressed in French finery, danced endless minuets, even cut back on billiards to take up archery, her favorite sport. Never mind the fact that he had a constitutional dislike of shooting arrows merely to hit a bull's-eye.

Boodle snatched up a scent bottle and waved it in the air. "This holds your personal scent," he cried, opening the stopper and taking a loud sniff. "The bottle is rock crystal and gold leaf. It came with this cunning travel pouch, which will enable you to refresh yourself before entering a ball, or if you find yourself in a crowd of odiferous persons."

"No," North said, keeping it simple.

"No?" Boodle's voice rose. "Why not? I spent hours preparing for your arrival. I even ordered you a frock coat with the new narrow cuffs!" He squinted at North. "I hope your shoulders are not as large as they appear to be, or the coat will not fit. Mr. Hawkes necessarily cut to your previous measure."

"No perfume." North glanced at the bed. "No yellow coats, Boodle, especially with all that embroidery."

"Yellow? It is not yellow. It's *saffron*."

North just shook his head.

An expression of extreme distress wrinkled his valet's face. "It's because of her, isn't it?"

"Her?"

"She's shamed and humiliated you, and thus you are hesitant to reenter polite society. I sympathize, my lord. I felt as much when I was on Bond Street, but I braved it out. I turned up my nose at anyone asking impertinent questions about you."

North stopped soaping and watched with bemusement as his valet threw a clenched fist in the air. "The solution is not to hide in Cheshire. No! We must order an entirely new wardrobe and be seen everywhere, talking to everyone! Courage, not retreat!"

Bloody hell. His valet was more passionate than the men in his regiment had been. "I feel no hesitation to go into polite society," North stated. Not that he meant to waste any time doing it.

If nothing else, service in the military had taught him the value of time.

Boodle didn't appear to have heard him. "From this vantage point, it is hard to remember that Miss Belgrave did appear to be a desirable match—barring the unfortunate circumstances of her ancestry."

That would be the grocer.

"Yet blood will out," Boodle said, shaking his head. "We see it over and over. Were Miss Belgrave on the stage, she would be an actress of some renown."

That seemed to imply cunning on Diana's part, as if she had wanted to be a duchess. She might have acted the part of a demure maiden during their courtship, but in North's opinion, she'd wanted neither him nor his title.

"I do not blame you for being taken in, my lord. I understand your shame. Who could have imagined the consequences . . . ah, the consequences!"

North was struck dumb.

"To be frank, it is only because I am the most loyal of creatures that I have awaited your return," Boodle said, turning to the bed and patting the saffron-colored coat. His mouth pulled so tight that it resembled a rosebud. "As the scandal grew and grew in your absence, I considered the reputation I had gained from transforming you into a gentleman of fashion. Your father offers no challenge to my creative genius. More than once, I contemplated not returning to your service, but if a valet is not loyal, what is he?"

It seemed to be a rhetorical question. "I gather you are vexed that Miss Belgrave returned to the castle with her son," North said.

"Had *I* refused to return to your service, it would have confirmed to England—nay, the *world*, because my reputation extends to the French court—that the scandal was justified. It would have confirmed the shame that has fallen on the Wildes as a whole."

North's mouth had fallen ajar, so he snapped it shut.

Boodle spun to face him, striking his chest with his fist. "If I left you, *I*, one of the most famous valets in all England, it would have confirmed the rumors that you took Miss Belgrave by force."

North let go of the soap and sat up so sharply that

water sloshed out of the bath. "What in the hell did you just say?"

"I would have thought someone informed you. There are those who say that you despoiled your fiancée." Boodle sniffed haughtily. "I have always denied it, and I shall to my dying day. I consider myself both loyal *and* discreet."

For the first time since he heard of the scandal, anger heated North's blood.

"You are the son of the Duke of Lindow," Boodle explained. "Had you been overcome by passion, it would not be for one such as her."

"There are *no* circumstances under which I would be overcome by passion, unless the lady shared my feelings," North said.

"I said as much! A future duke has no need to force his attentions on any woman, from the highest to the lowest in the land."

North stood up and grabbed the length of toweling before the valet could hand it to him. Boodle started babbling about his reputation again.

His reputation?

It was North who had apparently been accused of rape, though he could scarcely believe that nonsense.

"The prints have done the most damage," Boodle

was saying. "The sellers are like beetles, hiding under every rock. His Grace no sooner confiscates an actionable print than another is circulating the country."

His brother Alaric, the author Lord Wilde, had been plagued by etchings that depicted him wrestling a giant kraken and fighting pirates. Neither of which his brother had ever done.

"I gather the depictions of me are not as heroic as those portraying Lord Wilde," North said dryly.

Boodle snorted.

"What do they show?" Frankly, he didn't care if he never received another invitation to an event in so-called polite society. Not that he, as a future duke, would be shunned.

A weary inner voice told him that even if he *had* committed something as terrible as rape, many people would forgive him. Manage to forget. Decide to pretend it had never happened.

"There is one in which you are emerging from a trunk in a lady's bedchamber, supposedly that of Miss Belgrave. A scene taken from a Shakespeare play, I believe."

North frowned. "A trunk? I wouldn't fit in a trunk."

"That is hardly the point. It had an offensive title: *Lord Roland Seduces an Innocent, or the Despoiling of*

Virtue. From what I am told, it has proved extremely popular and sold copies throughout the country."

North suppressed the curse that rose to his lips. He saw no point in fighting the fascination people had with buying prints of the Wildes, not after his father's battle to eradicate images of his brother Horatius struggling in the bog that took his life.

Who in the hell would buy that print? Or one of a woman on the point of being "despoiled"?

He tossed the toweling over a bedpost and picked up the shirt laid out for him. It was exquisitely ironed and starched; Boodle was not wrong in lauding himself as one of the best valets in all England.

But its lace cuffs would fall over his knuckles.

"No," he said, dropping it back on the bed. "No lace. Rip off the cuffs or give me another shirt."

"That is not the *best* lace," Boodle observed, a note of cunning entering his voice. "It was made in your friend Mr. Sterling's factory. I judged that you would want to wear his product, as his reputation would be enhanced if the Marquess—if Lord Roland was seen wearing it."

"No lace, Parth's or otherwise," North said, holding up the saffron-colored breeches. It wasn't a color he liked, but he thought Boodle might faint if he suggested wearing his riding breeches to dinner.

After wrenching it up his legs, he managed to do up the placket. Glancing down at his front, he decided that he wasn't entirely against the idea of Diana seeing him in these breeches.

Yellow silk stretched so tautly over his crotch that everything he had was on display. Some dark side of him wanted her to compare him to the man she had before him.

"Your thighs are monstrous," Boodle moaned, concentrating farther down North's legs. "As big as gourds. It's all very well to pad one's calves—but thighs shouldn't look like that."

North and his men had spent weeks fortifying Stony Point fortress with logs cut and dragged into position. He'd known it was a fool's errand, but the commander wouldn't listen to him, and it was better to do something than nothing.

When the fort was conquered in a mere fifteen minutes, it wasn't for lack of logs. Just lack of intelligence, forethought, and soldiers.

It wasn't as if he'd been in that one battle only. But that was the one that stuck with him, that he revisited in the middle of the night.

Lucky him.

Boodle knelt at his feet, reaching out to button the

breeches below his knee, but North reflexively stepped backward. "I'll do it."

Alas, he no sooner bent over than a loud ripping sound indicated that the saffron-colored breeches had split from stem to stern.

To do him credit, Boodle didn't shriek or curse. He rocked back on his heels and let out a sigh. Without a word, he stood up, turned to the wardrobe, and pulled out a pair of breeches that North used to wear for hunting. They were plain buckskin, worn to just the right softness in the rear.

"I might do damage to Parth's reputation by being seen wearing his lace," North suggested, taking up the buckskins. "People might call it the lace of louts and loose screws."

The breeches were tighter than they used to be, but still comfortable. Even better, they weren't saffron-colored nor silk.

"Shall I tear the lace off the cuffs?" North asked, nodding at the shirt.

"No!" His valet gathered the garment to his chest with the protectiveness of a mother bear. "Don't touch it! The cuffs are removable and I shall unpick the stitching tomorrow." He picked up a sturdy shirt that North had worn under his uniform. "You can wear this, I suppose," he said sourly. "It's not as if anyone in the castle matters."

North gave him a chilly glance before he pulled on the shirt. Lady Knowe might not travel to London and attend society's events, but she definitely mattered. Diana . . . Diana mattered too.

"You'll never fit into the saffron coat," Boodle said with all the heartbreak of King Lear facing death on the heath. "You'll split it across the shoulders."

"I suspect you're right."

"If you'll excuse me, my lord, I believe His Grace left some coats in his wardrobe."

"Good idea," North said, dropping into a seat and picking up the book he was currently reading. He had never been a reader as a young man, but since leaving England he'd spent hour upon hour lost in a book.

It was better than playing cards, which he detested, or arguing with his superiors, which was even worse. Long days at sea had been tolerable only because of a tattered collection of plays by the Roman playwrights Plautus and Terence. When he couldn't sleep at night, he stayed up reading by candlelight.

After docking in London and being told by his superiors that no one—not even an American man fighting for independence—could show as much courage as a British soldier, he walked out of the Ministry, stopped by a bookseller, and left for Cheshire the same evening.

The book he'd purchased offered a depiction of hell, which felt bitterly appropriate after his experience of war. Dante Alighieri described hell as a series of circles, each containing sinners organized by their sins and punished in appropriate ways.

It was all very tidy and satisfactory. North would have put unthinking military commanders in one circle, doomed to run ceaselessly through battlefields full of dead and dying bodies, the air bitter with smoke from cannon fire.

He was considering a circle reserved for spies and intelligencers when his valet swung back into the room, a black coat over his arm.

After that, Boodle scampered about the room, pulling garments from two wardrobes that held North's clothing, most of which had been acquired during his courtship of Diana. Everything ended up in a huge pile on the bed, since North shook his head over and over.

No, he had no intention of returning to court in the near future, so he didn't need a coat embroidered with gaudy silver thread, with rubies for buttons.

"You may be right," Boodle agreed. "The newest coats are embroidered only on the skirts, the pockets, and the buttonholes."

No, he wouldn't wear that primrose silk again. Or azure satin with violet trim. Or striped stockings or stockings with clocks. Shoes with red heels? No.

"High heels have lost their acclaim," Boodle conceded, adding two pairs to the pile. "I won't even ask about this wig, so full-bodied, so fashionable," he mourned, holding up a wig that North's brother Alaric had described as a cross between a parrot and a fancy chicken.

No, no, and no.

"I have come to a decision," Boodle announced, after the stack grew to shoulder height. "I cannot serve a man who would countenance wearing those breeches to the dinner table, let alone one who shows disdain for lace cuffs. Forgive me, my lord, but I think we will both be more comfortable if I take leave of your service."

North put his book down. "I'm sorry to hear it, Boodle. I will hire my father's new valet, if you'd like to serve the duke instead."

"No," he said, with tragic emphasis. "I must express my talents for shaping perfection, sartorial perfection. Caring for His Grace was a trying experience, but I consoled myself with thoughts of the triumphs to come once you returned. I shall find a gentleman more appreciative of my genius."

North stood up and clapped him on the back. "I owe you great thanks, Boodle. You turned me into a paragon. I will happily give you a reference."

"I took a man who scarcely knew how to put on a wig and made him into a courtier who could have graced the court of Marie Antoinette herself," Boodle said, nodding.

"Without your help, I would not have caught the eye of Miss Belgrave."

That wasn't entirely true. Because of North's rank and fortune, every young lady began fluttering her eyelashes and giggling the moment he strolled into the ballroom.

He had enjoyed the fact that Diana hadn't gushed, but he'd had no idea that she was happier in the nursery than the ballroom, in a muslin cap than a wig. She had been as much an impostor as he, in his wigs and ribbons.

Impostor? He'd been a fool.

"It is hard to believe that *she* was a leader in fashion," Boodle said, shaking his head. "Lady Artemisia is never dressed to her station, never seen in a properly elegant frock. I have personally delivered illustrations of French children's garments to the nursery, but no. Miss Belgrave dresses the children as if they were beggars."

North had nothing to say about that; he hadn't paid any attention to what either child was wearing.

"I will dispatch a tailor from London to create a new wardrobe in your chosen style, unless you'd prefer to find someone in the village," Boodle said, adding with a touch of acid, "I hear that the baker's wife takes in mending on occasion."

"I would be grateful for a tailor," North said, sitting down and returning to his book.

In Dante's *Inferno*, the second circle was populated by lovers. Dante's chat with Paolo and Francesca was written in old-fashioned Italian and dashed hard to understand, but North came to the conclusion that either the wind was howling in their ears or they were being blown about the world by the wind.

Dante had caught something about the experience of falling in love. North might have denied falling in love with Diana, but in his heart, he knew perfectly well that he had experienced either a fit of madness or of love that had come over him with the violence of a summer storm.

He liked the idea of blaming a fierce wind for blowing him into the ranks of dandies. He couldn't believe that he had bothered to wear heels or a tall wig in an effort to court Diana. He had cared enough to wear *patches* on his face. It seemed inconceivable now.

Boodle caught his attention by waving a fistful of neckcloths in front of him, each edged with lace or ruffles.

"Don't I have any plain scarves?"

"*Plain* is not in my vocabulary," Boodle said, nose in the air. "I would hope that you will replace me with a decent valet. Whatever you do, I beg you not to consider the second footman, Cozens. The man had the impudence to inform me that he meant to become a gentleman's gentleman."

North grunted. In the back of his head, he was aware that he would be shortly dining with Diana.

For the last time, perhaps.

She would have to leave soon, taking that boy with her. His aunt was right. They needed to sit down in a civilized fashion and discuss her future.

But no more apologies.

"I told him," Boodle said, "I told him that you couldn't be a gentleman's *gentleman,* if you weren't a gentleman to start with!"

North made a mental note to hire Cozens.

Chapter Four

D iana slipped into the Prussian Dining Room to find it empty. A settee and a few chairs were arranged in front of an unlit fireplace, and a round table was set for the evening meal.

Supposedly the chamber had gained its name from oak panels painted Prussian blue, but North's brother Alaric had confided with a wicked twinkle that they all thought the name derived from the second duchess's seduction of a Prussian nobleman.

Diana skirted the table, noting absently that Prism had laid out the Leboeuf china, which Lord Alaric had recently sent from Paris.

Now that she was a member of the household, she knew far more about silver and china than she ever had before. The gold-embossed, porcelain plates were superb—and worth a king's ransom. Prism himself would wash them tonight, entrusting Mrs. Mousekin to dry each plate as he handed them to her.

Sometimes she felt overwhelmed by how much she hadn't known about the work required to manage a large house and its occupants. She had had no idea that a single muslin gown might take hours to press. She hadn't known that servants often stayed up until the wee hours to clean the library, if the master chose to work late at his desk.

She hadn't known anything important.

Catching sight of her tired black gown in the mirror over the mantelpiece made her wince, so she veered over to the window seat and sat down, leaning her chin on her crossed arms. Somewhere off to her left, Fitzy, the castle's irritable peacock, must be parading around his territory. She cocked an ear but didn't hear his screech.

During her first visit, she hadn't known that it took four gardeners and up to ten helpers to maintain the castle's gardens, the lawns rolling off to the west, the apple orchard, the ornamental pool that surrounded a Roman-style folly.

And yet she thought she could be the mistress of this ancient pile of stone, with its traditions, its priest holes, its sprawling nursery wing? It seemed unimaginable. Lady Knowe spent Tuesday—*all* of Tuesday, every Tuesday—going over accounts. Because the duchess spent most of her time in London with her husband, and North had gone to war, the duke's sister had stepped into the gap.

Which Diana, frankly, could not have done.

Her mother considered money the provenance of the middling sort and below. *Ladies* went shopping with a maid and a footman, who had charge of a velvet coin purse. Sometimes the merchant simply sent Diana home with the merchandise.

She had never considered how her beautiful shoes and silk stockings had been paid for.

Her mother had been deeply opposed to her daughters learning anything that had a smell of commerce, as if an understanding of currency would make everyone remember Diana's grandfather—whom no one forgot, anyway.

No wonder North had tried to ease her way with lectures on this and that.

One thing she had never fooled herself about was her ability to hold the attention of the man who would be lord of all this. North would have seen through her masks, wigs, and lip salve, and been bored to death by her, if not repulsed by her hair and freckles. It had been a terrible strain trying to appear duchess-worthy: intelligent, thoughtful, and all the rest of it.

Her own mother had acknowledged the truth in

their last terrible encounter, when Mrs. Belgrave had ordered Diana to be gone and to take Godfrey with her. Rose had been a true lady—cultured and intellectual, whereas Diana was impulsive and foolish. Apparently, their mother had always known Diana would muck up her marriage; she had just hoped it would happen when it was too late for North to cast her off.

Mrs. Belgrave had gone on to say something so cruel that recalling it sent a shiver through Diana's whole body, but she had become an expert at banishing that memory. Now she forced herself to savor the peaceful view behind the gardens. She was safe. Godfrey was safe.

Behind her, the door opened and Prism said, "Good evening, Miss Belgrave. May I offer you a glass of sherry?"

Diana scrambled off the window seat. "Oh, good evening, Prism!" When she returned to the castle, they'd come to a silent agreement that "Mr. Prism" wasn't appropriate when she was dining with Lady Knowe. "I would love a glass of sherry."

The butler poured her a glass, placing it precisely in the center of a silver salver before he carried it to her.

"Do you think that I could become a lady's maid, Prism?" Diana asked.

"With all due respect, Miss Belgrave, I do not." With

that, he bowed and made his way out of the room, maintaining a dignified silence as regarded his reasoning.

Diana sat down again with a sigh. She was prone to saying the wrong things at the wrong time—unless her mother was in the room to terrify her into silence. That wasn't a desirable quality in a lady's maid, who was expected to keep all her mistress's secrets.

Moreover, she couldn't even mend a ripped hem with any skill, thanks to her mother's ban on practical skills. Her governess had taught her to stitch a sampler, which was useless, in retrospect. She could paint a picture backward on a piece of glass, which was even more pathetic.

A few strands of ivy had crept up the side of the castle and grown into the room, where they would inevitably be snipped off by a housemaid. She couldn't help thinking that they were like her and Rose. Upstart sprigs, trying to enter the ton, to become part of polite society . . . likely to be clipped off.

Clambering up on her knees, she pushed the strands back out the window—and saw the nest. It was tucked on the stone ledge to the left of the window, hidden from the wind by a curtain of ivy.

Cautiously she leaned out a bit further. To her great pleasure, three spotted blue eggs lay in a soft, neat hollow lined with feathers.

Artie would be so excited . . . but quite likely Diana and Godfrey would be gone when the eggs hatched. Prism could arrange to have Artie brought to see the fledglings. Or she could tell North, now that he was home.

She had forgotten him for a moment. She'd actually forgotten he was back.

As if to prove that he was there in the flesh, strong arms wound around her waist from behind and hauled her back into the room.

Diana had never been embraced by North; their bodies had never even touched. But she knew instinctively that the hard chest at her back was his.

"What in the devil's name are you doing leaning out that window?" he asked, sounding perplexed instead of annoyed.

That raised the question of whether North *ever* became angry. Even when he'd found her in the cottage, she had thought his expression was bleak, not angry. He had been disillusioned, because he had put her on a pedestal, and she had tumbled all the way belowstairs.

His arms fell away and she looked over her shoulder. "There's a nest with three eggs in it, North. You are taller than I am, so you'll see it easily."

Somewhat to her surprise, he put a knee beside hers and braced his hands on the ledge. "A finch's nest."

"A finch!" Diana exclaimed. "How lovely!" And, remembering that ignorance was not a sin: "What is a finch?"

"A bird with a forked tail and a wheezy song, as I recall. My older brother was fascinated by bird nests and used to collect them."

"Did Lord Horatius sketch or paint pictures of the nests he collected?"

North shook his head. "Horatius would have thought such a womanly art was beneath him."

"What a shame," Diana said, getting to her feet and shaking out her skirts. "I can't paint well at all; it's above me. Perhaps there's a book about birds in the castle library. Artie would love to watch the baby birds hatch."

As would Godfrey, but she didn't want to mention her nephew yet because . . . here they were. The two of them. They had to discuss Godfrey, but the cowardly side of her wanted to stand beside North and pretend that she hadn't brought disgrace onto both of them.

"May I offer you another glass of sherry?" North asked.

Diana hastily finished the last of her drink. "Yes, please," she said, holding out her glass. "That's one thing I do not like about the servants' hall," she confided. "No wine to drink, except on Christmas."

North glanced over his shoulder. "Prism doesn't have a glass of wine in the evening?"

"Oh, yes, he does," Diana said. "The upper servants have their own sitting room, where they share wine and dessert, while lesser mortals drink small beer. I almost always retire to the nursery, as I am comfortable in neither place."

"Because you are neither upper nor lower?" North said, pouring sherry.

"As governess, I would sit with the upper servants or even the family, but as a nanny, I belong with the lower servants. Many gentlewomen become governesses, but they rarely become nannies."

"You are higher than all of them," he said, matter-of-factly. "You are Miss Belgrave, after all. Your father was a knight." He handed her a glass.

"Hierarchy is a matter of context, don't you think?" Diana asked. "There must have been times in the colonies when you were considered a lower mortal compared to your commanding officers. And yet, were you standing beside those men in a ballroom, you would be superior to them."

"My title led to complications," he agreed.

"Is that why you sold out?" Diana asked, and, seeing the barely perceptible tightening of his jaw, "It's not my business, so please forget that I asked. As for me, there are times when I think it would be easier to be the mistress of the whole castle than the governess of the nursery, but most of the time, I like having work to do."

His brows were drawn together, but his mouth eased. She was absurdly happy to see that.

"I know just what you're thinking," Diana said, babbling because her mother wasn't there to call her a fool, and North didn't seem to have much to say. "You're right. I would have made a terrible duchess. My mother was adamant that her daughters should marry into the gentry or the peerage, but I seem to be more akin to my grandfather. For example, I like hard work."

"Do you think that a duchess doesn't work?"

"Lady Knowe works very hard on Tuesdays, going over the castle accounts," Diana said. "But most ladies' labor is limited to dressing and undressing."

"Should that not count as work?" He took a sip, regarding her steadily over his glass.

"I don't consider it such. A lady stands motionless while one or two maids tie and pin her into a garment with as many as eight layers. It may take those maids three hours to clothe their mistress for dinner, and that's just evening clothes. There are all the other changes: morning and afternoon dresses, riding costumes, walking costumes, and so on." She shrugged.

"I thought you delighted in fashion," North said

dryly. "You were pointed out to me as the most elegant young lady of your Season, a celebrated paragon."

She took a bracing sip of sherry. "You assume that I was allowed to choose my own clothing. I can assure you, Lord Roland, that when it comes to hierarchy, a young lady ranks far beneath her mother."

"I understood that you would have no choice as regards your spouse, once I made my interest clear." His voice was rueful.

Diana had the sense that she was the only woman in the history of Great Britain to back away from marriage to a future duke. She'd been so unenthusiastic after their first meeting that her mother had threatened to cut off her sister and nephew without a shilling if Diana did not wed North.

"My mother insisted that I dress as a duchess well before you made your interest clear," Diana said, giving him a bright smile. "She was very pleased to discover that you were a model of elegance."

"I wasn't, until I noticed you," he stated casually.

Diana frowned. When she met North, he had been wearing a pale blue coat with silver embroidery, and she thought he was the prettiest man she had ever seen. And the most terrifying.

"I met you at Lady Rulip's ball," he said, "but I actually caught sight of you at a ball a few weeks earlier, before I asked for an introduction. On that occasion, I was wearing a brown velvet coat. My stockings were white, without clocks. Unimaginative wig, minimal powder."

"No patch?" she asked, fascinated.

He shook his head. "I asked who you were, and was told you were the most stylish young lady of the Season. Your cousin Lavinia said you were an expert in the art of dressing."

"She didn't know me very well," Diana said, taken aback.

"By the time you met me in Lady Rulip's ballroom," he said, "I had hired Boodle. I was wearing powder and patches, heels, and a lavishly embroidered coat."

Something about his face made her giggle. "You didn't appreciate your own sartorial success?"

"Hated it," he said calmly. "Loathed it. The worst was the lip salve. I tried that, and even for you, I couldn't do it. It had a flavor of cod-liver oil."

"Oil of roses doesn't," Diana observed.

He shrugged. "I hired Boodle the day after seeing you for the first time." He threw back the rest of his drink. "I stayed away from the ton while Boodle wrought his magic."

Diana stared at the strong column of his throat in disbelief. "I had no idea."

"Why should you? Would you like another glass?"

Her second glass of sherry was gone. A blanket of warm courage now hung about her shoulders, a relief after the trembling anxiety of the day.

"Yes, please." Watching North cross the room, Diana noticed for the first time that he wasn't wearing a high wig, the sort he used to wear. Instead, he had on a plain wig, not unlike one her grandfather would have worn. Small, unobtrusive, inelegant.

Earlier, in the nursery, she hadn't allowed herself to look at his body because, shameful though it was, Diana had been appalled by the idea of marrying North, but she had adored his body.

It was big and strong, like that of a man who labored in the fields. He had dressed like a fop, but he had never moved like one.

As a future duke, he had dressed in silk, often with sumptuous embroidery in gold thread.

Now?

He was wearing a black coat that fit his shoulders but wasn't so tight that he'd have to wrestle it on. He hadn't been willow slim before, but now he was strong and solid, as if he were a boxer.

"You look—" She stopped. Perhaps he had engaged in hand-to-hand combat in the war.

He came to a halt before her, a glass in each hand.

"We have both changed, haven't we?" He glanced at her. "A plain black dress. No emeralds. No wig. Those shoes."

They were sturdy, black shoes, made for a baker's wife. She had traded her last pair of satin slippers for the only shoes the cobbler had that fit her. She had disliked the showy, colorful clothing her mother made her wear—except for her shoes.

For some reason, she loved frivolous, brightly colored slippers, the more spangled and bejeweled, the better.

She didn't care a fig for North's opinion, but being pitied still hurt.

"They are long-wearing," she said, around a lump in her throat. "And appropriate to my station."

The sympathy left his face as if it had never been there. "We need to talk about that, don't we?"

"Not yet." She raised her glass and took a reckless gulp. She was beginning to feel tipsy. "I would like to pretend to be Miss Diana Belgrave for a short while longer."

There was an arrested look in his eyes, but she ignored it. Whether he understood or not, she would never be Miss Belgrave again. Not merely because her mother had informed her she was no longer a member of the family, but because something inside her had changed when her sister died.

She no longer had the faintest inclination to follow society's dictates. She was her grandfather's child now, for all intents and purposes.

"What would happen if you met me now?" North asked suddenly. She was still seated by the window, but he had withdrawn, most properly, to a chair across from her.

Diana almost laughed. He would have strolled past her. It was absurd to imagine that a future duke would have noticed her without all the jewels, the duchess-worthy attire, the face paint. Moreover, she had red hair, and without clever use of lip rouge, her mouth was too wide. He wouldn't have distinguished her from the wallpaper.

Or the wallflowers, more to the point.

"What do you mean?" she asked, stalling.

"What if we had not met during the Season? What if we had not met until this moment? Would you still run to the other side of the room every time I approached?"

Despite herself, a little puff of air escaped her lips.

"Did you think I didn't notice?" He raised his glass to his lips again. "I put it down to virginal shyness, which is somewhat absurd under the circumstances."

She had to tell him that Godfrey wasn't her son, but that could wait five minutes. Perhaps ten. "I am not terribly shy," she admitted.

"I seem to have been remarkably obtuse. At some point one of my brothers asked if you were an interesting woman, and I replied that I didn't want an interesting wife."

She cracked a wry smile at that. "I have certainly proved fascinating to the gossips. But I'm not interesting in the right ways. Your brother's implied judgment was correct."

"I don't think Alaric was implying anything, as you had scarcely met. What are 'the right ways'?"

"For a noblewoman to be interesting? Your duchess should be someone like Lord Alaric's wife. Willa is intelligent, and thoughtful, and never puts a foot wrong."

"So you *do* put a foot wrong?"

She widened her eyes comically. "The only way I succeeded during the Season was by keeping silent. I was terrified of misspeaking every time we conversed. It was easier to avoid you."

He flinched, just a small movement, but she saw it.

"The grand duke-to-be," she said, rushing into speech, waving her hands as she found herself doing whenever she had confessed something embarrassing that she would have preferred to have kept to herself. "Graceful and stylish, perfect in every way. I had been hoping for a baronet. A kind man with a coach and four and a comfortable house, who would overlook the grocer in my family."

"So it was disappointing when a gentleman who owned more than a coach and four made his interest known?" he asked dryly.

"My mother was not disappointed." She grinned at him, because she liked the unpretentious flash of humor he was showing now. She'd certainly never seen any sign of it when they were courting. "I knew you were too grand for me, but she felt rightly that your interest was confirmation of her brilliance."

"'*Her* brilliance'?"

"Remember, my mother is a grocer's daughter, for all she married a lord," Diana explained. "My mother put months into making me fit to marry a duke. The woman whom you courted was her creation, and she rightly took the credit."

She thought North's gaze was cold before, but now it was icy. Yet she refused to allow him to believe a lie any longer. "You weren't betrothed to *me*," she said flatly. "Your bride-to-be was a docile girl shaped by my mother to your specific requirements."

He scowled at that.

"Everyone knew that you were considering matrimony," she told him. "My mother studied Lindow

Castle and your family. She thought about tossing me at Lord Alaric's feet, but at that point we had no idea when he would return to England, and besides, your brother will never be a duke."

His shoulders moved sharply, as if he'd like to do something violent.

"She set a trap," Diana said.

"You were not a trap," he said. Stubborn man. He would never admit that he was foxed.

"I was not the trap, but the bait. I had the tallest wig in the room. Your sister-in-law, Willa, compared it to the roost in a barn. You couldn't help but notice me." She sighed. "At any rate, I thought that if my husband belonged to the gentry, rather than the peerage, he would be more likely to forgive me, once he found out who I really was."

"Who you really were," North said slowly. "Do enlighten me, Diana. Who are you?"

"You know what I mean."

"No, I truly don't."

"I'm not decorous or graceful. Remember how you told me, the last time I saw you, that I would be a wonderful duchess?" She smiled ruefully. "My sister would have made an excellent Duchess of Lindow, but my mother was forced to work with me instead. I make missteps all the time. I let slip the wrong things."

"I don't remember meeting your sister."

North was clearly annoyed, but he didn't seem angry to learn that he had proposed marriage to a mirage. His eyes were fatigued and she didn't like the smudges under them, but he had smiled twice and almost chuckled—she thought—once.

"I'll give you an image of what your life would have been like," she said, ignoring his comment about Rose. "Just imagine that your duchess is on your arm, and you're greeting Lord Hucklesburry."

"Who is he?" North inquired.

"I made him up. Lord Hucklesburry and his wife are not happy together." In the back of her mind she registered that North smelled good, like honey and spice and a clean man.

"What a shame."

He crossed his legs, leading Diana to notice his thighs. She'd always noticed North's thighs. She rushed into speech. "You and your wife know all the ignominious details of His Lordship's passionate love for one of the downstairs maids."

"No one tells me ignominious details," North observed.

"They always tell me," Diana countered, "and I will have related them to you. Now the thing you have to remember is that Lady Hucklesburry was not a virgin upon marriage, so her father added five hundred pounds to her dowry."

North was perturbed to find that he was on the verge of smiling at the absurd tale Diana was telling. She was so earnest, and so very pretty.

No, she was beautiful. How could he ever have thought she was attractive wearing a wig? This evening she had bundled all that copper hair of hers into a simple chignon, and soft curls were starting to escape and wave around her forehead.

"Yes?" he said, because she seemed to be waiting expectantly.

"Your duchess—the most important lady in the parish—says just the wrong thing."

"What would that be?" North inquired.

"A reference to the five hundred pounds."

"I can see that would be inadvisable."

"Back when Lord Hucklesburry discovered his bride had entertained a lover before they met, he insisted on renegotiating her dowry. So now that he has taken a mistress—downstairs maid or not—he owes his wife five hundred pounds."

North found his mouth reluctantly curling up. "That's absurd."

"Only because you're a man and not used to treating ladies as equal in value to their husbands."

"Are you adept at driving a bargain?" he asked, with reluctant fascination.

Her face fell. "I'm terrible with money," she confided. "You know Mr. Calico, the peddler, don't you?"

"Certainly." The visits of Mr. Calico and his bright green wagon had been high points of North's childhood.

"He scolded me when he was last here because I tried to give him back more than my original guinea in change. I got nervous and confused the coins. It was frightfully humiliating."

North took another swallow of sherry. He hadn't known his fiancée from Adam and it was beginning to sink in.

She caught the realization in his face. "Now you understand why I couldn't have been a duchess—"

He raised his head and cut off another list of her various shortcomings. "Are you telling me that you would have instigated a discussion of betrothal customs with the Hucklesburrys?" North put down his glass. "Or are you really saying that your mother would have added five hundred pounds had I asked her for it?"

He said it gently, because he didn't mean it to chide. He liked the new Diana, but her secret child was galling. It was one thing to put on fine feathers and play a docile role. That was no worse than when he put on powder and patches in a fruitless attempt to win a fair lady's heart.

It was another thing to have a child hidden in the country.

"Oh," she said. The pleasure drained from her face and her smile faltered. "That is not exactly what happened."

North glanced toward the door, but his aunt was nowhere to be seen. "Perhaps we should have that talk now."

Her fingers wound together anxiously. He liked it better when she laughed, her fingers fluttering in the air.

"Let's begin with how you ended up in a cottage. I understand from my aunt that your mother disowned you. I presume you and Mrs. Belgrave are still estranged, since she has not rescued you from your employment."

Diana felt as if her stomach had shriveled into a small, hard lump. Some errant, prideful part of her didn't want North to know how little respect her mother had for her.

Even after Rose had been summarily cast out of their life for the crime of carrying a child out of wedlock, Diana had kept making excuses, kept trying to love her mother, until she was sent off to a betrothal party in brightly colored silks and satins, while Mrs.

Belgrave remained in London to plaster over a vexing setback.

Rose's death.

"My mother will never relent," Diana said, allowing the familiar grief to resonate silently through her bones. "She thinks very poorly of me."

"Why didn't you turn to the child's family?" North asked.

"Godfrey's father and grandfather passed away in a carriage accident, and his grandmother died years before."

"You are Lavinia Gray's cousin," North continued, his eyes steady on hers. "You cannot tell me that Lavinia would not invite you to live with her. Even if her mother refused, she would share her pin money."

Diana managed a wry smile. "Lavinia and Lady Gray moved to France directly after our betrothal party. I tried to write to her, but I didn't have her address. I'm sure she wrote to me, but my mother would have destroyed the letter. I doubt Lavinia has any idea what happened after I jilted you, unless those terrible prints depicting us are circulating outside of England."

"Bloody hell." North reached up as if to run his hands through his hair, only to encounter his wig. Without pausing, he tossed it onto a nearby chair.

His hair was black and short. Without the white wig,

his eyes appeared darker and his cheekbones sharper. He had always been beautiful, but now—now he looked potent. Masculine.

Diana could at last imagine him on the battlefield. It had been impossible to picture the man she had known mincing around a battlefield in a tall wig and high heels.

But this man? He was a warrior, from his heavily muscled shoulders to his—to everything.

"Did you know that they are saying that I raped you?" He sounded as if he were gritting his teeth.

Diana almost apologized again, but she had the feeling he would snarl at her. "I have seen the print depicting us as characters in Shakespeare's *Cymbeline*. Could you dismiss them as an artistic flight of fancy?"

"No matter how fanciful, I dislike being depicted as a rapist."

"The print doesn't pretend to be accurate," she pointed out. "You are caught in the act of emerging from a little trunk, which seems to be crammed with jewels as well as you. And you are not a small man."

She let herself enjoy his broad chest from beneath lowered lashes.

His mouth had turned to an uncompromising line. "I don't find it amusing, no matter the size of the trunk."

"Well, you must change your attitude," she said

firmly, ignoring his curt tone. "The print is as absurd as those depicting Lord Alaric slicing off the head of a giant sea monster."

"Absurd they may be, but I feature as the villain instead of the hero."

Diana made a face at him. "You *aren't* a villain; we've already discussed the fact that our comedy of errors has a villainess, and I am she. I shall find some way to make the ton understand that you had nothing to do with Godfrey, nor with my employment. I promise you that."

"You needn't bother," he said flatly. "I don't give a damn."

"You can't have it both ways," she pointed out. "Either you are unamused by your depiction in a Shakespeare play, or you don't give a damn, in which case, the fact you extract yourself from a trunk half your size is as entertaining as your brother's subjugated sea monster."

Miraculously, his eyes went from frigid to amused. "Subjugated sea monster?"

She grinned, happy to see that glimmer of laughter. "Subdued squid? Licked leviathan?"

"In the midst of my lecturing, did I mention that the perfect duchess never points out when her spouse has ceased to be logical?"

"I'm sure you would have got around to it, given time," Diana said.

His eyes were at half mast, glittering at her with an expression in them that she hadn't seen before. It wasn't longing, or affection—

And it was gone.

"So that's the tale of how I ended up in the cottage where Lady Knowe found me," Diana said, circling back to his question. "There's no one to blame, I assure you."

Ever since Rose's death, she had spent a good deal of time thinking about blame. Whom does one blame, when life isn't as one wishes?

She could blame her mother. Or Archibald Ewing, for anticipating his wedding vows. Or the drunken coachman who overturned the Ewing carriage and killed Archibald and his father. Or . . . it was endless.

The one person she couldn't blame was North, and it was time to tell him the whole truth.

"Godfrey isn't your child, but he isn't my child either," she said, feeling a wash of pink traveling up her chest. "He is my sister Rose's child."

His eyes traveled slowly over her face. "Your sister's child." The words thumped down into the room, as if susceptible to gravity. "Illegitimate, I presume."

"Yes," Diana said flatly, adding, "Rose died of a

fever, two days before we were due to leave for the betrothal party."

"Your tears," he stated. "I am sorry for your loss."

She gave him a crooked smile.

"I will admit that I'm relieved to know you were not weeping over our proposed marriage. Is that why your mother didn't accompany you to the party?"

She nodded.

"I have no wish to take your grief lightly," he said, his voice dry as dust, "but the news that you jilted me in order to care for a child who wasn't your own seems tailor-made to knock down my ducal arrogance. Couldn't you have simply told me of the boy's existence, either before or after your sister passed away?"

Diana shook her head. "My mother felt that adding a besmirched sister to a grocer grandfather would make me *persona non grata* among the ton. Certainly not duchess material."

"That suggests that I am as shallow as the leaders of the ton," he observed. His face didn't show a hint of emotion, but she had the odd impression he was hurt.

"You are not simply you," she said, fumbling to explain herself. "You are the future Duke of Lindow."

She saw that strike home. He would have married her, because he was an honorable man. As yet for the future head of one of the oldest and most august families in all England, a lady with a besmirched sister ought to be out of the question.

"Why didn't you tell me the truth when I came to say goodbye before leaving England? You knew what conclusion I had reached."

Diana tried to summon up another smile and failed. "It seemed kinder to let you think that I was . . . that Godfrey was mine."

An ominous darkness crossed his eyes. "Because I would pine for you, unless I thought myself betrothed to an arrant whore?"

The last two words were spoken mildly, but they stung.

"I was ashamed to have jilted you without explanation." Her fingers were quivering again, but she didn't let her chin drop, kept holding his gaze. "I deserved to have you hate me. You *should* hate me. I mean, you probably already did, because—"

"I could never hate you," North said evenly.

Diana gulped. "That's—that's very good to know."

"So you let me believe the child was yours to spur my dislike."

"It was an impulse," Diana whispered. "A very stupid one." She cleared her throat. "I was determined not to accept help from you, and if you knew Godfrey was my sister's you would have felt compelled to . . ."

He raised an eyebrow.

"To be the hero," she said in a rush. "I deserved to be the villainess, don't you see?" She couldn't tell if he was incredulous or just plain scornful.

He gave a short bark of laughter. "Bloody hell, you were trying to save me, weren't you? You thought I was in love with you, and so I would fight to make you my wife."

Her fingers twisted so hard that she winced. "I thought that you had made a promise to marry me, and you would insist on seeing it through. I couldn't allow that to happen."

North threw back his drink, leaned over, and pulled the bell cord that summoned Prism. "I think they've left us alone long enough, don't you?"

"Prism has certainly been gone quite a while," Diana said, steadying her voice.

"My aunt likely has him tied to the balustrade."

"*What?*"

"Oh, not for erotic purposes, but so that he can't interrupt our deep and meaningful conversation. You hadn't noticed that you have made a conquest of my Aunt Knowe? She's hoping that I'll be overcome by the dregs of passion and compromise you."

The dregs of passion . . . She deserved that.

"It's impossible to compromise a governess," Diana

observed, desperate to talk of something other than their personal history. "Once a lady accepts a wage, she is no longer a lady."

"I don't think that's the case." He frowned. "My governess, Miss Raymond, had a voice like a frog and an unfortunate tendency to grow hair on her upper lip, but no one would have said she was less than a lady."

"The condition of being a lady is complicated, like the five hundred pounds that a lady must pay out of her dowry to excuse her indiscretions, even though a gentleman has no such requirement," Diana explained. "I can assure you that a woman can't be compromised—which implies marriage—by a man who pays her wage."

North's brows snapped together. "A gentleman who treats a lady with injudicious attention *has* compromised her, and *must* offer his hand in marriage." That was a growl. Diana decided not to remind him that the hour they just spent together would be considered fodder for a forced marriage proposal by any rule of polite society that she'd heard.

"It's different with us," North said, apparently reading her face.

"Oh, why?" She smiled into her glass; good manners dictated that a lady shouldn't smirk at a gentleman.

And she was still a lady, albeit one with a wage.

"We are old acquaintances, and my aunt will join us any moment," he said stiffly.

Diana wasn't impressed, and let him know it with a roll of her eyes. "If you return to polite society with that naive attitude, you'll be compromised before you know it. Actually, you're lucky my mother doesn't have a third daughter, because you'd be snapped up in a second."

"I disagree."

"You easily fell for her wiles the first time," Diana insisted. For some reason, she truly wanted to warn him. He deserved better than a wax doll like herself, a woman cowed into silence. She leaned forward and closed her hand around his. "Be careful choosing your duchess, North."

He turned over her hand, his thumb rubbing over calluses resulting from being a governess—not a lady. "*You* are offering me advice on how to succeed in high society?"

She withdrew her hand, feeling pink rising up her neck again. "Only from personal observation. My mother was driven by the notion of marrying me into the nobility. Sometimes I felt sorry for . . ." Her voice trailed off at the incredulous look on his face.

"You felt sorry for me?"

"Not sorry for you alone, but for gentlemen who have no idea how—how Machiavellian mothers can be."

"Do you know what 'Machiavellian' means?"

His incredulity made her bristle. "My mother believed that duchesses should be well-read in classical philosophy in order to facilitate conversation around a dining table."

He shook his head. "Your mother sounds like a general."

"I have often thought that she might have rivaled General Washington, if given a chance," Diana said. "You know better than I, but from what I read in the newspaper, he is a wily man who engages in thorough advance planning."

He said, his voice hard, "It seems the British newspapers have a better understanding of the war than does the Ministry."

Prism bustled in the door, followed by four footmen, each holding a silver platter covered by a dome. Lady Knowe came last, chattering loudly. She seemed to understand that Diana, for one, had talked enough of serious matters. Instead, North's aunt held forth with a flow of gossip about the family that had Diana in fits of laughter.

If she hadn't laughed . . . she would have cried,

thanks to the ache in her heart. The way she'd ruined her life as well as North's. And her sister no longer had a life.

Rose and North would have been perfect for each other. Absolutely perfect. Her sister had been sensitive and sensible, incredibly smart, and conversant in every courtesy. Rose had been beautiful too, with hair the gleaming color of corn silk.

If only Diana hadn't stubbornly refused to marry Archibald, Rose would have had her Season, married North, and been alive today. Lady Knowe would have adored Rose. Godfrey would have been better off; that went without saying. If he had a real mother, he'd be speaking by now. And North wouldn't have—

She pulled her mind away from that thought and fixed a smile on her face.

At the evening's end, Lady Knowe pushed herself upright and proclaimed, "We shall make a plan for you, Diana, but not until the duke and duchess arrive. We must wait for my brother's advice."

"I fail to see why my father should be part of a discussion addressing my former fiancée and her nephew," North stated, rising to his feet.

"Because we need a governess to replace Diana," his aunt said, adjusting the silk shawl that hung around her shoulders.

Diana suddenly noticed that the lady hadn't turned a hair on hearing that Godfrey was no relation to North. "You knew that Godfrey was not your relative," she gasped. "*And* that he is not my son!"

Lady Knowe snorted. "Child, you are many things, but a mother is not one of them. I am not a mother either, but I am well aware that a few months' acquaintance with a gentleman does not result in a baby that age. Furthermore, the boy doesn't resemble you."

"Why did you bring me here?" Diana gasped, her mind reeling.

"To my mind, you were almost one of us. I could not allow you to live in that hovel and you refused to allow me to help you financially. Granted, I didn't imagine that your stubborn insistence on being employed would cause such a fuss amongst the prudes who rule the ton."

Clearly considering the subject closed, she turned to North. "Our governess cannot leave us without a word of warning. Ophelia will need time to find a replacement. Artie is attached to Diana, and loves her like a second mother."

"I had no intention of throwing Miss Belgrave out the door," North said, his tone stiff.

His aunt rapped him on the shoulder with her fan. "Don't give me that pent-up mongrel glare. I remember you in nappies. I might remind you that you've been addressing Diana by her first name throughout the meal; it's too late for formality."

Diana was wrestling with a familiar wave of desperation at the idea of leaving Artie—and an unfamiliar one at the idea of living another day under the same roof as North.

The former North? The lord in a wig, patches, and red heels? She wouldn't have turned a hair.

But the North who'd thrown his wig onto a chair and never bothered to retrieve it? Whose eyes considered her face with such thoughtful interest? Who smelled like honey and sunshine?

He was dangerous to her in all ways.

"I will remain in the castle for two weeks to work out my notice, which will give Her Grace time to choose a replacement for me." She curtsied. "Good evening, Lady Knowe. Lord Roland." She emphasized the last name slightly because it was *not* too late for formality, and she had to remember that.

"Good night, my dear. We shall expect you at dinner tomorrow night," the lady said, nodding.

"I dine with you, Lady Knowe, when there is no one else in the castle. You and Lord Roland have much to discuss, I'm certain."

North's jaw tightened. He might have been grinding his teeth.

"I suppose I can't force you," Lady Knowe said, disappointed.

North didn't say anything, merely bowed in farewell. But the way his eyes glinted when she addressed him as "Lord Roland," and when she declined to join them for dinner?

She had a feeling that her wish had just come true: She'd seen North in a rage.

But she had done the right thing.

She had disliked North when they first met, because he was so stern and courtly. If he had revealed the raw masculinity he'd displayed tonight, she would not have fled their betrothal party.

All the same, their marriage wouldn't have been a success, because he had been attracted to a false version of her. From his own description, he chose a perfect lady, on the basis of her wig and clothing.

They were ill-matched, like white and black chess pieces trying to play on the same side.

She was happy as a servant, pleased to earn a wage, and she had to preserve her sense of contentedness. The evening had been enjoyable, but the experience was dangerously seductive.

No more North.

Chapter Five

Later that night, in the castle kitchens

"What on earth are you doing here?" Diana's voice startled him. North had just emerged from the pantry into the moonlit kitchen to find her standing in the doorway, a tray in her hands. He felt such a leap of desire that it was a good thing his shirt was hanging over his breeches.

"Reminding myself of the castle," he said. "Why didn't you summon a footman to fetch that tray?"

She glanced down as if she'd forgotten what she held. "I was setting the schoolroom to rights."

"At this hour?"

"It's my responsibility." She wore a thick flannel

wrapper tied tightly around her waist. Her copper hair was bound in a braid that fell over her shoulder.

"It's well after midnight," he pointed out.

"Truth to tell, I forgot to put the schoolroom in order, and had to get out of bed when I remembered." She gave him a lopsided smile. "I was thinking over what I ought to have said to you before dinner, the way one does."

Deep in his body, almost in his bones, he felt one word, over and over. *Mine. Mine. Mine.*

Ridiculous. The lady had soundly rejected him.

He leaned back against the battered wooden table that ran the length of the kitchen and crossed his legs before him. "What should you have said?" He kept his tone pleasant, as if he didn't give a damn about anything that had happened between them.

"I was so distraught over Rose's death . . . that's why I didn't write you a note when I ran away."

North didn't like hearing sadness in her voice. He shrugged. "If it ever happens again, just remember that when jilting a man, a woman explains her motives in writing."

"There's a protocol?" A smile eased her face. "Put it down to my poor education." She set the tray down on the kitchen table. "I am rubbish at making change, bathing a baby, jilting a man."

He straightened, because her smile made him even harder, and his breeches were pulling uncomfortably. "You really don't know how to make change?"

It was hard to tell in the moonlight, but she looked to be turning pink. "I can make a pressed-flower arrangement, and play the harp. My mother felt strongly that practical activities should be performed by servants, and never taught to ladies."

"Was the art of jilting too practical to learn?" he asked, enjoying the way Diana's lower lip was deeper in the middle, echoing her heart-shaped face.

"Actually, I wish someone had taught me the art of running away," she said, with a wary smile. "I was such a fool. I took nothing with me but a hatbox."

"What was in the hatbox?"

"A chemise, some money, a pair of gloves. I'm not sure why I brought the gloves along. I wasn't thinking clearly."

"How much money did you have?"

"A little more than a pound." She grimaced, and a streak of protectiveness went through him. "I had spent most of my pin money on gifts for my cousin Lavinia and Willa Ffynche, your sister-in-law."

"You fled the castle with one pound?" The dismay he felt was unnervingly deep.

"I was that much of a fool," she admitted. "Luckily,

I was wearing emerald earrings. I gave one to the innkeeper in Mobberley, and he bought me a ticket on the post all the way to London."

"I'll bet he did," North said, emotion boiling under his breastbone. "Your earring was undoubtedly worth far more than a ticket. Where did you go after you arrived in London? I went straight to your mother's house. You were not there, and I had the pleasure of telling Mrs. Belgrave of your flight."

"I know! It must have been awful. I'm so—"

He held up a hand.

"I had gone directly to the Foundling Hospital to look for Godfrey," Diana said. With a shake of her head, she added, "My mother had sent money with him, so he could be apprenticed at the proper age."

"You went to the Foundling Hospital?" North asked hollowly. No wonder he had been unable to find her. She had ventured into one of the worst areas of London, with nothing but a hatbox.

"First I went to Christ's Hospital, but they take infants only if they are legitimate. It took me another two days, but I found my way to Bloomsbury Fields and the Foundling Hospital there."

He felt sick.

And even sicker, once she told him about giving the hospital her other emerald in order to buy her nephew back. Taking the baby to her home, only to find her mother in hysterics after North's visit. "It was unnervingly like being in a bad play," she said, trying to smile and failing.

North fought his own stuttering breath, unable to find words. It was deeply ironic that the only woman who had no interest in his estate or title was the one he felt a deep, visceral urge to protect.

He had failed her.

"I hadn't been thinking properly since my sister died." Diana's fingers twisted together. "I tend to leap before I look, and my flight to London was one of my more idiotic moments in a life filled with lunacy."

He crossed the distance between them in a single stride, put his hands on her shoulders, and pulled her into his arms. "You did what you could to keep your nephew safe," he bit out. "There is nothing idiotic about that." She gazed up at him, her eyes wide, her eyelashes spangled in the moonlight. "When your mother threw you out, where did you go?"

"I took the post to my old nanny's home, but she had passed away."

Curses rose to his lips, but he cut them off. "I cannot believe that your mother threw you and her only grandson out the door without money."

"She gave me five pounds," Diana said. "She was

livid about the emeralds, and Godfrey, and my sister's death, though she wouldn't admit it. My mother never approved of me so much as when you courted me. I let her down dreadfully."

North saw no point in expressing his violent feelings toward Mrs. Belgrave. "My turn to apologize," he said, putting her away from him, because in another moment he would bend his mouth to hers.

"For what?"

"For wooing you so ineptly that you couldn't tell me about your sister's death. Lecturing you about being a duchess. For God's sake, Diana, why didn't you just tell me to shut up?"

"You were enjoying yourself," she said, her mouth quirking up in the teasing grin that he never saw when they were betrothed.

Because he was too busy being an ass.

"I didn't notice you were grieving, because I was trying to make you into a duchess." His voice rasped.

"I would have made a wretched duchess," she said, with obvious conviction. She touched his arm. "Are you well, North? I thought you'd be asleep hours ago. You seem dreadfully tired."

"It's not easy coming back to England after being at war," he said, surprising himself. "The castle is so quiet."

"I think it's loud." She wrinkled her nose at him. "I would have thought stone was silent, but the floors creak."

"The ghosts make noises too," he said, enthralled by the playfulness he'd never seen when they were betrothed.

Her eyes grew bigger. "Ghosts?"

"Has no one told you about the castle ghosts?"

"In *here*?" Her gaze skittered around the kitchen.

"There's supposedly a priest up on the ramparts who carries his head under his arm, but I never heard of him straying into the kitchens," he told her, adding, "My brothers and I made up more ghosts; unfortunately there was no evidence for their existence."

"Well, thank goodness for that," she said tartly. She turned to go.

A gentleman would escort her through those dark corridors to the nursery. But her wrapper had eased open and her nightgown was made of a flimsy cotton.

Diana had beautiful breasts, the kind that made a man's gut twist and yearn. Better he stay here, and let her go.

She hesitated, and left.

The space where she'd been assumed the shape of the ghost of the duchess he might have had.

The duchess he would never have.

Chapter Six

The following night

Months before, North had hoped that untroubled sleep would return to him during the interminable voyage back to England. If not then, once he'd returned to his boyhood bedchamber in the castle.

But no.

He had lost the gift of sleep at the battle where he'd lost most of his regiment. It didn't matter how often a man told himself that he had sworn a vow to follow orders, no matter how idiotic.

By buying a commission, North had put himself in charge of more than two hundred men. In making the vow to serve, he had put all two hundred lives at risk.

In following that vow, he had sacrificed a number of

them. He pushed the thought out of his head and fixed on another reason for sleeplessness: Diana.

Her story had a number of gaps in it. Her sister had given birth to an illegitimate baby, and died shortly before the betrothal party. He could understand that Diana believed care for Godfrey was incompatible with a lady's life.

She was wrong; Godfrey could have been established in a warm and loving home. Or, if Diana insisted on having him under her eye, North knew several examples of noble ladies raising their own or their husbands' bastards.

When he and Diana were betrothed, he had been desperately in love with his fiancée, figuratively at her feet. If she had told him of the Foundling Hospital, he would have fetched her nephew without hesitation, if only to wring a smile from her. Any lady with an understanding of the power women could wield over men would have known that.

Diana had had no idea. She had been naive, as well as impulsive.

At the moment he was so weary that he felt groggy and not a little queasy. Aunt Knowe had ordered only three courses at dinner, but even those were two more than he could eat.

Somehow, he had to return to being a man who

expected four or five courses as his due. A man who would be offended by a table laid without at least eight to ten dishes at every course.

Not offended for himself, he thought, stumbling through an explanation he'd never considered before Diana broached the subject. Offended for the title. Reflexively protective of the title. He was always waiting, he realized now, for someone to point out how ill-fitted he was to the role, in comparison to Horatius.

It made it all the more ironic that Diana had shielded him from her bastard nephew in order to protect the title.

The deeply shaming part, the nagging fact he kept revisiting, was that he had glimpsed Diana's desperate straits when he'd found her in that cottage. Nevertheless, he had ridden away in the grip of a savage rage, thinking she'd chosen a footman over him, over a *duke*.

Except that there hadn't been a footman, nor an insult to his bloody honor. If he hadn't been so defensive of his rank, he would have marched into that house and made sure she was taken care of, lover be damned.

He would have discovered that Diana had no lover. He would have learned of Rose's illegitimate baby.

Godfrey's parentage clarified Diana's future.

She was *his* problem, not his father's. Ophelia could

solve the problem of who would care for Artie—but he would solve the problem of who would care for Diana.

She didn't want him. She didn't need him.

No, she did need him. She was destitute.

His mind went around and around, like a rat in a trap. It occurred to him to send her to the family house in Scotland, but that felt terribly far away. What if something happened, and she needed him?

He swung out of bed and made his way to the writing desk that stood before his window. Down below him, out there in the darkness, was Lindow Moss, the peat bog that spread east of the castle. With the window open, he could smell the wind that scoured across it.

London air was choked with smoke and dust. The air over Lindow Moss smelled like peat, not entirely pleasant, but clean, in its own way.

He was damned lucky to have been jilted. Lucky that he wasn't in love any longer. Lucky that he recognized love for the mad wind Dante described before it was too late. Obviously, he hadn't been in love with a real woman. He had never met the Diana whom he'd encountered yesterday: funny, rueful, deeply loyal.

Even her hair was a revelation.

Before, he had always known where Diana was in any room, because of the tall white cloud that was her wig. He'd been so besotted that he had always marked her location.

Thinking about that idiocy, he shoved his hand through his hair. It was growing again. He used to shave it as that made it easier to tolerate heavy wigs, as well as to avoid the lice that plagued his men.

Diana's hair, her real hair, was dark red, with a sheen like a fox's pelt, but softer.

He stared out over Lindow Moss, counting stars as a way of curbing his own stupidity.

In love with a governess?

The worst governess the castle had ever seen?

Hell, no.

This was merely the disagreeable aftermath of being jilted. Whenever he had woken in his tent in America after dreaming of Diana, the edge of erotic longing he felt had made him furious. He refused to lust after another man's woman.

But as it turned out, she belonged to no man.

Godfrey, that plate-throwing boy, was her nephew, not her son. He almost liked the boy just for that. He himself had thrown a plate or two at Horatius, his infuriating brother—who was always right, always the best. Who wouldn't have thrown a plate at Horatius?

Even now, he would love to throw something at the fool for getting drunk and taking a bet he could gallop across Lindow Moss. No one could cross a bog on horseback in the night. They'd rescued his horse, although Horatius's body was never found.

Dead men, Horatius among them, crowded into his brain at night. He kept going over the names of those who died at Stony Point. John Goss, who was missing two front teeth. William Peach, mocked for the fuzz of his first beard. Peter Lithgow, the one they all called Gower.

Surviving prisoners of war from his regiment were due to be exchanged for American prisoners any day now. His father had pressured the Ministry to make certain that his men were part of the next exchange.

He couldn't bring them home; they would be sent to another regiment. But he wasn't sure they wanted to be home. They had joined willingly enough. He hadn't pressed anyone into service, or hired Hessians to fill his regiment, the way other lords had done.

He turned from the window and walked to the door, unable to even glance at his bed. If he lay down, he'd fall into dreams of smoke and cannon fire, weeping men and groans of the dying.

Better to go—

Anywhere.

Out in the dark, echoing corridors, he paced restlessly, tracing the path he had forged the night before.

He walked over stone flagging that stretched into irregular wings added by ancestors. Up and down staircases he went, through the kitchens again, and into the ballroom. The only floor he avoided was the nursery wing.

Perhaps he would summon Diana to the library on the morrow. Sit behind the great desk where he used to examine the estate's ledgers, and demand to know why she had fled the castle without asking for help.

Or he could summon her to the drawing room without warning. She might arrive with her hair falling down her back, and he could stare at its color surreptitiously while he inquired whether it was their kiss that had sent her running.

Why had she left all her jewelry except that pair of earrings? He remembered Diana wearing an emerald necklace that could have supported her for years. Yet she hadn't taken it in order to ensure her future.

No, she had fled the castle without a second thought.

Not unlike the way he bought a commission and left the country, a voice in his mind suggested.

He was making a third circuit around the Great Portrait Gallery—so called to distinguish it from the East Portrait Gallery, which was older and smaller—when he made up his mind to visit the nursery.

Diana wouldn't be awake, but he could check on Artemisia. Or Artie, as his little sister wanted to be called. Poor Artemisia had been given an even worse name than Betsy, whose real name was Boadicea. "Betsy" was acceptable on the marriage market, but what gentleman would want to court "Artie"?

The names resulted from the duke's determination to name all his many children after warriors. Horatius and Alaric had been lucky. He had chosen North over Roland. Leonidas turned himself into Leo; Alexander and Joan accepted their names, as did Erik. His stepsister Viola had joined the family with her name intact. But what about Artie and Sparky? Presumably Spartacus no longer allowed himself to be called Sparky. He'd been complaining about that before North left for the war.

Making his way to the nursery wing, he surprised himself with a bark of laughter, thinking of Artie, Sparky, and Betsy.

He descended stone steps, walked a long corridor, and headed up the wooden staircase to the nursery floor. At the top, he stopped in the dim light and felt under the ornamental knob atop the newel post that graced the top of the stairs.

Sure enough, the big H was still there. Years ago Horatius had carved his initial, claiming the castle in some foolish game they'd played.

Except it was never foolish to Horatius. He had relished the role of future duke, strutting around like a bantam cock from the age of five. Dressed in velvet, most of the time. Keeping himself clean while Alaric, North, and the duke's ward, Parth Sterling, rolled in the dirt.

North's hands tightened on the knob, making the white scar that bisected his right hand gleam in the low light of the lamp burning in the nursery wing.

Within a month or two of landing in America, he'd known that the war was hopeless—and immoral. That country belonged to its rough and ready inhabitants, not to the red-coated British. He could have lost all the fingers on his right hand—or his life—and the war wasn't worth that, let alone the lives of men on both sides.

With a half-suppressed sound of disgust, he walked down the corridor. The nursery bedchamber was in the middle on the right. He pushed the door open and stood for a moment, accustoming himself to the dim light.

An empty rocking chair was placed next to the fireplace. Presumably a maid sat up all night only when a baby was in residence. Around the large room, pushed against the walls, were small beds, each with its own set of curtains. There were as many as one might find in a small orphanage, thanks to his father's three fertile duchesses.

Only one had its bed curtains closed, so he stepped over and quietly drew back the fabric. Artie lay fast asleep, clutching a wooden doll with brown hair and violent red spots on its cheeks. The doll wore a night-dress printed with small blue flowers that matched Artie's. North was instantly certain that Artie's governess had made it for her.

He had clear memories of his sisters' bedtime. They went to bed shining clean, their hair tightly braided. Artie's face was clean enough, but her hair was a tangled cloud on the white pillowcase.

In the house he meant to offer her, Diana would have a cook, a maid, a nanny. She probably needed two maids. It couldn't be a cottage, because she would need room to house those servants, so that she and Godfrey could be comfortable and happy.

That was crucial. She had been *his*, for a short time. He had believed she would be his for life, and it was a hard idea to shake.

He straightened and softly pulled Artie's curtains back in place.

Godfrey must have refused bed curtains. He himself loathed the stifling feeling of sleeping surrounded by heavy draperies. To this day, he preferred his bed curtains tied back, and a window open as well. Even the brutal conditions of an American winter hadn't changed his mind about the delights of fresh air.

The next bed was empty, which surprised him. He'd have thought Artie and Godfrey would sleep near each other, but perhaps that wasn't proper.

The following bed was also empty, and he made his way more quickly to the bed beyond that. A conflicted feeling was rising in his gut. Dread. Guilt.

Damn it, she couldn't have left without warning a second time, could she? His gut twisted at the thought of Diana gone, this time with a little boy instead of a hatbox.

Surely she wouldn't have handed over Artie to be cared for by that ill-tempered nursemaid.

"Hell and damnation," North muttered when he inspected the last bed, keeping his voice quiet so that Artie wouldn't wake up. He glanced around the room one more time, then pushed open the door to the nanny's bedroom.

It was empty.

The nursery at Lindow Castle was made up of a sprawling suite of rooms that included the children's bedchamber, a bathing alcove, the schoolroom, the dining room, and even a priest's hole.

He suddenly remembered that his governess, Miss

Raymond, had had a sitting room of her own, where she used to retreat when four energetic boys—Horatius, Alaric, he, and Parth—wore her out. In retrospect, she had done an excellent job, handing out butterfly nets and sending them on daily rambles around the countryside.

Once in the corridor, he turned right, passing the dining room and the schoolroom. Next to it was the door to Miss Raymond's chamber.

He had no memory of ever being invited to enter, nor, indeed, wishing to. He and his brothers hadn't devoted any thought to their governess, although now he wondered if she, too, had been caught between the family and the household, not fitting into either place.

His heart sank. The door stood ajar. No lady left her private chamber door open.

Curses spun through his head. Diana was gone, and he would have to chase after her. He pushed open the door, thinking that Prism had to have been aware of her departure. Nothing happened in the household without the butler's knowledge. Yet no one had informed him?

An indefinably flowery warmth hung in the air. Bread had been toasted at the fire in the not-too-distant past.

She hadn't left.

His heart hitched in a way that sent a shock down

his spine. It was merely because he was grateful not to have to chase the woman down, he told himself quickly. That would have been a bother.

The chamber was good-sized, with a small desk by the window. A narrow bed was nestled in the corner, but he didn't allow his eyes to rest on it, looking instead at the fireplace flanked by two padded chairs, worn enough to have been there since his childhood.

It had been a chilly evening, and a fire was still giving off enough light that he could see watercolor paintings propped up on the mantel. They were likely gifts from his sisters, considering their dashing colors and complete lack of talent. The room was full of reminders of his siblings, from a broken bow to a pile of children's gloves awaiting mending.

The fireside chairs were wide enough that a slim governess might read aloud to one or even two small children, and in light of the stack of children's books on the hearth, that happened on a regular basis. An unfinished sampler, perhaps belonging to Joan or Betsy, lay across a stool, a bag of embroidery thread beside it. A roughly carved wooden boat leaned against one wall, waiting for its creator to return from Eton, presumably.

Big plump pillows were piled to one side so that a child could throw herself on the floor and read a book.

A grin spread across North's face—such an unfamiliar facial movement that he noticed it—when he realized that one wall was taken up with a gallery of prints depicting his brother Alaric, or "Lord Wilde," as he was known to readers of his books as well as playgoers who saw the infamous *Wilde in Love* which, before being shut down, was the most sought-after theater ticket in all London.

He drifted across the room, knowing that he shouldn't be here. Intruding on a lady's bedchamber. Unheard of. Appalling.

No gentleman would consider such a thing. Perhaps an aftereffect of war was that a man lost his standards. Years before, if he had inadvertently entered a lady's chamber without express permission, North would have promptly retreated from the room.

Here was Alaric planting the British flag on an impossibly tall mountain, Alaric wrestling a sea dragon, and Alaric entertaining the Empress of Russia in her bedchamber.

He turned to the paintings that crowded the mantelpiece. A sketch of kittens was propped next to a stick figure. Another engraving of the sort that adorned the wall. He held it closer to the fire so he could see the subject. A downtrodden girl was seated on a bench, a small child clutching her skirts.

The girl was recognizably Diana. Those straight eyebrows weren't hers, but the pointed chin and full lips? Undeniably Miss Diana Belgrave. On the doorstep behind her, an aristocrat lounged.

It could have been any man in a wig and heels. He didn't think his lips curled in such a thin, fantastically cruel line. At least he hoped not.

He had horns. Wonderful.

One of his hands was out of sight. He tilted the page toward the light to see whether . . .

Damn it.

"You're the wicked baron," a sleepy voice said from the other side of the fireplace. "Naturally, your hands are wandering."

North's head jerked up. Diana had pulled the dressing gown she wore the previous night over her nightdress. Her face was in shadow but he was acutely aware of her body and its curves. Once a man had glimpsed Diana's breasts, they couldn't be unseen.

"I thought you'd fled the castle," he said, putting the print back on the mantel. "Forgive me for entering your chamber, but your nephew isn't in the nursery and I was concerned about you." He corrected himself. "Him."

"Godfrey is here," she said, nodding toward the bed. "He crawls into my bed when he feels uncertain or afraid. Since he doesn't yet speak, I'm never quite sure what took him out of his own bed."

"How old is he?" North walked over to the bed because, after all, he'd expressed interest in the boy's welfare. In reality, he didn't feel more than the usual curiosity one male feels about another who has usurped his place in bed.

"Almost four years old," Diana said, an edge of worry clear in her voice.

North had a shockingly strong impulse to comfort her, but he couldn't think what to say. "When do they usually begin speaking?"

"'They' being children in general?" Her voice had a thread of laughter in it, like pure spun gold. "Artie began before she was a year old, but I understand that boys are often slower to speak. I think she is as unusual in her own way as Godfrey is in his."

Diana had turned away to light a lamp, and now she brought it over and stood at North's shoulder. The boy was curled up like a snail, fast asleep. He had red hair and his long eyelashes lay on his cheeks like tiny fans.

"Did you and your sister have the same hair?" North asked, for something to say.

"Oh, no, she was truly beautiful. Rose had lovely hair, the color of yellow primroses in spring. Godfrey was unfortunate enough to inherit that hair from his father."

What did she mean by saying her sister was "truly beautiful" or that Godfrey was "unfortunate"?

"Was Godfrey's father . . ." North hesitated. "A member of the household?"

"No." She reached out and pulled the covers over the boy's little shoulder. "Her fiancé, as it happens." Her voice was wooden. "A gentleman, supposedly."

Right there was the reason men of honor ought to behave with propriety, especially with their betrothed. "He died before they could marry," North said, appalled.

"He did."

"That's bloody bad luck."

A soft sound, like a choked giggle, escaped her. "I never heard you curse while we were betrothed. In fact, I didn't think you *had* thoughts violent enough to justify the lack of dignity."

There was enough humiliating material there to destroy whatever fragments of self-worth he had clung to after being jilted.

She seemed to recognize it, because after a pause, she added, "Only because you were beautifully behaved, North. Seemingly effortlessly proper."

Had she really thought him so proper that a curse wouldn't cross his lips? North found that galling.

He cut her off before she could further pare his manhood down to the size of the boy in her bed. "And yet, here I am, in your bedchamber uninvited, in the middle of the night." A gleam of dark amusement eased his exhaustion. "You could say that I'm playing the role of that Shakespeare character I'm depicted as. Not Hamlet, obviously."

"I have no idea who the character is," Diana said. "My mother considers dramatists to be dissolute by nature. She included Shakespeare in that group, so I haven't read the plays. I must say that the plot of *Cymbeline* seems to confirm her opinion."

"Hinges on a ravishment, as I remember it," North said.

"I don't suppose you're planning to reprise the role?"

It took a moment for him to work out what she was saying. His head snapped around and he met her eyes, only to feel his incipient fury—did *everyone* think he was capable of rape?—melt away. Her eyes were dancing.

For a moment, rash words trembled on his tongue. His better nature prevailed, and he gave her a lopsided smile. "I only ravish fair ladies after emerging from a trunk. It's a prerequisite."

"I understand," she said, her voice somehow turning laughter into words. "A gentleman must have standards."

"Dukes require trunks full of diamonds," he said, walking back toward the fireplace. He should go to his dark, quiet bedroom and the memories hovering in its corners. Instead he crouched down and put another log on the fire, poking at the embers to make it catch. "I wouldn't have entered, but for the fact your door was ajar."

"I leave it open for Godfrey," she explained. "He can't tell me his emotions, you see. It makes it difficult."

North almost opened his mouth and said something absurd. Instead, he forced out a different sentence. "Who was your sister's fiancé?"

He was beginning to formulate a plan to break down the door of the rake's house and force his family to support their illegitimate grandson. He would take care of Diana, but the boy's grandparents could set Godfrey up in comfort.

Their son had been a reprobate. Or perhaps merely imprudent, in love, and deeply unlucky.

Diana drifted to the other side of the fireplace. "Would you like some honey toast?"

He frowned at her. "What?"

"Honey toast. When Artie is as tired as you are, I feed her honey toast." If her voice had been sympathetic, he would have left the room. Instead, she was matter-of-fact.

She went over to a table on the side of the room and began sawing at a loaf of bread. North poked at the fire again, trying to remember if he'd ever seen a lady slicing bread. He rather thought not, since he'd never been served by any hand other than a servant's.

After a minute or two, Diana returned to his side holding two long forks of the sort he remembered from Eton. Thick, uneven slices were stuck on the tines. One side of his mouth curled up at the sight; servants knew how to cut a loaf of bread properly, which Diana did not.

She nudged him with a fork handle. "Your bread, Your Future Grace."

Diana Belgrave had the most beautiful smile in the world. Tonight, she hadn't braided her hair for bed, any more than she'd braided his sister Artie's. It was loose, a silky mass thrown over one shoulder.

"Do you need me to show you how to make toast?" she asked, a wry note entering her voice because he hadn't moved, frozen in place.

"No," he said, taking his fork and hers as well. She

opened her mouth to protest, shrugged, went back to the table and clattered about. The rich smell of fresh butter and a sultry waft of honey filled the room.

He felt a pang of hunger, perhaps because they were such simple foods. Since landing in England, he had discovered that his stomach revolted at mushrooms *à la béchamel*, hare cake in jelly, and even lamb cutlets *à l'échalote*, which he used to enjoy.

Pigeons *à la poulette* made him feel physically ill. Giblets of beef *aux fines herbes*? No.

But farmer's bread, turning brown and crispy around the edges, made him hungry. "My brothers and I used to tramp across the countryside carrying bread and roast beef tied up in handkerchiefs," he said, over his shoulder.

He propped up the forks and pulled one of the chairs close enough that he didn't have to crouch on the hearth. "We were forbidden to build fires, so naturally we always toasted our bread."

He didn't watch as she settled into the other chair. She might have told him, foolishly, that a lady couldn't be compromised once she accepted a salary. That didn't mean a man couldn't seduce her. Not ravish: seduce.

The question was irrelevant, as he had no plan to do either.

"That sounds like fun," Diana said, curling her legs underneath her. Her toes were delicate and pink. "I always manage to burn my toast, but you're getting an even brown. Were your brothers as skilled at cookery as you seem to be?"

"Horatius would painstakingly toast his bread to a perfect color on all sides. But I am still waiting for an answer to my question, Diana. Who was your sister's fiancé?"

"I don't like to think about him."

North glanced up, just to be sure that the castle governess had refused to answer his question. Or, to put it another way, that his former fiancée was stirring a jar of honey and ignoring him.

He flipped the toast, and thought about that. Then he tried a new tactic.

"Will you please tell me his name? We needn't discuss his qualities."

"Why do you want to know?"

He glanced up as the jar of honey thumped onto the hearthstone next to a plate containing a slab of butter and a dented knife.

"His family ought to support Godfrey," he said, slathering butter onto a perfectly toasted slice. "I shall make that clear to them. And to your mother as well, by the way."

"Rose's fiancé had only a father, who died with him. Why would anyone accept responsibility?"

"Someone must have inherited his land, and along with inheritance comes responsibility. Rose was not any woman; she was a lady and his betrothed. I don't understand why she didn't go to his family, if your mother threw her out."

"My mother continued to support her. Rose sank into a melancholy when her fiancé died, so my mother postponed her plan to bring both of us to London for the Season. And then Rose found out she was carrying a child."

"That must have been a shock."

"Rose was happy about it. My mother was not, but she finally accepted it; she was there when Godfrey was born. When she and I moved to London for the Season, Rose couldn't live with us, obviously, or people would find out about Godfrey. But Mother rented a house for them in Lincoln's Inn Fields, and we saw them as often as we could."

North pulled the dipper from the jar and drizzled honey over the toast. "Is this honey from the estate?"

"Yes." Diana smiled, clearly relieved to drop the subject. "It smells like balsam and sweet alyssum. Lady Knowe experimented last year with planting lavender near the hives."

North offered Diana a slice of toast, ignoring the bone-deep satisfaction he felt at feeding her.

Her smile grew, reminding him sharply how dangerous this impromptu visit was. Shadows in the room had drawn around them warmly, and even the bed holding her nephew seemed to have retreated from the circle of flickering golden light coming from the fireplace.

It was as if they were in a small boat on a large sea, just the two of them.

He dragged his gaze away after she took a bite of toast, which left her lips glistening and soft. If they kissed, she would taste like butter and honey. His toast had begun to burn, so he pulled it out and slapped on a chunk of butter, which promptly melted and ran down his wrist.

Without thinking, he raised his hand and licked it off, just as he would have as a boy.

"What happened to you?" a curious voice asked.

She was smiling again, damn it.

"You would never have *licked* yourself in front of me before. Was it going to war? Or is it because I'm not your betrothed any longer? Or because I'm no longer a lady?" There wasn't any condemnation in her tone, just genuine curiosity.

The damnable thing about the silent castle in the middle of the night was this feeling of seclusion. A boat in the middle of the sea, with no one for miles around.

He'd grown up knowing that the Wildes were an object of curiosity to all England. Attention had become more fierce after he became his father's heir, and it leapt again after Alaric became famous as an author of travel memoirs.

Printing presses churned out prints that turned them all into objects of public fascination. Privacy had been in short supply for most of his adult life.

"I feel comfortable with you," he said, taking another bite before he could say something stupid.

"I suppose it's because we have a past." Her voice was thoughtful. "You can trust me not to be chasing after you with ducal lust in my eyes."

He finished the toast, knowing damned well that he'd like to see any kind of lust in her eyes.

"You'd better eat this as well," she said, handing over her piece, minus a couple of bites. "I'm not hungry."

The warm bread was in his stomach a moment later. "Whether or not Godfrey's family knows he exists, they must pay for his care," North said, pulling out a handkerchief and wiping his hands. He sank back in his chair feeling inexpressibly exhausted. "He's blood of their blood. Their relative took advantage of a lady, the lady whom he should have treasured most in the world."

"Do we have to discuss it?"

"Yes."

He opened his eyes a slit, just enough so that he could see the way golden strands wove through her red hair. See *her*, curled in the other chair.

The silence lasted so long he nearly closed his eyes, but not to sleep. He rarely slept these days, and certainly not in a woman's room. He hadn't shared intimacies with a woman since . . . since he saw Diana for the first time.

Her expression was unreadable, the way it used to be when she was covered with face paint and powder. Without thinking, he scowled at her.

"What?" she asked, surprised.

"Your face took a turn into your mother's idea of a perfect duchess," he said, allowing more than a tinge of cynicism into his voice.

She hunched up one shoulder. "I suppose I can tell you about Rose and her fiancé. It's not easy to have a grocer as a grandfather," she said, coming at the subject from the side. Naturally.

Diana's voice was like velvet, with nothing of a grocer audible. Her accent was the purest King's English, her voice resonant with the inherent confidence that supposedly results from generations of aristocrats.

"He loved proverbs," Diana said, working toward an answer in her own way. "He would say, 'One volunteer is worth two pressed men.' Have you ever heard that before?"

He had. He had refused to have any "pressed" men in his regiment—those boys snatched from the streets and forced into service. Lethargy was stealing through him. "Perhaps we should discuss it tomorrow," he murmured. Lord knew how long it would take Diana to get from proverbs and pressed men back to her sister.

"I don't want to discuss this ever again," Diana stated, so he opened his eyes. "That proverb is just as relevant for ladies as it is for sailors. I was blackmailed into service, if that makes sense, but Rose was a volunteer." A tight note in her voice filtered through his hazy exhaustion.

"I don't understand. She fell in love?"

"Not initially. You see, I was supposed to marry him, but I didn't want to. Rose volunteered. My mother was furious because Rose was truly beautiful. She would have won the highest in the land had she debuted in London, and my mother was acutely aware of Rose's value."

He was so absorbed by Diana's casual depiction of a mother who assessed her daughters like horseflesh that he almost missed the implication that *she* wasn't beautiful. Diana couldn't have meant that.

"Of those men available to marry, *I* was the highest in

the land during that Season," he said flatly. "She couldn't have won me, because you had already done so."

Her laughter blended into the honeyed, quiet air. "That's only because you never met Rose. She was not only lovely, but she had flawless manners." Her voice was warm with affection and love.

North was damned sure he would have ignored Rose if Diana had been in the same ballroom.

"My mother refused, of course, but Rose took matters into her own hands. My proposed spouse and his father paid a second visit to our house, and Rose smiled at him."

North squinted across the fire. Diana was curvy and soft, everything he'd dreamed of as a boy. Her hair shone like a river of fire and her mouth . . . well, poems had been written about lips like hers. Only half of them were appropriate in polite company. In fact, none of them were, because any man reading the poem would know—North cut himself off.

"I miss her so much," she said.

"I miss my brother, but you would have hated him," he observed. "You seem to think that I'm pokerfaced, but Horatius was fifty times more pompous than I am."

"We've both lost a sibling," Diana said in a surprised tone, not taking issue with his summary of her feelings about him.

Had he really been that pompous? Or that much of an ass?

Another wave of exhaustion hit him and he shut his eyes again. "So was it a love match?"

"Rose deliberately flirted with him to save me from a marriage that I didn't want," Diana said flatly. "She showed every sign of being affectionate toward him. For his part, he couldn't believe his own good fortune."

The story didn't make sense to North but he was too tired to ask for an explanation. "His name?"

For once, she answered. "Archibald Ewing."

The name sifted into his consciousness and floated there for a moment. He sat up straight. "Archie Ewing, as in the future Laird of Fennis?"

"Yes. Did you know him well?"

"There aren't so many of us," North said. He tried to sort through his memories of a pugnacious schoolboy with a thick Scottish accent and a chip on his shoulder. "How did he die?"

"Drunken coachman," Diana said, getting up and moving around behind him. "Not his fault. He had no siblings."

"This castle is haunted by dead people," he said, knowing he sounded drunk. His eyes closed again, and this time he couldn't open them. "Horatius and Rose. Archie and the rest of them."

"The rest of them?" Her voice floated to him so softly that the words didn't sound like a question.

He found himself answering. "John Goss, William Peach, Gower . . ."

"Who are they?" A warm blanket settled over his chest and he sank into a darkness that smelled like home: a moldering castle and English honey.

"My men," he answered. "My men."

North woke when the first birds were singing. The fire had burned itself out. He stood up, and the blanket fell to the floor. He stretched and raked his hand through his hair, conscious of an unfamiliar sense of bodily well-being.

It was dawn, and he had slept at least five hours, longer than he had in months.

Diana's bed was empty. She hadn't gone to sleep in the same room as a slumbering man, of course. She was a respectable governess. He'd driven her out of her own bedchamber.

He rubbed his chin, guilt making him feel awkward. He had entered a lady's bedchamber without knocking, stayed for an irresponsible, improper conversation, and fallen asleep.

The high-pitched laughter of a little girl came from somewhere down the corridor. Diana was with

Artie. Diana with her curves, her sensual mouth, her tender . . . He clenched his jaw and cut the thought off.

When he managed to make his way down the corridor without being discovered, his relief was directly proportional to the surprise of having had a refreshing five hours of sleep.

Chapter Seven

Late the following morning

Diana pulled Artie out of the bath and wrapped a warm towel around her wiggling body. She was determined to spend the day focused on her future, and not give a thought to her past.

North was her past. After he'd fallen asleep, she had picked up Godfrey and carried him back to his own bed, and slipped into one of the nursery beds herself. Before she fell asleep, she had decided that she could not allow North to approach the laird's family.

It was only after Diana flatly refused to marry Archibald Ewing that Rose took matters in her own hands. Within half an hour of their second meeting, Archibald was desperately in love, Rose was agreeable, and only Mrs. Belgrave was furious.

Mrs. Belgrave had mandated a long betrothal, perhaps hoping that the marriage would fall through. Instead, Rose fell into Archibald's bed, and when he died, months later, she was carrying his child.

If Archibald weren't dead, Diana would love to kick him. Perhaps, if everything had gone differently, if she and North had married, North would have whipped Archibald to within an inch of his life for having the temerity to take her sister's innocence before marriage.

Yet she had never seen the point of building castles in the air, and marriage to North would have been an ethereal castle, indeed.

"We will be fine," she said aloud.

Artie patted her cheek. "Mama coming later?" she asked hopefully. She asked every day.

The Duchess of Lindow—or Ophelia, as she insisted Diana call her—returned to the castle as often as she could, and whenever she was in residence, she spent much of the day with Artie, Godfrey, and Diana.

It was unheard of among ladies, to the best of Diana's knowledge. Her mother had seen her only during weekly appointments during which she and Rose displayed the skills their governess had taught them, playing the part of young ladies before they were dispatched back to the nursery. Mrs. Belgrave's sojourns in London had been a source of relief for the entire household.

"Your mama will arrive very soon!" Diana said, giving the little girl a kiss and a celebratory twirl, holding her tight and spinning in place until Artie screamed happily. Then she put her down and suggested that Artie change her doll out of her nightdress while Diana bathed Godfrey.

Artie's brows were like tufts of embroidery floss— until she began making a low noise like a teakettle on the hob. Then they turned into a straight line.

"What is the matter?" Diana asked, keeping her voice calm.

"You promised a story about Fitzy!"

The castle peacock reigned in solitary splendor over the lawns south of the castle, deigning to approach the Peacock Terrace on occasion. In their ongoing bedtime story, Fitzy led a thrilling life, in which he solved petty crimes and went to the theater in his spare time. He liked to show off for the queen, or so the story went.

"I tell you a story when you're tucked into bed, not in the morning," Diana said.

"No!" Artie's face was turning red. "I want Fitzy *now!*"

Last night Godfrey had crawled into her bed, and

now Artie was having a fit of temper, though she wasn't hungry. Godfrey couldn't tell her what the matter was, but Artie could.

Diana collected her little charge and sat down in the rocking chair. She immediately discovered that Mabel had informed both children that Diana would soon be leaving the castle and taking Godfrey with her.

"I want Mama," Artie sobbed, collapsing against her chest. "*And* I want DeeDee."

"I'm right here," Diana said. "I'm still here, Artie."

The girl curled her fingers into Diana's apron front and pulled so hard that a few pins gave way, and the apron sagged over her bosom. "I want you to stay. Papa will *make* you stay!"

Goodness.

Somehow a two-year-old already knew the power that dukes had over lowly folk like herself. Diana rocked back and forth.

After a while, Godfrey came over to join them, and Diana began a brand-new story about Floyd, the friend whom Fitzy had left behind when he came to the castle.

"Who's he?" Artie asked thickly. She was snuggled against Diana's breast, her thumb in her mouth.

"Floyd is a beautiful peacock," Diana said, thinking of a certain lord's cheekbones in the light of the fire, and how strong his back and shoulders were.

North had worn no coat the night before, and all that snowy linen made his face gleam in the firelight. He wasn't thin, but somehow she didn't think he was eating properly. His skin was drawn taut over his cheekbones.

Floyd had been to war and back, it turned out.

The children were fascinated.

Chapter Eight

That evening

North paused in the door of the drawing room. The room was crowded with furniture, but he was used to seeing it thronged with family and guests. In their absence, it was startlingly silent.

"There you are, darling!" Aunt Knowe waved at him from a sofa facing the gardens.

He bowed with a flourish. "My best of aunts."

"Oh, pooh, do sit down. I'm just going over a letter sent by Wilkins, the estate manager in Wales." She folded the paper and set it on a table that dated to the first Wilde, an intrepid fellow who had survived a siege by bringing in food through Lindow Moss, the bog east of the castle. According to family legend, his enemy's bodies disappeared without a trace in the same place.

"I was under the impression that Alaric was going to help Father run the estates," North said, as he sank into the seat beside her.

"My dear, he was miserable. So heroic, but your brother is an adventurer. I saw instantly that darling Willa was the perfect match for him. I simply had to convince him to follow his own instincts."

"So you have been overseeing the estates?"

"I have," his aunt said blithely. "I should have been doing it all along, but when Horatius died, your father was so terrified that he wanted to keep you close, and handing over management of the estates did the trick. Of course, Wilkins, Butterick, and Shell do a great deal of work."

North digested that in silence. In retrospect, his father had given him oversight of three estate managers within weeks of Horatius's death.

"I wrestled the ledgers from Alaric's grip," his aunt said. "After that, nature took care of itself; Willa is an adventurer just like her husband."

"I would never have guessed," North said, picturing his civilized sister-in-law. "Thank you for taking on my responsibilities."

"They weren't yours, but your father's. I have no

intention of giving them back," she said, tapping his knee with her fan. "You know how much I love telling people what to do. I took up the sketches you had made for water mills and had them built, by the way. I've increased profits by eleven percent in the home estate, and I'm hoping to eke out a few more percentage points in the next years."

"Brava," North said.

He was free. The thought sank in slowly. If his aunt truly meant it, he was free. Until he inherited, hopefully a great many years hence, he had no need to stay at home.

Diana and Godfrey wouldn't be living in the castle. Not that the fact was relevant.

"I just had a letter from Alaric," his aunt said. "Willa leads him about with a crook of her little finger, but luckily for the marriage, her passion for travel seems to be as great as his."

He'd always wanted to see the Colosseum. He could be on a boat in a few days. Leaving Diana behind.

"Yes, you ought to travel," his aunt said, noticing his expression. "Everyone is abroad these days. Did Diana tell you that her cousin Lavinia and her mother moved to Paris?"

He nodded.

"Lavinia conquered the French court as easily as

she did the English." His aunt rarely left the castle, but she could generally be counted on to know any gossip worth repeating.

Prism entered and bowed. "May I offer you refreshment, Lord Roland? Sherry, perhaps, or champagne?"

North glanced at his aunt, who was sipping a glass of liquor that shone like old pennies in the candlelight. "I'll have the same as my aunt."

A moment later he held a substantial glass of brandy.

"Prism believes ladies should drink sherry before dinner," his aunt said, as the door shut behind the butler. "I am a constant disappointment to him."

"What does Prism think of Diana's role in the household?"

"I never interfere with domestic matters," his aunt said, quite untruthfully. To his memory, she was always getting involved with a lovelorn maid—or dropping a new governess into the household without warning. "Diana has turned the household upside down, but he seems to be managing. She's remarkably impulsive."

"How so?"

"Last summer, she decided the children should have the experience of caring for a pet—this was when your younger siblings were on leave from school—so she brought a young goat into the schoolroom."

"And?"

"He remained in the castle for two days, in which time he managed to eat the wardrobe belonging to Artie's doll, three pairs of slippers, the schoolroom curtains, a hearth rug, several nappies, and a few prints of Lord Wilde's adventures."

No wonder Diana had sewn a nightdress for Artie's doll. That might explain the ugly shoes Diana was wearing as well.

"Moreover, when your brothers were home from Eton last August, Diana had the idea of taking them to the country fair. They played the coconut shy until they won a sow and all ten piglets."

"Impressive."

"Diana had given them an impromptu lesson the afternoon before, using turnips. The boys decided they needed more practice, so in the evening they absconded with the melons Buckle was growing under glass. Many of them split, naturally enough, and Buckle was not pleased."

North laughed.

"The boys wanted to keep one of the piglets, but Diana persuaded them to give the sow and her piglets to Buckle."

"Who paid for the coconuts?" North asked.

"Diana," his aunt said. "The boys repaid her out of their pocket money, but Diana also bought flowers for the housekeeper when she was ill. She bought a potion from a Gypsy that was meant to cure one of the footmen's toothache."

"Did it work?"

"It did not. She bought a lace collar for Agnes, the second housemaid who is courting, and a blue Dresden bowl for the castle butcher, on the occasion of his marriage."

"She doesn't understand money," North said.

"Not unusual in a young lady," his aunt commented.

"What do you know about her sister Rose?"

Lady Knowe took a sip of brandy. "Since I knew that Godfrey couldn't be yours, I hired a Bow Street Runner to investigate. At some point that boy is going to want to know who his father was and why he is not playing a role in his life. Rose Belgrave became a mother at fifteen years old."

Fifteen was shockingly young to bear a child, although young ladies often were affianced at that age.

"Godfrey's father, Archibald Ewing, was the only son in a family that was here before the Norman kings, with estates in Scotland and England," his aunt continued. "Barring an inebriated coachman, Archibald would have become the Laird of Fennis. Do you know who *is* definitely going to be the laird?" She tipped up her glass and finished it.

North frowned. "Surely not."

"Illegitimacy is not grounds for disinheritance in Scotland," his aunt said. "The eldest male inherits. Godfrey will be the laird someday."

They sat in silence for a moment. "Why haven't you told Godfrey's remaining relatives of his existence? Presumably they have no idea."

"I decided against it. I haven't said a word to Diana either."

"Why not?"

"An heir who can't speak? Better to be an illegitimate scion of the Wildes than a laird who can't lead his clan. I am hopeful that Godfrey will talk eventually. Horatius didn't bother to speak until he was three. One day your nanny came shrieking downstairs to report that he had informed her that the soup was cold and should be returned to the kitchen."

"He was a stiff-rumped fellow, wasn't he?"

"Came out of the womb a little duke." Her voice didn't wobble or break, but her eyes grew shiny.

"I am glad you brought Diana here," North said, taking his aunt's hand. "I'll take care of her from now on."

"I doubt she'll accept your help. She's as stubborn and proud as you are, and that's really saying something."

North's jaw clenched. She *would* accept his help. He'd make bloody sure that she was safely housed, with servants he would choose.

Prism reappeared in the doorway, signaling that the evening meal awaited them.

"Your father sent a groom ahead; he should arrive tomorrow," his aunt said, rising. "I want to hear about your military service tonight." It wasn't a request, it was a demand.

North bit back his instinctive refusal.

His aunt tucked an arm through his. "Keeping it to yourself won't help," she said briskly. "Tomorrow morning we'll go around the estate on horseback, so you can see the improvements I've made. Perhaps hunting the day after. The partridges have become so numerous that they're fluttering out in the road and startling the horses. Two or three days of good shooting and we'll have enough to give one bird to every tenant."

North grunted. She was trying to ensure that he slept, but exertion had no effect on his nightmares. The only thing that had helped, he thought with bemusement, was a plate of toast and honey.

"Do you have any of those prints of me?" he asked. "I've only seen one, and I'm curious."

"Leonidas brought home a few at Christmas."

"And?"

"Not as bad as they could be." His aunt patted his arm, smiling mischievously. "You figure as the devil incarnate in high heels. All the prints purport to warn of the nobility's wicked ways, so every young woman in the kingdom is collecting them feverishly, and nightly dreaming of conquering your cruel heart."

North swallowed another curse.

"I'll show you my favorite later," Lady Knowe said, her grin broadening. "It's entitled *Too Wilde to Wed*. You're dressed for court, with patches, rouge, and a wig fit for the Lord Chancellor."

North groaned.

"A young woman representing Diana is kneeling at your feet, her hands clasped in entreaty. Very dramatic. All you need is a playwright to pen your life in order to sell out a theater. A play about your depraved habits might well outsell the play about Alaric's love life. Or perhaps they could do a back-to-back matinee! *Wilde in Love* followed by *Too Wilde to Wed*."

"Thank goodness, the only dramatist we know is not free to write that play," North said, adding, "She isn't, is she?"

A couple of years ago a deranged playwright named Prudence Larkin had fallen in love with Alaric and been unable to curb her jealousy. The Duke of Lindow had eventually placed her in a comfortable sanitarium.

His aunt shook her head, her face sobering. "I'm afraid not. The poor girl has fastened her attentions on the chaplain."

"Has she written a play about him?" North asked, fascinated. Having met Prudence, he could imagine her smuggling a play out of the asylum and having it presented at Theater Royal in Drury Lane.

"Worse. A few weeks ago she tore off her gown in the chapel. He was mortified, and the mistress of the house wrote me that Prudence had to be given a sedative, as she is convinced she is being kept from her lover."

"It sounds uncomfortable for all concerned," North said. He wasn't overly sympathetic, because Prudence had nearly murdered both Alaric and Willa.

"Especially for the poor chaplain," Aunt Knowe said, gurgling with laughter. "Apparently he's sixty-seven and has led a blamelessly chaste life."

"The first set of breasts he saw as an adult were Prudence's?" North asked with a real smile on his lips. "That could rival Alaric's play. *What the Vicar Saw, A Comedy in Three Acts.*"

Aunt Knowe threw back her head and laughed. "I'm so glad you're home." She stopped and put a callused hand on his cheek. "We were all terrified that something would happen to you over there, so far from home."

North managed a crooked smile. "Here I am, safe and sound."

"Safe, anyway. Sound will come, darling. It will come."

Three hours later, North felt as if the heaviness that had settled into his bones would never leave. As the castle grew darker and quieter, the ghosts grew louder.

He paced in circles in his room, cursing his own stupidity. This weakness wasn't *him*. He loathed weakness. He had never been weak, not when Horatius died, and not when young Peach had died in his arms.

An hour or so after the castle fell into complete silence, he found himself moving swiftly through its deserted corridors. This time he didn't pace around the picture galleries—either of them—or visit the kitchens.

One lamp affixed to the wall in the nursery corridor had been turned low but left burning. He stopped for a moment, wondering if it was a sign, a welcome for tired visitors who had sailed from a far continent and washed up on this dark little island.

At the end of the corridor, the door of Diana's room was slightly ajar. He pushed it open, because the needling instinct he felt to go to her was stronger than the prideful instinct to avoid the woman who had jilted him.

He breathed easier as soon as he entered the room.

It smelled like a tallow candle, and he made a note to tell Prism that servant though Diana might be—at the moment—he didn't ever want to see a tallow candle in her room, or in the nursery as a whole, for that matter.

It also smelled like woodsmoke, honey, and Diana. She didn't wear a complicated perfume concocted only for her. Her scent was light and joyful, flowery with a hint of lemon.

Her bed was empty, but a jar of honey and a plate of melting butter had been left on the hearth. One chair—*her* chair—held a sleeping person wrapped in a blanket.

He moved soundlessly across the room and stood with his back to the fire. The blanket was snuggled to Diana's ears. Her hair was partly caught under its folds and partly tumbling down her side.

God, she was beautiful, her skin so translucent and delicate that he could see a pulse fluttering in her forehead.

For some reason he felt weak in the knees, so he dropped to a crouch. No wonder the monstrous Mrs. Belgrave had known she could launch her daughter onto the marriage mart and catch the biggest fish of all.

Diana had the beautifully knit bones of royalty, along with a fresh sensuality to her mouth. He'd never seen the like.

He was close enough to touch her knee, but he didn't. It wouldn't be proper.

The damnable thing was that he didn't think he had been spellbound by the clear planes of her cheekbones, or her straight little aristocratic nose, back when he first met her. It was her laugh.

He'd asked her to marry him when she was covered in a bucket of face paint and rarely murmured more than a sentence at a time.

So what could have entranced him, if not her laughter?

Archie Ewing had been a decent lad, which didn't explain why he had debauched his own fiancée. But if Diana's sister was as beautiful as she, Archie had likely fallen in love with Rose, never imagining that Fate would send a drunken coachman his way.

North was staring absently at Diana's rumpled hair when her eyes opened. She met his gaze with no sign of embarrassment or surprise. Instead, the corners of her mouth tipped up, and his heart eased in a way that should have given him great concern, and didn't.

"Come for more toast, have you?"

There was nothing pitying in her tone, or even sympathetic. It was as if men often wandered the castle at night, washing up at her doorstep like jetsam thrown from a ship.

"Yes," he said, keeping it simple.

The castle chef had served up lambs' tongues in aspic that evening, which caused North to lose his appetite entirely. He wanted more from Diana than toast. The conviction made itself known deep in his gut, but he refused to listen. If he *did* listen, he would pick Diana up and then sit down again in the chair big enough for two.

She'd be in his lap and he could rest his chin against all that rumpled hair. Something deep in his bones told him that her weight on his legs would keep him from marching over battlefields in the dark.

"I laid it out for you," she said, sounding less sleepy. She extracted one arm from under the blanket and waved at the fireplace.

Next to him was a plate of inexpertly cut slices of bread, a jar of honey that was silky and liquid after being warmed at the fire, and butter that had melted into a low hill surrounded by a moat.

"May I make you a piece of toast?" he asked.

"I'd like a bite or two," she said, curling her feet under her. "I was dreaming that I was back in a London ballroom. It should have been a nightmare, by rights, but it wasn't."

North wrestled the first slice of bread onto a fork. She had known he would come. He should feel wary. A future duke visiting the governess. The governess confident that the lord would arrive. Leaving her door ajar.

"Was I in the dream?" That was a reasonable question. After all, they had once been betrothed. Before coming to Lindow Castle for their betrothal party, their only conversations took place in and around ballrooms.

Likely because he didn't lecture her there, his conscience reminded him. But he had never meant to lecture her, and hadn't thought he was. He was only . . .

He *had* lectured. Damn it.

"You were in my dream," she said.

He waited, turning over the toast.

She leaned forward and touched his upper arm with a slender finger. "Aren't you going to ask?"

North turned his head slowly, because from this distance he could have leaned over and claimed her mouth with a kiss. As the queen of the impetuous gesture, she hadn't anticipated that. He saw her eyes widen as she took in a silent breath.

I could steal the air from your lips, something deep inside him growled. But he kept his face bland. "I trust that I comported myself adequately on the ballroom floor?"

She settled back in her seat, acting as if she didn't know about the rosy flush on her cheekbones. "You were a graceful dancer, Lord Roland, as always."

North narrowed his eyes at her.

"You weren't wearing your high wig," she said in a rush. "Nor those silk coats you always wore, with the tight—" She waved her hand at the lower part of his body.

"Tight?" Amusement leaked into his voice.

"Breeches."

"I believe a young lady is not meant to notice."

"Everyone notices." She pulled up her knees and hugged them. "Presumably that is just the attention you wanted. Why would any gentleman wear tight breeches unless he wanted attention?"

"I'm almost sorry for the loss of my newest pair," he observed.

"The loss? What happened?"

"Boodle handed over some yellow—no, *saffron*—colored breeches and the back split in two pieces a moment later."

She broke into laughter that cascaded around his ears and made him feel warmer than the fire did.

"Boodle took that pair and all the others with him to London. After," he added scrupulously, "I told him that I would never wear them again."

Her mouth fell open. "Boodle *stole* your pantaloons?"

"I prefer to think that he gave himself *un pour-*

boire." At her raised eyebrow, he added, "A tip of staggering proportions."

"Did he take all those fancy coats you used to wear as well?"

He grinned at her over his shoulder. "The neckcloths edged in lace. The boxes of patches. The heeled shoes and clocked stockings. The ornate perfume bottle that he'd decided I must carry with me wherever I went."

"I don't like to judge people," Diana said, sounding as if she was confessing to one of the seven deadly sins. "Boodle is somewhat foolish, but he is not evil. Still, by any measure, that is theft."

"Prism is remarkably displeased, and went so far as to suggest that I take action," North said, turning the toast. He was unable to make himself care.

"You have lost a tremendous amount of money," she pointed out. "We all heard about the perfume bottle that came from France and was meant to protect your nose from the unwashed hordes. Will you send the sheriff after Boodle?"

North shook his head. "He helped me win you."

"Under the circumstances, you wouldn't be blamed for wishing him locked up for life," she said, her eyes falling to her hands.

"Hmmm." He didn't feel like clarifying his feelings, so he set to work on the first piece of toast, which was now evenly brown, as perfectly cooked as the lambs' tongues he hadn't brought himself to taste.

"Talking of theft, my mother wrote me a letter accusing me of stealing the emerald necklace and diadem I wore during our betrothal party," Diana said in a rush. "I didn't! I only sold my earrings."

He glanced at her large, vulnerable eyes. "She repeated as much to Aunt Knowe, who finds your mother repellent, and didn't believe her, any more than I would. Prism returned your jewelry with all items intact, under the care of your maid and one of my father's grooms."

He spread butter on her toast, thinking that he'd like to lick butter off her chin. Or at the least, watch her lick it off her lips.

"I did take the matching earrings I was wearing that day," she said, her voice dropping. "I *am* a thief, though my mother exaggerated the matter considerably."

"Did the earrings belong to Mrs. Belgrave?"

"My grandmother gave me the set for my eighteenth birthday, but my mother always acted as if they were hers."

North dripped honey carefully on the toast, thinking about a vituperative woman with the audacity to accuse her daughter of theft when the jewels in question were a birthday present.

"A gift should stay a gift. I don't like your mother," he observed.

"I don't either." Her voice was miserable. "I think accusing me of theft is a way of making herself feel better about not supporting me," Diana said. "She's not terrible. She wouldn't want me to be destitute."

"All evidence to the contrary," he said gently.

She was silent.

"Eat this." He handed her a piece of toast, dripping with butter and golden honey.

She took it gingerly. "I know what you're doing."

"You do?"

It was lucky that the saffron breeches had already met their maker, because they would be splitting apart, and not in the back. What was it about Diana's velvety laugh and gray eyes that made him feel like the kind of dissolute rake he had never been?

Like a man who had never heard of rank or title and didn't give a damn . . . a man closed in a dark room with a warm woman?

"You're trying to fatten me up, aren't you?" Diana said, mock scowling at him. "Lady Knowe has probably complained to you. She keeps telling me that I'm overly thin."

North felt a pulse of alarm. Diana had nothing to lose, from his point of view.

"That's a ferocious glare you're leveling at me," she said mildly. "You and your aunt should go head-to-head."

"You don't need to lose weight," he stated.

"I could say the same to you." She took a bite from one corner of her toast, and licked her lips afterward.

Honey toast was the food of the gods. Every nerve in North's body was attuned to Diana's shining lips.

"Lady Knowe is a worrier," she said, taking another bite. "I'm no smaller than I was the last time I saw you. All my gowns fit precisely as they used to." She giggled. "If I was in the habit of wearing breeches, they wouldn't split!"

Diana in breeches . . . slim legs enclosed in tight silk. Round bum—

He wrenched his mind away. The word "proper" had lost all force, and he knew it. As if it had been a magic spell, and now the magic had worn off and he didn't give a damn about what was an appropriate subject of conversation, and what was indelicate.

He did give a damn about whether Diana had lost weight, because if she had, she was working too hard while enslaved by the evil lord of the manor: himself.

North propped another slice of bread close to the fire and inspected her face carefully. Her delicate jaw and cheeks weren't taut.

She smiled at him, lips glistening, and swallowed. "Agree with me?"

"I'd need to make a closer inspection," he said, allowing desire to show in his eyes. In the wavering firelight, she looked like a goddess. Diana, emerging from the woods to strike a mere mortal man silent with her beauty.

She snorted. It was ladylike—but definitely a snort. "Here, you eat the rest," she said, pushing the toast at him. "I had supper and I'm guessing you didn't. Besides, you've burned your piece."

Sure enough, the bread had turned black on one side.

"Try another," Diana said. "I thought you never burned toast!"

"I was distracted by the question of whether you were withering away," he retorted, discarding the blackened bread as a bad job. He ate the remains of Diana's piece in three huge bites. He hadn't been hungry for months, but now he felt ravenous.

"I sliced the whole loaf," she said, reaching forward with a slender foot and nudging the plate closer to his leg. She met his eyes with a bland smile. "In case you burn another piece."

"I would snort," he said pointedly, "but gentlemen try to express themselves in words. They never mock a lady's comment."

She leaned forward, elbows on her knees, chin cupped in her hand. "Would you like to know more about what you were wearing in my dream?"

"I believe you said that I was naked from the waist down. I was hoping that you were in *dishabille* as well."

"No, I didn't!" she squealed. "You may not have been dressed like a dandy, but you were certainly wearing clothing!"

"*Quel dommage.*"

"Too bad?" she asked. And, at his nod, "I don't speak French. My mother considers it a language spoken only by debauchers and lechers."

"You're the one dreaming about naked men," he pointed out.

"As I said, you weren't naked! You simply weren't wearing silk pantaloons. Nor a wig, or jewels, or even a patch."

"Boodle would have considered me naked," he said. He waved another piece of toast at her, but when she shook her head, he made short work of it. After that he arranged a log on the hearth so that he could toast two more pieces and watch her at the same time.

"I should have kissed you more when we were betrothed," he said, telling her what he was thinking.

"That would have been most improper!" Pink crept into her cheeks.

He was a little taken aback by the vehemence of her comment. "Why?" Then, frowning: "Because of your sister's plight? I can assure you that I am capable of kissing a woman without losing control." He managed to sound indignant, though he knew he would have trouble stopping at one kiss, if he ever managed to get Diana into his arms again.

But only Diana. No other woman. And only if she were willing.

"Those prints suggesting that you despoiled me are rubbish," she said, leaning forward and wrapping warm fingers around his forearm. "No one who matters thought twice about them."

North turned his two pieces of toast, thinking of Boodle's assessment of who mattered. "Who matters?"

"Lady Knowe and your family," she said without hesitation. "Leonidas has bought as many prints as he could find. Last Christmas he added devil horns in crimson ink and posted them all around the house. I'm told he did the same for Alaric's prints before I joined the household."

It was oddly comforting to remember that. "Did I get a tail as well? I remember that Alaric had extra bits top and bottom."

"Bottom," she said, chortling with laughter. "That's quite naughty of you, Lord Roland!"

He turned back to her. "I can be far naughtier than that, Diana." He knew his eyes were hungry and dark, and not for honey toast. For her.

Diana frowned, and he wasn't sure whether she understood what he was thinking. Probably not. She was one of the bravest, most independent women he'd ever known, and at the same time, she was startlingly naive. She didn't seem to recognize when a man was staring at her with stark lust. She didn't think of scandal when she took employment in the nursery of her former fiancé's home.

"Leonidas's decorations had to be removed," she said. "The younger girls began examining the Shakespeare print depicting you as the rapist leaping out of a trunk, which led to conversations about men who might ask you to store trunks of jewels in your bedchamber. Spartacus thought it would be funny to jump out the wardrobe in the nursery when Viola was asleep."

North ate two more slices and another one while Diana's voice washed over him like a benediction, sweet memories of family and home and people who loved each other and laughed together.

Apparently all the girls had screamed bloody murder. He hadn't grown up with so many little sisters without learning what girls' screams sounded like. Diana tried to describe the chaos, and he drank the mug of milk waiting on the hearth, even though he hadn't drunk warm milk since he was a boy.

But Diana had put it out for him, so he drank it.

He put a couple more logs on the fire, and poked it until he thought it would keep burning until dawn or thereabouts. Diana was still wrapped in that blanket, and part of his mind made a forcible suggestion that he should unwrap her like a present.

It wouldn't be the right thing to do.

She glanced up at him, startled, and he could tell that she hadn't thought this far ahead. For Diana, she had been fairly organized. She had not only got a loaf of bread from the kitchen, but she had sliced it, and there had been the mug of milk as well.

But she hadn't thought of the moment when a man would be staring down at her, unable to stop his lips from curving.

"You're so large," she said faintly.

Several responses came to mind and he discarded each. For the moment.

Instead he bent down and picked her up. She went still all over, eyes round, as he got the right grip on an impossibly soft and curvy body.

"No," he said to her, answering the question he hoped she wasn't thinking. "I am not going to hurl you onto the bed and have my evil way with you."

"I didn't think you were," she said, dignified. "That is our past, not our present."

Still holding her, he sat down in the seat she'd been in and nudged her head onto his shoulder, until his cheek could rest on silky hair. "During our engagement we were never near a bed, more's the pity."

"You know what I mean." Diana was gazing at the fire, and he had the sense that she felt shy. Yet she wasn't a shy woman.

"No, I don't."

"Romance is our past," she explained, keeping her eyes fixed on the burning logs. "You know, when you . . . well, when you met my mother's creation, and thought I would be good enough as a duchess."

Good enough?

Her view explained why she was so comfortable to be here, with him in her bedroom. It made it clear that the woman who jilted him was still the woman of his heart. The truth of it unfolded slowly inside him, the way dye colors water: first just a bright drop, then spreading in every direction.

He loved her; he still loved her; he'd never stopped loving her.

Not that she had any idea. His future wife—if he could persuade her to consider him again—was damned unobservant. He'd have to look out for her.

For the moment, Diana was in his lap, smelling like honey and lemon. She was safe and warm in his arms.

"If we're not lovers, what are we?" he asked.

"Friends," she said, with such certitude that he knew that she'd given it thought. "You need a friend to take care of you right now. Alaric would do it, if he were here. Or Horatius. Or Parth—I saw him at Christmas and I liked him so much."

North grunted. Was her voice particularly animated when she talked of Parth? He had the feeling she had ruled out marriage to the peerage, but Parth wasn't a member of polite society.

Parth probably owned most of England by now, but he stayed away from anything smelling of the ton.

Smart man.

Not the right man for Diana, however. North's arms tightened around her. "This is so improper," she said, with a little squeak. "I wouldn't allow it to happen, North, except for you . . ."

"I can't sleep," North said, ruthlessly using the truth against her. "You are helping. Alaric could scarcely curl up in my lap, could he?"

"You slept last night, with no one in your lap," she pointed out with a gurgle of laughter.

"I'm going to sleep even better tonight," he said. "Talking of our past, tell me of our betrothal party."

"What of it?" She didn't sound eager to elaborate. "It was lovely. Your parents were so kind."

"But your sister had just died. Were you able to go to her funeral?"

She shook her head, and he felt warm breath on his neck as she sighed. "My mother insisted that I continue on to Lindow Castle, since Lady Gray, Lavinia's mother, could act as my chaperone."

"Even if your mother had kept Godfrey's existence to herself, why not explain that one of her daughters had passed away? The wedding might have been put off for six months, or we could have made it a small affair since you would have been in mourning."

"Perhaps she would have, if we had been a real couple."

North had thought they *were* a real couple. He still thought so.

"We would indeed have gone into mourning, and you were likely to find out about Rose's son," Diana said wearily. "I would be tainted by his existence. As my mother saw it, you might use it, at some point during the mourning period, as grounds to break our engagement."

"Why would your mother question my honor?" he said, hardness entering his voice.

She was silent.

"Diana."

"You were infatuated with the perfect duchess-to-be that she presented you with. That wasn't real; it wasn't me. She and I both knew it. The longer we allowed the betrothal to carry on, the more likely you would discover the truth."

He did snort this time.

"You had purchased a special license," she said softly.

North frowned. Hair had fallen over her eyes and she was tracing a circle round and round on his chest. "How did you know that?"

She took a deep breath. "My mother bribed Boodle. She knew everything you did. She knew when you asked your stepmother to give you your grandmother's ring. On the morning you asked me to marry you, I put on a special dress, a gown fit for a duchess, with real pearls sewn among the embroidery. Your valet had sent a messenger two hours earlier."

North was stunned into silence.

"I'm sorry. But my mother was not the only one. Boodle likely took bribes from three or four other women who wanted their daughters to be duchesses, and accordingly kept track of your daily activities—if only to make certain that they accepted the same invitations you did."

North waited to feel angry, but he couldn't muster the emotion. "Did my purchase of a special license frighten you?"

"I had strict instructions," she said in a low voice. "If you brought up the special license, I was to eagerly agree. It felt wrong, and every hour it felt worse. I think I went a bit mad." She was tracing circles again. "There was no one to mourn Rose, so my mother didn't hold a funeral for her."

"Except for you," North said, tightening his arms. "Except for you, Diana. No wonder you ran away. I can't even remember the first week after Horatius died. The family hardly slept. Someone was always crying somewhere."

"You are so lucky to have your family," Diana said, her voice falling to a whisper. "Even if Horatius didn't live very long, he was lucky too."

"I kept thinking that it must be a jest," North said. "I hoped I would wake up to find him strutting around the drawing room, provoking Aunt Knowe to snap her fan at him."

"I know," Diana said. Then: "I'm afraid marriage to you became mixed up in my mind with grief for Rose."

"Your dream would have been to wake up before you ever met me," North said, his hand stroking down her back and curling around her side. He put his head back, a wave of exhaustion closing over him.

Diana threaded the fingers of one hand through his, and he felt her body relax against his. Their closeness wasn't sensual, not just now. Her fingers wound around his with strength, and her slight weight felt like a mountain pinning him to the here and now.

To this room, this castle, this woman, this contented moment.

"I'm sorry, North," she said, when he was on the very edge of tumbling into sleep.

"No apologies," he said groggily. "You don't love me. I understand that. You can't choose how you feel, any more than the mad playwright chose to be mad."

"Are you talking about the author of *Wilde in Love*?" she asked, her voice confused.

But sleep overtook him before he could answer.

Chapter Nine

The next day

It was close to two in the afternoon before they heard a rumble of carriage wheels in the distance. Diana sent up a silent prayer of thanks, because she was at her wit's end. Artie was driving her mad.

They had found Fitzy irritably stalking around the Peacock Terrace. They had visited the finch's nest four times. The first three times, a little brown bird was snug on her nest. The last time, its mate had been poised on the edge and flew away when they poked their heads from the window, so the children were able to count the eggs.

At the sound of a carriage, Artie looked up at Diana. "Mama?" she asked, for perhaps the fiftieth time.

"Yes!" Diana cried, after a quick look out the window. A plume of dust in the far distance translated to the train of carriages that accompanied the Duke of Lindow's family: carriages holding the duke and duchess, at least four and possibly seven Wilde offspring, personal maids and valets, six or seven grooms, a few footmen, and anything else deemed necessary for travel.

Artie screamed with ear-piercing joy and spun in circles until she made herself dizzy. Then she grabbed Godfrey's hand. "Downstairs, Free!"

"Wait!" Diana looked over both of them. Just because they didn't always dress to their rank didn't mean that they hadn't proper clothing, no matter how Boodle used to complain.

They were clean and their curls brushed until they shone. Artie was wearing an enchanting ruffled gown with a translucent silk overlay embroidered with rosebuds. Godfrey wasn't dressed as expensively, since Diana paid for his clothing, but he had on neat brown pantaloons, a dark blue jacket with red cuffs, and a lacy collar to his shirt.

She held out a hand to each. "Let's go dazzle everyone with Artie's new teeth."

Artie jumped up and down, clapping her jaw together so her teeth were on display. "I want my feather!"

"I'm not certain that a peacock feather will suit your gown," Diana said coaxingly.

Artie disagreed; her lips pursed in a testy pout. Diana gave in, crushing Artie's curls with a strip of cloth that tied in back, allowing a peacock feather glued to the fabric to wave in the air. Then they all started down the stairs, Artie clutching her doll and Godfrey his wooden horse.

As the stream of carriages bowled down the avenue of ancient chestnut trees that led to the castle, Prism began ushering the household out the front door. In short order, more than a hundred servants stood outside in the sunshine, grouped according to their positions in the household.

Lady Knowe, clad in a magnificent purple gown with no fewer than four plumes on her bonnet, was striding from group to group, offering praise. To everyone working in the castle dairy, "Milk has been fine lately, and I commend the cheddar!" To the chef, "Splendid meat pies last night, but no more lambs' tongues. Curious though it seems, my nephew turned green."

Diana looked over the crowd, but North was nowhere to be seen. "Where is he?" she heard Lady Knowe demanding, her braying tones carrying on the breeze.

Artie, Godfrey, and Diana walked over to join the

children's favorite footmen, Frederick and Peter. Soon Artie was bouncing and squealing on Peter's shoulders, and Godfrey was waving happily from his perch on Frederick's.

One might think that the duke and duchess would travel in the first carriage. But no, that door flung open before the liveried groom could approach. As Leonidas and Alexander Wilde sprang out, sun shone on thick black hair, on strong jaws and noble noses, on cheekbones that would make a king gasp with jealousy, on lips that would make a queen feel faint.

It really wasn't fair. How could one family be gifted with so much? But then, they had lost Horatius, Diana reminded herself.

North appeared at last. He strode out of the front door and headed toward his brothers. The three of them met in the middle of the castle courtyard, engaging in the rough-and-tumble greetings that young men liked.

Watching them, Diana thought that Leonidas and Alexander were like young lions testing their strength, whereas North had the burly strength of a leader of the pride. The idea was so foolish that she felt her cheeks heating with embarrassment.

All the same, she couldn't take her eyes away from North. He wore no coat, and the muscles in his broad back showed through his linen shirt. His breeches weren't nearly as tight as those he used to wear, and yet they emphasized the muscles in his thighs.

He had a wildness that seemed new to her. No matter how she racked her brain, she couldn't remember anything *wild* about the man who had courted her.

That man, with his heels and patches . . . he had been civilized, urbane, utterly controlled.

The new North grabbed Leonidas and fairly crushed him against his chest. One arm slung around his brother's neck, he turned to the other vehicles. Seven carriages had come to a halt inside the courtyard walls, with another three drawn up just outside the gate, as they couldn't fit safely inside.

All of Prism's organization was for naught, because the ladies' maids ran to their friends. Grooms flocked forward to meet those who'd accompanied the family to London. A group clustered around one horse's hoof.

Young Wilde ladies burst out of their carriage, running to North and surrounding him like a bouquet of flowers that squealed and cried. The duke strode over to join them. His Grace's hair was silvered at the temples, but he wore his fifty-some years with grace. He was as broad-shouldered as his son, but leaner, equally strong.

Looking at the two of them made her heart twist because North's father loved him so much. It was there, in his strong embrace, and in the way the duke and the whole family had stopped whatever they were doing to return to the castle. Leonidas and Alexander had even come from Oxford.

She'd bet anything that Spartacus and Erik would arrive from Eton later today or tomorrow. The duke would have sent a ducal carriage for them, and the school wouldn't dare to quibble.

Just now His Grace had his head bent, arm around his son's shoulders, telling North something with a rueful smile. News from the Ministry, perhaps. Something about those fools who'd underestimated General Washington.

North looked around, as if for something or someone, and paused on her. The force of his stare made her shiver, because—

No.

She certainly could not recognize desire in his eyes at this distance. Or anything else.

All the same, she didn't tear her eyes away. She kept watching as His Grace turned his head toward her as well. He nodded. Perhaps Diana should have curtsied, but she was all the way across the courtyard and it felt awkward.

Instead she reached up and took Godfrey's hand because at any moment—well, in the next hour or so—

North would have to inform the duke and duchess that Godfrey was not his son.

Unless they, like Lady Knowe, already knew.

Of course they already knew. A mixture of relief and shame flooded her.

North turned away, listening to something his father was saying. He tipped his head back and laughed. She'd seen him smile, but she'd never seen a belly laugh. He had dimples at the corners of his mouth.

His brothers were beautiful, but he was so much more so, like Adonis or a half-mad Greek god caught chatting with a mortal.

Now the courtyard was full of people running back and forth. The duchess had Artie on her hip. His Grace turned around, his face lit up, and held out his hands. Artie leaned toward him with a happy cry.

Artemisia Wilde would be fine when her governess, no matter how beloved, disappeared from her life. Diana knew that in her bones, in her hollowed-out, sorry-for-herself bones.

Godfrey dropped her hand because Leonidas, one of Godfrey's favorite people, was headed in their direction. Sure enough, Leonidas grabbed Godfrey from Frederick's shoulders and transferred him to his own, walking back to the duchess, who smiled with the kindness they'd always shown the boy.

The raging sense of envy Diana felt had nothing to do with the comparison between her work-worn fingers and the duchess's delicate ones. It was the fact that Ophelia was surrounded by love. Her children loved her, and her stepchildren loved her.

Leonidas was grinning as he told her some awful joke that he'd learned at Oxford. Her Grace was laughing so hard that she was leaning on her husband. Artie was reaching toward her again. And the duke . . .

The duke had a possessive hand on his wife's back. He'd put it there without thinking, most likely.

Diana's thoughts tangled together like a vine. That was a *forever* hand. It was a simple caress that said, *I will always be yours. And you will always be mine.*

The gesture spoke of love that overflows onto children and stepchildren, and even onto the household, and certainly onto Lady Knowe, who was beaming and listening to whatever Alexander was telling her about his first term at Oxford.

Prism began waving footmen and maids back into the house, so Diana made up her mind to retreat as well. Mabel could take care of Godfrey for an hour or two when Leonidas tired of him, and the duchess wouldn't let go of Artie for hours.

That evening, there would be rough ground to cover, as Lady Knowe would say. Diana would have to give notice, offer apologies, and make up a lie about where she was going next.

One thing she knew absolutely, watching the family mill around each other, was that she could not live near the Wildes. If she and Godfrey were to be happy, they had to go far away. They could not hover on the edges of all that joy.

Leaving the courtyard, she skirted the castle on the west side and hurried along the path to the apple orchard, trying to run ahead of her tears.

On the other side of the orchard, she scrambled down the hill toward the lake and hauled on a weather-beaten rope tied around the trunk of the willow tree until an old punt scraped the edge of shore. It was the work of a moment to climb in and use the pole to push off from the shore, without undoing the rope from the trunk.

The boat drifted from the shore, the rope's length stopping the vessel under a fountain of leafy green willow spears that hung so thick and low that they brushed the surface of the water.

Tucked under a length of oiled canvas were two pillows, allowing a person to slip off the seat and comfortably sit or even recline in the middle of the flat-bottomed boat. She put down the pillows, kicking off her uncomfortable shoes, peeling down her thick black stockings and tucking them under the gunwale at the end of the boat.

Finally, she pulled up her skirts and relaxed, propping her crossed ankles on the rear seat. She watched the shifting green leaves and the twinkling bits of sunlight that filtered through, until slowly her jealousy and sorrow eased.

She didn't like herself when she got mired in sadness.

North would be comforted by his family and have no need for toast and honey. That was an excellent thing, no matter how much her heart tried to say otherwise. She was happy to have been able to help him in any way, in view of the damage she'd done to his reputation. And perhaps, to his heart as well.

Twenty quiet minutes of thought told her that she would never be able to find another position as a governess. No respectable family would hire a governess with a bastard child, nephew or not. What elderly lady would want a companion who had a child?

Fear burned in her chest, but she pushed it away. She wasn't destitute. She could ask Lady Knowe for help and receive it, with no questions asked.

Or North.

She could ask him for help. They had become friends, of a sort, in the last few days.

She was thinking that over when a thrashing noise broke the silence. Someone tugged on the rope. Hastily she sat up, curled her legs to the side, and made certain that her bare toes were covered.

"Leonidas!" she called. "I'm here."

The boat broke free of the willow fountain, and Diana looked up with a smile on her face.

To be met with a scowl.

"*Leonidas?*"

"North!" she squeaked.

"You have an assignation with my *brother*?" North's mouth was a furious, thin line.

"No," Diana stated. "I do not have an assignation with your brother."

"What in the bloody hell are you doing here, then? Shouldn't you be in the nursery?"

"Of course." That was the first time he made her feel like the governess. She snatched up her shoes and stockings and hopped onto the rear seat. She refused to meet his eyes as she jumped to shore.

She'd never done that before, flinging herself recklessly into the air. North moved smoothly sideways to catch her, his hands landing on her upper arms. "Let me go," she ordered. She couldn't back up, as she'd be in the lake, but she wriggled sideways.

For a moment she thought North might shake her.

Had she ever wished to see his face angry? She refused to let him think her intimidated. "Let me go," she stated again, head high, "so that I may return to the nursery. I can assure you that upper servants are allowed a break of several hours each day."

His response was pithy and blasphemous.

"That's enough!" she said fiercely. "Let me go, Lord Roland. You have no right to speak to me this way. You are not acting like a gentleman!"

"I'm not a bloody gentleman," North growled. But he let her go.

She moved sideways, and then, because she was angry at him, curtsied. "Good afternoon, Lord Roland." Her tone was scathing.

Large hands jerked her close to him. "Don't *ever* call me that."

Before she could respond, North's mouth closed on hers. She was too startled to speak—but her body made a decision for her.

It wasn't his open, rough kiss, as much as the way his arms went around her, as if they would protect her. As if she could stay in his embrace and he would keep away the world and its cruelties.

"Brawny" wasn't a word that could be applied to nobility . . . but the arms that encircled her were thickly muscled. Even when they were betrothed and she didn't want to be a duchess, she had secretly craved North's touch.

Not that he'd ever touched her like this. They'd kissed once. But never like this.

His grip tightened until she melted into his arms. The force of his kiss tilted her head back; he devoured her mouth, desire and anger speaking to her as clearly as if he'd shouted at her.

For the first time, the very first time, she kissed him back, up on her toes, hands curling around broad shoulders. She lost her head and kissed him back, a raw sound coming from her throat as her fingers slid down and spread over his chest, loving the powerful muscles under her touch.

He was kissing her so hard that her mind blurred and she felt engulfed in his heat and strength. She had never imagined a kiss could be so raw. So real.

When they both needed to breathe, he nipped her lip, his gaze direct and smoldering. She closed her eyes and snuggled against him, which made him groan, a hungry sound that weakened her knees. Her eyelids swept closed as he captured her lips again, tongue exploring her mouth as if she was . . .

As if she was his. Holding her as if she was his.

Until he wasn't.

Chapter Ten

"What were you doing in that boat?" North demanded, noticing the hoarse note in his own voice with incredulity.

He'd heard Diana call to his brother with that happy note of welcome and . . . Bloody hell. He'd lost his mind. He couldn't remember when he'd gone so white-hot with anger. Not for years.

"You weren't waiting for Leonidas," he answered himself. "That was . . . I apologize."

Diana was staring at him. She put her hands on her hips. "Your brother is a friend. Whenever your siblings are on leave from school, I spend a great deal of time with all of them, and that includes Leonidas."

"He told you about the island," North said, gathering the threads of his sanity together.

"What are *you* doing here?" Diana demanded. "You should be with your family."

"They are bathing and such. As you pointed out, it can take a lady three hours to change clothing."

She shook her head, slowly. "You are a terrible liar."

"There are so many of them. They're very loud." His hands were clenched at his sides, because if he didn't keep them in fists, he would reach out and pull her into his arms again. Kissing Diana, as it turned out, was like eating honey toast.

Curative, if not irresistible.

She surveyed him in a silence broken only by a cricket.

Then, to his utter shock, instead of answering, she took a step forward and tucked her head under his chin. He didn't move, as frozen as if the cricket had landed on his palm. Diana wrapped her arms around his middle and relaxed against him.

Uncurling his fists, North slipped his arms around her, resting his cheek against her head. Her hair had the sweet, elusive scent of sunshine and under that, lake water. Something wound very tight in his chest relaxed.

"It's going to be all right," Diana said against his chest, her voice so low that he hardly heard her over the lapping of water at their feet.

He kissed her hair, and kissed the one ear he could

see. Then he put his cheek back down on her hair and they stood in the late afternoon sunshine and listened to silvery-green willow spears rustling in the breeze. The cricket went to sleep or forgot its own tune.

After a while he stepped back. "Do you really need to return to the nursery immediately?"

He'd always thought Diana's eyes were a clear gray, ringed in midnight blue. But with the lake behind her, they turned misty blue. She shook her head. "Artie is with your mother. Leonidas almost certainly took Godfrey to the stables; they have a tradition of greeting every horse when he comes home."

North digested that. Godfrey had become a member of the family; no wonder his aunt hadn't told Diana that Godfrey would be a laird. The situation was something akin to when the second duchess took Joan to London, perhaps planning to abscond with the baby to the continent.

One of their own was in danger of being stolen away. Lady Knowe, let alone the duke, would never allow it.

Accepting that thought, North decided that he would like to take Godfrey for visits to the stables. The thought of a little boy on his shoulders felt right. He and Diana had to talk about that. They had to talk about many things, but not at the moment.

"You weren't punting to the island?" he asked.

She shook her head. "I don't know how to maneuver the pole. I came here with Lavinia once during the betrothal party. We just pushed the boat away from shore until it drifted under the willow tree, where all the branches dip below the surface. I escape here sometimes."

"I don't suppose there's much privacy when you are living with very small children."

"No," Diana said with a wry smile. "As you know, Godfrey ends up in my bed. Sometimes they both find their way there."

North looked down, and she curled her bare toes in embarrassment. "I've seen your feet," he pointed out. "Under your night robe, which is a good deal more improper than this."

She had dropped her ugly black shoes on the grass. She was looking at him—at his mouth?—so he stretched out one foot and gently kicked one of her shoes right over the bank and into the lake.

Diana gasped. "Those are my only pair of shoes!"

He gave the other shoe a harder kick, and it flew off the bank and into the water with a splash, like an ugly clod of dirt.

"How dare you," Diana cried, narrowing her eyes and placing her hands back on her hips, the drowsy-eyed temptress replaced by an eagle-eyed governess.

North tried to kick one of the serviceable black stockings next, but it didn't go far, and Diana grabbed it. "You're out of your mind," she gasped, clutching the stocking to her breast.

For some reason, the idea didn't bother him, the way it had for months. Instead the corners of his mouth curled up and he tugged at the stocking she held. "This is too practical to be worn by you."

He didn't want anything like that on her body. Near her.

"I have only two pairs of stockings," Diana said, obviously marshaling her patience. "I'm no good at darning. These are my best pair. What am I going to do without shoes?"

She didn't ask the question to him, but to herself. The words had a quiet desolation to them that chilled North to his core. He wrapped his arms around her and pulled her against his chest. "I am going to buy you shoes, the kind you used to wear."

"No, you are not." She didn't bother to shake her head, but North could feel rejection of that idea through her whole body.

"One of my sisters will give you a pair."

She pulled herself free. "I shall borrow Mabel's second-best slippers until I can acquire another pair. Do you understand what you've done, North?"

He shook his head.

"Those shoes were my possession, and I have very few possessions. Just because you can afford to allow your valet to steal your breeches doesn't mean the rest of the world can be as cavalier. A pair of slippers, like those in your sisters' wardrobes, costs far more than I can afford."

"I want to buy you shoes. I knocked your shoes in the lake, so I will replace them." He hesitated and then told her the truth. "Please. It will make me feel better."

North had the unnerving sense that Diana knew exactly how pared to the bone he felt. The panic that blanketed him when his loving, exuberant family flooded into the drawing room and made that enormous room seem like a narrow cavern with towering stone cliffs.

She sighed. "Kicking my shoes into the lake *ought* to make you ashamed. It's something Artie would do in a temper."

He couldn't stop himself and kissed her again until she let the stocking fall to the grass and wrapped her arms around him.

"Stop worrying," she said sometime later, eyes intent on his.

"Because all will be well?" He couldn't muster a smile.

"It will pass." She turned away without giving him

a sympathetic smile, which he would have hated, and pulled on the rope; the boat had drifted from shore again.

He leaned over her and gave one tug that beached the boat on the bank.

"I never get the boat to come onto the shore so I have to jump." She nimbly climbed back into the boat. "I wish I were as strong as you are."

North pulled off his boots and threw his stockings on the bank next to hers. "Strength is not something I think about very often," he said, climbing after her. She had seated herself on the forward seat. He sat down facing her. "It's a family trait. In one of my earliest memories of my father, he was taming a horse. In my mind it was the size of an elephant."

"I have no memory of my father," Diana said wistfully. "Now poke the shore with the oar, pushing us in that direction." She nodded toward the thick waterfall of leaves.

The prow of the punt slid into the green wall. Leaves closed around them as the boat reached the end of the rope, coming to a halt in the midst of a sea-green cave, as if they'd slid underwater and entered a mermaid's parlor.

North slid down and sat in the generous well between the two seats. Stuffing one of the pillows behind him, against the rear seat, he waved the other pillow at Diana.

"This is so improper," she observed.

"Less so than your chamber last night." He put his feet on the seat beside her, giving her a nudge with his bare ankle. "Off the footstool, my lady."

Diana slid to the bottom of the boat opposite him, taking the cushion he handed her and putting it at her back. Then she carefully arranged her skirts so that they draped over her toes.

"I like your feet," North said thoughtfully. His eyes narrowed. "Did you take off your shoes when Leonidas showed you the island?"

"Oh, for goodness' sake," Diana said. She threw her head back and looked up at the maze of willow branches over them.

He had felt trapped by bed curtains and military tents, but this living tent felt right.

"Yes, I'm jealous," he confirmed.

"I am not yours," Diana said, keeping her eyes far above them.

He admired the long smooth line of her throat. Some of her hair had fallen from its bun and a strand or two trailed over the wooden seat, forcing him to imagine locks of her hair falling over his chest, winding around his arms, brushing . . .

Well.

"You're my friend," he said gruffly. "Alaric's abroad, and Parth is in London. I trust you."

She lowered her chin and leveled her gaze at him. "That says little for your intelligence, don't you think? Has anyone other than myself told lies about you?"

"Probably not." He reached over his head and stretched, enjoying his lack of a coat. "Except for those engravers who depicted me as a ravisher emerging from a trunk."

"Would you mind if I put my feet on the seat beside your shoulder?"

He grinned at her. "The way I have done, without asking permission?"

There was a thread of erotic tension between them that grew hotter and tighter every time their eyes met. And when she stretched out long, slender legs and put her feet beside him?

The sight of Diana's ankles jumbled his thoughts so much that all the blood in his body headed downward. He had to be careful and not frighten her. Though if that kiss hadn't frightened her . . .

She slid farther down, so her head rested against the cushion. Her cheeks were pink and her lips had the curve, the laughing curve, that he remembered from when he first saw her.

How could he not have realized that she was griev-ing during their betrothal party? How blind had he been? In the last three days he had learned every curve of her face. If she felt miserable now, he would know.

"You have freckles," he observed, because if they didn't talk, he was going to pull her into his lap and probably capsize the boat.

"Yes, I do."

There was a heaviness in her voice that he didn't like. "I would like to kiss every one."

Diana rolled her eyes. "You're a terrible liar, as I told you earlier."

"I'm not lying."

She snorted. "Tell me five things about yourself, and I promise I can identify each one for truth or falsehood. Do you know, when we were betrothed, I was never quite sure what you were thinking? Now I know that the trick is to watch your eyes."

That was a delighted smile on her face. North took a careful breath, exerted control over the lower half of his body again, and said, "A gentleman does not fling about his emotions, treating everyone in the room to a display."

"Why not?"

It was a simple question, and once he thought about it, perplexing to answer. "Perhaps," he said after a minute, "because so little that we do is private. Ophelia told me once that if she sneezed at the opera the gossip columns would report that she was dying of consumption."

"The burden of being a duchess," Diana said, looking delighted at having avoided that fate. Did she truly believe that a coronet wasn't in her future? Looking into her clear eyes, he knew the answer to that.

Yes. Yes, she did.

Diana believed herself to be his friend. She enjoyed their kiss. She instinctively knew how to make him feel better.

But she did not consider them to be still betrothed, or betrothed again.

It was a pretty tangle, but he had time to work it out. "I'll tell you five things about myself," he said, "and you may guess whether they are true or false. From the expression in my eyes." He grimaced.

"You can't try to fox me," Diana said instantly.

"Of course I can! What's the point otherwise? What do I get if I trounce you?"

"What do *I* get? You might as well give up now!"

"You get a new pair of slippers," he said, nudging her bare feet with his shoulder. "And I get a kiss."

"A kiss is not equal to a pair of shoes."

"To me it is," he said. "A kiss is better than shoes."

She wrinkled her nose. "I don't mean to be rude, North, but you say that because you've never earned a wage."

"I was paid for my service." His voice was raw.

Diana didn't say anything, but what she did was better than words. She turned a little to the side and wrapped a hand around one of his ankles. He had the sudden feeling he'd had the night before: She was tethering him to the ground.

"Very well," he said, clearing his throat. "Number one: I lost my virginity to a barmaid."

"False," she said, smiling at him. Her fingers loosened around his ankle, but he still felt her touch as if she were stroking his leg.

"Number two: I lost my virginity to a married woman."

"Fal—" She began, and then narrowed her eyes. "True! I can scarcely believe that, North. I would have thought you would respect marriage vows. You seem so . . ."

"Self-righteous?" he suggested.

She dimpled at him. "If the shoe fits."

"I was a wild stripling. Horatius was alive, and the future was my own. A young beautiful lady, married to an elderly gentleman, had her way with me, to my great enjoyment. Taught me quite a lot too," he added.

Diana didn't turn a hair at this statement, which in his estimation would have had a great many maidens fainting, or at least pretending to be shocked. She gave him a wicked twinkle. "It doesn't seem fair that a lady can't avail herself of the same instruction before marriage."

North kept silent a second while he registered the protest that flooded his body at the mere idea of Diana taking instruction from any man other than himself. Diana taking instruction? He had the sense that she would teach a man—*him*—things that couldn't be learned from an adulterous affair, no matter how genial.

"I would be happy to teach you anything you wish to know," he said, keeping it simple.

"Men!" she said, laughing. "You instinctively turn the simplest remark into an invitation, don't you? Leonidas—" She jolted to a stop, like a colt encountering a wall too high to jump.

"My brother Leonidas," North said, his heart pounding steadily, "is just your age, isn't he?"

"He is a month or two younger," Diana said, her eyes wary. "He's a terrible flirt, but no more than that."

North was fairly certain that his face was inscrutable. "Three: I have every faith that Leonidas would not try to seduce my former fiancée."

"False," Diana said, with a small but triumphant

grin. "You look uncertain around the eyes. Leonidas has only tried to seduce me if offering witticisms count. I suppose if I were a silly, green girl I might have fallen in love with him. That's number three, and so far I've been right every time."

North pulled himself together because he was behaving like an irritable toddler. He picked up one of her feet.

"No!" she said, trying to pull her legs back, which made her skirts slide up, much to North's approval.

Grinning at her, he dug his thumbs into the bottom of her foot. "Those shoes must have been miserable to wear."

She froze on the verge of pulling away. "That feels so good," she breathed.

The warm, happy sound of her voice jolted sensation down his body and into his loins. "Number four: I bought a special license because I planned to talk you into marrying me as quickly as I could."

She examined his face. He consciously tried to slow his breathing, aware that it had grown ragged, a result of the slender foot in his hand and her delighted response to his touch.

His fingers trembled, poised to trail caresses from her feet up her legs.

"False?" she asked, uncertain.

He couldn't stop a smile. "Very astute of you, Miss Belgrave. I bought the special license because I had a vague feeling that you would try to back out. I thought—wrongly—that you were fearful of my family, or the attention given to a duchess."

"Not the former, but a woman would have to be mad to want the latter."

North had known many women greedy for precisely the attention that duchesses received. "I meant to use the license only if you couldn't bear the idea of a ceremony in the cathedral, if you felt strongly that you could not face public scrutiny. I had not imagined," he said wryly, "that you didn't want to marry me at all. A measure of my arrogance, I suppose."

She did not soothe him with a falsehood about herself. Instead, she gave him a rueful smile, wriggled her toes, and nudged her left foot into his hands. "One question more and I will have earned a pair of slippers." The gleeful sound in her voice made him laugh.

"Fifth and final: I loved you."

The words hung in the lazy summer air.

"How can I answer that?" she said, her eyes on his. "You've since told me and Lady Knowe that I did not break your heart. So obviously the answer is no."

He kept silent.

Diana let an audible puff of air escape her lips. "Yes?"

North didn't know what he was doing. What game he was playing. Was he playing for a pair of slippers, a kiss, or something altogether more costly?

"Skip that one," he said. "Five: Aunt Knowe is one of my favorite people in the world."

She laughed, palpably glad that the tension was broken. "That's true. She's your mother, isn't she? For all intents and purposes?"

He nodded and shifted position, managing to come to his knees without rocking the boat overly much. "I'm going to claim my kiss now."

"You didn't win a kiss!" she said indignantly. "I won shoes."

He came to her side and tugged her lower into the well of the boat. Propping himself on an elbow, he leaned over enough to kiss her straight nose and her rosy cheek. "I said that I would kiss every freckle," he reminded her.

"That was foolishness."

"I love your freckles," he murmured. Her skin was warm and very smooth, like taut silk. "They're on the bridge of your nose, but not on the tip."

"No one loves freckles, and it's unkind of you to remind me of them."

He buried his free hand in her hair and looked into her eyes. Meeting those eyes was frightening, like leaping off a cliff. They were so beautiful, a clear gray once again, now that the lake was not in sight.

But more than that, they were the most honest eyes he'd ever seen. True eyes. Eyes that had never lied to him, even when most women would have pretended to have had tender feelings during their betrothal, in order to please him.

More fools they, because that implied he had no thirst for the chase. He *loved* a chase. There were battles he would never again undertake, and there were others that he welcomed joyously.

"I was in love with you," he informed her, deciding that he might as well make everything very clear. Her breath was warm against his, but she didn't say anything, just regarded him with the same peaceful silence that enveloped him last night, and the night before. Did she understand that she was his only source of comfort?

Her silence was an invitation. If Diana didn't want to be kissed, she would tell him. If she hadn't wanted to comfort him, she would have thrown him out of her chamber instead of offering him toast.

When her mouth opened under his and her arms went around his neck, he felt a distant pang of triumph. It was distant, because the touch of her tongue sent his brain into some other place. His body took control and he relaxed into the warm dregs of the afternoon and the gentle rocking of the boat.

They kissed like explorers this time, learning taste and sound. He memorized the small squeak that came from the back of her throat whenever his tongue tangled with hers. The shudder when he licked her neck. The whimper when he gave her more weight, pinning her hips to the bottom of the boat.

He loved kissing the freckles she hated, pressing kisses on her eyelids and her cheekbones and her finely wrought jaw.

But he kept returning to her mouth and crashing inside, tasting her the way no other man had. His heart was beating so rapidly that he could hear it in his ears.

Her hands were twisted in his hair.

When her hands moved, sliding down his back, sending waves of feeling down his body, he no longer needed to be held to the earth. Everything in him was embodied, pressing her to the bottom of the boat.

She seemed to like it, nipping back at him, combating his tongue with hers, kissing him as deeply as she could, her body arched against his chest.

He wanted to run a hand down her leg so badly that he was shaking all over. But . . . kisses were kisses. His sister-in-law had been kissed by any number of suitors;

his brother Alaric had used that as an excuse to marry Willa by special license.

That, and Alaric had been madly in love.

"North." Diana's voice was little more than a breath of air that traveled as far as his ear and no more.

"Darling." He kissed his way along her cheekbone and back to her mouth, and the conversation stopped.

By the time she spoke again, North was gritting his teeth because she was rocking against him, arching her back and—

This was no courtship kiss.

"We must stop," Diana murmured.

"Mmmm." He was propped over her now, elbows on either side of her head, in the right position to ravish her mouth. One of her slender knees was bent, and her dress had fallen back on her legs.

A gentleman wouldn't put a hand on her ankle and run it up her calf.

Her arms were looped around his back, but one of her hands caught his before it could go higher.

"No." The word sounded in his ear with dismaying strength of character.

He groaned. "May I say that your ankle is one of the most beautiful things I've ever touched?"

Enjoying the compliment, Diana squinted down at

where his golden-brown hand encircled her ankle. Her foot had strands of grass stuck to it—and freckles.

"My foot is freckled," she cried, dumbfounded, sitting up. "Hell's bells! Things just get worse and worse around here."

North threw back his head and fairly bellowed. That was the first laugh that she had got from him, and she loved every joyful second of it.

"My room is dim, and I hadn't seen," she explained. "They must be from taking off my shoes and lying in the boat. It's a good thing my mother isn't here."

"For many reasons. Just think of the freckles that would sprout if you took off all your clothing." North managed a leer so exaggerated that she giggled.

"Freckles are anathema," she told him, since he had clearly missed this crucial piece of information.

"Anathema," he said thoughtfully. "A big word for a small spot."

"They are a terrible blemish."

"I like them. Smallpox scars would be worse."

Diana was taken aback by that. "I've never seen any."

"Queen Elizabeth covered up her scars with thick white paint, just the way you did your freckles when we first met. Your freckles should be proudly displayed," he said, dropping kisses on her nose.

His lips moved to her cheeks, and she lay back again, loving the caress. North began peppering her cheekbones with kisses.

"You're not still kissing freckles, are you?"

"Yes," he said dreamily. "Like flecks of sweet sugar."

"No," Diana breathed. "That can't be right." He'd given her far more kisses than five. But with a sinking stomach, she realized that it could be. From the time she was a little girl, her mother's abhorrence of freckles had resulted in bonnets that stifled any ray of sunlight.

But here? At the castle? She had formed a habit of escaping to the lake and the punt for an hour or so while the children napped. Lying on her back and allowing filtered sunlight to warm her face.

The tallow candles in her room meant that she'd spent little time looking at her face. The five freckles she used to have must have multiplied.

"They are beautiful," North said soothingly, a large hand gently stroking her hip. She hadn't realized she had gone rigid. Her mother wasn't here. There was no chance that Mrs. Belgrave would sweep into any room where Diana might be and express disgust.

Children didn't care about freckles.

North didn't care either—though that was irrelevant.

"We should return to the castle," she said. Her feet

were freckled, her face was freckled . . . She peered down at her chest, what she could see of it.

"No freckles," North said helpfully. "Perhaps I should examine it more closely." He pulled aside the fichu tucked into her modest neckline.

"North!"

"Why did you ever . . ." His voice trailed off.

Diana stifled a grin. He was gazing at her bosom as if he was ravenous. North was a predator, a top-of-the-food-chain predator, and she probably ought to worry about that look.

"Are you licking your lips?" she inquired. Frankly, if she was going to fuss about indiscretions with North, she should have started two nights ago.

"Yes," he said, and a puff of laughter escaped her mouth, because his finely chiseled jaw was practically hanging open. "Lavinia Gray flaunts her breasts, and every man in her vicinity appreciates it, Diana. Why didn't you, when we were betrothed?"

She scowled. "Why were you looking at Lavinia's breasts?"

He dropped a hard kiss on her mouth. "They were there, on display, and no man could overlook them. But yours are even more beautiful."

"So they should have been on display?" she asked tartly. "Is that what you wanted your fiancée to do?"

"I have numerous sisters, and I've had two step-mothers," he said with exaggerated alarm. "I wouldn't dare make a suggestion about what a woman should wear."

She sighed. "Breasts are indelicate and immoral. My mother's judgment, in case you're wondering."

"Immoral?" North managed to tear his eyes away. "How can a part of one's body be immoral?"

Diana rolled her eyes at him. "Don't be absurd! You don't go around with that exposed." She waved her hand toward his breeches.

His lips curved. No, he hadn't been using lip color, as she and Lavinia had once surmised. That dark rose color was his own.

"Just because I keep my tool wrapped up doesn't mean it's immoral," North stated, his tone purely wicked.

"I must return to the castle," Diana said. But she couldn't stop herself: "'Tool'? *Tool?* That's absurd." Giggling. She always seemed to be giggling around him, like the green girl she wasn't.

"What term do you prefer?" His eyes met hers, curiosity warring with desire. "I haven't discussed the subject with a young lady before."

"Nothing! It shouldn't be mentioned," she said, hastily stuffing her fichu back into her bodice.

"Cock?"

His deep voice hung in the air, the silence broken only by the cricket and the gentle lap of water against the boat. Diana's cheeks turned so red that her ears felt hot. "North!"

He grinned, unrepentant. "Some men talk about their willy, but I think that word references something Godfrey's size."

"I see," Diana said. Her inner voice screamed at her to remember that she wasn't a shy miss any longer. She was an independent woman. A mother. Sort of. She cleared her throat. "I must return to the nursery."

Any gentleman would apologize for embarrassing her, but North showed no signs of doing so.

"Are you speaking those words to me because I'm . . ." She couldn't work out what she wanted to say. Did she want to ask if he felt free to bandy words with a governess because she was part of the household? He didn't, and she knew it. Did she mean to ask whether he thought she was ruined? He didn't.

"Never mind," she amended.

"I'm expanding your vocabulary because I'm a born teacher," he whispered, leaning over and brushing his lips on hers.

Despite her resolution to return to the castle, her mouth opened. His tongue skimmed her bottom lip and slipped inside. Heat simmered in her belly and down her legs, because he tasted so good.

She loved the way he was holding her shoulders, holding her still so he could kiss her deeply, as if they were one person instead of two.

She put her arms around his neck, and he kept his hands where they were. All they did was kiss. And kiss some more. She took a breath now and then. He muttered something low, but dived back into her mouth before she understood.

An hour or so later, he pulled back and said, "I suppose you must return to the castle." His voice rasped, as if he were pushing a rock up a hill. Performing an amazing feat of strength.

Diana had completely lost her head. Her heart was pounding and she felt happier than she had in months . . . no, in years. She smiled, took each of his hands in one of hers, and slid them down her front, brushing her scarf aside.

Her corset had forced her bosom into a single mound, squished together like a bundle of laundry.

But her breasts emerged from the top, because a corset couldn't subdue Diana's generous curves. She dragged his hands down, just enough so they rounded her bosom, her hands cupped over his.

The emotionless duke-to-be was gone. Looking back at her was a man whose eyes were turbulent and full of desire.

There was more there, but that desire . . . he wanted *her*. Freckles and all. With no paint, no wig, no jewels, no silence. His desire was for the real Diana.

To this point, she'd been focused on giving North whatever he needed to heal from injuries she felt responsible for. Acceptance. Kisses. Toast.

But she hadn't thought . . .

"I believe we should leave the boat now," North said, his voice low. He slipped his hands from under hers.

She stared at him as he rose in one smooth movement and hauled on the rope. One tug and the boat skimmed onto the grass bank.

North leapt out and turned, one foot on the boat, hand reaching toward her. Diana crawled onto the backseat.

He made a stifled sound, a groan, and she looked up at him. "I don't want to fall out," she explained. "I can't swim."

"Bloody hell."

"I know," she sighed, straightening, but still on her knees. "I shouldn't go anywhere near water. I wouldn't let Artie and Godfrey in the boat, I promise you."

Her eyes dropped. His breeches were tented in front

with something very large. Hard. Right at the level of her eyesight.

Slowly she looked up and met his eyes.

North leaned forward, with one hand holding the prow and the other swinging around her waist. Before she knew what happened, he grabbed her, took a step back, swiveled, and placed her on her feet.

"I don't have a willy," he said, a wry twist to his lips.

"No," she breathed.

"I'm sorry that you no longer have shoes," he said, dropping her hand. He bent over, and before she could stop him, her stockings flew over the bank, floated on the surface for a few moments, and sank.

Of course they sank. They were heavy and hot. They made her legs itch and her calves sweat.

"North," she said, marshaling arguments that would address his arrogance and thoughtlessness, not that sweet expression in his eyes and the way he looked at her as if she were a queen, ugly shoes or not.

"Now I owe you a pair of shoes and a pair of stockings," he said, as if that excused him. As he pulled on his silk stockings, having retrieved them from the grass, she remembered how smooth the silk stockings she used to wear had felt on her legs. Her favorites were embroidered with pansies, and tied over her knees with ribbons embroidered with the same design.

They had been a pleasure to wear.

North was stamping into boots that had voyaged to the New World and back, and yet, because they were so well made, looked hardly the worse for wear.

"I am a governess," she said, resolving to make herself understood to him. No matter how much she missed wearing silk stockings, they were part of her past and not her present.

He pulled her arm through his as if they were strolling through Hyde Park, whereas in fact they were heading up a small hill and would be making their way through an apple orchard. They were quite improperly alone, in other words.

"I don't have very many belongings and you cannot take them."

His brow furrowed. "Don't we pay you a decent wage?"

"It is absurdly generous, considering my poor credentials. But everything costs money." Godfrey's clothing, for one. Any treats she bought him—or Artie, for that matter. Prism had told her to inform him about what she spent on the children, but how could she do that? Godfrey was in the castle under false pretenses.

"My aunt was furious about the clothing that Boodle took," North said.

She stole a sideways glance. He was rubbing his

chin. How had she thought his face unreadable? That quirk on one side of his mouth was rueful. "She has a good point, but . . ."

The slumberous expression in his eyes made her stomach twist. "Boodle made it possible for me to catch your attention," he said. "He took a man who didn't know a French wig from a pile of straw and taught me everything."

"I paid no attention to your wigs."

He shrugged. "I thought you were fashionable. It wasn't really you, I know now."

Diana looked at her freckled feet, strolling through the thick grass of the west lawn. Two gardeners spent days every month rolling it flat and thick. But somehow that fact slipped away.

Her mother had forced her into a duchess mold, set her out to trap a duke, and succeeded. She hadn't realized that North had done something like it—but for *her*, not for an abstract title.

"That wasn't me," she agreed.

"I didn't know about the freckles on your nose, for instance."

She glanced up at him. "Would that have changed everything?"

"Absolutely." His mouth quivered but he didn't smile.

"Imagine if you had known that I have them on my feet."

He pulled her arm tighter, against his body. "I would have had to throw you in a carriage and set out for Gretna Green." Looking at her with lustful eyes. "In order to save any other men who would be fooled into thinking there weren't freckles under all that face paint. A sacrifice for the greater good of mankind."

They rounded the corner of the castle and Diana pulled away. Hopefully no one had seen them strolling across the lawn. She certainly wasn't going in the courtyard arm in arm with the heir to the dukedom. She headed toward the side entrance that led to the kitchens.

"Who would have thought you were so saintly?" she asked. "So willing to use the small tools you have to help your fellow man!"

He burst into laughter. "My cock, such as it is, is always at your service, Diana."

She gasped. "I didn't mean that!"

"I did."

Chapter Eleven

Frederick, the footman who had earlier been carrying Godfrey on his shoulders, was manning the front door. "Is my family still in the drawing room?" North asked him.

Now he could tolerate a room full of Wildes. An hour or two drifting in a punt had settled his spirits.

That, and kissing a beautiful, befreckled woman.

"I believe the ladies accompanied Her Grace upstairs," Frederick said.

North took the stairs two at a time. Shoes. His girl needed shoes.

He found the female members of his family—his aunt, stepmother, and all four sisters—in the duchess's bedchamber.

North happened to know that his stepmother slept

with his father, though no one would mention such a disreputable fact.

Her chamber had been designed to be a reception chamber, back in the sixteenth century. An enormous bed jutted from one corner of the room, surrounded by a low railing that served as a barrier in times past. Ladies' maids and ladies-in-waiting would have been allowed inside the railing, whereas guests could only hover outside.

Naturally, his sisters were all over the room like chickens in the hen yard.

Artie was balancing on the railing, her mother waiting to catch her. Viola, Betsy, and Joan were clustered on the bed, the first two watching Joan cut something up. The bed was scarcely large enough to hold the three of them and their skirts. Aunt Knowe was seated on a settee to the side, poking at a bedraggled piece of knitting.

They all looked up as he entered. Ophelia smiled and caught Artie when her welcoming wave toppled her from the rail. Viola hopped off the bed, came over to him, and put an arm around his waist.

As she was Ophelia's daughter from her first marriage, Viola wasn't really his sister. But from the moment he'd met her fourteen years before, a painfully shy child, she'd been his special girl. She had walked into the nursery holding her mother's hand, her mouth somewhere between vulnerable and just plain terrified.

"Viola," he said, giving her a squeeze and a kiss. "You're what . . . . sixteen now? Is that possible?"

Betsy, the oldest of his sisters, pranced over. She had turned into one of those women so beautiful they blind a man—and she knew it. Every swish of her hips said, *Watch me.*

North bent down and gave her a kiss as well. "I understand that you have mowed down every man in London, forced them onto their knees, and tossed them out the door."

"That's right," Joan shouted from the bed. "She chews them up and spits them out."

"You are disgusting!" Betsy told her little sister, tossing her curls again.

"No lady should marry in her first Season, and possibly not in her second either," their aunt observed.

"I can't get up to greet the conquering hero," Joan said, blowing him a kiss. "I'm busy making you a present."

"Good afternoon, shortcake," he said, going over to the bed and dropping a kiss on her cheek. Then he saw what she was doing and an involuntary groan came to his lips.

"Miss Gray—Willa's friend Lavinia—did it with Alaric's prints," Joan told him. She was busily cutting around the outline of an aristocrat with a snarling expression of disdain and a wig so high it grazed the ceiling. "I bought five in a stationer's shop last week, and we already had some."

"I donated mine," Betsy said, adding impishly, "I'm the only one who owned the naughty one."

He didn't curse, but it was a near thing.

"Just as well it's being cut to pieces," Aunt Knowe said, sounding unusually severe. "That print is almost as bad as my knitting. Does anyone know how I could have ended up with a hole in the middle?" She held up a ragged scrap.

Viola sat down beside her. "I'll fix it, Aunt Knowe," she said in her sweet way.

The duchess's bed was covered with snippets of paper. One discarded fragment showed Diana kneeling, presumably at North's feet. He picked it up. A memory of her kneeling before him on the boat seat flashed into his head, sending a streak of pure heat down his body.

"What do you plan to do with those versions of me?" he asked, poking around in the mess and rescuing three more images of Diana.

"I oughtn't to ruin the surprise, but I'm making you a memory box," Joan said. She spread six or seven versions of him like a fan. "I'm going to glue them onto the lid of a box so you don't forget the year when all of England thought you were the devil's brother."

"Just like that pantomime we saw at Haymarket last year," Betsy cried. Then she sang, *"I can bark like a dog, I can grunt like a hog!"*

"No one would want to hear *you* singing onstage," Joan said with dampening emphasis.

Ophelia came over and kissed North's cheek. "Good afternoon, dear." Artie was on her hip, blissfully sucking her thumb.

"Good afternoon, Duchess," he said, and tapped Artie's nose. "Where's your accomplice, Godfrey?"

"Leo," Artie said, the word muffled by her thumb.

"After the stables, Godfrey wanted to stay with Leo," his stepmother explained, "so they went to his bedchamber. Leo said he's going to teach Godfrey to tie a neckcloth, but I think he was joking."

"I need shoes," North said, abruptly remembering why he had come into this bower of femininity.

"None of our shoes will fit you," Betsy said with a giggle. She was practicing the steps of a country dance, sashaying forward and backward to music only she heard.

"I threw Diana's shoes into the water," North said, keeping it simple.

But nothing was simple with six women in the room. "That was very naughty of you!" Joan exclaimed, and even quiet Viola said, "You oughtn't to have done it, North, because she doesn't have any others."

When the recriminations had died down, his stepmother said, "Who has shoes that might fit Diana?"

"Not I," said Joan. "There's a reason you all call me 'shortcake,' and Diana is delightfully tall."

"Not as tall as I am," Lady Knowe said. "My shoes will never fit Diana, though I will echo the rest and say that you shouldn't have done it, North." His aunt's feet were as ungainly as her hands, another unenviable inheritance that came with being the duke's twin. Not that the size of her feet ever seemed to bother her.

"Diana isn't as tall as she used to be when she wore high wigs," Betsy said. "Oh, I envied her so much. Parisian wigs! And now look, she lets Artie suck her hair, which is *disgusting*."

"Shoes," North ordered. "I left the poor woman barefoot."

After that, everyone but Joan ran off. Ophelia put Artie down and began rummaging through a trunk that appeared to hold nothing but shoes.

North was conscious of a desire to buy a trunk full of shoes for Diana, but he was used to waiting. That day would come.

"Rats!" Joan cried. "I accidentally cut off Diana's hand. Not that it matters." She threw the scrap to the side.

He rescued the mangled Diana, adding it to the others he held. He must be losing his mind.

Perhaps he could make a memory box for Diana, whatever that was. He pictured his bold, self-reliant former fiancée's reaction to a box covered with kneeling images of herself and snorted.

Betsy stuck her head back in the room. "Come on, then!"

Ophelia handed North a basket with two pairs of shoes and put Artie back on her hip. Joan grabbed the remaining prints and her scissors, and Lady Knowe put aside her mangled piece of knitting.

"Artie, may I have the inestimable pleasure of carrying you to the nursery?" North asked.

"No!" Artie said, snuggling against her mother's shoulder and sucking her thumb.

Ophelia smiled at him. "I'm perfectly able to climb the stairs with her, North, but thank you."

They trailed up a flight and down a corridor and arrived at the steep flight leading to the nursery.

By the time the three of them reached the nursery corridor, a burst of high-pitched voices could be heard coming from the schoolroom. Ophelia stopped, and

North halted as well, even though Diana's laughter drew him like a kite string.

"I am very fond of Diana," his stepmother said. "As is Artie."

Artie's head rested on her mother's shoulder but she roused enough to nod. "DeeDee." That nod seemed to take all her strength. Her eyelids closed.

Was he meant to chime in? "Fond" wasn't the word for what he felt for Diana.

"Diana is a wonderful woman, but she would not be a happy duchess," his stepmother said firmly.

Another burst of laughter from the schoolroom underlined North's stab of pure impatience with Ophelia's interference. "I thank you for sharing your opinion."

She put a hand on his arm. "Don't become stiff with me, North. I love both of you, and I *am* a duchess. I know what the position entails."

"I have not asked her again to be my duchess," he stated.

Ophelia's eyes softened. "Not yet."

"Are you warning me not to propose marriage?"

"I am telling you that Diana Belgrave would not be happy as a duchess. I leave Artie behind when I accompany your father to London; babies cannot thrive in London because of the smoke from coal fires. As Duke of Lindow, he attends endless dinners and hosts them as well, and he needs me beside him. That is part and parcel of being a member of the House of Lords."

North had already decided to stay away from Parliament, though it had little to do with Diana, and everything to do with an aversion to hours spent in an airless chamber listening to tedious speeches.

"Yes, you will," his stepmother said, reading his face. What happened to the days when no one could read his expression?

"There are more than enough asses in the Parliament chambers already."

She shook her head. "You Wildes are stubborn enough to choke, but you never shirk your responsibilities. Your father would vastly prefer to be here. It breaks both of our hearts to leave Artie. But he has been fighting to get an anti-slavery bill through the House." She readjusted her sleeping daughter.

North frowned.

"Exactly. How could you not take up your seat? Or refuse to attend the dinners necessary to persuade selfish men to think of someone other than themselves?"

"I take your point."

"I presume that throwing Diana's shoes in the lake was a courtship ritual of some sort." Ophelia's eyes crinkled at the corners, and he had the random thought that his father was a damned lucky man.

"You could call it that."

"I will be very displeased if my home was no longer a refuge for Godfrey and Diana."

"She cannot remain your governess. If I do listen to you, I still have to marry someone, and what woman would marry me under those circumstances? Most of England thinks I took advantage of her!"

"I understand." Ophelia nuzzled her daughter's cheek. "I will find another governess."

"You should bring Artie to London, governess or no."

"I can't." His stepmother's hand curled around Artie's head. "The smoke."

"London is full of babies, and our townhouse borders on Hyde Park. The smoke must be better there. Or buy a house just outside London, if you want. Send Father in daily to the Parliament. You could join him when you absolutely had to."

Ophelia's breath hitched. "What if she grew ill?"

"Then you would return to the country. Look at Joan. There's nothing wrong with her lungs now, is there? Artie needs you, and Diana cannot remain here to be her second mother."

Pain flashed through Ophelia's eyes.

"Exactly. If there's one thing that I learned in battle, it's that time is precious. Anti-slavery laws are a noble pursuit, but I'm certain there is a way to keep your family together."

Instead of going on to tell her that he meant to find a way to have Diana, he strolled into the schoolroom and watched as Diana rejected offers of shoes for long minutes until she gave in and accepted a pair of cream slippers cross-hatched with black thread.

"You should have these as well," Viola said, waving a heeled shoe at Diana. "Yellow clashes with my hair."

"That's not yellow," North said. They all turned and looked at him. He grinned. "Saffron, Viola. Saffron."

He was an agile man, and deftly caught the shoe when it flew through the air at his head.

"These are more than enough," Diana said, happily wiggling her toes in the cross-hatched slippers.

"Take this pair as well," North said, holding up the yellow shoe. "Viola is right. The color would make her skin appear jaundiced."

In the resulting mêlée, as Betsy defended the color of Viola's skin, and Joan protested that Viola's chestnut hair went extremely well with yellow, he handed the shoe to Diana and watched her slip it on.

It was a frivolous shoe, delicate and spangled. Peeping from the hem of Diana's worn gown, the yellow silk was a glimmer of sunshine.

"You must." Viola gave Diana the other shoe. "Yellow is brilliant with red hair, but *not* with chestnut, no matter what Joan says."

"Yours is copper, but Godfrey's is more like a rusty gate," Betsy said. She was helping Godfrey arrange his horses, and she reached out and tousled his hair.

"Diana's sister might have had darker red hair." Joan had brought her scissors with her, and was busy cutting up one of her last prints.

Diana's eyes flew to his and he knew exactly what she was thinking. He nodded. Yes, they all knew.

And no, they didn't care.

Chapter Twelve

For the next two nights, Diana set out bread and honey. It was as if she were feeding a house elf, she thought amusedly on the first night. One of those Norse sprites she'd read about in a storybook given to Artie. A housewife might set out milk and honey as thanks, or to trap an elf into granting her wishes.

They were tiny men in red caps, and nothing about North was tiny. But he had answered one of her wishes, at least: She had longed for new shoes, and now she had them.

North didn't come that night, nor the second night either. Diana woke up in the cold dawn, shivering in her robe, wondering why she had slept in the chair again.

No one had eaten the bread, and the milk soured on the hearth.

She had spent both days with the duchess, the lady's daughters, and Godfrey. Without direct conversation on the subject, she was no longer the castle governess. If Artie needed a new nappy, Her Grace summoned Mabel, or changed it herself.

Within a day, Artie began using the chamber pot, whereas Diana's previous attempts to persuade her had resulted in Artie protesting and, at one point, kicking over the pot. Diana tried not to mind. The important thing was that the family treated Godfrey as lovingly as they did Artie. He was visiting the stables twice a day, once with Leonidas, and again with North.

Her mind couldn't get around that last one.

It turned out that North, her foppish, prim fiancé (to call a spade a spade), was a superb horseman, who managed a large breeding program at Lindow Castle. There had been an excursion or two on horseback in the early days of the betrothal party. But she had managed to avoid them, throwing herself on her bed so she could cry in peace, grieving for her sister.

She'd never even seen North on horseback.

On the third day, North didn't return Godfrey to the nursery after their daily trip to the stables. When Diana found her nephew, he was sitting on the edge of the billiard table, happily watching Leonidas and North knock balls about.

North looked up and caught her eye, but just nodded and wished her good afternoon, with all the emotion of someone greeting . . .

Well, greeting a governess.

That night, she looked at the loaf of bread she'd fetched from the kitchen and felt like a fool. Obviously, North no longer had a problem sleeping.

True, she thought the smudges under his eyes were darker than they had been the day before. But what did she know? With a twinge of humiliation, she put the loaf to the side, uncut. Thank goodness he had no idea that she'd sliced bread for him the last two nights, and then fed them to Fitzy in the morning so that no one would know.

She had deluded herself into thinking that she could help with whatever had happened to him during the war—because she felt guilty. Absurd. Yet guilt was such a familiar companion.

Closing her door firmly, Diana bathed, tightly braided her hair, and climbed into bed. Ophelia had informed her in the afternoon that she intended to bring Artie to London. In the next few months, the duke would buy a new house near Kensington Gardens, where the air was cleaner.

"The girls will need to be in the townhouse for the Season," Ophelia had said. "But I can go back and forth. Artie can join us at the townhouse now and then." Ophelia had looked at Diana with pleading eyes. "Do you think Artie's lungs will be harmed?"

"No," Diana had said, and then, with a wry smile, "Although you mustn't consider me an expert in child rearing! All I know is that it will make Artie so happy. She misses you awfully."

"I cannot bear to leave her again," Ophelia had said, relief written on her face. "I simply cannot."

Diana went to sleep thinking about the joy in Artie's eyes as she curled like a dormouse in the duchess's lap. Yes, Artie loved Diana. But not the way she loved her mother.

North had survived two nights without venturing into the nursery wing.

His family was here now. They had been cross with him for tossing Diana's shoes in the lake, but if they learned he had invaded her chamber at night?

No gentleman did such a thing. He'd only done it in the grip of madness.

It reminded him of Alaric's pithy summing up of the duke's eldest sons: Horatius had been arrogant but true; Alaric foolhardy and adventurous; North rakish and half mad. And North couldn't quibble with Alaric's appraisal.

"Rakish and half mad" were obviously making an appearance again, even though North would have said his childhood was far behind him, buried in a deluge of ducal responsibilities.

At midnight, he was no closer to sleep than he'd been at nine o'clock, when he'd drunk a large amount of brandy and beat Leonidas and his father at billiards, only to lose to Betsy. His sister had laughed madly, cackling about Marie Antoinette's love for the game—and went on to beat them all handily.

He threw an arm behind his head and stared at the gathered canopy over his bed. Of course he would sleep. It was just a matter of closing one's eyes and allowing darkness to descend. He'd wake up in the morning refreshed.

Bloody hell, why had he ever complained about anything when he could *sleep*? The last two nights he'd lain wide-eyed until the darkness outside his window lightened to gray, followed by a faint pink.

He could remember times when he had caroused until dawn and slept until two in the afternoon. Granted, those halcyon days came before he inherited Horatius's title and its responsibilities, back when he was earning Alaric's characterization.

Finally, he gave up. He got out of bed, pulled on his breeches and shirt, and started pacing.

His bedchamber was forty-four steps long, and thirty-eight steps wide. He distracted himself by designing perfect bedchambers in his head. Now that he was free to leave the castle, he'd gone back to planning a mansion of his own. His bedchamber would be large, with a separate room for bathing, and a water closet off that room. There would be a dressing room for him, and a boudoir for his wife.

Despite his resolution to stop thinking about Diana, he pictured the gowns she used to wear, doubled the size of the boudoir, and then added a sizable alcove that could house a large wardrobe.

The bathing room would hold a ceramic tub like those Alaric had described seeing in Florence. He moved his imaginary mansion to Italy, on a hill overlooking fields of silver-leaved olive trees. He enlarged the windows and raised the bathtub so that it looked down the hill at the ocean.

A large bath, big enough for two.

His mind obligingly presented him with an image of Diana smiling at him, hair spilling over the side of the bath, cheekbones flushed by warm water and desire.

He began pacing again. Forty-four, turn. Forty-four, turn. Forty-four . . . He flung open the door and moved into the corridor. His bedchamber was in one of the oldest parts of the castle, where the corridors were stone, and a chill wind whistled around the window glazing in the winter. Snow sometimes found its way in. He padded barefoot through the castle, not even the clip of his boots accompanying him.

One hundred and twenty-three steps later, he started down a pair of winding stone steps that looked as if they belonged in a production of *Hamlet,* or at the very least, in a melodrama with a ghost.

A desperate man will do anything. He was a desperate man.

Intent came over him the way hope might come over a dying man, or love a desirous one. Like an unexpected visitor who can't be denied.

The fastest route from the east wing to the nursery was across the echoing ballroom, through the ladies' retiring room, up one flight and down another, and down a long crooked corridor. He emerged at the servants' staircase leading to the nursery, which was just as steep and narrow as the one designated for family.

There was no welcoming lamp turned low in the corridor.

The door to Diana's bedchamber was shut tight. Yet surely she hadn't locked it, in case Godfrey came to her bed with a nightmare. He and Godfrey, both plagued by nightmares and both in search of a single remedy.

He turned the doorknob as deliberately as if he'd entered a hundred maidens' chambers, though he hadn't. "Rakish" had never involved virgins, and Diana was a virgin; he was certain of that.

Whether she remained so was up to her.

Intent again.

She was curled under the covers, facing away from the door. The fire was low, and he saw with a quick glance that no jar of honey and half-melted butter were to be seen. The stab of disappointment he felt was wildly out of proportion.

It wasn't as if he needed toast. The chef had made six or seven dishes per course, as was normal when the duke was in residence. In the midst of all the French cooking, there had unexpectedly appeared simple English dishes, the kind he used to have as a child.

So he had eaten cottage pie, followed by a pasty with a wonderfully flaky crust, and then a bit of suet pudding.

He toppled a log on the fire before moving silently to Diana's bed, scarcely breathing. Her skin glowed in the moonlight like the inside of a periwinkle seashell they had in the nursery when he was a boy.

His breeches were on the floor in a moment. But his shirt . . .

He didn't want to be that character in the Shakespeare play, the one parodied in the etching. If he slipped naked into bed with her, was he any better than Shakespeare's ravisher?

Yes, he was.

He would never take what wasn't freely given.

He left his shirt on, lifted the covers, and slid beneath them. Diana didn't move, which surprised him until he remembered that she was used to another body, albeit a small one, slipping into bed beside her.

Sure enough, she murmured something and rolled over, one arm coming around him—

And froze.

North waited, enjoying himself the way he hadn't since he was a young man just free of university, sharing his God-given talents with any woman generous enough to smile at him.

Her eyes opened slowly. He brought her fingers to his mouth. If the lake turned her eyes blue, moonlight restored them to a beautiful silvery gray color.

"I must be dreaming," she muttered.

He eased forward and kissed her, his tongue sliding over her lips and then past them. Heat blazed down to his groin. His cock was hard; it had been hard from the moment he'd entered the room and breathed the flowery honey scent that was Diana.

"I must be dreaming," she said again, her voice

husky with sleep, "because no duke's son would be so lost to propriety, so indelicate, and so immoral as to enter a woman's bed without her express invitation."

The words were indignant, but her tone wasn't. And she was looking at his mouth, not at his eyes.

"I had the idea from a print that my sister Betsy bought in London," North said, keeping his voice serious.

"Who would have thought a future duke had a theatrical bone in his body?" The words were a retort, but her voice held such pure longing that he responded to it instantly. This time he kissed her gently and sweetly, waiting for her to open her mouth.

Which she did.

They kissed until his loins ached to arch toward her softness. His fingers trembling and his cock thicker and harder than it had ever been, he murmured, "May I kiss you in other places, Diana?"

She pulled back. Her eyes had darkened from moonshine to . . . to the color of gunmetal. Or a mouse, with fur the color of tarnished silver.

"What are you asking?"

"For more kisses."

"Where, exactly?"

"Everywhere." He edged closer, enough so that he could feel the warmth of her silky skin, and nudged her until she rolled on her back. He thanked her with a kiss. A raw, hungry, possessive kiss.

When he raised his head, she was looking at him in a dazed way. "As long as you understand that I'm never going to be your duchess."

"So you've said." He didn't allow himself a scowl.

"No, I need you to acknowledge what I said, not simply repeat it."

He groaned. "Diana Belgrave refuses to be a duchess. I know it, and so does most of England. She'd prefer to do menial labor, such as cleaning chamber pots, than allow me to buy her all the shoes her feet deserve."

Her eyes softened and she laughed. "My feet don't deserve fancy shoes."

"Saffron-colored shoes are not good enough for you," North murmured, one hand sliding under her head so he could cradle it. "Your toes should be in diamond-studded shoes and pearl-adorned slippers."

He kissed her cheekbone, heading toward her chin, heading . . . down.

"I spent the last two days with the duchess," Diana said with a little gasp. Her fingers curled in his hair. "His Grace came to find his wife every few hours. Sometimes just for a kiss, but often to ask her something about the estate."

North murmured something. He was unbuttoning her nightdress and she wasn't stopping him.

"Yesterday he made an absurd excuse and bore her away with him," Diana whispered. "I think they went to his bedchamber. In the middle of the day!"

North raised his head. "I'm certain they did."

"Most of England believes that you have seduced me," Diana said. "From that point of view, you're somewhat behind schedule, although my edict stands: I will not be your duchess."

A moment of stunned silence followed. She was looking at him expectantly, a smile on her lips.

She meant it. The small part of his brain capable of logical thought registered utter determination. "I want you to be my wife," North said. "I want to lure you away in the middle of the day."

"I know . . . I mean, I know you used to want that," she said. Her hands slipped from his hair. "I'm enormously fond of you, North. I am. But I don't love you the way a wife ought to love her husband. Now that my mother is no longer in control of my life, I mean to marry for love, or not at all."

Her eyes were bright, clear—entirely honest.

He felt it like a blow to the gut, the kind that felled a man. She wasn't saying anything he didn't already know.

Diana's face was uncertain. He leaned forward and brushed her lips with his. He was thinking fast. She wanted to marry for love.

As he saw it, toast and honey was a way of saying, "I love you." Making love was another way.

"You refuse to be a duchess," he said softly.

She nodded, her eyes on his. "I would be terribly unhappy." Her hand curved around his cheek. "If anyone could convince me, it would be you, dear friend."

"You lost Rose and I lost Horatius," he said, kissing her again. "So we are clinging to each other like shipwrecked sailors with one raft."

She giggled, and her arms wound around his neck. "I don't want to hurt your feelings, but I am relishing my freedom."

"I know you don't love me," he said, keeping his voice even. "Just so you know, I do love you. I think it is a lifelong condition."

Her eyes filled with remorse, but he shook his head. "Love should never be regretted. But what might be regretted by you is this evening, Diana. You wish to marry for love. Won't the man you choose expect you to come to him without knowledge of men?"

Never mind the fact that he had every intention of being the man she chose. Look what happened to Godfrey's father. What happened to the men in his regiment. Life should never be taken for granted.

"Whoever marries me will already know that I jilted a ravishing future duke," she said firmly, and then, with a twinkle, "You can take 'ravishing' in two ways."

Who would have guessed that his melancholy fiancée could have such a naughty grin?

"My husband will love me enough not to care," Diana said, her eyes shining with faith.

Everything in North chilled at the idea of Diana being loved by another man. *Loving* another man. He cleared his throat, because he had the feeling she wouldn't approve of her romantic ambitions making him homicidal.

"Miss Belgrave, are you giving me permission to ravish you?"

She dimpled at him. "Yes! I requested just that, Lord Roland."

A gentleman wouldn't agree. But that perfect gentleman likely wasn't as focused on winning as North was. Sometimes winning involved breaking some rules. Taking risks. Thinking creatively.

Diana kept stealing glances at his lips.

"A gentleman never refuses a lady," he said, making up his mind. He rose onto his knees, pulled off his shirt, and threw it over the side of the bed. "What do you know about intimacy?" he asked, enjoying the way she was looking at his chest, wide-eyed.

"Everything."

It took a moment for the word to register.

"I'm glad one of us is an expert," North said, suppressing the wish to smile. He'd bet his life that Diana was a virgin. He bent and traced her lips with his tongue. The expert was shy, and he chased her mouth, demanding entrance. When her mouth eased open, he kissed her, deep and wet and desirous.

And let his hands wander.

Every caress made Diana jump—and then moan. He wrapped a hand up one lush hip. She startled, and then smiled, letting her legs fall apart.

"You're perfect," he said, the word rasping in the quiet night. His hand slid down and curled around a plump thigh. "Not scrawny."

"I like buttered muffins."

"I will have muffins sent to your bedchamber every morning."

His hand slid over the softest skin he'd ever felt, making him reel with the desire to tear off her nightdress and leave kisses all over her pale skin.

She let out a little scream when his finger stroked her core. In his head, North was shouting something incoherent, made up of a string of curse words, forged from soft, wet, plump, trembling, heat. *Heat.*

With every caress, her eyes got larger and larger. He paused, his hand cupping her, one finger poised at her entrance. "Is this all right?" he whispered.

"Is that allowed?" his expert whispered back, stunned. Her hips arched, just enough so one broad fingertip sank inside.

"Oh, my," Diana gasped, her hands curling around his arms, fingernails biting into his skin.

North stroked her again, loving the way her hips were twisting. "I need to kiss you," he said, his voice a jagged sliver of sound.

Diana's thighs were rising toward his hand. He took her gasp as agreement; he sat up and eased his hand away.

"North!" She sounded fierce, like a thwarted warrior queen.

He drew up her nightdress, allowing moonlight to glimmer over giving, soft thighs. Perfect thighs.

A groan burst from his chest. Between her legs was a twist of red hair, strawberry-colored, lighter than the hair of her head. Below it, the perfect pink of a wild strawberry, gleaming with moisture and desire.

He came up on his knees, letting her see everything he had: thighs and chest corded with muscle, and arms the same. No softness, because if there had been any, it had been carved away by war.

His cock was thick and broad, standing out from his body and straining toward her. He watched her eyes go up and down his body, fascinated. Pause on his balls, which felt heavier than ever before.

Back to his cock.

"Even an expert like yourself might still have a question or two," he said, reaching down and gripping himself. He felt as if his loins were on fire.

Her eyes widened as he ran his hand down his cock, and pulled upward with a twist of his wrist. It was all he could do to keep his eyes on her face. Not to look down her body.

She sat up and her slender hands closed over his.

"Do it again," she whispered. A moment later she batted away his hand and took over, her hand surprisingly strong, pulling his cock just right.

He forced his hands to stay still and allowed her to play with him however she wished. She stroked him, one hand clenching, the other wandering. Each time a groan erupted from his lips, she would repeat what she'd done less tentatively, until she had him trembling like a boy of fifteen, head thrown back, his entire body focused on the deep burn in his balls.

Hell, the only mistress he'd had, years ago, hadn't figured out how to pleasure him like this.

When he couldn't take it any longer, he shifted over her in one smooth movement, pushing her gently onto her back. "If you touch me like that much longer, I'll come. I could do the same for you, and we can save the ravishing for another day."

"This isn't ravishing?" Diana's eyes were sparkling and her lips had the curve that he'd fallen in love with, as if joy was air she breathed.

"I am ravished," he said, meaning it.

She pouted, an expression he'd never seen and instantly approved of, and said, "I want more."

His body flamed with the absolute determination to give her whatever she wanted.

"Please, North."

Without hesitation, he shifted back, pried her luscious thighs apart, and lowered his head so that he could lick her. She tasted like tart honey, perfect Diana: fresh, lovely, and unlike any other woman.

He banished that thought. He hadn't had another woman since he met Diana. He didn't even want to *think* about another woman, ever again.

He concentrated on this moment, this pink, beautiful pussy in front of him, Diana squealing, writhing, grabbing his hair to hold him in place. Her hips arching in the air, her hands tightening, a breathless cry, another—

Silence because she was shaking so hard she couldn't make a sound. If he'd had to guess, he'd say that Diana was an expert in many things, but perhaps not in this.

Sure enough . . .

"What *was* that?" She sat upright, sweat-drenched hair, wild eyes, happy mouth.

"*That* was the beginning." He couldn't wait any longer. "I'm going to make love to you now, so this is your last chance to avoid being ravished."

She fell backward. "If that was the beginning, I could never refuse."

"I'll take that as a yes." Still, he bent over her, catching her eyes, because, damn it, they weren't married. He was taking a risk, a gamble, and so was she. He was gambling with his heart, and she with the virtue that no one believed she still had.

"Yes." She sighed, and tangled her fingers in his hair, pulling his mouth to hers. "Kiss me, North."

Chapter Thirteen

Diana and Rose had been young girls when their mother addressed the topic of conjugal intimacies with them. She had been brisk but detailed. Very detailed. She had bluntly told her daughters that she hadn't married into the gentry by being a prude.

"Your daughters can be prudish," she had told them. "*You* still need to overcome the grocer." That was how Mrs. Belgrave referred to her own father, as "the grocer."

Her mother's instruction had gone on to detail the services a woman can offer her husband.

So far this night, North was playing Diana's body as if it were a violin, and Diana hadn't used any of her expertise. Fragments of her mother's advice drifted through her head.

"He might wish to spurt on your breasts. Hold them

like this." Her mother had pressed her hands together. "Let him spank you."

North was smoothing a French letter onto himself, just as her mother had demonstrated on a cucumber.

"Did you bring that with you?" she asked.

He nodded, and gave her a smoldering but bluntly honest look. "I started carrying it lately. Just in case you allowed me to seduce you."

Given her sister's experience, there was something to be said for waiting until marriage. Unless—Diana thought with a surge of independence—your reputation is already ruined, and you've turned down the only marriage proposal you've ever received. Twice.

"Diana," North said softly. He had secured the French letter and was hovering over her. "Are you quite certain?"

Her smile came straight from her heart, meant for this thoughtful, intelligent, blindingly handsome man who had become a true friend in the last few days. A friend was so much better than a betrothed.

"Yes," she said. "I just want you to know that I *will* put all my expertise to work when I catch my breath. I know I haven't been doing it right."

He had an odd look in his eyes. "There's no right or wrong way." When he finished kissing her again, they were both panting. Diana braced herself.

Her mother had been very clear about this moment. "Scream whether it hurts or not," she had said. "The man deserves your virginity, and sometimes the pain is a mere pinch. He *expects* it. Without the knowledge of your lost virginity, your marriage is already on the wrong footing."

She and Rose had looked at each other, mouths open. "It's deranged," she had told her sister later. "Your husband wants you to be in pain? Absolutely deranged."

"I'm ready." She smiled at North, smiled because he would never want her to experience pain in the act of making love.

Sure enough, he hesitated. "There may be some discomfort."

She burst into giggles. "I was just remembering that my mother told me to scream so you would know you got your money's worth, to put it bluntly."

His jaw tightened, and he muttered something about her mother.

Diana couldn't stop laughing.

"Do you know what happens to your breasts when you giggle?" North asked, his voice strangled.

She looked down. "They wobble like pudding?"

"I love pudding," he murmured, moving his mouth to her breast. Diana forgot about giggling; heat blazed up her body, making her aware of sweat at the backs of her knees, and trembling in her fingers.

Her legs fell apart and suddenly, North wasn't doing enough. She needed more, she needed him, all of him, *now*. The fact she could feel his cock nudging her below made it worse.

Her hands went to his shoulders and curled over all those muscles and then she arched toward him. She was breathing fast and shallow.

"Easy," North murmured, leaving one breast and switching to the other.

Not easy.

"Lie still." He sucked hard. She couldn't lie still. Even though her mother—

Enough. She banished every thought of Mrs. Belgrave.

"I can't just lie here," she gasped. Her hands slid down his back, loving the way corded muscles flexed under her fingers. "Please, North, *please*."

"I'm afraid I'll lose control." His voice growled from deep in his chest.

"Please do." She arched her back again, and he slid a little way inside.

His brows knit. "I will go as slowly as I can, Diana. I've never felt . . . ." His voice trailed off and she realized his braced arms were shaking.

She wiggled impatiently. "Hell's bells, North, what are you waiting for?"

He choked out a laugh and thrust slowly forward. Pulled back and pushed again, and again, until finally his hard, heavy cock bumped home.

Diana had never imagined anything like it. A wave of feeling spread out from her hips. He paused, eyes wild. He more than fit. He fit *her*, in every way possible.

"Pain?" he rasped.

"No! No." And: "*Please*, North."

He drew back and lunged, his heat and weight sending another streak of feeling down her legs.

"I love the way that feels," she cried, when she had her breath.

With a choked laugh, he pumped again, and again, and with every movement of his hips he buried himself inside her, and every time, the sensation spread through her. She couldn't keep her legs flat on the bed. First she bent them, and even then they shook uncontrollably, until she wound them around his hips.

When she arched her back, he bit back a curse, his eyes fixed on hers.

"Too fast?" he growled.

She shook her head.

"Too strong?"

"No!"

He bent his head to her nipple again and sucked hard.

Diana grabbed him, trying to find purchase on his sweat-slicked back, greedily welcoming the pleasure she felt with every thrust.

Her heart was thundering in her chest, and she couldn't get her breath. All she could do was cling to him, shuddering, a jolt running through her body every time he filled her.

He dropped his forehead until it touched hers, a guttural moan breaking from his chest. "I've never felt anything like you, Diana. You're killing me."

"Don't stop," she cried, only half listening because she was concentrating on the burning sensation in her limbs.

She was vaguely aware of a bitten-off groan, but then he reared back, and one hand settled on her hip and pulled her up just enough so that he could pump into her at a deeper angle. Diana squeaked, need pulsing through her.

Her breath was sobbing from deep in her chest when her legs began to pulse, frightening her a little. North leaned over. "Give it to me, Diana," he ordered, that big hand holding her body up to meet his thrusts. "I want all of you."

"I can't," she sobbed, disoriented.

"Open your eyes."

She forced them open. North was staring down at her, jaw taut. He thrust forward slowly, pressing down in a way that made her let out a little shriek. "Why not?" For all the uncontrolled ferocity in his eyes, his voice was tender. His throat corded with the strain of keeping himself still.

"I'm afraid," she whispered.

A smile curled the edges of his lips. "Don't ever be afraid of me, Diana."

"Not you," she managed, and then, "Oh, God!" because he was slowly, slowly bearing down on her again, filling her up. She tensed, waiting for the moment when he was fully inside. Uncontrolled fire raced through her body.

"No," she sobbed. "It's too much. I can't." Her legs were pulsing and she was close to being . . . to something frightening.

North lowered himself onto his elbows, his body deep inside hers, and brushed his lips across hers. "There's nothing to be afraid of, darling."

How could he say that? He was between her legs, filling her. He was looking at her as if she were the only woman in the world. As if he owned her. Loved her. He *did* love her. He said so.

She was shaking.

"Diana," North said, kissing her again. "Do you want to stop?" His voice was hoarse, hungry for her, but calm too.

That was North. "Your eyes are a beautiful dark blue," she said, gasping.

He waggled an eyebrow at her. "They're only one color. Your eyes have two."

She was pulsing between her legs, her body sending frantic messages, but Diana ignored that for the moment. "When we were betrothed, I used to sneak glances at your body," she gasped. She was sweating, so it was absurd to feel heat rising in her cheeks, but she did.

North planted one hand on the bed and thrust forward again.

Diana arched and cried out. Her body felt fluid, like water, like fire, rising to meet his, wringing grunts from his chest every time he pumped into her. He was relentless, savage with hunger and lust. She gritted her teeth, almost surrendered, caught herself, because . . .

"I love the way this feels," she gasped, her voice raw. Her fingers curled around his arms, holding him as tightly as she could.

"Hell, Diana." Something rasped in his voice. "You're unmanning me."

"You don't feel unmanned." She rubbed against him like a wanton woman, shameless because it felt so good. The delight of it spread to her fingertips, reminding her that he was still there, connected to her. And if she tightened—

This time his curse was a good deal harsher.

"You can feel that?"

His lips curled back from his teeth and he grunted. Diana smiled to herself and tightened again. He pulled back and buried himself to the hilt, again, again . . .

The sensation wasn't as terrifying this time. She kept her eyes on North's face. He was braced on his elbows now, only his hips pumping slowly. It began building again, and she couldn't stop herself from rising greedily to meet him, her fingernails clutching his forearms, their ragged breath interlocking.

He was ravishing her and she loved it. It was worth every exhausting moment as a governess. "Do you know why this is so good?" she whispered.

"Because it's you," North growled, not looking away from her eyes. "Because I'm making love to you."

"Because I'm not giving you this in order to lure you into marriage. Because we both—" She broke off with a sharp gasp.

He lifted her hips again and drove into her. She couldn't . . .

The ripples she felt encompassed the two of them. She saw in his eyes, felt it in the sharp jerk of his body, the way he thrust faster, harder, making the feelings racking her body last longer, until her body spasmed and milked his over and over.

When Diana let go, a shudder of relief, joy, plain damned lust, went through North like a bolt of lightning. When she finally quieted, head back, gasping, he carefully rolled the two of them so that she was on top. His expert was so tired that she didn't sit up—in fact, he had the idea that she'd never imagined such a thing.

She could ride him some other time. What he wanted was to be skin to skin, the weight of her trembling, sweet body anchoring him to the bed.

When she raised her head, eyes hooded and satisfied, he rolled his hips up and watched her eyes widen. Her throaty giggle was heaven.

He grabbed her head, winding his fingers into her hair, holding her still so he could slide his tongue into her mouth. "Next time we're in the punt in the lake I'm going to lick all your honey until you scream into the open air," he told her, his cock pumping up, filling her again and again. "Then I'm going to roll over on my back and you're going to ease down on me, greedy for what I can give you."

"I'm greedy now," she whispered.

He filled his hands with her round ass and pumped, holding her tight so she couldn't move, watching to make sure she didn't wince.

Her eyes fell to half mast.

"Frightened?" he whispered.

"No."

She clenched around him again, holding him in every way there was. Pure need cascaded through him.

He flipped her at the last second so that he could pin her down with his solid bulk, own her, keep her, take her mouth. His lusty, independent girl. Not his duchess.

His Diana.

He let it all go, giving himself, spilled himself, heart and soul, deep inside her.

"Hell's bells," she whispered, an eternity later. There was awe in her tone, exhausted pleasure.

Love.

He took care of the French letter, cleaned them both with a cool cloth . . . went to sleep.

Chapter Fourteen

The next morning, Diana found Mabel unenthu-
siastically dusting the nursery. "Her Grace took
both children to see the peacock."

The nursemaid's eyes skated down Diana's black
dress and she shook her head. "You need to wear
something different." Mabel straightened, tucking the
duster under her arm. "At breakfast this morning, we
decided you still have a chance."

"'A chance,'" Diana echoed. "What do you mean?"

"A chance at being duchess," Mabel said. "A chance
at him, at Lord Roland."

Diana's mouth fell open.

"I know, it seems barmy, doesn't it, after all that happened? But listen to me," Mabel said, lifting a finger.
"First thing, he's a gentleman. More than others are,

if you know what I mean. Not as wild as most of the Wildes. Right?"

Diana nodded.

A second finger. "He's not angry. We thought as how he might get nasty about the fact you ran away, and about the boy, but he didn't. He knows it all, and he doesn't even care."

"Lord Roland is a remarkable man," Diana said, nodding.

"Third, and this is the important one, the man went unhinged over there in the colonies. You may not have seen it," she said, in response to Diana's frown, "but it's the truth. You know Daisy, the upstairs maid? She says that he doesn't ever sleep. And he doesn't eat, either."

"I don't think he's unhinged, but even so, what has that to do with me?"

"You were the one who told Chef to make those English dishes, weren't you? Prism said that's all he ate last night, the things you ordered. He'll likely starve if you don't marry him."

She raised her fourth finger. "No real lady is going to want him after the scandal. They all think he turned up your apron and then left you in the nursery."

"Turned up my apron," Diana said, rather faintly. "He didn't."

Mabel shrugged, her thumb up. "He watches you all the time. We reckon that if you put on a pretty dress, he might forget that you've been downstairs and kiss you or something, and then he'd have to marry you."

A memory of the "something" North had done to her hours before drifted through Diana's mind.

"Mr. Calico is in the village today," Mabel finished. "If you buy some fabric, we will help you sew a dress, Mrs. Mousekin too, and you know she's got a way with a needle."

Diana couldn't help it; her eyes grew teary. She had thought that North was her only friend, but perhaps she just didn't know what friends looked like. Maybe they came in the shape of somewhat lazy, sharp-tongued nursemaids, dignified butlers, and kindly housekeepers.

"I take your five points, but Lord Roland and I would not be a good match. I will never be a duchess," she said, her voice wavering a bit, "but I'm grateful for your advice and help."

"You *did* jilt him," Mabel conceded. "It might sour the marriage. Still, I think a new gown will do it." In an odd echo of Mrs. Belgrave, she added, "If you look like a duchess, he won't be able to hold back. Now, since you're awake, perhaps you wouldn't mind finishing the dusting, because I should deliver an important message."

"To the dairy?" Diana gave her a hug. "Thank you."

After luncheon, Artie put on her peacock-feather headband and ran around the schoolroom in imitation of Fitzy.

Mabel had returned from the dairy looking glum; now she rolled her eyes. "I've a headache like you wouldn't believe."

"I could take the children to the village, so you could take a nap," Diana told her.

"Don't forget to buy cloth that looks as if it will rot by next Christmas."

"Why?"

"You need a dress that will tear in a strong breeze," Mabel said authoritatively. "Did Lord Roland really throw your shoes in the lake?"

Diana nodded.

"There you are," Mabel said, satisfied. "I didn't believe it of a grown man, but it's just like any lad of seven who falls in love. I'll nip down and say hello to Jack while you're in the village. That will cure my headache."

"Lord Roland and I would not be a good match," Diana said.

"I want to go see the peddler!" Artie was hopping on one leg, holding Godfrey's shoulder. "I shall buy a peacock for Fitzy."

"No room for a peacock in Mr. Calico's cart," Mabel told her.

"We'll find something wonderful," Diana promised as she wrestled Godfrey into his nankeen coat.

"No buying the children treats from your own money," Mabel reminded her. "Mr. Prism said he wanted an accounting after what happened when the fair came through the village." She looked down at Artie. "You were too small to care last year, but Mr. Calico carries wooden dolls in his wagon."

This time Artie's shriek truly rivaled Fitzy's. Mabel winced. "Tea," she moaned. She moved in the direction of the door.

"Shall we go?" Diana asked, holding out her hands.

Artie's and Godfrey's eyes were shining with excitement. But: "Fitzy first," Artie demanded.

"Do you have your bread crumbs?" Diana asked.

"Yes!" Artie held up a little cotton bag.

Diana usually took the children through the library out to the south terrace, where Fitzy roamed the lawn. But it struck her that they might encounter North.

Last night, he'd again asked her to marry him, and she'd refused.

Though that wasn't what was making her feel shy this morning. She had been completely exposed to him in all ways, body and soul. He had wrapped her up in warmth and safety. She had never felt like that before.

Loved was one way to describe it. He'd said he loved her, and she'd felt it in his every touch and kiss.

The idea made her feel dizzy.

"Let's go out the side door today," she said when they reached the bottom of the stairs. "After greeting Frederick and Peter, of course."

"Morning," Artie shouted. She was much given to shouting. "No curtsy," she reminded herself.

"That's right," Frederick said, grinning down at her. "You don't curtsy to me. Now if I was 'Lord Frederick,' what would you do?"

"Curtsy!" Artie cried.

Godfrey didn't say anything, but he waved.

"No bow," Artie told him. She turned back to Frederick. "We're going to see Fitzy, an' then the doll man." She started hopping up and down, causing her feather headband to slip over one eye and then fall off. She looked so funny with her fluffy yellow curls and startled eyes that all three boys started laughing.

"No laughing," Artie cried. When Godfrey just laughed harder, she darted over and tickled him. He writhed, giggling madly, until Peter rescued him by swinging him up onto his shoulder.

Diana managed to hold Artie still long enough to

retie her headband so the feather stood up tall behind her head.

"Master Godfrey isn't ready to go," Peter said sadly. He was holding Godfrey upside down by his ankles, and the little boy was twisting around, giggling madly and trying to grab the footman's waist.

"Peter," Diana said with some alarm. "Remember that he had breakfast not too long ago."

"Oh, he won't—Lord Roland!" Peter nimbly turned Godfrey right side up, and put him on his feet.

"Good morning, Peter." North turned to Diana. "Miss Belgrave, children." He had that severe look again.

He *wasn't* severe, Diana reminded herself, hugging the knowledge inside herself. He had slept with his legs tangled around hers, one hand on her bottom.

He had slept.

"Good morning, Lord Roland," Diana said, dropping a curtsy. "We are going to say hello to Fitzy before walking to the village."

"Mr. Calico is visiting Mobberley," North said, nodding. "I shall accompany you. He is one of my favorite people in the world."

Artie leaned back, hands on her hips, staring up at her brother. "To see Fitzy?"

"Absolutely," North said. "Are you a peacock?"

"Yes," Artie told him. "'Cause Fitzy is lonely. Bread." She held up her cotton bag.

"That's very kind of you."

Diana caught Godfrey's hand. "Lord Roland, we wouldn't dream of distracting you. I'm sure you have much work to do." Which was a gracious way of saying, *Please withdraw your offer.*

North ignored her and turned to Artie. "Artie, would you like a ride to the lawn?"

"No," Artie said, grabbing Godfrey's other hand.

"No, thank you," Diana prompted.

"Uh-huh," she said, dancing up and down. "Fitzy will be hungry!"

When they reached the terrace, Fitzy was waiting for them, though given his magnificent girth, his appetite was debatable.

Over the last year, he had grown used to seeing the three of them every morning. He cocked his head and looked suspiciously at North.

"Please stay back," Diana said. "Fitzy is not fond of men."

"He doesn't dislike us," North remarked. "He's just a competitive beast by nature." But he obediently backed away.

"Come, come, Fitzy," Artie crooned. Slowly the

peacock advanced on his spindly legs, his great tail dragging in the damp grass. "You're a good peacock," Artie told him, holding out a fistful of bread crumbs. "The best peacock ever!"

Godfrey had no interest in Fitzy, and began attempting to hop the entire length of the terrace without putting down his right foot.

North moved until his shoulder bumped Diana's. "Why is Artie so much nicer to that bird than she is to her own brother?"

"She's known him all her life," Diana reminded him. "She scarcely knows you."

"Friends *should* feed each other." His voice was ripe with innuendo.

"Good Fitzy," Artie said, gently patting the peacock's beak. They'd discovered that Fitzy didn't care to have the top of his head touched, perhaps because of his magnificent crown of blue feathers.

The children skipped ahead as they headed across the south lawn toward the path to the village. "Do you like peacocks or dukes better?" North asked idly.

"Isn't it an overlapping category?" Diana asked, giving him a mischievous smile. "I enjoy the absurdly dressed, though I'd rather not be one of the flock. London would be very tiresome without the odd peacock to gawk at."

"I find clothing to be a matter of indifference," North said, an unmistakable ring of truth in his voice. He bent closer. "Unless I'm trying to capture one particular woman's attention, of course."

The path leading to Mobberley was an easy ramble between two meadows. The moment they were out of sight of the house, North tucked Diana's arm into his elbow. His eyes dared her to say something. When she didn't, he pulled her closer.

"Behave yourself," she warned. "So you don't care about clothing. What do you care about?"

"A beautiful woman who manages to look regal in a worn black dress."

"Pooh," Diana said. But she let the compliment warm her heart. The children were galloping ahead now, Artie occasionally swerving to pick a flower and add it to a messy handful.

"Almack's is full of women who would happily be my duchess," North said musingly. "Like an ocean of perch trying to leap into my net, and the one fish I want swims as fast as she can in the opposite direction."

"You are terribly arrogant," Diana said.

"Would you say my observation is inaccurate?"

Diana chose not to answer that.

"When one becomes a reluctant heir to a dukedom, fish with shining scales try to jump into one's boat, so many that one could easily capsize." He glanced at her, but she held her tongue. "I was savaged by a trout in the first year after Horatius's death. You might know her better as Lady Catherine Weathersby."

Diana snorted. "You were 'savaged'?"

"She locked us in her father's library and did her best to compromise me."

"How did you escape?"

"She had not envisioned a gentleman leaping from the window, which I did."

"That is," Diana said, trying to find an appropriate word, "regrettable," she concluded.

"I managed to keep my virtue, such as it was," North stated, a smile playing around his mouth.

"I'm glad to hear it," Diana said. "Artie, please don't go into the ditch! You'll get your pinafore dirty."

"It's already dirty," North said.

That was undeniable.

"Do you mind my asking why my sister sticks out so far in the front?"

"She carries her doll, Hortensia, in a bag slung around her neck under her gown. Hortensia has been lost several times."

"Right," North said, nodding. "Let's return to the fish and peacocks. I'm lost in a welter of comparisons, but my main point is that unless I fall overboard and am eaten by a shark with a wig, I plan to marry neither a fish nor a bird."

"Really?" Diana asked. "You want to add a shark into the mix? I think they aren't fish, by the way."

"Yes, they are fish. Did your mother consider marine life as unladylike as pounds and ha'pennies?"

"Yes, but I am learning. I've been reading aloud to Godfrey from a book about animals that I found in the library."

"Must have been Horatius's," North said, guiding her around a rabbit hole in the path. "He was always thinking about birds and the like. A shark would have interested him."

"What sort of books did you read as a boy?"

His mouth flattened. "You'll find a collection of books about classical architecture somewhere on those shelves. I meant to design houses."

"Really?" Diana was startled. She knew that houses had to be designed—sometimes architects were knighted by the king for their work—but not by noblemen.

He glanced at her with a rueful smile. "What should I have done with my life?"

"Noblemen don't *do* things," she said, without pausing to think. "No, that's not quite true. They pay calls in the morning, and go to their clubs in the afternoon. They bet on horses. They go to the opera in the evening, or to a ball. They attend court now and then."

"Noblemen run this country," North said in a measured voice. "It could be that, in the future, the House of Commons will take a greater role. But at the moment, the House of Lords is vital to every decision the Prime Minister makes. We are judge and jury in many parts of the country, we muster militia, we send our men to war, we employ thousands of people."

"I stand corrected," Diana said. And she meant it.

The children had reached Gooseberry River, the small watercourse that separated the duchy from the village. They were seated on the low stone bridge, legs dangling, looking down into the water.

"Hell," North said, drawing her to a halt. "I just lectured you, didn't I?"

"I am woefully ignorant when it comes to the aristocracy," she said. "Always better for a lecture, or at least, so my mother believed."

"The cruelest cut of all," he groaned. "You are likening me to a woman who discarded her daughters and stole their dowries."

Diana frowned. "My father's will merely requested that she provide for us. No dowries were specified and, in any event, I haven't married."

"She is *not* providing for you. You are working."

"It was inappropriate to compare you to my mother, and quite unfair," she said, not answering his point.

"I was trying to tell you," he said, walking her to the bridge in order to join the children, "that I know you aren't one of those women who flutter their eyelashes and fan out their plumage. That doesn't stop me from wishing you would."

They stood shoulder to shoulder, staring down into the Gooseberry River. As one might expect from the river's name, the water was a curious pale green. Thick incursions of mare's tail made a low-flowing stream even slower.

"Thank you," Diana finally said, because it was that or kiss him in public, which would be frightfully improper, and she was trying to curb her impulses. She was tired of being a person who spoke or did things first and thought better of them later.

She crouched between Artie and Godfrey and peered at the water. "What do you see down there?"

"I can't see fish. Godfrey can," Artie said.

Diana had no idea how Godfrey conveyed his opinions to Artie. "I can see the peddler's wagon," she said, and nodded toward the village square.

The children scrambled to their feet and ran off the other end of the bridge.

Mr. Calico's wagon was painted bright green, and

had yellow lathe sides on hinges that, when raised, revealed shelves crowded with wares. He himself was a thin, elderly gentleman wearing a wondrous coat that sparkled in the sunlight.

As they neared, Artie hung back, holding Diana's hand, but Godfrey ran straight over to him and bowed in an abrupt up-and-down motion, waving his hand at the peddler's coat.

"It's covered with pins," Mr. Calico told him, "shiny pins from all parts of the world. Good morning, Miss Belgrave."

"Good morning," Diana said, smiling at him. "May I introduce Lady Artemisia? She is very excited to meet you."

Artie performed a credible curtsy without taking her thumb from her mouth, a skill one didn't see in Almack's.

North stepped forward and bowed as respectfully as if he'd met a local squire. "Mr. Calico, it is a pleasure to see you once again."

The peddler bowed with a flourish. "I am happy to see you returned safe and sound from such a perilous adventure, Lord Roland."

"War is no adventure," North said dryly.

"I've heard the same from other acquaintances," Mr. Calico agreed. He turned to Godfrey and Artie. "My young friends, I have something to show you."

He picked a large basket from a shelf in his wagon and placed it on the ground.

Artie fell on her knees. "Dolls!"

Godfrey's whole being reverberated with approval. He reached out and picked up a horse that had a raised foot and an open, crimson mouth.

"What do you lack, Miss Belgrave?" Mr. Calico asked, gesturing toward the shelves lining the side of his carriage. "I've everything a lady might desire: pins, powder, lace, even a wig or two, and lengths of fabric."

"Miss Belgrave has been suffering from a melancholy complaint," North said, his eyes clear and innocent. "Perhaps you have a tonic. Cod liver oil is thought to be an excellent remedy, is it not?"

Diana couldn't halt her startled little puff of air.

Mr. Calico's thick eyebrows jerked up and down. "I have just the cordial for the lady. No fish oil, but a mixture of herbs with the power to soothe the most wicked of beasts, or elevate the saddened spirits of a young lady. I have one bottle left."

He walked to the other side of his caravan and began rummaging about, causing a great tinkling of bottles.

"Revenge," North whispered in her ear.

"I did nothing to incur such a terrible fate!"

"You pointed out what a tedious, lecturing bastard I am." His eyes held hers.

Diana caught her breath. His expression made warmth boil up in her belly, all the way to her fingers and toes. She felt dizzily happy. The perfume of a jasmine bush growing next to the church drifted by, and she could hear Artie's happy stream of talk as she supplied both her side of the conversation *and* Godfrey's.

But in reality the only thing Diana was registering was North.

"We noblemen are prone to terrible revenge," he went on.

A monologue coming from the other side of Mr. Calico's wagon indicated that perhaps he had sold that last bottle of miraculous elixir.

Just as well, because although Diana had money in her pocket, she preferred not to buy a cordial with it. "*You'll* have to drink it, if he finds it," she informed North.

"I'll give it to Aunt Knowe. She maintains that Mr. Calico always has the perfect treasure in his wagon for the deepest desire of your heart, which—in one example—was a riding hat she didn't know she needed, but realized on inspection was precisely what she had been longing for."

"I wouldn't describe that as miraculous," Diana said.

"Another example. He brought Sweetpea to Willa, and arguably the baby skunk helped save Willa's life.

That was after you left the castle, though I suppose you heard the story?"

Diana nodded, feeling a pinch of guilt. But only a pinch.

"Moreover, when we were boys, Mr. Calico brought Alaric a box of curiosities that my brother says provided the genesis of his desire to travel. In a way, Mr. Calico is responsible for Lord Wilde's adventures."

"What has he brought you?" Diana asked.

"Those books on architecture I told you about. One a year, carried from London. Until Horatius died, and I became heir to the dukedom, that is."

"And thereafter? What did he offer you?"

The bleak expression in his eyes was replaced by a rueful smile. "Aunt Knowe bought me canary-colored stockings, which I didn't think I wanted. Later I wore them to woo you in the style to which I was certain you aspired."

It felt so good to laugh about their brief betrothal. Ever since North proposed to her, their relationship had been a source of nothing but anguish, guilt, and anxiety.

But now he stood grinning at her, his black hair gleaming in the sunshine. Diana felt a deep wash of happiness, almost as if . . .

No. After closely watching Ophelia, she had a deep conviction that she would be unhappy as a duchess. She had to stop looking at North's lips and his shoulders and his eyes . . .

Right now.

She had stepped away and crouched down next to the children, when she heard the clop-clopping of hooves on cobblestones. At a quick glance, it seemed to be the castle pony cart, the one she'd taken to the village when she'd made her escape from the betrothal party.

With a shock that nearly made her topple over, Diana realized that *Lavinia* was holding the reins, Leonidas lounging on the seat beside her. Her cousin Lavinia, whom Diana hadn't seen since she ran away to London, hatbox in hand.

Lavinia was dressed in what must be the newest in French fashion, since she'd been living in Paris for the past two years. Her golden hair fell in shining waves, topped with a tall purple hat, cocked at a rakish angle. Her traveling costume was navy blue with a wide purple belt and four buttons that drew attention to her bosom.

Diana froze, painfully aware of her shabby dress. Scorching embarrassment swept over her like a fever. It was one thing to be a governess. It was another to meet her dazzling cousin while wearing attire that some maidservants would scorn.

She didn't even have a bonnet, let alone a French

hat like the one on Lavinia's head. The housekeeper had replaced the floppy cap that North had absconded with, and Diana had pinned it on top of her bun that morning without even looking in the mirror.

Lavinia tossed the reins to Leonidas and hopped down. "Hello, North! Where's my cousin?" she cried, not bothering with a formal greeting. "Prism said I could find her down here. Isn't it beautiful? It's not raining! It usually rains for the entire month of May, but not today!"

As Lavinia, Leonidas, and North greeted each other, Diana remained in a crouch, trying to get herself to straighten up.

Artie had paid no attention to the arrival of the pony cart. She was clutching four dolls to her small chest. "May I have them?" she cried, in great excitement. "May I, DeeDee? Please? Please?"

Godfrey had discovered a rearing horse with front hooves raised high, and improbably blue eyes. He held it up silently.

"We must bring that ferocious steed home," North said, appearing at her shoulder. "Choose one doll, but not all four, Artie. You three must not have noticed, but Leonidas has arrived with Miss Lavinia Gray."

Diana stood up, hearing her knees creak as if she were an old woman. She pasted a smile on her face, and started toward her cousin. "How wonderful to see you, Lavinia," she managed.

"Diana," her cousin breathed, looking at her from head to foot, which was precisely as humiliating as she could have imagined.

"I'll leave the two of you to talk," North said, striding after the children, who had dashed over to Leonidas on the other side of the wagon.

Diana took a deep breath. "You look beautiful, Lavinia. I love your hat."

Her cousin looked her over once again, her expression appalled. "Oh, darling. Why didn't you write to me?" Tears welled in her eyes as she reached out and pulled Diana into her arms. "I would have rescued you," she cried, her voice breaking. "Why didn't you tell me? Why didn't you *ask*?"

"I did write to you, but I didn't have the proper address in Paris," Diana said, hugging her back. "Don't cry, Lavinia. I've been very happy caring for Artie and Godfrey."

"It's worse than I thought," Lavinia said, her voice wobbling. "You're wearing that ghastly dress, and you have had to take a position in order to support yourself!" She pulled back. "Have your fingers been worked to the bone? Are you well? Oh, Diana, I don't know how you'll forgive me, but please do!"

"Of course I forgive you," Diana said, finding she was smiling as hard as she could, and she didn't care about the humiliation any longer. "It's mostly my fault. I didn't know how to write to you in Paris, but I could have tried harder. I could have asked Lady Knowe."

"My mother got a bee in her bonnet directly after Willa married, and insisted on visiting Paris." Lavinia brushed away tears with the back of her hand. "I had no idea you were in such straits; I assumed you returned to your mother when you left the castle. I never imagined that your mother would reject you. *And* her only grandson as well!"

Diana pulled out her handkerchief and wiped Lavinia's cheeks, her heart melting. "I knew you would have helped me if you could."

"I feel like the worst cousin on the face of the earth. I wrote to you twice, but you never answered. I should have known something was wrong!"

"My mother did not forward your letters," Diana confirmed. "How did you find out where I have been living?"

"That was *wrong* of Mrs. Belgrave," Lavinia said savagely. She was sunnily cheerful by nature, but at that moment, she looked positively murderous.

Diana summoned up another smile. "My mother

sometimes makes rash decisions that I'm certain she regrets later." In fact, Diana's lack of forethought was a legacy from her mother. "Never mind that; however did you find me here?"

"A fortnight ago, Lady Hofstra arrived in Paris with one of those terrible prints depicting your situation, and we began packing the next day," Lavinia said. "There are no words to describe your mother!"

Diana tried to think of something to say in defense of her mother but failed.

"We spent two days in London while recovering from the voyage, and everyone we met was aware that you had been disowned for caring for your sister's child. That's better than what Lady Hofstra said in Paris—she thought that *you* had a child with *North*!"

"It's a complicated situation," Diana said.

"*No one* will ever receive Mrs. Belgrave again," Lavinia said, with grim satisfaction. "My mother made her opinion clear among all her friends."

Diana's heart sank. She couldn't help feeling sorry that her mother had lost her foothold in the society she treasured so much. "How did everyone learn that God-frey is not my own, but my sister's child? In all those prints, North is blamed for seducing me."

Lavinia pulled Diana back into her arms and held her tightly, rocking her back and forth. "I can't bear to see you in this dress." Her voice wobbled again. "You were the most fashionable woman in London."

Diana kissed her cheek and gave her another handkerchief. A wise governess carries at least three tucked into her waistband at all times. "I should have tried to write to you again, but it was so expensive, and I hadn't the faintest idea what your Parisian address might be. And then afterward, once the scandal broke . . ." Her voice trailed off. "I thought your mother might prefer not to acknowledge me."

"My mother may be indolent, but she is a *good* person," Lavinia cried. "She would never have tolerated this state of affairs had we been in England. As it was, she is dreadfully affronted by your mother's lies. And we had no idea Rose had died. I'm so sorry about her loss." More tears slipped down Lavinia's cheeks; Diana mopped them up with her last handkerchief.

A short distance away, North stood watching them, his eyes hooded and serious. Diana had the feeling that if he believed meeting Lavinia was distressing her, he'd come to her rescue.

Just as a friend ought to, she thought, happiness spreading through her.

"How could Her Grace allow you, a *lady*, to become a domestic in her household?" Lavinia demanded.

"The duchess didn't know for over a month," Diana

explained. "By the time she arrived at the castle, I was ensconced in the nursery, caring for her daughter, and I wouldn't have given up Artie. I love being a governess."

"You *do*?"

"I thought you would have married by now," Diana said, thinking of all the proposals Lavinia had received during her first Season.

"My mother decided that I needed Parisian polish before we embarked on another Season."

Diana laughed. "You were already one of the most elegant ladies in London. And now you look ready to go for a stroll with the queen!"

North strode over, his eyes on Diana's face. "Everything well here?"

"As well as they can be, considering that my cousin, Miss Belgrave, has been relegated to your servants' hall," Lavinia said, a sharp edge to her voice.

"I spent those years in America, and my family chose not to inform me that Diana was employed in the nursery," North said.

Lavinia searched his face. "You had no idea?"

"I did not."

"It seems everyone in London has discovered the truth about Godfrey's parentage," Diana put in, trying to break the tension.

"Truth is always relative." Lavinia's face took on a characteristically mischievous look.

"Don't!" Diana said, pinching her.

"Ouch," Lavinia said loudly. "I hadn't properly greeted your—"

"He is not my anything," Diana stated.

"I am charmed to see you again, Miss Gray," North said, bowing.

Something chilled in Diana's heart, just a little. She didn't want to be a duchess. Not at all. But Lavinia . . .

Lavinia *had* wanted to be a duchess. She had once told Diana that she wished North had fallen in love with her at first sight. It had been a joke, nothing but a joke.

"I hope you don't mind my addressing you as 'North,' as Willa and I did two years ago," Lavinia said, her eyes sparkling. "I daresay you've seen all the prints depicting you? One of them sells for four times its customary value."

North groaned. "The Shakespeare one."

"Exactly! I understand that you are depicted emerging from a trunk, like a genie from a bottle, all chest and no legs." Her gaze rested appreciatively on North's upper body.

"I have a copy of that print in my lodgings in Oxford," Leonidas said, joining them. At twenty, he was a younger version of North, with the familial slashing eyebrows and startling dark blue eyes, but a lanky build.

"I must buy one," Lavinia said. "I gave up most of my Lord Wilde prints, all but two favorites, but now I shall start a Wilde collection. I can dazzle Willa's children someday."

North groaned.

"Mr. Calico may have the *Cymbeline* print," Leonidas suggested. "He has a huge pile over there. I saw a few of Alaric and one of Father riding to hounds, which is absurd because he gave that up years ago."

Lavinia tucked her hand into Leonidas's arm. "Lay on, Macduff!"

"Wrong play," North said wryly.

Lavinia turned toward Diana. "If we do nothing else, dearest, we are buying whatever fabric Mr. Calico can sell us so you needn't wear that dress even one more day. We might start a fashion for togas while a proper wardrobe is being sewn."

"Miss Belgrave, may I ask you to join us, please?" Mr. Calico called.

"I'll be back in a moment," Diana said to Lavinia. She was contemplating whether she could accept a gift of fabric. Everything in her revolted against the idea of charity. But Lavinia had come all the way from France to rescue her.

"He's got a peacock for Fitzy," Artie said, coming up, grabbing Diana's hand, and dragging her toward the peddler.

"Well, no, my dear, *I* don't have a peacock," Mr. Calico said, when they reached his side. "I did see a peacock just outside the village, though. It was tied to a fence. When I saw this young lady's fanciful hair ornament, I thought perhaps the castle's peacock could use a friend."

"Tied to a fence?" Diana repeated, frowning. Fitzy would hate to be restrained.

"Let's go!" Artie cried, hopping on one foot. "Now!"

Godfrey took Diana's other hand and nodded vigorously.

Diana wanted more than anything to escape. Lavinia was so kind—but she gleamed with the beauty that was possible when one had a maid, or even two maids, devoted to one's care. Quite unlike herself, who scarcely found time to wash her face, let alone apply rosewater masks and pineapple tonics.

She was certain her freckles stood out like ink dots. Lavinia must have seen them. And she *hated* being rescued. It made her feel helpless, rather than bold and independent.

From the corner of her eye, she could see North and Lavinia bending over a print, their shoulders brushing. They looked like china figurines, a matched pair of aristocrats.

"We could walk to the edge of the village, and ask the bird's owner if he's for sale," Diana said.

"Yes, please," Artie cried. "Please, DeeDee."

Lavinia, North, and Leonidas were sorting through the stack of prints, pulling out any that featured a Wilde. "Mr. Calico, I wouldn't want to interrupt your customers. Would you inform them that the children and I are strolling to the other end of the village? They should feel free to return to the castle without us."

"Certainly," he said. "Lord Roland will pay for the toys, so you may take them with you."

"I shall pay for the horse," Diana said, taking out a handful of coins.

Mr. Calico looked as if he was about to refuse, but Diana gave him a direct look, and he accepted her money. "Before you go, I wonder if you would have any use for this fabric, Miss Belgrave," he said. "I believe it would suit your hair."

He pulled a bundle of cloth from a lower shelf. It was pale blue gossamer silk, shot through with silver threads, the sort of thing her mother would have rejected as fit only for a strumpet.

"Pretty!" Artie said. Godfrey was squatting on the ground, making his horse buck its way through the dust.

"It must be very dear," Diana said, hating that she hadn't the faintest idea how much it ought to cost.

"A trifle," Mr. Calico said promptly. "One pound ten."

Diana just managed to swallow her shock. That was more than two weeks' wages. "I can't," she said regretfully, returning it to him.

"One pound?" he asked.

She shook her head. "A governess doesn't make enough money to justify silk."

"Isn't that the truth?" he said, putting it back on a shelf that held bolts of silks and calicos, all mixed up. "Walk past the church, Miss Belgrave, and you'll come across the peacock soon enough."

On the other side of the wagon, Leonidas was waving a book. He and North seemed to be discussing a Greek playwright.

If North hadn't truly known Diana when they were courting, it was clear she hadn't truly known him, either. She would have said that he was a man of action, not one to read books, or design houses.

"Thank you," she said to Mr. Calico. She walked away, Artie and Godfrey trotting beside her.

Chapter Fifteen

"**W**hat do you mean, 'They went for a walk'?" North asked, frowning. He had given Diana time to recover from the shock of Lavinia's arrival, only to discover that she and the children had disappeared.

"A short walk," Mr. Calico said. "You needn't worry about Lady Artemisia's safety, my lord. Miss Belgrave will stay within the bounds of the village."

North had no such worry. He'd been talking to Leonidas, thinking absentmindedly that he wanted the right to touch Diana. To hold her arm, hold her hand, tuck a curl behind her ear, dust a kiss on her cheek.

Diana had looked mortified when Lavinia arrived, and he wanted to comfort her. Pull her against his side and face the world as a couple.

Which they were not—and never would be, if she had her way.

"I'll pay for the toys, Mr. Calico, as well as this book." He had found a book describing ancient Greek temples. He had spent hours as a boy tracing buildings on paper before going on to model them with mud and twigs. He'd tried to make a miniature Parthenon once.

"Miss Belgrave has already paid for the young gentleman's wooden horse," Mr. Calico said.

North couldn't stop himself from growling. "You shouldn't have allowed that. She can't afford to pay for trinkets."

"Governesses deserve better wages," he replied, unperturbed. "Miss Belgrave is prudent with her money. She admired this bolt of fabric, for example, but decided it was too dear for a governess."

"She's not a governess," North said, giving the peddler a dark glance.

Lavinia joined them. "Where has Diana gone?"

"She went on a walk with the children," Mr. Calico said, turning away to help Leonidas with the stack of prints he had selected.

"What did you say to her?" Lavinia demanded.

North frowned at her. "Nothing. I said nothing. I was with you."

She folded her arms over her chest. "Were you truly unaware of her plight?"

"I believed that she had jilted me for love of another

man, with whom she had borne a child," North replied. "My aunt employed her in my absence. Do you truly believe I would have allowed Diana to enter the servants' hall if I'd known of it?"

Lavinia was fearless; his tone didn't intimidate her at all, although it would have sent his regiment scurrying into formation. She looked him over, and finally her mouth eased. "I suppose I'm trying to blame you rather than myself."

North nodded.

"I had better return to my mother," Lavinia said. "I left her in Her Grace's hands." She paused. "North, I shall assume that you have encountered marriage-minded mothers before." Then she said, as if to herself, "Well, of course you have. You must know Diana's mother, Mrs. Belgrave."

"Yes."

"My mother traveled from France to rescue her niece, but I would be remiss not to inform you that she was delighted to discover that you are still in need of a wife."

North managed to choke back a response, but his lips moved in a curse.

"I have to repair Diana's reputation before we can take her away from Cheshire, thus we cannot leave directly."

"We have to right her reputation," North said firmly.

She eyed him. "I gather you are not holding a grudge over Diana jilting you."

He shook his head.

"Or that she apparently allowed the world to believe that the child was yours."

He shrugged. "I would have been proud to have fathered Godfrey."

Lavinia put a hand on his arm and smiled at him. He was forgiven.

"In my opinion," she said, "it would be disastrous if we were to leave before the rumor about Diana being a governess is quashed."

"I agree," North said, thinking that Lavinia would have made a good general.

"It would be enormously helpful with respect to my mother if you would play the part of a suitor of mine until we fix things up with Diana," Lavinia said, straightening her hat. "Don't worry; I won't compromise you."

"I'm not worried."

"In that case, would you see me back to the castle? My mother will be looking for me, and it will warm her heart to see the two of us together."

North looked around again, but Diana and the children were nowhere to be seen. "Do you subject your mother to your sardonic sense of humor?" he asked, escorting Lavinia to the pony cart.

"My mother does not understand subtleties," Lavinia said with a sigh. "Leonidas, come over here!"

"You seem to know my brother very well," North said, trying to delay in case Diana returned. Where had they gone?

"Of course. He's too young for me, unfortunately."

"Isn't he just your age?"

"Yes, but I seem to prefer grumpy and older," she said lightly.

Diana probably needed time to think over Lavinia's reappearance. He doubted that she would cheerfully climb into Lady Gray's carriage, return to London, and resume the life of a lady.

"I was going to hand the reins to Leonidas, since he made such a fuss on the way here, but why don't you take them," Lavinia said to North.

"She drives like a madwoman," Leonidas said, jumping onto the seat. "Don't allow her to drive unless you're feeling immortal. We almost overtook a hare on the way down the hill."

"It shouldn't have been hopping down the lane like that," Lavinia retorted. "I thought it was quite fun, and so did the pony."

Diana was still nowhere to be seen, and North was wrestling with an unusual bout of . . . of emotion.

In the midst of the Battle of Stony Point, he had wrenched off a dead soldier's coat, snatched the paper that identified the man as a Yankee, made his way through enemy ranks, dived off a cliff, and swum a mile to get help. The HMS *Vulture* had been unable to return in time to save the outpost, but it wasn't for lack of trying.

Throughout, he had stayed as calm as if he were in a ballroom. It was only around Diana that he got these infuriating surges of emotion.

Lust. Anger. Frustration.

"You might as well drive," he said to Lavinia. "My brother has overturned the cart more than once."

"Not since I was twelve!"

All the way home, as Lavinia enjoyed herself by sparring with Leonidas, North tried to pull his thoughts together. He'd never experienced anything like last night. It had felt as if he and Diana were two halves of the same coin, fitting together perfectly. But it didn't seem to have changed her mind.

Diana went her own way, despite what society would think. What's more, she was impulsive, and her spontaneity was only matched by her determination.

He would have imagined himself falling in love with a woman of tact and composure, not one who turned fiery red when she embarrassed herself, which seemed to happen with alarming regularity.

Yet North would happily spend his life fishing her out of the corners she fled to, luring her to their bedchamber, and making her turn rosy red for a different reason.

After they reached the castle, they found Lady Gray and the duchess taking tea in the drawing room. He managed to sound enthusiastic enough about Lavinia's visit that he caught his stepmother eyeing him. Then he sought out Lady Knowe.

His aunt had her own sitting room, a messy, comfortable room crammed with books and curiosities Alaric had sent her. Since she didn't leave the castle very often, his adventuresome brother tried to send the world to her.

She looked up and smiled, waggling her quill to show that she had to finish her missive.

North went to the window. Like his bedchamber, Lady Knowe's sitting room looked east, over Lindow Moss. In winter the bog was often covered with a thin sheet of ice that delicately outlined every blade of cottongrass that hadn't been flattened by rain. Now, in late spring, the grass spread like a rolling sea, if oceans were greenish-brown and full of life.

At this distance, he couldn't distinguish the fluffy tufts of hare's-tail cottongrass or the darker green clumps of maidenhair moss. He couldn't see the midges dancing over the surface, or hear the warning gurgle of an underground stream.

"That's done!" his aunt said cheerfully. Following the death of his mother—the first duchess—his aunt had never been precisely maternal. She had never made any obvious attempt to be a mother to her nephews, but all the same, she had become the fulcrum around which their days turned.

He bent over the desk and kissed her cheek. "Good morning, Aunt."

"How are you getting along with Lavinia?" she asked, her eyes twinkling. "I'm so happy she and her mother have come to pay us a visit. I do believe she's one of the most direct people I've ever met. She says exactly what's she's thinking, but with utmost tact. I adore her."

"Lady Gray is of the opinion that Lavinia would make an excellent duchess," North said.

"She has every possible air and grace; she's absurdly beautiful; she knows how to run a large household. You could do much worse."

North nodded.

His aunt waved at a tall stack of letters. "I've been

attending to my mail. My correspondents can be divided into two camps: those who feel that an appropriate betrothal with any young woman of quality will mend your invidious reputation, and those who think you are irremediably beyond the pale."

"According to Lavinia, my reputation is on the mend."

His aunt's eyebrow flew up. "How so?"

"Polite society has learned that Archibald Ewing fathered a child on a daughter who was disowned and died shortly thereafter. It would seem that disowning one daughter is acceptable, but two is criminal; Mrs. Belgrave is being shunned."

"Excellent!" Lady Knowe cried. "I couldn't have wished for a better bout of gossip."

There was something about her face . . .

"Aunt," North said. "What did you do?"

She grinned. "Nothing much."

"Aunt Knowe."

"I blackmailed Boodle," she said, chortling. "Told him to gossip all he wanted, and to make sure that the news reached the right ears, because otherwise I would have to inform the sheriff of his light-fingered ways. I wrote to some friends myself, but I haven't had replies to those missives yet."

"My dearest of aunts," North said, "did you ever

read the fable about the frog who gossiped so much that he burst?"

"I'll look it up when I next find myself at leisure," she promised, twinkling at him.

"So you didn't actually blackmail Boodle?"

"Not unless you count a promise not to prosecute," his aunt said. "With that hanging over his head, I expect he scurried around London as quickly as he could. On a different subject, I have decided to throw a ball in honor of Lavinia's visit, during which we shall make it clear that Diana has been in the castle as a dear and honored guest ever since you left for the colonies."

"Who would possibly believe that? The prints depict her as a scullery maid."

"No one would dare gainsay myself, the duke, or the duchess to our faces. If we say she has been our guest, then that is the case. Mrs. Belgrave will still be blamed, but frankly, my dear, she deserves no less. I'll invite everyone for miles around. All they need to do is meet Diana in her current incarnation—albeit properly gowned—not as the miserable girl who first arrived here."

North grunted. Of course they would love her. Diana—when she was being herself—was irresistible.

"I was prepared for trouble when I brought her

and Godfrey to Lindow," his aunt said, "thinking the household would dislike a lady living below-stairs. But my fears were unfounded: She won them all over, even Prism, who is far more straightlaced than we are."

"Whoever heard of a duchess who was happier in the servants' hall?"

"The question is, my dear, what do you mean to do about it? I should add that, considering Diana's disinclination to marry you, she will appear at the ball as a dear family friend. You will have to bestow your charms on Lavinia in order to quell gossip."

North nodded. "She told me the same, though her goal was to soothe her mother."

"You wooing Lavinia, while Godfrey is freely acknowledged to be Diana's nephew rather than her son, will kill the scandal like cold water on embers."

"Paying court to Lavinia in order to entice Lady Gray into a longer stay in the castle is one thing, but I dislike the idea of wooing her in public view."

His aunt was never interested in remarks that disagreed with any of her plans. "I have a letter from Willa here." She poked around in the piles that covered her desk. "Here it is! She and Alaric are very happy and well. She says they might pay us a visit before traveling to India; wouldn't that be wonderful?"

"Do you think that the scheme will raise false expectations in Lady Gray?" North asked, ignoring her attempt to distract him.

"Lavinia has no interest in marrying you. By the way, I am writing to Parth to insist that he pay us a visit."

"He won't come," North said, startled. "He hates balls."

"And he dislikes Lavinia with a passion. What's more, the feeling is mutual," his aunt said, looking delighted.

"Then why . . . ."

"For interest, my dear boy. To liven things up around here."

"I asked Diana to marry me again, and she refused."

"I thought as much." His aunt rose and touched his arm, in fleeting sympathy. "Frankly, darling, she's not fitted for the role. I've never seen a woman more at the mercy of her impulses. If Diana took on the title, she'd have to change. I worry she'd be flattened."

North cursed silently. His aunt was right, of course.

What had he done, making love to Diana last night? He had thought he could change her mind. If she realized she loved him, she would agree—but that wasn't good enough.

His aunt was right.

The idea presented itself with some force. The rebellious, loyal, stubborn Diana whom he'd come to know?

She wouldn't want to open the townhouse in London for eight months of the year to host elegant dinners for political allies and opponents, as Ophelia did. Or if she did, she'd probably have the politicians shouting at each other within half an hour.

These weren't the things he had lectured her about when they were betrothed. He had talked about knotty problems of etiquette, such as how to respond if a member of the royal family was profoundly drunk.

It wasn't as if he couldn't understand her reluctance to be a duchess. Cold hopelessness had replaced his grief after Horatius died. Back when he remembered how to sleep, he used to have fitful dreams about the estates, the Duchy of Lindow, the House of Lords, the hundreds of dependents. Not to mention the beautiful, clean lines of the houses he had dreamed of designing.

He had to let her go. He loved her too much to snare her in the same trap he was mired in.

"Mr. Calico was in the village," he said. "I bought you a present."

His aunt clapped her hands. "Oh, that's wonderful!" She untied the twine wrapped around brown paper, revealing a length of glimmering blue silk.

North had the sudden impulse to snatch it back from her and give it to its rightful owner.

His aunt stroked her hand over the shining threads.

"What a beautiful piece," she said. Then she looked back at North. "My dear nephew, this fabric will never suit me."

"Why not?" North asked, keeping it short because obviously he'd made a mess of things.

"It's for the young. This silk is meant to flutter and flow around delightful feminine curves. It's meant to drive men mad. That is not an honor to which I ever aspired."

North cracked a smile, despite himself. "Aunt Knowe, if you wished to make men mad, you could certainly do so."

"Yes, I think I agree," his aunt said, grinning back. "I oversee the medicinal herb garden after all, and you'd be surprised how a pinch of henbane can scramble the wits. My point is that you didn't buy this cloth for me."

She pushed it toward him.

North sighed. "Perhaps I should give it to Lavinia."

"You could always cut it in half, the way Solomon threatened to do with the baby." His aunt rose, her eyes dancing with laughter. "I shall be *most* interested to see who appears in a silk gown at the ball."

His aunt was built along such generous lines that North scarcely had to bend his head to give her a buss on the cheek. "Are you certain that you don't wish to fashion it into a gown for yourself?"

"Absolutely," she replied. "Willa will be so sorry to have missed all these interesting developments! I shall have to write her daily now that Lavinia has arrived."

"I can't imagine what you write about," North said.

"Certainly not about my personal life. I attempted a diary once, and had to fill it with lies in order to keep myself interested."

North burst out laughing.

"I shall write of you," his aunt said. "You and darling Diana and the lovely Lavinia. And Parth, of course."

Chapter Sixteen

Fitzy's new mate didn't care for her leash. The bird kept flapping its wings, very nearly jerking Diana's arms from their sockets. Even worse, Mrs. Fitzy tried to peck Artie, which led to Godfrey hitting it on the beak with his toy horse.

After that, Diana kept the children well away. By the time they got back to the castle, they were all hot and tired. Artie and Godfrey were gray from head to foot because Mrs. Fitzy liked to stop and scratch the ground, sending billows of dust into the air.

The only clean spots on Artie's face were the two tearful streaks leading from her eyes to her chin.

As they made their way into the courtyard, the door was opened by Prism. His eyes moved from Artie to Godfrey to Diana . . . to Mrs. Fitzy. "Goodness me!"

Artie trudged forward. "Mr. Prism," she said, sniveling a little bit. "I'm tired." She leaned her dusty cheek against his immaculate white stockings.

Prism bent down and picked her up. "I assume that this bird is an addition to the castle aviary?"

Diana was so exhausted she couldn't marshal words and merely nodded. Artie put her dirty thumb in her mouth and said indistinctly, "Fitzy's wife."

Prism frowned; perhaps he felt that the castle didn't need another such bird. But he didn't admonish them; instead, he turned to his footmen. "Frederick, take the bird to the stables. Peter, we need hot water in the bath in the nursery, as well as in Miss Belgrave's chamber."

Diana handed the rope to Frederick with a feeling of acute relief. "There are sores around her neck; perhaps the stablemaster could apply some salve."

The bad-tempered bird took one look at Frederick and stopped scratching the ground, which was insulting.

North was working in the library, and he had kept an ear out for Diana and the children's return from the village. More than once, he had almost called for the pony cart to be brought around again. What could be taking them so long?

What if . . .

But then he thought about Diana's firm chin, and that she didn't need or want him to follow her about.

All the same, he bolted from the library when he

heard the front door opening. He reached the entry hall just as Prism entered, carrying Artie in his arms. Diana followed, clearly exhausted. Her face was dirty, and her hair had come loose and was falling down her back. Both it and her dark dress were noticeably dusty, and there was a smear of blood on her cheek—

"What happened?" he thundered. "Were you attacked?" Fear and anger beat inside his chest. He shouldn't have left them; he shouldn't have listened to Calico. He rubbed his thumb across the smear on her cheek. "How were you hurt? Artie? Godfrey?"

"It's nothing," she said. "Please stop making a fuss, Lord Roland. I have to bathe the children."

"*Diana.*"

She met his eyes with obvious reluctance. "It's just a scratch."

He waited until she uncurled her right hand; a wicked, red-raw laceration crossed her palm. "What happened?" His voice was deadly quiet.

"DeeDee pulled and pulled, 'cause Mrs. Fitzy is a *bad bird*," Artie said, around her thumb.

North brushed a finger across the part of Diana's palm that wasn't rubbed raw from rope, and then curled her hand shut. "Right. Upstairs, all of you."

Diana pulled her hand away. "Godfrey!"

North followed her gaze and saw the child curled

on the marble bench where footmen usually sat. It was hardly comfortable, but he seemed to be sleeping peacefully.

Diana sighed and bent over him. "Godfrey, I need you to wake up."

North brushed her gently to the side and picked the child up. Godfrey smelled like dirt and sweaty little boy, an odor North remembered in his bones.

"We wanted to ride," Artie told Prism, "but DeeDee said no, 'cause Mrs. Fitzy is a *bad bird*."

Prism led the way upstairs, murmuring quietly to Artie, which brought to North's mind a sudden memory of Prism—considerably younger and some-what slimmer—talking to Horatius.

Horatius had adored the butler, and had often sat for hours in the butler's pantry while Prism polished silver. In the white heat of grief, North had never thought about how much the loss of Horatius must have af-fected their butler. Every person in the castle had red eyes for weeks, but Prism would have had to keep the household going, no matter how he felt.

By the time they reached the nursery, the tin bath was half filled with steaming water. Peter upended the can he held. "That should do it. I filled the pitcher as well, Miss Belgrave, and your tub is waiting."

"Lady Artemisia, I will see you tomorrow morning," Prism said, putting Artie down on a bed.

Before he straightened, Artie patted his cheek and said, "Thanks." Then she closed her eyes and went to sleep.

Prism made a sound that in a less dignified man might have been a chuckle and left the room, silently closing the door behind him.

North's little sister was an excellent duchess-in-the-making: fearless, with an effortless assumption of rank combined with genuine charm and affection.

"Well then," Diana said, her voice strained with weariness. "If you'll excuse us, Lord Roland, I must bathe the children."

"Prism has gone, which means I'm North, not Lord Roland. I'm not leaving until your hand is properly washed and bandaged."

He placed Godfrey on his feet and the boy swayed.

"How far did you walk these two?" he asked, picking Godfrey back up before he fell over.

"You make it sound like an accusation," Diana said, slowly unpinning her cap.

"Why didn't you wear gloves? They would have protected your hands." He determined that the bed next to Artie's must be Godfrey's. He laid him on his side, and the boy's eyelids fluttered closed. "How easily they sleep."

Diana put her muslin cap, gray with dust, on the nursery table. "They usually nap much earlier than this."

"Why didn't you wait for me?" he asked, the question coming from his mouth without permission. "I looked around, and the three of you were gone, even though we had walked to the village together." He was fairly certain that his voice had a tone of civil inquiry.

"There you are again," she said.

He frowned. "What?"

"You've turned duke. Hoity-toity. One moment I think you're human, and then you remind me of your rank."

"I apologize," North said. "I didn't mean to 'turn duke'."

Back when he was in the nursery, with four boys living in proximity, someone was always getting hurt. In those days, the cupboard in the corner held a good supply of clean white cloths, a bottle of vinegar, and a jar of his aunt's comfrey salve. Sure enough, they were still there.

He brought them back, and poured warm water from the pitcher into a bowl. "Put your hands in the water. Please."

She was wearing the dress he had come to hate, black, and frayed at the neck. The very sight of it put his teeth on edge.

Diana plunged her hands into the warm water and hissed under her breath as it met the raw wound on her palm.

North had seen men succumb to infections that had settled in wounds that had not initially seemed grievous. He gently washed her hand with soft soap, making certain that no strands of rope or dust were left. He dried her hand, then poured vinegar over the laceration, ignoring her squeaking protests.

"Infection is a terrible thing," he said, keeping his voice low so as not to wake the children. Her hands were beautiful, with slender fingers that felt incredibly fragile. His hands were battered and scarred, whereas even her calluses were delicate.

"This is merely a scrape," Diana protested.

North patted her hands dry again with a clean towel and looked carefully for dirt that had escaped him. "Why weren't you wearing gloves?"

She threw him a dark look. "Governesses do not have an unlimited supply of gloves, Lord Roland."

A flash of heat went down his back. Diana, his Diana, had injured her hand in order to conserve a pair of gloves?

He added a mountain of gloves to the trunk of shoes he planned to buy for her, duchess or no. "I gather that you brought home a peahen?"

"A mate for Fitzy," she said, watching as he carefully dabbed salve on her palm.

"Why didn't you return to the castle and inform Prism that there was an appropriate bird for purchase?"

"She was tied to a fence with a short rope. She has no feathers left around her neck. Her tail is missing feathers as well; I think they were deliberately pulled out and sold. I couldn't leave her."

Tail feathers? Typical Diana, he registered. For good and ill.

"Did you steal it?" He rubbed her palm.

"Ouch!"

"I'm sorry."

"I thought about it," she said in a rush. "But the owner appeared. He was a horrid man, far too young to be so cruel."

"Cruelty is not the preserve of the old," North pointed out, vivid scenes from the war racing through his mind.

"I gave him money, and he said we should take her now, because otherwise he couldn't be responsible for her safety. He said she'd pecked him one too many times. What could I do at that point?"

"If we'd still been in the village with the pony cart, we could have helped. Damn it."

"There was no reason that you should have stayed," Diana told him. "When we returned to the square, Mr. Calico had shut his caravan, so we began walking. It's not far, but the peacock—did you call her a peahen?— was unexpectedly strong, especially for a bird that seemed half starved. Every time she spread her tail—"

"Does Mrs. Fitzy have a tail that might rival our castle cock?" North interrupted.

"No, she's missing at least a quarter of her feathers," Diana told him, frowning at the way he was winding muslin around her hand. "You can't do that. I have to bathe the children as soon as they wake up."

"You may not bathe the children, because you mustn't get your hands wet at least until tomorrow."

She snorted. "Please try not to be ridiculous. I have to bathe *myself* as well."

"I shall help you," he said, his voice silky. He tucked the end of the muslin under the bandage, and Diana pulled her hand away.

"No, thank you," she stated.

"Where is your nursemaid?" he asked.

"Mabel? She's probably in the dairy. She's in love with one of the men who work there. Or perhaps with two," she added. "She talks of them both."

"Adventuresome," North commented. "She can bathe the children after they wake from their naps. You mustn't get your wound wet, Diana. An infection can be very dangerous."

He could feel a tic in his jaw. Because, damn it, she had to be safe. "I'm not usually like this," he said roughly.

The white bandage made a glaring contrast to her dusty dress. "Mabel will help me undress, but thank you." Diana's eyes crinkled at the corners because she was smiling, and God help him, her smile made him a bit dizzy. "Was there something else?" she asked, when he didn't move.

"Mrs. Fitzy?" he prompted. "You were telling me of the peahen with the battered tail."

"Yes." Anxiety crossed her face. "Do you think that His Grace won't want another peacock? I do realize that Fitzy makes a terrible racket. I didn't think when I saw her tied to that fence, and all the feathers on her neck worn off from trying to break free."

"*You* didn't think? Shocking."

She scowled at him.

"How much did you pay for it?"

Diana bit her lip, suspecting she might have paid too much. The peacock had cost more than the silvery fabric—but how could she say no? With Artie looking up at her, confident she would rescue Mrs. Fitzy, and Godfrey likely thinking the same thing?

"You paid too much," North concluded when she didn't answer. "I'm sorry to tell you that Mrs. Fitzy is no mate for Fitzy."

Her mouth fell open. "What?"

"The bird you describe doesn't sound like a peahen. More likely, he's a male in his prime, with or without all his tail feathers."

"Are you absolutely certain? How do you know?"

"Peahens don't have tails—or rather, nothing at all like the males'. Did you know that peacocks are quite territorial?"

"Are you saying Fitzy will be insulted by the arrival of a new bird?"

"We males tend to be like that."

"Hell's bells," she breathed.

"Indeed."

Diana's stomach tightened into the size of a walnut. She felt like an idiot. What if the duke was angry to learn that beloved Fitzy had a rival?

"It will be good for the old bird," North said, dropping a kiss on her dusty nose. "The scoundrel needs something to give him a new lease on life."

In an uncharacteristic show of timeliness, Mabel happened into the nursery at that moment. North pointed to

Diana's bandaged hand and announced that Mabel was in charge of the children until the following morning, and then he left.

Diana ignored Mabel's smirk. She refused to ask Mabel to help her disrobe. Or to help her bathe. She had never liked having a lady's maid, and had happily left hers behind when she'd fled the castle last time.

A duchess, she reminded herself, almost certainly had *two* maids. Duchesses were summoned to the court on a regular basis.

It turned out that she did have a maid. When she slipped through the door to her bedchamber, North was seated before the fireplace, reading one of her books. "*The History of the Peloponnesian War?*" he asked, holding it up.

"I'm trying to educate myself," Diana said. "I don't know anything about peafowl. Or Shakespeare." She hesitated. "Or war."

He stood up, putting the book to the side, came over, and began briskly unbuttoning her gown. "Isn't it a good thing that we've already been intimate, so you needn't feel shy?"

Diana felt shy anyway. It was one thing to make love in the middle of the night, and another to undress with afternoon sunlight slanting in the window.

"Are you happy Lavinia has arrived?"

"Of course I am."

"How many bloody buttons are on this dress?"

Diana glanced down just in time to see his hands settle on her neckline and tear the tired fabric right down the front. She barely managed to suppress a scream that Mabel might have heard. "What are you doing?" She was so exhausted that tears came to her eyes. "This is like my shoes. You don't understand."

North pushed off the pieces of worn cloth, made quick work of her corset, and sat down in the chair with her in his arms, wearing only a chemise. "I hate that dress."

"It's mine," Diana said shakily. "I had three, and now I only have two."

"You've forgotten that Lavinia is in the castle now," he pointed out. "Your cousin will faint if she sees you in that rag again."

Despite herself, tears started down her face. "I made do," she said, sobs shaking her voice. "I worked hard. Now everything is changing, and Godfrey and I will have to live with Lady Gray."

North tucked her closer to his chest, pushed a handkerchief into her hand, and thought about his plan to buy a house for her, with room for servants, in any part of the country she wished. She didn't have to love him, or marry him, but she couldn't stop him from taking care of her.

"It's not that I dislike Lady Gray. I just don't want to do it again," Diana said, hiccupping. "Dress and undress all day long, with endless dinners in the evenings, playing cards, which I hate." Her voice trailed off in a sob.

North put his chin on her dusty hair and rocked her back and forth. Every word she said struck arrows into his heart, but they reinforced his decision. He had to let her go. He couldn't tie her to a fence until she lost all her feathers trying to escape.

"You needn't live with Lady Gray," he said, when her sobs quieted.

"I ca-can't marry you, North."

"I know," he said, the words leaden in his voice and heart. "I know you can't. I understand."

"Almost certainly your father will live to be ancient, but North, you *know* that people don't always live as long as they should. And *I* know it."

His arms tightened. "True."

"I wish I could," Diana whispered. "I mean, I could, but I would be such a terrible duchess and you'd come to hate me. My mother did." She stopped.

"Hated you?" North had to remind himself that Mrs. Belgrave was not an enemy combatant. He couldn't take revenge.

"I never did anything right," she said, burying her

face in his chest. "The only way she could find me a husband was if I promised not to say a word."

"Your mother is a fool."

"Lavinia said Mother's been shunned by polite society." A huge sob shook Diana's body. "She must be so unhappy."

North rocked her some more. Given a choice, Diana never would have married for the sake of a title. She was like his aunt in that.

Unless someone forced her to.

"How did Mrs. Belgrave make you behave as she wished? She didn't harm you?" His voice fell an entire octave.

Diana squeaked. "Absolutely not!"

"Then?"

Silence.

"*Diana*."

"She threatened not to support Rose and Godfrey," she said, her voice desperately sad. "I promised I would behave just as my mother wished, and wear whatever she wanted, and after I married, my mother would give Rose her dowry."

A growl came from low in North's throat.

"She thought I couldn't do it, but I could and I did. I would have done anything for Rose. And Godfrey too."

"Rose was very lucky to have you," North said.

Tears wavered in her voice again. "I don't know why she got that fever. She had money for a doctor."

"People are fragile," North told her. "They die easily. You mustn't blame yourself."

"You blame yourself, and you're telling me not to? You lie awake at night thinking about the men you lost, don't you?"

He rubbed his cheek against her hair. "Something like that."

"Leaving Lindow Castle, leaving you, was the cruelest thing I could have done to my mother. I'm sure it broke her heart." She took a deep, shuddering breath and wiped her eyes again.

"I think it is grossly optimistic to assume that your mother has a heart," North said flatly. He stood up and placed her on her feet. "The water must be cooling. May I bathe you, Diana?"

She put her hands on his chest, and he tried very hard not to look down at her breasts, scarcely covered by her light chemise. Just as he had before going to war, he tried to memorize *her*, everything from her rounded lower lip to her curling eyelashes. "God, you're so beautiful," he said hoarsely.

Up on her toes, she pressed a kiss on his mouth. "I would be grateful for help bathing."

North nodded, turned around, and locked her door.

Then he followed her to the bathing alcove. She was lucky enough to have a sturdy wooden tub, not a flimsy one made of tin. She looked over her shoulder before she pulled her chemise over her head and threw it to the side.

If he hadn't had a cockstand simply from being in her presence, it would have leapt to attention now. Her body was like a beautiful instrument, her breasts tapering to her waist, curving out again in a generous haunch, beautiful arse, legs . . .

He watched her lean over and test the temperature of the water with one finger and managed not to groan. Another glimmering smile over her shoulder, and she stepped into the bath, carefully keeping her right hand well above the water.

North shed his clothes faster than he ever had. She watched him, eyebrow raised. "None of my other maids have disrobed."

"It's an efficient way to bathe."

North had never felt so large as when he squeezed into the bathtub, Diana between his legs, his erection pressed against her hip. She was soft and small, compared to him, and the flood of pleasure he felt was almost unbearable. When he picked up the ball of soap—honey-scented—his fingers trembled.

Having Diana in his arms was a shock of joy. Like

being struck by lightning, and all the more precious because it couldn't be done again. His calm center—the part that navigated battlefields fearlessly—informed him that this would be the last time. She was not his, and she could never be.

He made a lather, leaned forward, and soaped the delicate arch of her right foot. "You left your betrothal ring behind," he said. "You could have sold it for a great deal of money."

"We grocers' granddaughters don't think it's polite to sell a ring that a gentleman has given in promise of marriage." Diana had her right hand well out of the tub, but the fingers of her left caressed his wrist, gently following the curve of his arm from wrist to elbow and sliding back again.

"You broke your promise to your mother, rather than tell me the truth," he pointed out. "I would have gone with you, Diana. I would have forced your mother to support you and Godfrey."

"I panicked. I did think of telling you, but how could I word it? 'Excuse me. I'm so sorry, but I have to rescue my sister's bastard and raise him as my own'?"

"I would have done something." He picked up her left foot.

Diana found herself smiling reluctantly, because North was as stubborn as she was. "Hidden Godfrey away in some cottage in the country so he could be brought up to an honest trade, perhaps as a cowherd?"

"You believe that I—that any Wilde—would do such a thing to a member of our family?"

She turned and put a kiss on his shoulder. "I didn't know you, any more than you knew me. I wouldn't have trusted any gentleman with that knowledge."

"None of us?" he repeated.

Diana allowed her head to fall to the side so she could look back at him, but North merely looked thoughtful. He had finished soaping past her knees and he was sliding up her thighs.

She smiled.

"We cannot make love again after today," he told her, his voice quiet and reasoned. "Not unless we are to marry. I understand that you can't be a duchess, Diana. I do understand. If I didn't have to be duke, I would throw you in a carriage and take you to Gretna Green."

"What would we do after that?" she whispered.

"Would you care to travel?"

"I would love to."

"I would take you and Godfrey to Greece and Italy. I had planned to take a Grand Tour, but I was needed at home. Now my aunt is managing the estates." His hands had slowed; they were tracing patterns on her inside thighs and made her want to squirm.

"After a few years, we would come home. Perhaps we'd have a baby by then. I would rent a house while choosing land to build the house I had designed for you."

Diana could scarcely breathe. Her heart felt so full she thought it might burst.

"We would have many babies and cheerful nurse-maids, unlike Mabel."

"She's not terrible," Diana objected. "She just doesn't like her work."

"Since we wouldn't go to London for the Season, Ophelia and my father could leave Artie with us."

"We might keep a flock of peacocks," Diana suggested. His fingers kept coming closer to the heart of her and then sliding away. She couldn't keep herself from squirming, her knees pressing outward against his legs like a wanton.

"May I touch you, Diana?" he whispered.

"Please," she said, gulping air.

Just as his right hand slid between her legs, his left splayed over her breast, and two fingers trapped her nipple. She turned wetter than water, and her moan was echoed by the groan that came from his throat as he caressed her.

"I can't, oh, I can't," she panted.

"Watch," he commanded, and Diana watched his

sun-bronzed hand caress her breast, roughly enough to make her arch toward his fingers. His other hand covered her most private part, one broad finger . . . .

"Oh," Diana whispered.

Because she *could*.

And she *did*.

The aching sensation unfurled inside her the way a rose does in the morning sun, streaks of heat spreading languidly down her legs, up her belly. Her head fell back on his shoulder and she clenched around his finger, squeaks coming from her throat that might have been embarrassing, except his breathing was harsh in her ear and there was no place for embarrassment between them.

North loved the way Diana was rubbing her arse against his cock, pleading for more. Her eyes were soft and unfocused. When she finally lay bonelessly in his arms, he washed her hair and rinsed it carefully before he lifted her from the bath, toweled her off, and pushed her gently down on her stomach over the side of the bed.

Diana didn't have time to ask questions, because North's hands settled on her hips and then—

And then.

They made love for hours, and it wasn't until the end that she really understood it was for the last time.

"Condoms aren't perfect," North said, propped on his side looking down at her. Her hair had dried in crazy corkscrews and kinks. It was all over the pillow and he kept winding his fingers through her curls.

Diana felt drugged by the times he'd pushed her into making that leap of joy; her mind foggily sorted through his sentence.

"We can't make love after today, or you might end up with child. And Diana, no child of mine is going to be born out of wedlock." His voice wasn't angry, or even sad. Just accepting.

"I understand," she said, knowing that was the truth. North would set her free, but not under those circumstances.

His gentle caress down her arm was like a lullaby promising a bedtime story. "I keep thinking about the night we met."

"My mother was exuberant on the carriage ride home," Diana said, sighing.

North had that imperturbable expression again, as if nothing she could say would shock him. Perhaps it wouldn't. He'd been the heir to a dukedom for years, after all. He knew the schemes of marriage-minded mothers.

If anything, his eyes were sympathetic.

"You asked me to dance," she continued, because she

wanted him to know the truth. "My mother had found out that you had bought a horse earlier that day. I asked you about the lineage of Arabian horses. We knew that you are very close to your brothers, but did not enjoy hearing lavish adoration of Lord Wilde's books. I managed to inform you that I had heard of your brother, but had not read his books."

His thumb stopped its caress and the side of his mouth quirked up again. "That *is* thorough."

"Thorough is the fact that my mother didn't allow me to read Lord Wilde's books, both in deference to you as his brother, and in case she decided to target the famous explorer instead. She thought he would never marry a lady who had read his books or had seen the play about him."

A full smile now. "My sister-in-law Willa had not read the books, because she disliked the sound of them. She thought Alaric made up his adventures."

"My mother believed that ignorance of his work would prove irresistible to Lord Alaric."

"What did she think would be irresistible to me? Surely not simply ignorance of my brother's books."

"No."

"I am curious about the key to my personality, the key to making me fall in love."

She glanced up at him, shamed to the bottom of her

soul. North had been direct and honest with her, and she had been nothing but devious. It made her feel ill, because her mother's pressure was no excuse. She had been, and was, a grown woman.

"Diana?"

His voice was agreeable, but it held the undertone of a future duke. A man to whom few people would say no. She owed him the truth.

"My mother decided that the dominant trait in your personality is protectiveness," she said. "You lost your older brother, under circumstances that were preventable."

His face closed tight, jaw locked.

"She judged that since you had been in the vicinity when Horatius became inebriated and made his reckless bet, you would blame yourself. Everyone said that you were actually not in the room, nor, in fact, even in the tavern, but she thought proximity would add to your urge to protect."

"I was upstairs in the inn with a cheerful woman with blond hair," he said, voice utterly emotionless. "To this day, I dislike yellow hair."

She nodded, reached out, and took his hand. "That is why she reasoned that you were likely to find me appealing."

"Your red hair?"

"Absolutely not. She hated my hair. She thought you would be likely to respond to a woman who was uncertain of her place in society. Your protective instincts would be aroused. Indeed, you did spend a good deal of time trying to teach me to be less—"

She stopped. Started again. "Not less, but more: more aristocratic. All those lessons on being a duchess."

"Your mother was wrong."

"It went exactly as she predicted. The second time we danced together, I confessed that someone had made an unkind remark based on my parentage, or more specifically, on my grandfather."

His brows knit.

"You were determined to bring me to the highest ranks, proving them wrong and protecting me against criticism. So you told yourself that you were in love with me. It didn't hurt that I dressed and looked precisely like a duchess in a French painting. Also, I never disagreed with you, only raised subjects of interest to you, and on the surface at least, gratefully accepted your advice."

"I was a complete ass," he growled.

She shook her head. "You were a man whose impulse toward kindness was taken advantage of."

"Now shall I tell you what I remember about that evening?" His voice was gentle, not angry, not bitter.

"No." She realized that she was clutching his hand and let go, but his fingers tightened and he grabbed her other hand as well.

"The height of your wig did not serve as an attraction; rather, it was your laugh. Your eyes danced, and your bottom lip was the color of a peony. I had already noticed you a few weeks before, as I told you. But at the next ball I attended after first seeing you—now dressed by Boodle—I watched you for a while before I asked for an introduction. Lavinia was making you laugh. I think she was probably telling you bawdy jokes."

Diana felt her cheeks growing pink. Lavinia had been telling her about a private toy that one of her ancestors had made for his wife. Bigger than Lavinia's forearm, or so she had said.

"You were watching?"

He nodded. "Care to share the joke?"

"No," Diana said hastily. "That is . . . no."

"I searched out our hostess and asked for an introduction."

Her eyes flew to his.

"Mrs. Belgrave's machinations were uncalled for." His voice was tender, his eyes anything but. They were fierce, but a ferocity that had nothing to do with her mother's schemes.

"Oh!" Diana said, idiotically.

His eyes drifted from her forehead all the way to her toes. When they met hers again, they were on fire. "All she had to do was put you in front of me."

"A waste of research and coin, in that case. If only Mother had known that all she needed was my bosom and my red hair."

His face was not elegant or foppish. It was harsh and masculine but for his eyes, which were caressing her. He bent his head over hers, his lips brushing her mouth. "I wanted you from the moment I saw you. You didn't let me see much of the true Diana, but I saw enough. I would make myself into a dandy for you all over again, if you wished."

"I'm sorry that I wouldn't be good as a duchess," she said, whispering it against his chest.

"I know." His voice rumbled from his chest. "You're far too spontaneous, and you don't even understand how to distinguish male from female peafowl. That's requisite biology for everyone who might own a castle someday."

"Recognizing peacocks is not the same as joining the highest ranks of the peerage. Being watched by crowds of people, judged, and tallied for what you are not doing correctly."

"A duchess is at the top of society," North said, nodding. "She leads and others follow."

"The idea of people looking up to me like that is terrible. I would—I would do things wrong."

He paused for a moment. "I shall ask you again. The third time." He didn't have to add that if she refused him, there would be no fourth time.

"Will you be my duchess, Diana? To have and to hold, in good times and ill, as long as we both shall live?"

"No. Though I think I love you," she added desperately.

A moment of silence was broken only by the singing of a bird building a nest outside.

Something in his eyes was unbearable, so Diana found herself looking at the window instead.

"You don't love me," he said, almost kindly.

She opened her mouth to protest, but he moved his head, just a fraction of an inch, and she stopped. "If you loved me, you would brave the role of a duchess. I think, in fact, that your anger at your mother outweighs whatever you feel for me. You refuse to become a duchess because that's what she wanted you to be. That's what she schemed for."

The blood drained from Diana's face. Could that be true? Her mind reeled, trying to make sense of it. She *was* angry at her mother, but . . .

He nodded, watching her. "Your mother's actions

toward your sister Rose were monstrous. Anyone would feel strongly."

He got to his feet and pulled on clothing. He kissed her for the last time.

She still hadn't said a word when he left.

Diana stared at the closed door. Part of her wanted to run after him, screaming, reckless, willing to agree to anything to keep him.

But another part of her . . .

She could clearly see how unhappy she would be as a duchess, and it didn't have to do with proving her mother right or wrong. She had survived her Season because her mother literally dictated everything she said. Without that . . . without that she would make mistake after mistake. Buying the wrong peafowl was the least of it.

The real problem wasn't her impulsive behavior. Perhaps more importantly, she had no wish to direct a huge household that encompassed several estates. She didn't want to meet the queen.

She wanted to sit in the sunshine and tell stories about an adventuresome peacock. In the summer, she wanted to live in a small cottage on the Isle of Wight, not in a ducal estate in Scotland.

Did it mean that she didn't love him, the essential North? The idea shook her to the core. But at the same time, that part of her that had bent to her mother's demands was protesting.

Making itself heard.

North had donned heels and powder for her, but that wasn't the same as turning over one's life to the enormous endeavor called a duchy. He himself had told her about the administration, the work, the House of Lords. Never once did he speak of those things with joy or even interest.

This time she couldn't hold the tears back, because she was selfish. The man she loved—and she *did* love him—was trapped in a duchy, and she was refusing to join him. Refusing to be his partner.

In the end, she sobbed until there weren't any more sobs, until she stared dry-eyed into the silent room.

Chapter Seventeen

The next morning Diana got up at dawn with Artie and watched listlessly as the little girl tied ribbons on the tails of Godfrey's toy horses. Her nephew was still asleep and hadn't yet learned how his precious playthings were being "decorated" when Mabel emerged from her bedchamber.

Diana handed the children over to Mabel's care, pleading a headache, and returned to her room. Her head did hurt, and her heart hurt even more.

Lavinia found her there an hour later. With one look, she held out her arms and Diana toppled into them, sobbing so hard she couldn't speak.

"Hush," her cousin said, hugging her. "It will pass, I promise you."

A while later, as she washed her face, Diana asked

huskily, "How do you know it will pass, Lavinia? Perhaps I'll regret refusing North for the rest of my life."

"I fell in love with the wrong man once," Lavinia said, her voice thoughtful. "It was a salutary experience. I *was* sad. But not as wretched as I might have been, had I married him, not that he asked."

"Oh," Diana said, sinking into a chair and pressing a damp towel against her burning eyes. "I didn't know that."

"I didn't tell anyone," Lavinia said. "*You* are not to tell anyone either. The right man will come along. I promise you that."

"All right," Diana said shakily.

"For now, I want you to stay away from North, if you possibly can. For one thing, my mother is convinced the man is courting me. If she's in a sweet mood, it's so much easier for everyone."

Diana had to ask, though her voice came out in an ashamed whisper. "He isn't, is he?"

Lavinia snorted. "No. But you must keep a distance both for your peace of mind, and the sake of your reputation. Lady Knowe is a wily old bird. She's invited half the country to this ball."

"I have nothing to wear."

"You'll wear a gown of mine, of course. Thank goodness, we have the same bosom, so I doubt my clothes will need more than a stitch here or there to fit as if they were made for you instead of me."

"Thank you," Diana said.

"At the ball, I want you to dance with everyone, but only once with North. You have to keep an indifferent, if not bored, expression on your face. Do you think you can do that, Diana?"

"I can try."

"I will tell him to stop watching you," Lavinia said. "I came to fetch you because we need to begin altering a morning dress immediately. If I see you dressed like a rusty crow again, I'm going to tear the garment off you myself."

Diana stared at her. "Did you know that you are re-markably like North?"

The pillow Lavinia threw missed Diana and bounced off the wall. "I have nothing in common with North; for one thing, I enjoy wearing pretty gowns and presumably he does not. Were you really happy being a servant and wearing that ghastly dress?"

"Not entirely," Diana found herself saying. "But I wasn't comfortable being a lady either. The idea of being a duchess is horrible."

"You are so peculiar," Lavinia said. Then she grinned. "You must be a relative of mine!"

"North spent most of the time we were betrothed

trying to teach me how to be a duchess," Diana said morosely. "'Peculiar' is not a desirable trait in a duchess."

Lavinia pursed her lips. "No wonder you fled the betrothal. Perhaps I should give him some helpful instruction before he tries to find another wife."

"You would be much better at keeping him on a string than I was," Diana said.

"Keeping him on a string? Behind me, like a footman?" Lavinia grinned naughtily. "Have you noticed how much North has changed? There is something very male about him now. I might have trouble keeping him behind me, except in bed!" She burst into a fit of giggles.

Diana found herself laughing too, even as her mind was reeling over the memory of North ravishing her from behind. She had been on her hands and knees, her hair falling over her shoulder. He had been thrusting—

"A woman could guide him easily," Lavinia said, so overcome by hilarity that she wrapped an arm around her tummy. "'Get thee to the North of me!'"

It didn't make much sense, but Diana dissolved into laughter as well.

"What's funny?" a little voice asked.

Artie was standing in the doorway, thumb in her mouth.

"Where's Mabel?" Diana asked.

Artie shrugged.

"And Godfrey?"

"Sleeping."

"Ladies' jests," Lavinia said, beaming at her. "Diana, you must introduce me, because we didn't properly meet yesterday in the village."

"May I introduce Lady Artemisia Wilde?" Diana obeyed. "Artie, this is Miss Lavinia Gray."

The two of them regarded each other for a moment, and then, to Diana's utter astonishment, Artie pulled her thumb from her mouth and dipped into a curtsy. Or what passed for one in a miniature person with extremely chubby legs.

Lavinia immediately rose and curtsied as well. "Lady Artemisia, it is an honor."

"Tell me a lady's joke," Artie demanded, putting her thumb back and coming over to lean against Diana's knee.

"I can't," Lavinia told her. "All the best jokes are forbidden to young ladies of your age."

Artie's brows drew together, and Diana's heart sank. When Artie was thwarted, she had an unfortunate propensity to fall to the ground and drum her heels on the floor.

"When you are old enough, I shall invite you for tea and tell you many jests. All of them," Lavinia added quickly.

Artie nodded. Crisis averted.

"That was an excellent use of ladylike restraint," Lavinia said warmly.

Artie likely didn't understand, but she smiled and took a step toward Lavinia. Diana held her breath. Artie didn't care to be held by strangers, but she had just invited Lavinia to do so.

Once in Lavinia's lap, Artie relaxed against her shoulder with a sigh and began sucking loudly.

"Artie," Lavinia said. "Stop sucking your thumb. You're making me feel sick."

Diana watched, curious but wary. She'd never tried to make Artie stop sucking her thumb. There were so many things to worry about, like curtsying, and she assumed Artie would drop the habit by herself in good time.

Artie withdrew her thumb, looked at it, then put it back in her mouth and closed her eyes, apparently deciding to ignore Lavinia.

"It's not easy to be a governess," Diana confessed. "I had never imagined a situation in which my commands were routinely ignored."

"I see what you mean; servants do precisely as I ask, and I trust my husband will as well," Lavinia stated. Her eyes darkened. "The only person—other than this little scrap—who has heedlessly ignored me is Parth Sterling. Do you remember him?"

"Certainly," Diana said. "He seems agreeable enough, though I remember you disliked him."

"Lady Knowe invited him to the ball," Lavinia said, an edge to her voice.

"I like him," Artie said, around her thumb.

"Is there some reason that my gown feels disturbingly wet?" Lavinia inquired.

"Oh, no," Diana groaned.

Artie smiled.

Chapter Eighteen

Five days later

North had become convinced that Dante had omitted one circle of hell—the one he was in. He saw Diana often, but never in his bed, and never to talk to.

She usually had Godfrey and Artie with her, and Lady Knowe had had no success in persuading her to join the family for supper or, indeed, any meal.

He lured himself into fitful sleep by thinking of her. She was like a dream that he wanted to live in.

No one really knew what it was like to be a duchess, or a duke, until one found oneself in the role. How hard it was to be fawned over any time one wasn't in the midst of family.

How lonely it was.

Diana had a right to refuse that life.

On the fifth day, when he went to the nursery, planning to collect Godfrey for their daily trip to the stables, he found Diana in the schoolroom, mending a pair of children's gloves. Her nephew sat on the floor nearby, silently playing with his toy horses.

"Godfrey has already been to the stables with Leonidas," she said, barely glancing up at him. She was wearing a gown made of some sort of sheer purple fabric embroidered with violets at the hem. It must have been Lavinia's, if only because Diana had tucked a fichu into the bodice. Lavinia flaunted her magnificent bosom and Diana hid hers.

"Those horses were mine and Alaric's," North said walking over and crouching beside Godfrey. "Aha, I remember this fine steed. His name is Christopher." He held up a wooden horse with a faded red bridle and one splintered leg.

Godfrey shook his head.

"You gave him a different name?"

The boy looked at him.

"Of course you did."

Godfrey plucked Christopher out of his hand and put him back in line with the other horses. They were all wearing little saddlebags, clumsily made.

"You made these saddlebags, didn't you?" North

asked Diana over his shoulder. "I think I recognize your flawless stitches from Artie's doll's nightdress."

Diana sighed. "Sewing is not one of my accomplishments."

North rose and went to her, thinking about wooden horses. He saw no reason not to give Godfrey the battered herd. He liked the idea of this solemn little boy taking a part of his childhood with him, wherever he went.

Godfrey leaving. Diana leaving.

This was hell: loving a woman so much that you would willingly die for her, yet letting her go.

Dante had it wrong when he put lovers into Hell in pairs. What was hellish about that? North would whirl endlessly in that high wind if he could hold Diana's hand, comfort her, love her, protect her. He would wind himself around her so that she didn't suffer.

"I am looking forward to dancing with you again," he said, despite himself.

"I'm not the woman you danced with in London two years ago."

No, she wasn't. This woman had proud eyes and a mouth that looked as if she smiled frequently. He wanted her so much that his hands trembled with the instinct to pull her close.

He cleared his throat. "We danced well together, even if we rarely spoke."

Diana looked up with a smile. "Yes, we did."

North bowed.

The next day he returned to the nursery, because that was the whole point of Dante's Hell: one was cursed to repeat the same thing, no matter how painful. Diana's presence in the castle was like an itch he couldn't reach. Damnably irritating. Always there, driving him mad.

He heard her laughing from outside the schoolroom, and something in him stilled and quieted. He entered, scowling at the thought.

Lavinia and Diana were seated on the sofa. Artie was asleep between them, her head on Diana's lap. Lavinia was leaning over and whispering something in Diana's ear. A bawdy jest, based on her impish expression.

If they heard him enter the room, they gave no sign. Lavinia's silk dress billowed on either side of her, trailing on the floor. Pearls were wound in her hair, and her bosom was displayed like fruit on a platter.

Diana wore the same purple gown she had worn the day before. It flattered her complexion and made it glow with the pale perfection of moonlight. Her russet hair was unpowdered, but an elegant curl fell over one shoulder. Her eyes shone with laughter, her cheekbones marked not by rouge but a natural flush.

It was no wonder that he'd seen her across the ballroom and instantly wanted to marry her—before he knew that she was loyal, intelligent, and brave.

Diana had given up everything for her sister. Never having met Rose, North couldn't say whether she deserved it. But Diana would have been completely loyal to her sister anyway, because that's how she loved someone.

She hadn't given her heart to North—as everyone in the kingdom knew—but presumably she would give it to another man, one day. He stood staring at the two women, contemplating the death of a man he didn't know, when Lavinia looked up.

She held out a hand, smiling. He came closer and bowed before them, kissing the back of Lavinia's hand. "Good afternoon, ladies."

Diana murmured a greeting and looked down at Artie.

"We have been contemplating the difficulties of herding gentlemen," Lavinia said, with a husky chuckle.

Godfrey dashed over, and North swooped him into the air and put him on his shoulders. "Ladies," he said, "we men will leave you to your discussion."

From on high, Godfrey caught a handful of North's hair and squealed.

North took the boy to the stables where they visited each horse, stroking its nose, feeding it a handful of grain. He returned the boy to the nursery only when Godfrey started knuckling his eyes.

Godfrey went straight to Diana and collapsed into her lap. "You're tired," she crooned.

North should have left then, but he didn't. He sank onto the sofa and watched as Diana washed Godfrey's face and then put him down for a nap. The little boy snuggled down, closed his eyes, and fell asleep.

It was mesmerizing. North was still gazing at the bed when Diana sat beside him. "Still no sleep?"

"It's better," he lied. Weakness was a damnable thing.

"I feel as if it's my fault," Diana said, her hands twisting.

He turned to look at her, a smile crossing his face. "How did you come to that conclusion?"

"I jilted you, and you went to war," she said flatly. "You certainly never mentioned that you had ambitions to raise a regiment when we were betrothed."

North found himself in the grip of genuine amusement.

"Don't laugh at me!" Diana said. "Am I wrong?" Her voice was hopeful.

"There may be men who would fling themselves into combat on account of a broken heart."

"But you aren't one of them?"

He shook his head.

Diana let relief flow through her like a cool river.

"Did you make love to me out of guilt?" North asked.

She looked at him, incredulous. His face told her that it was a sincere question; she moved over just enough so that she could lean against him. His arm went around her and she laid her cheek against his shoulder.

"Is that a no?"

"I offered you toast in the hope it would fill your stomach and act as a soporific. Artie can't sleep if she's hungry. But intimacies? No."

He was silent. Then: "I cannot abide suet pudding, but everything else you told the chef to make was perfect."

"I merely suggested plain English food."

His arm tightened. "When I was a boy, I dreamed of two things: architecture and war. Alaric came home and offered to take over the ducal estates, so I was free."

"Except you'd already asked me to marry you," she said, seeing the problem. North would never have betrothed himself and then taken on a hazardous venture like war. Most heirs to duchies wouldn't consider risking their lives.

"I wanted to serve my country. When you broke our betrothal, I was most unhappy. But I was also free to buy a commission."

Soft laughter bubbled out of Diana, relief coming from deep inside her. "I was terrified that you would die or be maimed, and it would be my fault."

He kissed her hair. "The way you blame yourself for Rose's death?"

"If I had accepted Archibald, she wouldn't have decided to marry him." She whispered the next. "My mother felt that Rose's death was the direct result of my selfishness. I can't seem to forget that."

North cursed under his breath. "That's a monstrous thing to say, and she's wrong. How well did Rose know Archie when she chose him?"

"He had dined with us. I had consistently said that I didn't want to go to London for the Season. My mother told herself that a Scot would take no notice of my hair. Archie was the highest ranking eligible Scotsman with an English estate nearby, and she knew his father."

"If Rose was anything like you," North said, "she made up her mind about Archie during that dinner. She waited to make certain that you didn't want him—I am assuming that a peskily self-sacrificing trait runs in your bloodline—and then she smiled back at him. Likely that was enough."

Diana frowned, trying to remember the dinner. She'd been so cross at her mother that she'd scarcely paid attention to the suitor Mrs. Belgrave had produced. "I can't even remember if Rose and Archibald spoke."

"I'll warrant they did. Archie wasn't a bad fellow; she chose well. They were just unlucky. He was a stubborn Scotsman. I'd warrant that if he had betrothed himself to you, and decided thereafter that he was in love with your sister, he would have jilted you and taken her to Gretna Green."

It was an interesting thought. Another river of relief, cool and forgiving, washed over her. Diana brushed a kiss on North's neck by way of thanks. It was strong and corded, nothing like the birdlike necks of courtiers. "Will you tell me why you sold out?"

"There's not much to tell." His voice rasped.

She snuggled against him and waited.

"The war with the colonies isn't just. We should give the country to its citizens. Our incompetence is another issue. We're fighting the war with an army made up primarily of German mercenaries, and we consistently underestimate the enemy."

She waited some more. Across the room, Godfrey snuffled and turned over in his bed.

"My regiment was last stationed at Stony Point. My commander thought that the Yankees wouldn't climb a rocky cliff to attack, and they did. We were overcome in fifteen minutes. The enemy could have shot my entire regiment, because the men were caught with weapons in hand."

Diana shuddered.

"Instead, they showed mercy. Our orders had been to shoot any enemy taken with a weapon. After that, I disbanded my regiment."

Three sentences that contained a world of pain.

No wonder he was in the army for so short a time. A man like North would not tolerate a lack of ethics or plain stupidity.

She said nothing, and neither did he. After a while, she glanced up and saw that his eyes were closed.

Maybe he was asleep.

Chapter Nineteen

June 1, 1780
The Duke of Lindow's ball

I n the time that Diana had lived in the nursery wing, the castle had been en fête twice, but this was the grandest occasion of all. The green salon, the drawing room, and the ballroom shone with candles and masses of lilacs in vases that stood as tall as a ten-year-old child. There were tubs of bluebells and tulips, and even a fairy grove of miniature willows on one of the galleries overlooking the ballroom.

Diana stayed in the nursery until the last minute, declining to join the family for a private supper beforehand—because she was not a member of the family, and she had to remember that.

Lavinia's and Lady Knowe's plan was to restore her reputation this evening. She would be a lady again, under the chaperonage of Lady Gray.

Her soul shriveled at the thought.

One of her cousin's evening dresses had been altered to fit her. It was silk, in a color that Lavinia, who knew everything about fashion, called the "stifled sigh." Diana would have called it pale lilac.

Its bodice was almost nonexistent, but its skirts, overlaid with cobweb-thin lace, swelled from her hips. The skirts were just the right length to flirt with the air and show off her ankles. Best of all were the slippers that Joan lent her: silk lutestring, with lace accents and a small rose on each toe. A cluster of tiny amethysts in the center of each rose provided the finishing touch.

Joan's shoes were frivolous and heeled. They made Diana's ankles look delicate and her calves deliciously slender. She loved them with a passion.

She wore no wig. No plumes, no basket of fruit, no sailing ship. None of the objects her mother had insisted she balance on her head in the name of fashion. Just a few silk roses tucked here and there, each adorned with glittering amethysts.

Before her debut, two maids had spent most of the afternoon making a fuss over her. With a white robe thrown over her dress, one maid applied color to her lashes, her lips, her cheeks, while the other worked on her wig.

Now Mabel came in to help her with her corset, and spent the time complaining because Godfrey had brought two toads into the nursery, only one of which could be found.

"Sooner or later, it will leap out of a pitcher of milk," Mabel said sourly. "Jump on my leg perhaps. Or hide in one of the beds!"

Diana murmured at the right moments while Mabel first powdered the back of her hair, then the front. She thought about lip rouge, before remembering that she didn't own any.

"You look lovely!" Mabel said, sounding faintly surprised.

When Diana stepped before the glass, a lady dressed in a gown the color of a sigh smiled back at her.

"He'll be sorry he gave you up," Mabel said with great satisfaction. "I'd better get back to Godfrey. A body never knows what mischief that boy will get up to next."

Diana should go to the ballroom now. One moment she felt like a crusader, ready to do anything to clear North's reputation and her own. The next, she was rigid with humiliation, her heart withering at the idea

of greeting people whom she had first met as the fiancée of a future duke.

All the neighboring gentry were coming, some from
as far away as Manchester and Rochdale. Both wings
of the castle were filled with guests spending the night,
those who would dance until dawn and climb into their
carriages after a leisurely breakfast.

She could not continue to hide in her bedchamber, if
only because Lavinia would drag her down to the ballroom. She had to descend the stairs and pretend that
she was and had been a guest of the duke and duchess,
and that rumors of her employment were an unfortunate, and wholly misguided, result of her deep love for
her orphaned nephew.

With a gulp, she forced herself from her chamber.
Lavinia was waiting for her at the bottom of the marble
steps leading to the entry, and spun her in a circle,
crowing about how exquisite she looked.

Diana had never felt beautiful, not compared to
Rose. Certainly not during the Season, when her towering wig and extravagant attire drew everyone's gaze.
In her cousin's shining eyes, she saw the truth. She was
beautiful when she was allowed to be herself.

Lavinia was wearing a white gown overlaid by translucent silk gauze, embroidered with scattered tea roses

in precisely the right shade to complement her lip color. She looked like one of those naughty French angels in paintings who lounged on clouds wearing nothing but a few wisps of carefully painted silk. Were those angels?

Diana's knowledge of art was as scant as her understanding of peafowl. Perhaps those ladies were actually courtesans.

"Look at this!" Lavinia whispered, pulling her in front of a mirror in the entrance hall. "We look so much alike!"

"Not really," Diana objected.

"We must owe our bosoms to some formidable ancestress. I hope she made as good use of them as we will tonight!" Lavinia's giggle threatened to split what little silk was holding her breasts in check. "Oh, my goodness," she exclaimed. "Where is your lip color?" She stuck a hand in her pocket and brought out a tin no larger than the tip of her thumb. "Here."

"My mother always made me wear pale shades," Diana said dubiously. "That red will make my mouth look even larger."

"Your mother is a fool, and if we agree and move on, we'll all be better off," her cousin said briskly. "There is nothing a man loves better than naughty lips on a chaste lady."

Diana obediently pulled off her right glove and

dabbed dark rose on her lips, trying not to think about how swollen it made them look. As if she'd been kissed for hours.

"There is no reception line tonight," Lavinia said, "which means we will walk straight into a thicket of gentlemen. Don't forget our plan: You must flirt with every man I introduce you to. I shall dance numerous times with North, making my mother happy and quelling any rumors about the two of you."

Diana nodded, conscious that she didn't want North to dance with Lavinia. Dog in the manger, she told herself, not for the first time. It was shameful not to want him, and not to want any other woman to have him either.

"You shall dance more than once with Lord Hon, the Baron of Houston." Lavinia said, inspecting Diana's lips. "You look utterly delectable."

"I shall dance with whom?"

"Lord Hon is a distant cousin of mine on my mother's side, so you won't have met him, most likely. His title hails from Scotland. Renfrewshire, I think. I'll introduce the two of you. All you have to do is say something clever and smile at him, and he'll be entranced. He's not a useless aristocrat, like the ones you disparage. He rebelled against his family and got a degree at Edinburgh, so he's a practicing physician. You might even address him as Doctor Hon if you prefer, high-brow that you are."

"I'm not a highbrow!" Diana protested. But she had to admit that Lord Hon sounded interesting.

"Later this evening, I shall deposit North directly at your feet. You will dance with him, but you must look utterly bored the entire time. Exchange a word or two at the most. You are like brother and sister to each other, or so the duke decreed over supper."

Taking a deep breath, Diana marshaled the strength she had inherited from her grandfather. Lady Knowe strolled to meet them as she and Lavinia entered the ballroom.

"Good evening, Miss Gray, Miss Belgrave," she said, dropping into a curtsy. Diana's silk skirts puddled on the floor as she curtsied, in a way that the stiff bro-cades her mother favored had not.

"Since I never go to London, I had forgotten how imaginative everyone is," Lady Knowe said. "A woman just told me on the best authority that Godfrey is the son of the Duke of Cumberland, brother of King George."

"My mother probably started the rumor," Lavinia said. "She has far too much imagination for her own good, and counts it a poor day when she doesn't circu-late at least one story that she created herself. Doesn't Diana look exquisite?"

Lady Knowe looked Diana up and down. "Fifty times better than you did during your first Season, if you'll forgive my bluntness, darling. I will assume this triumph should be laid at your feet, Lavinia?"

"Yes," Lavinia said with undisguised pride.

"My cousin is my fairy godmother," Diana said. "If Lavinia dressed the ton, a ballroom would be an altogether more beautiful place."

"I shall ask you for advice," Lady Knowe said to Lavinia. "And now, Lavinia darling, why don't you dance with a few of those men who are eyeing you so hungrily? His Grace has assigned me to instruct Diana about her role in tonight's drama."

Lavinia gave them a dimpled smile and swept into a curtsy. The moment she moved a step away, two gentlemen leapt to her side.

Peter appeared with a tray of champagne. Diana accepted a glass, but Lady Knowe waved him away. "I've a flask in my side panniers in case I want a drop of something. Did Lavinia explain the part you're to play, Diana?"

"She told me that I must dance once with North and look bored while I do it."

"You have a nervous disposition," Lady Knowe elaborated. "You didn't run away from North; that is an unfortunate rumor. Your nerves, compounded by grief at the death of your sister, led you to retire to your mother's country estate. You then returned to the castle to be nurtured as the future duchess."

"'Nurtured'?" Diana echoed. She couldn't help smiling.

"Because you adore your orphaned nephew, you spent a great deal of time in the nursery. However, when North returned from war, you and he came to an amicable parting of ways."

Diana turned the story over in her mind and nodded.

"The rumors about your *working* in the nursery arise from the fact that you sleep in that wing, as it is quieter. None of my friends was surprised to learn of the demise of your engagement; they had all noticed your tepid affection for your fiancé. Of course," she added, "that was one of the reasons North courted you in the first place."

"I see," murmured Diana, though she didn't see at all.

"North doesn't feel the title is truly his, thus he dislikes it when young ladies drape themselves about his person as if he were a ducal coat stand," Lady Knowe explained. "You never acted that way, because you didn't like him."

"That's not true!" Diana protested, before she thought.

Lady Knowe's mouth curved in a toothy smile that made Diana think of an old crocodile waiting in the sun. "Really? You jilted him in a surprising fashion for someone who cared tuppence for the man's feelings."

"I did not think before I acted," Diana said, adding pointedly, "no more than you did, when you hired me as a governess."

"You have me there." She shrugged. "Between us, we managed to ruin North's reputation, so let's put it right."

Over the lady's shoulder, Diana saw North standing with Parth Sterling, his boyhood friend and Lavinia's great nemesis. As she watched, North turned, caught sight of her, and instantly started in her direction.

His face was expressionless, his wig unobtrusive, and his coat and breeches an austere black. A coat that unremarkable shouldn't emphasize how broad his shoulders and chest were, but it did so nonetheless. Pristine white stockings flattered his powerful legs.

No patch. No powder, no rouge, no lip color. His bottom lip was a natural color that should be available for purchase.

North's expression grew speculative as he neared them, as if he had read her mind.

"Diana," Lady Knowe said with exasperation.

"Forgive me," Diana said, pivoting back to her.

Lady Knowe groaned. "You!" she said to her nephew.

North bowed and kissed her hand. "Yes, my best of aunts?"

"I'm your only aunt," she pointed out.

"Which allows you to shine without interference."

She rapped him on the shoulder. "Pish! I have just been reminding Miss Belgrave of her nervous complaint, and the rest cure she took before you left for the colonies."

"I'd like to know more of Miss Belgrave's nervous complaint," North said, a rumble of amusement running through his voice. "Did it arise as a reaction to an aggressive peacock? Prism has just informed me that Fitzy has a new lease on life, thanks to a spirited fight that has vanquished young Floyd from the terrace."

"You are supposed to appear sympathetic to Miss Belgrave's afflictions," Lady Knowe said, ignoring this frivolity, "but also uninterested. No more staring at her as if she were a gazelle and you a hungry lion."

North looked only at Diana. "Nervous complaints cause a racing heartbeat. I know any number of ways to soothe that symptom."

He smelled wonderful. Clean male, she thought, a little dreamily . . . so much better than turnip mash or dirty nappies.

Lady Knowe huffed and turned to leave. "Neither of you is good at following directions; I don't know how my brother overlooked that signal fact. If you don't fall in line, you'll ruin the plan."

North didn't take his eyes from Diana's face. "I can demonstrate it to you."

Diana raised an eyebrow. "Your remedy for a racing heart? I would want to sample more than one remedy."

His smile was a caress, as if he brushed her with warm silk. "I volunteer to demonstrate them all." He picked up her hand and kissed it.

"I shall gather evidence from more than one provider," she said sweetly, pulling away.

Blue eyes darkened like a storm over the ocean.

"Now," she said, enjoying herself, "my mandate tonight is to flirt with every male in the room except for you. *You* bore me."

"You are recovering from a nervous complaint," North said, his jaw tightening. "If you flirt with many men, you will not look like a recovering patient."

"You mustn't look at me in such a heated fashion," she whispered. "We are no longer betrothed."

"I never looked at you this way when we were betrothed," he said.

It was true enough. If he *had* looked at her that way, she might not have run away.

The truth must have shown in her eyes, because he said, "Damn it, I played it all wrong, didn't I?"

His brows were slashing, black, arrogant.

Rather irresistible, she decided.

North's attention made her feel light-headed, warm-cheeked, slightly dizzy . . . as if she were suffering a true nervous complaint that could be cured only by intimacies.

"Darling," Lavinia cried, inserting herself between them and deliberately turning her back to North. "I must introduce you to Lord Hon! I am convinced that you will greatly enjoy each other's company."

Diana blinked at the tall man bowing in front of her. He had kind eyes and an intelligent forehead. He was a doctor.

He wasn't a duke.

She sank into a curtsy.

Chapter Twenty

Dancing with Lavinia was no hardship, North admitted to himself; she was spirited, sardonic, and a wonderful dancer. During their third dance, she confessed that her mother thought he would ask for her hand at any moment, and then went into peals of laughter at his expression.

North watched surreptitiously as Diana danced with every gentleman in the room, his father twice, and the baron three times. He didn't like that, especially when the baron took her in to supper.

Prism had set up a magnificent feast in the antechamber to the great hall, where a number of small tables had been set about, sufficient to accommodate every hungry guest. North collected a plate of food for Lavinia and then escorted her to a table where Parth and his sister Betsy sat.

He would have thought twice about steering Lavinia in that direction if he'd realized that Parth would greet her with "My dear Lady Disdain! Are you yet living?"

Without answering that Shakespearean salvo, Lavinia turned to North and served up such a performance of sweetly intimate conversation that anyone watching would have assumed they were already betrothed.

Parth sat opposite, scowling. Betsy rolled her eyes. North put in a word now and then, while watching Diana out of the corner of his eye and trying to avoid the effusive smiles of Lady Gray, who was seated not far away.

"Who's that baron who took Diana to supper?" North asked Lavinia, during a lull in her gushing flirtation. He suspected her performance was really directed at Parth, rather than the guests seated around them.

"The Baron of Houston? He has a degree in medicine from Edinburgh. I believe he holds some other titles as well." She turned to Parth. "How are the children who used to be employed in that lace factory of yours?"

Her face and voice were as cordial as ever.

"The children are happily living in the country," Parth said. Then he added, with an edge, "You might even say that *you* are supporting them, Miss Gray.

Lace factories depend on those who indulge their every desire, six or seven bonnets in a single afternoon."

Parth didn't have the smoothest manners in the world, but that was surprisingly impolite.

Lavinia smiled, her face showing nothing but kindness. She leaned forward and cooed, "Alas, you assume that I would wear Sterling lace. Even for the charitable reasons you mention . . ." She shook her head sadly. "No."

North stood up. "I must beg you to excuse me. I have just remembered something important."

"I agree with you," Lavinia said.

North wasn't sure what to make of her mischievous smile. He kissed the ladies' hands and nodded at Parth. Then he made his way over to Diana's table and leaned down to murmur in her ear.

She looked up, frowning slightly. "They'll be in bed," she whispered back.

"We never slept in the nursery during a ball. You can hear the music."

The others at the table were looking at them curiously. "Miss Belgrave is a devoted aunt," North said smoothly. "My butler tells me that her little nephew is awake and asking for her. I'm sure you can understand that the noise echoes around the castle."

They nodded at her approvingly, except for the baron, whose frown conveyed disapproval. The man clearly thought that there was something fishy about North's interruption.

There was.

Lady Knowe's plan had worked, and Diana's reputation had been successfully restored. Accordingly, Lavinia and her mother would whisk Diana away, perhaps as early as the following day.

Lavinia was fundamentally honest, and when a reason to pretend that North was courting her no longer existed, she would break the news to her mother, and take Diana to London or to Lady Gray's country estate.

North walked away from Diana without a backward look, playing the role of a mere friend. He returned to the antechamber and Prism's feast. Recruiting Peter with a tray, he made an effort to collect a bite or two of everything: frangipane tarts that looked like tiny sunbursts; grapes frosted with sugar that sparkled in the candlelight; meringue of preserved apples, cunningly presented in tiny glass bowls; chocolate creams; and even violet creams too, because although he loathed them, they were so pretty.

He added glasses of lemonade to the tray, along with nougat almond cake, and a bowl of vanilla blancmange, because it had a sensual wobble that reminded him of

Diana's breasts. Not a square inch remained on the tray to add another thing.

Peter didn't blink an eye when instructed to carry the tray to the nursery. North lingered long enough to seize a bottle of champagne and a pair of goblets, and then took the back stairway to the nursery in order to avoid meeting even a single guest.

When he reached the nursery bedchamber, he found Artie and Godfrey in a nest of blankets before the fireplace. Godfrey was hovering breathlessly over the little tarts, and Artie's eyes were fixed on the sparkling grapes. Diana was seated on a low stool at their side, silk skirts spreading around her like a field covered in violets. Peter had come and gone, and there was no sign of Mabel.

"Champagne for Miss Belgrave, who is once again welcome in polite society," North said, handing her a glass.

"Thank you, Lord Roland," Diana said.

He lowered himself to the floor beside them. For a few minutes there was no sound other than squeals of excitement from Artie. North put the blancmange to the side, but they demolished everything else.

"The baby finches will be born t'morrow," Artie told North.

"You say that every day," Diana said. "It takes time to hatch baby birds, Artie."

"It's true, though." The little girl licked her fingers and ate the last grape.

Diana was unable to stop smiling, for all the world as if she'd drunk an entire bottle of champagne. "This picnic was a splendid idea," she said to North, wishing she could kiss him.

He gave her a heavy-lidded look that suggested he wanted to do more than kiss. Perhaps he had decided to give her one last night.

Artie lay back, her tummy distinctly rounded. "I want to go to balls every night," she said sleepily. She reached over and grabbed Godfrey's hand. "I'll dance with you, Free. We'll go round and round, then we'll eat everything."

Her eyes closed, and she missed Godfrey's scowl. Apparently he didn't see himself as a dancer. North came to his feet and scooped Artie into his arms, put her in bed, and drew the curtains.

"Where's Mabel?"

"Not here," Diana said. "The upper servants are entertaining the ladies' maids and valets staying overnight."

"I'm sure she'll do a good job," North said wryly. He tucked Godfrey into bed, then stooped and caught up the white pudding he had set aside. He held out his hand. "Your chamber, I think." He pulled her into the corridor. "One last time."

"It's dangerous," she muttered, meaning it all ways.

"If you conceive a child, we marry."

"Are you hoping it will happen that way?" Diana asked.

"No," he said. "But I would like one last memory. Unless you disagree?"

Diana shook her head. "I too would like that," she whispered.

He undressed her as tenderly as any devoted lady's maid and laid her on the bed. Being completely naked when a man in formal attire stood by was shiveringly erotic.

"Diana." North's voice made her toes curl. It was deep and dark and full of promises.

"Yes?" Diana rolled onto her stomach and dropped her head over the side of the bed.

"What are you doing?"

"Pulling the pins from my hair," she answered. "If I shake my head like this, I can get rid of most of the powder."

She wriggled a few more times, making sure to tilt her arse into the air. Then she edged fully back onto the bed, rolled over, and raised her hands to give her hair a final shake. A bosom as generous as hers was at its best when her arms were over her head.

"Bloody hell," North grated, staring down at her. "Every time I have the upper hand, you find a way to counter me, don't you?"

She smiled and drew her fingers through her hair again, letting it fall around her on the pillow.

"You are a little devil," North said hoarsely, coming down on one knee. "I need to tame you."

Diana laughed aloud at that one.

Then he explained how sweet and cold the pudding was, and how it reminded him of her breasts, and she fell silent, caught in an erotic haze. She enjoyed every moment as North painted her breasts with delicious blancmange and then licked it off, pretending to ignore her gasps and wriggles.

"Oh, look at these nipples," he crooned. "So red, so abused. We'd better cool them down again." So he did. Diana could scarcely remember her own name by then. She kept trying to pull him down to the bed, but he evaded her.

She pleaded and begged, but he merely held up the bowl and looked her over. "I wonder where else you might enjoy a cooling sensation?"

Diana promptly allowed her legs to fall apart.

"Are you asking for something, Miss Belgrave?"

"Hell's bells, North," she cried, losing all control, "give *me* that bowl, won't you?"

"All you had to do was ask."

She kept her eyes on his face, slid her finger through the pudding, and applied it to the hottest part of her body. It felt so good that she let out an involuntary moan.

North responded with a good old-fashioned Anglo-Saxon oath. He put a knee on the bed, but she held up her hand.

"Remove your clothing, if you please."

She swirled her finger while she watched the most beautiful man at the ball disrobe. She pressed down as his breeches flew to the ground. A thin line of hair bisected his muscled stomach, leading to his tool.

Cock, he called it.

He pulled her legs apart, and replaced her finger with his tongue.

And later, his tongue with something else.

"I love pudding," she murmured in the middle of the night, when the castle had quieted and the musicians were gone.

"I love you," he said, so softly she almost didn't hear the words.

Chapter Twenty-one

Nまっorth woke the next morning curled around a sleeping Diana. He got out of bed, taking care not to wake her, and hauled on his breeches, thinking about all the vows he'd made to himself that he had broken. Making love again hadn't changed anything as far as those vows were concerned.

Diana hadn't enjoyed herself during the ball, for all she danced with every man available. Even from afar, he could tell. Lady Gray wouldn't pay for her niece to have her own establishment; why would she?

But *he* would. In fact, it was the only thing he would accept. Diana needed a house of her own. He could send that young footman, Peter, along with her, because he trusted Peter and she would need help. Perhaps Frederick too. Not Mabel.

Maybe—

No.

He would give her a house and an annual allowance, and then he would leave for Rome, and not visit her until he was married. Perhaps after he had children.

Diana's eyes opened then and she smiled at him. He couldn't bring himself to smile in reply because, damn it, there were limits to a man's endurance. A rumpled Diana, with swollen lips, skin reddened by his stubble, and sleepy pleasure in her eyes?

"We must discuss your future," he said, sitting down on the edge of the bed.

She blinked, and pulled herself upright, tugging at the sheet to cover herself with. It didn't quite reach her breasts, so he pulled it free.

"I don't believe you'll enjoy living with Lady Gray," he said, pushing away the idea that he might have seen her breasts for the last time.

"Artie will be awake, if she isn't already," Diana said, avoiding the topic. "She sometimes wakes at dawn."

"She is no longer your responsibility," North stated. "Your reputation is restored, and ergo, so is mine. Being seen caring for Artie, when there are so many guests in the castle, would be to undo those repairs."

Diana nodded.

"You risk confirming the rumors that I trapped you into servitude," he added.

"I understand."

"You must behave like any other guest in the castle. That means archery this afternoon, dinner and card games tonight. Whatever Ophelia has planned."

"I understand," she said again. Her voice was dull, and everything in North rebelled. But he couldn't seduce her again; last night shouldn't have happened.

Diana climbed out of bed, went to the basin, and poured water from the pitcher. North silently watched her wash herself, a rough cloth passing over all the places he'd licked and kissed and caressed the night before.

But for quiet splashes when Diana rinsed the cloth, the room was silent.

She put on a chemise and stays, and then pulled a yellow morning dress over her head. It wasn't saffron-yellow, but softer, the color of cowslips in springtime.

Still, he sat silently, watching with hungry eyes as he memorized every soft curve. The way she lifted her silky hair from the neck of her chemise. The way she drew the strings of her stays together, and how it supported her breasts. The way her gown's bodice complemented the swell of her breasts.

Only when she began brushing the last of the powder from her hair did he find words and return to the subject he'd raised earlier. "You won't be happy living with Lady Gray."

"I may marry in the near future." Her tone was indifferent. She had once told him that she would marry only for love. He choked back a response.

"If I am not enjoying life with Lady Gray," she said, looking into the glass but not meeting his eyes there, "I shall leave, but I would never take money from you, North, if that's what you are intending to offer."

The firm, set lines of her face made him want to howl as no gentleman should. "You are my responsibility."

"No, I am not."

"I want to buy a house in the country for you. I'll send Peter with you, to ensure your safety."

"You have no responsibility for myself or Godfrey," she said, steadily brushing her hair, as if the conversation was trivial.

"If I had never asked for your hand, would you be in this situation?"

"What is the point of that sort of thinking?" she asked. "If I hadn't refused Archibald, would Rose be alive? My mother thinks so." Her voice grew tight.

"Your mother is deranged."

"If you hadn't called up a regiment, would those boys you told me about be alive?"

"Perhaps not," North said.

"I was not for sale when my mother tried to sell me to a Scotsman, and I am not on the market now," she said. "You have absolutely no responsibility for me whatsoever."

North stood up and went to the window, his back turned. "Is anything to be gained from splitting hairs?" he said, wheeling around. "I saw you; I lusted after you; I *bought* you with a combination of my rank and wealth. Your mother was angry when you spoiled the transaction."

Diana's self-respect strangled any response she could have made in her own defense. She wasn't for sale, but the wax doll her mother had created? *That* Diana had been for sale. North had bought her. He was right.

To hide the tears that had sprung to her eyes, she bent over and pulled on her stockings. She used to think North was an unbending poker of a man. Now she knew he was all that on the surface, and a protective, primitive warrior underneath.

"This is all the fault of my impulsiveness, and has nothing to do with you," she said, once she had her emotions under control and her stockings in place. "I ran away from you, thinking only to save Godfrey. We both know it was a foolish decision—as was allowing Lady Knowe to believe Godfrey was yours."

She moved toward the door. "I must go down to breakfast."

"Three hundred a year? And a house, or even just a cottage?"

She froze, a hand on the latch. Three hundred pounds? Once upon a time, she wouldn't have known what that meant. That was when she was an heiress, able to buy any frivolous pair of shoes that took her fancy.

Now she knew differently. With three hundred pounds and a cottage, she could live comfortably with Godfrey. The blaze of longing that accompanied the thought was the final straw in her humiliation.

When she turned around, North's face was blurred from the tears that came with rage, or at least that's what she told herself. Somehow she had been stumbling along, hanging on to her self-respect. Telling herself that she had had no choice when she agreed to be a governess.

Would he pay visits to the house he was paying for? Probably not, because he was a decent man. If he did, they would go to bed together, because she couldn't be in the same room without thinking of it.

Even now, erotic longing clawed at her. She wanted him. She wanted to fall backward on the bed and pull up her gown and chemise, let her legs fall open. She wanted him to pounce on her with his thick, hot length and . . . and service her.

A cottage in the country, and North walking in the back door, that glint in his eyes?

Hell's bells. Yes.

No.

The three hundred pounds would come at a terrible price, for herself and Godfrey. She took her rage and let it fill all the fearful, aching, lonely spaces in her heart that seemed to have imprinted themselves with North's image.

"I admit that I took this position under false pretenses. I gave no thought to how it would affect your reputation. But I have worked hard for my wage. No one has ever given me money."

He moved toward her as she blinked away the tears. "We're friends, Diana. *Friends*. Why can't I help you?"

"No."

"What else can you—" He sounded exasperated.

"I am not that woman," she snapped, trying to stop him from saying whatever he had in mind.

A look of horror crossed his face. "I would never ask you to be my mistress."

His recoil shouldn't have felt like an insult. In fact, if she had been capable of it, she would have been amused by the evident distaste on his face.

"I know that," she answered. "But nothing that has happened between us requires you to be responsible for me."

"My rank made it impossible for you to refuse my offer of marriage," he said, obstinate as a mule.

Diana almost laughed. "If my mother hadn't been blackmailing me, you would have been refused so quickly that your wig would have spun around." Then she flinched. Would she never learn to hold her tongue and not say the first thing that came to mind?

"I see," he said stiffly, the future Duke of Lindow very much in evidence. "Is that why you gave such little weight to your promise to wed me?"

"I would have kept my promise, under ordinary circumstances." By which she meant, if she'd wanted to marry him.

If she hadn't been forced by her mother.

If she'd loved him.

His eyes, furiously angry now, were locked on hers. "What if we had married? Would you have played me false because you didn't really mean your vows, owing to these 'out of the ordinary circumstances'?"

"No!"

A harsh sound came from his throat. "I don't believe you. You took the easiest road, allowing people to believe what they wished, and the devil with the consequences. It was easier for you to accept my hand than not, so you did so, telling yourself your promise wasn't important, because of 'circumstances.' When I no longer served your purpose, you left without farewell or explanation."

"I'm sorry," she whispered.

"It was easier for you to tell my aunt that your nephew was mine, rather than tell the truth. There are those who would say that you sacrificed my reputation as a man and a gentleman in order to allow you and the child to live in comfort in my family's home."

"You think—" she cried, and stopped. She had done all those things, though they hadn't been easy. None of it had been comfortable. "I meant to marry you, and I would have been faithful," she said, her voice shaking.

His eyes met hers, level. They weren't contemptuous or bitter. He had assessed her—and she had been found lacking.

If anything, he looked sad.

Nausea washed over her.

"It's not really your fault," he said, as if he could hear her thoughts.

She couldn't find words. North pulled a handkerchief from somewhere and blotted a tear from her cheek. "I apologize," he said, sounding tired. "My emotions are overwrought. My lack of insight is no excuse for be-having like an ass."

"It didn't cross my mind to leave you a letter, but I shall always regret my lapse."

In another man, that might have been a recoil. His eyes turned a shade darker.

"All my attention was on Godfrey," she added des-perately, her stomach twisting. No matter what she said, she seemed to be making it worse and worse. She *hated* that he was making her feel not just humiliated and apologetic, but crushed. And yet she felt she de-served every word he said.

"Whereas all my attention was on *you*," North said, between clenched teeth. Then, abruptly, as if he couldn't stop himself, he stepped forward and drew her into his arms. His kiss was violent and possessive. Their tongues warred, making her body ache so that she writhed against him.

Her back thumped against the door and the wood creaked again as he thrust his hips against her. Again and again, until she was aching for him to tear open his breeches and thrust inside, holding her so tightly that she wouldn't have to make a decision and could simply surrender to the moment. To the pleasure.

But he stopped the kiss as abruptly as he had begun it.

Diana fell back against the door, one hand instinctively coming to her lips. They felt hot and swollen. North stared back at her, his face once again unreadable.

"I will support you and the boy, Diana," he stated, his voice harsh. "If you need anything, *anything*, you will write to me, and no one but me."

Her breath was so lost somewhere in her ribs that she couldn't shriek at him, which was just as well. The children were not far away.

"I will never again treat you as any less than the lady you are." He sounded as if he was making a promise to himself.

North might promise to treat her as a lady, but his promise was as thin as hers to marry him. He had kissed her as if he couldn't control himself. The night before, in a fog of champagne and desire, she had grabbed the pudding, and had done—other things.

Unladylike things.

He opened the door and strode down the corridor without a backward glance.

If he were to hide her away in a cottage, it would be found out. He was dreaming if he thought a sordid fact like that would remain a secret for long.

Even worse, she suspected they would be unable to resist each other. She'd be damned if she let him turn her into a notoriously fallen woman—again.

The fact she had loved every sinful moment they'd spent together?

Not the point. Women loved all sorts of things that were bad for them. She smoothed her skirt with trembling fingers.

Rose would have wanted Diana to raise Godfrey with love, even if love came with uncertainty and dirt. Diana had no particular fondness for hard work, but it was tolerable.

Intolerable would be if she—if North kissed her like that again, after she had taken money from him.

She had to get out. Now.

発

Chapter Twenty-two

The next day

"I don't wish to live with you and Lady Gray," Diana told Lavinia. Her cousin's face fell. "I am so grateful that my reputation is restored. I truly am. But I don't want to marry the Baron of Houston, nor dance with him again. I'm not made for this life."

"Because you are in love with North?"

Diana was folding Godfrey's shirts and putting them in a valise. "No." She looked up. "Did you enjoy the ball?"

Lavinia scowled. "Parth Sterling was rude to me."

"Why does that always happen?" Diana asked. "He is such a gentleman to me, and I mean that in the best of ways."

"He saves his true self for me," Lavinia said, then shook her head. "Enough of him. If you don't live with us, Diana, where will you go? Obviously, I will support you and Godfrey. No more governessing."

"I don't mind work," Diana said.

"I mind you doing it," Lavinia retorted. "I don't ever want to see you in a dress like that black rag again."

"I thought I might live in Manchester," Diana said, avoiding the subject of work. "It's not terribly far away. I can bring Godfrey to pay visits to Artie."

"But not when North is in residence," Lavinia said shrewdly.

"It wouldn't be good for either of us."

Lavinia pressed her lips together, thinking it over. "I shall accompany you to Manchester," she said, finally. "I must know that you and Godfrey are safely housed before Mother and I return to London."

"Doesn't your mother need you?" Lady Gray had declined in the last two years. She rarely left the sofa, and spent most of her time pressing cool cloths to her forehead and demanding special broths and preparations.

Lavinia shrugged. "I shall buy her a new bonnet, and she will be satisfied."

"We could tell everyone that we are going to Manchester to visit the shops," Diana said, inspired. "Godfrey can remain in the nursery with Artie."

"Yes!" Lavinia clapped her hands. "We will find you a charming house. Whatever you do, you mustn't run away the way you did last time."

Diana replaced Godfrey's shirts in the wardrobe. She had been dreading telling the duke and duchess, let alone North and Lady Knowe, about her decision to move to Manchester.

It would be much easier if she had already found a house. Perhaps she could work for the milliner Lavinia loved so much. She didn't want to be dependent on anyone.

"We want to come with you," Artie protested, when Diana told them she was leaving for a couple of days. "Mama could come too."

The three of them had never been separated since the moment Diana entered the nursery. "I'll be back very soon," she promised.

"The baby birds might be born while you're gone!" Artie cried.

In the end they gave her tight hugs and covered her face with kisses. By contrast, North betrayed no emotion when Diana informed him that she and Lavinia were going to Manchester for a couple of days.

Prism assigned Hickett, one of the senior grooms, to take them to Manchester. Hickett was a stout man with a wrinkled face whose habitual expression resembled Artie's when she needed a nap.

She and Lavinia climbed into His Grace's solid, bulbous traveling coach with the ducal crest on the door. It was terribly generous of him to allow them to use it.

"Knock if you need the coach stopped," Hickett said, securing their valises in the boot. "We should reach Manchester in two hours if we aren't delayed. We'll stay at the Royal George."

Lavinia plopped down on a seat, looking unusually vexed, given that she had a generally sunny disposition. The moment Hickett closed the door, she burst out, "Sometimes I cannot *bear* my mother!"

"I can understand," Diana said, seeing no reason to prevaricate. In her opinion, Lady Gray was intolerably selfish.

"She had a tantrum that would have been shameful on Artie's part. Weeping, and carrying on about how selfish I am, merely because I am leaving her for two nights. What will she do when I marry?"

"I suspect she'll find a companion, and badger *her* instead," Diana said.

"That's why you won't stay with us," Lavinia gasped, her eyes rounding. "Oh, Diana, you're right to move to

Manchester. She's my mother, so I have no choice, but you would be made miserable."

"Truthfully, I do not believe your mother and I could live harmoniously together," Diana admitted. "I think I am unfitted to be Lady Gray's companion."

"I wouldn't have told you this, Diana, but she is simply *beastly* about Godfrey. As if it's his fault that his parents weren't married!"

Diana was unsurprised, since Lady Gray emitted an audible moan if anyone mentioned Godfrey's name in her presence.

"She refused to give me any money to spend in Manchester," Lavinia spat, her hands curling into fists. "I swear I am going to marry the first man who asks me."

"Perhaps we should turn back," Diana said, her brow furrowed. "I'm not sure I have enough to pay for the Royal George."

"The duke's coachman will cover everything. She merely did it to be unpleasant. Because she knows I love that milliner, and she wants to make me unhappy. She screams at me, and then she accuses me of giving her a nervous spasm, takes her soothing drops, and doesn't wake up for a whole day, sometimes."

Diana moved across to sit beside Lavinia and took her hand. "Obviously, you could marry within a month of returning to London if you wish. Your suitors are legion."

"My suitors have probably married by now," Lavinia said morosely. Then she shook herself. "Do forgive me. I am weary of the way my mother treats me. I am an heiress, after all, yet she won't give me any pin money."

"You can always live with me in Manchester," Diana said, kissing her cheek.

Lavinia's cheerful smile broke out again. "I made up my mind not to be thwarted by her. Look at this!" She reached into her knotting bag and drew out a long strand of pearls.

"They're lovely," Diana said, somewhat puzzled.

"I intend to sell them," Lavinia announced. "I know how it's done, because one of my friends is always selling her pearls when her allowance runs low, and buying the string back the next month. I'll take them to a jeweler, an excellent one, of course, so he doesn't cheat me."

"Are you sure that's a good idea?" Diana asked. "You won't be able to buy them back next month; you'll be in London, not Manchester."

"I've never liked these pearls. My aunt Mildred gave me the string with a withering remark about how it would draw attention to my only asset."

"That was unkind, and equally untrue."

"I shall happily turn her gift into money. We will have to pay the house agent, after all. We can't count on His Grace's coachman for that!"

Diana had a guilty feeling that the duke oughtn't to pay for their stay in the hotel, but she couldn't deny that she felt better with every turn of the coach wheels taking her farther from North, and the castle.

"Perhaps we should ask Hickett to find us a less costly hotel than the Royal George," Lavinia said a while later, showing that she didn't feel entirely comfortable about relying on His Grace's generosity either.

"I agree," Diana said, with relief. "After all, neither of us is a true guest of the duke. I came to the castle under false pretenses, and you arrived in search of me."

"My mother told me to instruct His Grace's coachman to pay for everything, including meals and gratuities for our chambermaid," Lavinia said. "I don't know if you've noticed this, but neither of our mothers is precisely ethical."

"A depressing inheritance," Diana agreed. "My mother will never forgive me for taking employment as a governess."

"It would have served her right if you'd become a duchess, and never acknowledged her thereafter," Lavinia muttered.

Hickett was too experienced a servant to betray any surprise when they explained their new plans. His sister and her husband owned an inn, he told them, and he promised to get them a clean, safe room there. Moreover, he voiced no objection to taking Miss Gray to visit one of the best jewelers in the city.

To the dismay of the grooms at the Royal George—a magnificent establishment that would probably cost the equivalent of one of Lavinia's pearls for a single night—the Duke of Lindow's carriage trundled off to a considerably humbler establishment, the Beetle & Cheese.

Hickett's sister, a Mrs. Barley, set them up in a cunning little room tucked under the eaves, and Lavinia declared herself perfectly delighted. "Just look how adorable this sloping ceiling is," she cried, bouncing on the bed. "I wish Parth could see me now. He wouldn't think I am such an extravagant person, would he?"

Diana wasn't sure what Parth had to do with it, but Lavinia took herself off with Hickett, refusing to permit Diana to accompany her to the jeweler's. "They'll know from your face that you would accept a low price."

Having nothing to do until Lavinia's return, Diana ventured downstairs, where she had a fascinating conversation with Mrs. Barley. "The problem is keeping barmaids," the woman lamented. "They run off with men, they go home to their mothers . . . Tonight is the same story. I have no one to stand behind the bar and draw pints."

"How hard can it be?" Diana asked. "I should think you'd have no trouble filling the position."

"It's *work*," Mrs. Barley explained. "In my opinion, there's many a lazy piece that would rather lie in, even though a good barmaid can make over four shillings a night!"

Diana gaped at that information. "More than any governess is paid."

"That's for an excellent barmaid," Mrs. Barley said. "One as tempts the men into giving her tips, if you see what I mean."

They parted on the best of terms, and Diana resolved that once she moved to Manchester, she would definitely stop by the Beetle & Cheese occasionally to say hello to Mrs. Barley.

Not merely because she might learn all the gossip from the castle either.

Back in their little room, she took a nap and dreamed of North. She jumped out of her skin when her cousin threw open the door to their room. "They are counterfeit!" Lavinia cried.

Diana sat up, blinking. "What?"

"My pearls!" Lavinia shut the door behind her.

"They aren't worth more than a few pence. What's more, my earrings . . . do you see these earrings?"

She sat down beside Diana. "Rubies?" Diana ventured.

"Red paste that isn't worth tuppence," Lavinia stated. "My father gave me these on my fifteenth birthday. I thought the other day that they weren't sparkling the way they used to."

"Oh, no," Diana cried, slapping her hand over her mouth.

"That's right," Lavinia said grimly. "My rubies have been stolen, as have the pearls. The jeweler sees it all the time. A thief finds work as an upstairs maid, and over a few months, the woman takes away one piece of jewelry and then another to be copied. Do you know how often my mother dismisses the domestic help?"

Diana shook her head.

"I can think of thirty or forty suspects, on both sides of the Channel. My jewelry is gone, and I'm sure that my mother's is lost as well. Gone for good."

"Oh, Lavinia, I'm so sorry!" Diana cried.

After a moment, Lavinia's brow cleared. "I've never loved bedecking myself in jewels anyway. A woman should *be* the jewel, don't you think?"

Diana smiled at her. "I know many women who would be in hysterics."

"My mother has all the talent for hysterics in my family," Lavinia said dryly. "The problem is that we haven't money to give to a house agent. Hickett can pay for our room and board, of course. My mother will repay him."

"Your mother will be terribly upset about your jewelry," Diana said, imagining the scene.

"She's already peculiar about money," Lavinia said, nodding. "This will give her another nervous turn."

"I have an idea!"

"No," Lavinia said, a moment later. "Are you cracked, Diana? Completely deranged? You are a *lady.*"

"Not tonight," Diana said, grinning. "Tonight I shall be a barmaid. I shall *earn* the price of our room!"

Lavinia shook her head. "I had no idea how impulsive you really are."

"It's a bit mad," Diana conceded. "But how hard can it be? A barmaid merely stands behind the bar all night long."

"I think there's more to it than that," Lavinia said. "What if someone we know sees you, Diana?"

"This is the Beetle & Cheese, Lavinia!" Diana said. "Who would see me? Think about it."

"You can't do it alone. I'll join you behind the bar."

"*No,*" Diana said. "Absolutely not. You would be

ruined, and you are a member of polite society. I can try something as mad as this because I don't care."

Lavinia chewed on her lower lip. "It's improper."

"You wanted to be ethical," Diana said encouragingly. "Besides, Lavinia, I could always walk out if I feel uncomfortable."

She found herself laughing at Lavinia's incredulous look. "You *really* are not a lady," her cousin exclaimed. "You're excited at the idea, aren't you?"

Diana nodded.

"Why? That's what I don't understand. No lady would wish to be a barmaid!"

"I don't want to be a barmaid. I'm just curious to see what it's like."

"Mad," Lavinia said with conviction. "Utterly deranged."

"You mustn't be seen in the tavern," Diana told her.

"It will not affect my reputation." Lavinia looked supremely confident. "I am perfectly capable of stopping by a public room for a glass of lemonade, properly escorted by the duke's servants, of course."

"Not at night," Diana said.

Lavinia gave in. "Well, either Hickett or a groom has to stay with you in the room, then."

"Very well," Diana said. "That's reasonable. I'll ask

Hickett to put a groom in the corner where he can keep an eye on me."

Lavinia clapped her hands and her eyes lit up. "What do you think a barmaid wears, Diana? I don't believe I've ever seen such a costume."

Chapter Twenty-three

N orth spent the day going over the estate books his aunt had been keeping while he was gone. They confirmed what she had told him: that income had increased in two of the six ducal estates. At the sound of an excited cacophony of voices in the entry—the greater part of his family, by the sound of it—he remained bent over the ledgers.

He didn't look up until the door to the library opened.

His father stood there. "North."

North came to his feet. "Father?"

"Hickett has returned from Manchester."

North's fingers curled hard around the edge of the desk. "By himself? He left Diana there?"

"Hickett reports that she has decided to play barmaid for the night," his father said wryly. "He failed to persuade her that it was a poor idea, so he returned to the castle." Then he added, as if to himself, "If my sister couldn't change Diana's mind about being a governess, poor Hickett was bound to fail."

A *barmaid*? North was speechless.

"Diana is no duchess, but she may be one of the most intrepid women I've had the pleasure to meet," his father said, a smile playing around his lips. "Oh, and Godfrey's great-uncle has just arrived. That would be the Laird of Fennis."

North strode into the entryway. It was full of Wildes, talking at once. His eyes went to Godfrey, who was crying. Artie was holding his hand, and the duchess was trying to soothe him.

The moment he saw North, Godfrey dropped Artie's hand and ran to him. North scooped him up. "We'll go to her," he said, as the little boy buried his face in North's neck, his body shuddering with sobs.

North raised his voice. "Prism, I need a carriage. A fast carriage."

"Hickett has the small traveling coach ready for you, my lord," Prism said.

"Please have my bag put in the carriage, along with Godfrey's necessities."

His father joined them, accompanied by a middle-aged man with hair like a rusty gate, liberally sprinkled with white. "May I introduce my son, Lord Roland," His Grace said. From the tone in his voice, he was highly amused. "North, this is Diarmid Ewing, the Laird of Fennis—Archibald Ewing's uncle and thus Godfrey's great-uncle."

North nodded. "Please forgive me for not bowing, my lord." Godfrey's narrow shoulders stilled under North's comforting hand but he kept his face hidden.

"I traveled from the Highlands in hopes of gaining some acquaintance with my great-nephew," the laird rumbled in a strong Scottish accent.

"We will return tomorrow evening," North said. "Godfrey will be happy to spend time with you then." He ignored the way Godfrey shook his head.

"I have urgent business in London," the laird said, his face settling into disappointed lines.

Godfrey clung harder to North.

Hickett broke in. "I couldn't convince Miss Belgrave, my lord." His forehead was sweaty. "My sister's just the same, and neither of them would listen. I left a groom in the public room, but if we leave at once, we'll arrive within an hour of the pub's opening."

"Believe me, I understand," North said. "I don't blame you."

"We can change horses at the King's Elbow, in Headington," the coachman said anxiously.

"I'm coming," North said, with a nod.

From the other side of the entry, Lady Knowe cried, "Put on your pelisse, Ophelia! We have to arrive in time to see Diana draw a pint! There's a sight not many will see in their lifetimes." She began shooing everyone out the front door into the courtyard.

It seemed that the whole lot of them were traveling to Manchester with North and Godfrey.

"May I suggest that you accompany us to Manchester?" his father asked the laird. "The Wilde family intends to join Godfrey's aunt, Miss Belgrave, there."

The laird looked aghast. "I was led to understand that Miss Belgrave was forced to work in a nursery to support my great-nephew. Are you saying that she has become a *barmaid?*"

North strode out the door, leaving his father to make explanations.

The family was sorting itself into two large carriages. Leonidas was bellowing with laughter and threatening to open a tavern of his own, to be operated by the family. Artie was refusing to leave because the baby finches still had not made an appearance. Aunt Knowe was directing a groom to ride ahead and alert the Royal George that the Wildes would be arriving in two or three hours, and would require an entire floor. Another carriage would follow in an hour with changes of clothing, as well as the ladies' private maids.

The Wildes were going *en masse* to rescue Diana.

Not that she needed rescuing.

Hickett was standing next to a small carriage at the entrance to the courtyard, so North made his way through the crowd, Godfrey still clinging to him.

"North!" his aunt shouted.

He bent and deposited Godfrey on the seat and turned. "You'll be there in no time," Lady Knowe said, coming over to him. "If she's safe and well, don't make her stop simply because of fool ideas about what a lady can and can't do."

North gave his aunt—who had never, in his memory, paid more than lip service to ladylike behavior—a kiss and a nod before he climbed into the small carriage.

It wasn't easy to be in love with Diana, he thought ruefully. Not only could he not make her a duchess, but he couldn't stop her from barmaiding either.

They were trundling down the road in a minute; Hickett was obviously hell-bent on reaching Manchester before Diana wearied her arm drawing pints.

In fact, North wasn't worried . . . much. Diana was curious and impetuous, but she was also highly intelligent. He had a feeling she might develop an acute distaste for beer.

Godfrey soon fell asleep, so North occupied himself by imagining what the men gathered at the public house would make of Diana's delightful figure. And her voice. She had an elegant accent, as refined as any duchess's. Yet she spoke with a husky lilt that hinted at her irrepressible nature. She was a study in contrasts.

When they stopped to change horses, North left Godfrey nestled in a blanket on the seat inside, assigned the groom to sit next to him, and leaped up beside Hickett, taking the reins. He could drive faster than the coachman.

After another twenty minutes, he sensed that Hickett had something he needed to say. "You'd best make a clean breast of it," North advised, steering the phaeton around a slow-moving mail coach.

Hickett clung to the side of the vehicle. "Miss Belgrave isn't a barmaid. But she knows what it is to earn an honest wage."

"I agree," North said, leaving the mail coach behind.

"She's better off earning it in my sister's tavern than in some cottage of yours, my lord. If you want to let me go for saying it, so be it."

"'Cottage of mine,'" North repeated slowly.

"I heard as how you offered her three hundred pounds and a cottage. Mabel overheard it."

"Mabel misunderstood."

"Miss Belgrave, she isn't that sort. She's an innocent. Even Mabel wouldn't say anything about her that way. She tells the boy stories of his mother at bedtime."

"My offer to support Miss Belgrave implied nothing improper," North said, his voice turning frosty despite himself. Like his aunt, the coachman was merely expressing the protective affection that Diana inspired in everyone around her.

"You didn't just imply it," Hickett said flatly. "From what I heard, you said it out and out, *and* had her up against the door as well. You can't blame the girl for taking fright and running to Manchester. She can do better than that, my lord."

Better than you was the unspoken implication.

"She doesn't care to be your duchess," Hickett continued. The man really didn't know when to shut up. "Nor the other thing either. She won't marry you, but that doesn't mean she won't make some other man a good wife."

"A man she meets in the tavern?" North asked curtly.

Hickett narrowed his eyes. "There's many a man in the Beetle & Cheese who wouldn't make a lady an offer that's a disgrace to say aloud."

After that, North concentrated on driving.

Chapter Twenty-four

The Beetle & Cheese

The moment Diana took her place behind the bar, someone had roared, "Her Majesty's arrived!" With that, men crowded up to take a closer look. Given their greedy eyes, she was glad for every inch of the stout barrier between them.

Diana took a deep breath and addressed the man most directly in front of her. "What will you have?"

"Mumphss," he said.

"I beg your pardon?" she asked. His Manchester accent wasn't easy to understand.

"Mumphiskiss!" he repeated, with emphasis.

Diana poured the first ale that came to hand and pushed it across to him. He flipped a coin at her, which she put into a box behind the bar, as Mrs. Barley had instructed. Two more men were shouting and shoving farther down the bar, and someone to her right slammed a tankard so loudly that it made her jump.

She hurried to the other end of the bar and managed to serve the two obstreperous men. Then she ran back, summoned by the slamming tankard.

After two hours of this—during which she could scarcely pause for breath, let alone sit down to rest— she had a new, profound respect for barmaids. She had spilled beer down her front, which the men appreciated. Three or four of them were motionless on their stools, their eyes locked on her breasts. One of them kept shouting at her and breathing heavily through his mouth when he ordered, which rendered his demands impossible to understand.

At some point, her hair had come unfastened and fallen down her back. She let it go. She didn't have time to bother, not when she had to run back and forth along the bar, dodging to avoid grasping hands, pushing tankards of ale across, collecting coins.

She had no idea what she was meant to be charging. Mrs. Barley had gone over it quickly, but Diana couldn't remember what she'd said. As a result, she just said, "No change," over and over.

One customer, who informed her his name was

Harvey, kept his eyes glued to her breasts and his tongue plastered to the back of his front teeth. Every time she stood in front of him, he adjusted his breeches and eyed her like an obscene owl.

Mrs. Barley had been serving the tables. At some point, she raised an eyebrow, and Diana nodded, signaling she was finished. She pushed another tankard across the bar, as Mrs. Barley made her way across the room.

Her arms ached and—insult to injury—beer had soaked all the way through to her chemise. "I'm useless as a barmaid," she told Mrs. Barley, with a tired laugh. She used to think she was exhausted at the end of a long day in the nursery, but she hadn't truly understood the meaning of that word until now.

"It would have helped if you knew how to return change," Mrs. Barley said, smiling at her. "But you've kept the beer flowing, and it's given the lads something to talk about for many a day. I'm that grateful."

"Don't leave us, Your Majesty!" the men lined up at the bar shouted. They were the agreeable ones, with jovial rather than lustful eyes.

"I'll just run over to the inn and get one of the lads to help me for the rest of the night." Mrs. Barley rushed out the door.

Diana pushed open the half door that separated the

bar from the rest of the room. Harvey slid from his stool and shambled toward her.

"Good night," Diana said.

"It's going to be a good one for us, I promise you that." His speech was slurred but more or less intelligible.

"I beg your pardon?"

"Us," he said, reaching her side and wrapping his fat fingers around her arm.

Diana looked down at this trespass on her person. "Unhand me."

He guffawed. "You're as good as a play."

She did sound like a heroine in a drama. "Do you need me to say, '*Unhand me, Villain*'?"

"I like the way you talk," Harvey said, swaying closer so that his hot, beery breath washed over her cheek. "Fancy-like. I'm going to pretend I'm tupping the queen, you know? In fact, I might pay you more if you say some queen things."

"What are you talking about?" Diana snapped. "Let go of me this instant!"

That provoked another guffaw. "I paid for you, no time to regret now."

"You did not pay for me!"

"Oh yes I did!"

She laughed. "You're out of your mind."

"You took the coins yourself. You're paid for. Bought and paid for. Mine for the night. I want the queen."

"You are a disgusting little worm," she stated.

"That's right, Your Majesty," Harvey panted. "Everyone saw you taking my money." His grip on her arm tightened; she knew he would leave bruises—injury added to insult, rather than the other way around.

Across the room, the groom Hickett had left to watch her was rising to his feet, and the line of men at the bar had all swiveled around, but Diana believed she could take care of this boor herself. She reached out her free arm, picked up an abandoned tankard sitting nearby, and brought it down on Harvey's head.

"Hey!" he cried.

Huh. She would have guessed it would do more damage than that.

The door to the yard slammed open and a man came in with such speed that Diana saw no more than a blur. He caught Harvey by the shoulder, spinning him away with such force that the drunk flew over a table and slammed into the wall.

Her deliverer stood with his back to Diana, hands on his hips, surveying his handiwork. She blinked at him, her eyes moving from broad shoulders down to taut waist, dusty breeches, tall boots . . .

A gentleman's coat. *Not* a gentleman's body.

North.

He was blocking her view of Harvey swaying on the other side of the room.

"Who the hell are you?" Harvey slurred. "I paid for her. Paid for the night. Paid enough for a whole night, I mean."

A low growl came from North, potent and full of menace. Harvey's eyes widened and he fell backward a step. "Aw, bollocks. She's cheating on you? Belongs to a gent."

Diana stepped out from behind North. "I had no idea that you were overpaying for your ale."

North pushed her behind him. "There seems to have been a misunderstanding."

"I want *her* as I paid for. I even held back on the brew so I could do the deed!"

Diana edged to the side once again. "You could hit him again," she suggested to North.

He glanced at her, a flash of amusement going through his eyes. "I have your permission?"

"I didn't get to see it the first time."

"I wouldn't want you to miss the spectacle."

Harvey squeaked like the coward he was and started to move around the table between them. "Mayhaps there's been a mistake," he suggested.

"Oh, there has been," North assured him.

416 · ELOISA JAMES

"I can let the money go," Harvey offered.

"You can," North agreed. He reached out and dragged Harvey across the same table the man had flown over not two minutes earlier.

It was terribly primitive and ungentlemanly, and Diana had an impulse to applaud. Only, she told herself, because she had enjoyed boxing matches at the county fair, those her grandfather used to secretly take her to when she was a little girl.

Those no lady would enjoy.

"What's happening here?" Mrs. Barley cried, running in. "Here you all!" she shouted to the men who were standing around, enjoying the spectacle. "Why aren't you doing something?"

North grinned at her. "We're just cleaning some rubbish out of here, and we'll be on our way."

"Oh, you fool, Harvey," the lady said, folding her arms over her chest. "You've gone too far this time, you old dunce."

"I ain't a dunce," Harvey said indignantly.

"I would think very carefully and then apologize to the lady," North said, giving Harvey a shake, "because if you don't, I shall be obliged to satisfy her bloodthirsty desire to see you flat on your back again."

"I apologize," Harvey said quickly.

North pushed the drunk away. "I'm sorry to disappoint you, Miss Belgrave, but a gentleman always accepts an apology, however poorly it is expressed."

With this he turned to face Diana at last and opened his arms. "Did he injure you?" he asked, holding her tightly. "If so, I'll kill him."

"I'm unhurt," Diana said, contentedly leaning her head against his chest. "He has disgusting teeth, though." North smelled good and clean, like starch and safety, like expensive wool and the very best soap.

"I have to admit something," she told his coat. But this wasn't the place for a serious conversation. "I am not a good barmaid."

There was a moment of silence, and then a roar of laughter.

Chapter Twenty-five

North escorted Diana to the Beetle & Cheese's private parlor, where he had left Godfrey in Hickett's care. The boy slid from the coachman's lap and ran to Diana as if it had been weeks, not hours, since he'd last seen her.

North left to ask the innkeeper, Mr. Barley, to prepare a hot bath in his best bedchamber. He was talking to the man in the front entryway when two carriages drew up and a stream of Wildes poured out. Plus one laird.

"They are with me. We'll need a lot of tea," North said to Mr. Barley. "And food," he added, thinking of his younger sisters and brothers, who always seemed to be hungry.

Five minutes later, the room was churning with Wildes lamenting they'd missed seeing Diana draw pints. Lady Knowe was deep in consultation with Mr. Barley, who was insulted at the very notion they might retire for supper to the Royal George, and was promising a very fine roasted sirloin and some plump chickens.

"I neglected to tell you that we have an unexpected visitor," North said, making his way to Diana. "Miss Belgrave, may I introduce Diarmid Ewing, the Laird of Fennis, Godfrey's great-uncle?"

Diana's eyes rounded and she made a deep curtsy. "I'm honored to meet you, my lord."

"It's a true pleasure," the laird said. His eyes were gentle, but his voice was a burr accustomed to being obeyed. "My dear, we had no idea that Archibald had left a child. I gather that your mother felt it too disgraceful to acknowledge his birth. We Ewings would be happy and proud to welcome both of you to our family."

Godfrey grabbed North's hand, scowling up at the old Scotsman. He couldn't have made it clearer that he considered himself a Wilde.

"That is tremendously kind of you," Diana said.

North reminded himself that he had learned patience during the war, because it seemed remarkably difficult to keep silent.

"Miss Belgrave," the laird continued, "will you and

Godfrey come home with me? We'll be most glad to have you." He paused and looked down at his great-nephew, still clutching North's hand. "Though it might be that you have other plans."

Patience be damned. "I want to marry Diana," North said, adding, reluctantly, "however, she does not wish to be a duchess."

A high but firm voice cut across whatever Diana might have said in answer. "If my aunt doesn't want to be a duchess, then you shouldn't be a duke."

Diana let out a startled gasp, and Lady Knowe came out with "Bloody hell." A roomful of Wildes went silent perhaps for the first time.

North stared down at the little boy holding his hand. His mind reeled—not only because Godfrey had just uttered his first sentence, but because what he said was so simple.

And so *right*.

Out of the mouths of babes, indeed.

Diana fell to her knees. "Oh, Godfrey, you spoke!"

The laird chuckled. "On the way here, these kind people told me that you didn't talk, lad. I'm glad to find they were mistaken. It'll be easier to lead your clan."

Godfrey leaned into Diana's embrace, but he continued to stare expectantly up at North. The Wildes, even Artie, remained quiet. Astonishment and a heady feeling of joy spread through North's body. The solution was obvious, now that a little boy had revealed it. Of course he shouldn't drag Diana into a trap; instead, he should get himself out of it.

His father and aunt were regarding him with uncannily similar expressions. "I shall not be a duke," he said slowly, hearing the words come from his mouth as if spoken by another man.

Aunt Knowe's face creased into the biggest smile he'd ever seen, and she elbowed her brother. "It's called renunciation of the title," she said merrily. "We've been waiting for you to throw up your hands for, oh . . . five years now?"

The duke nodded, his eyes on North's face. Ophelia joined them, Artie on her hip. "Your father didn't feel it was right to suggest something so weighty. You had to say it yourself."

"I was getting desperate," his aunt said with a chuckle. "I was on the verge of joking in front of you about the Earl of Harebottle, that madman who renounced his title because he thought the stress of it was making him bald. And then he died without a hair on his head anyway."

North smiled at that as he helped Diana back to her feet. "Will you marry me, Diana, if I renounce the title?"

"You'd be giving up so much," she whispered.

She didn't say no.

"As it is, I would be giving up *you*, and you are worth more to me than forty dukedoms." Diana made a choking sound. He pulled her into his arms and clasped her as tightly as he could. She was *his*.

At this, the room burst into excited chatter.

"Alaric will do the same," Lady Knowe said to no one in particular. "No question about that."

"Well, *I'm* not taking the title," Leonidas announced, in the most decisive tone North had ever heard his young brother use. "I'll flee to Scotland and help Godfrey head the clan instead. Or open a tavern!"

"Erik wouldn't make a terrible duke," the duke said thoughtfully.

"Truly?" Diana whispered against North's chest.

"Yes," North answered, deep joy resounding in his bones. There was too much noise and excitement in the room; he walked his future wife from the parlor and out the front door into the courtyard.

It was dark, and the now-empty yard was illuminated by lanterns hanging from the stone walls.

"I've never heard of anyone giving up his place as heir," Diana said. "What if you come to regret it in a few years?"

"I promise you, I won't." He grinned down at her.

"Why would I want to be duke? Parth has turned my inheritance into an outrageous fortune. You and I can live like a duke and duchess, if we wish, but in private."

"I don't wish for that."

"I don't wish for more than you," North said.

Godfrey ran out the door, having followed them. Diana held out her hand to the little boy, but kept her eyes on North. "The odd thing is that I was about to tell you . . ."

"That you love me enough to become my duchess," he stated, giving her a kiss.

"You guessed?"

"I love you enough to give up the title, and you love me enough to take it on."

"I *will* be your duchess," she promised. "I'll be a good one too. If I can weather being an inept barmaid, I can certainly manage, at some point in the distant future, to be an inept duchess."

North looked down at Diana, her beautiful, impulsive face solemn and earnest, and bellowed with laughter. He scooped up Godfrey, who started laughing too, a spiral of boyish giggles that floated into the night air.

"Stop that, you two," Diana cried. "That was a heartfelt offer. It's possible I would be a *good* duchess. I just don't want to make promises I might not be able to keep."

"I don't want you to be an inept duchess," North said, catching his breath.

"You don't?"

"I want you to be next to me, to be my partner, not my duchess. I want to grow old with you, and love you, and argue with you."

He set the boy down and squatted before him. "You'll be my son, Godfrey. Is that all right with you?"

"Yes," Godfrey said, as nonchalantly as if he'd been speaking for years.

"We shall live in a different house, not the castle, but Artie can visit you."

"Yes."

Diana came down on her knees. "We will be a family."

A moment later, the door swung shut behind Godfrey, who was headed to the parlor with orders to be polite to his newfound great-uncle, and stay close to Artie and the duchess.

Diana wound her arms around North's neck. "You needn't give up the dukedom," she said. "I can do this. You know I can."

"I would hate being a duke." The rough emotion in his voice told its own story.

"But Horatius . . ." Her voice trailed away.

"You're a wonderful mother to Godfrey, but you

aren't the same mother that Rose would have been, are you?"

She shook her head.

"I tried to be Horatius, but it was impossible. Fortunately, my father was farsighted enough to have many sons. Erik is only eight, but he does have an air of command. He won't be Horatius, but he might take on the title in his own way."

"From a governess's point of view, I can assure you that Erik is quite devilish," Diana said.

"An excellent attribute for a future duke. I needn't renounce the title immediately; there's time for Erik to grow up as a normal lad, not the Marquess of Saltersley. Perhaps Alaric will decide that he wants to be Duke of Lindow. Perhaps Leonidas will change his mind. I don't care. I see no reason to formally renounce a title I never assumed until my father passes away, hopefully not for many years."

Diana's mind was clearly whirling with questions, but she smiled, came up on her toes, and kissed him. "I haven't answered that question you asked me."

Their eyes met and she knew there was nothing to tell him. He knew. He was her heart, and the joy she felt was as natural as the morning.

A number of kisses later, the innkeeper emerged and informed North that a steaming bath was waiting in his best bedchamber. They followed him inside. North stopped at the parlor, looking around the room full of people laughing, talking, and welcoming the Laird of Fennis to the Wilde family, until he caught his aunt's eye.

Lady Knowe grinned and nodded toward Godfrey, the boy whom he would soon adopt as his son. "All's well," she called.

Diana tugged on his hand, and he took a last look at the people he loved so much. And then turned away to follow the person he loved most of all.

Chapter Twenty-six

North carried Diana into the inn's best bedchamber in the middle of a kiss, managing to kick the door shut behind them.

Diana was having trouble breathing. Her lungs were moving in and out, but she was taking in *North's* air, and that made all the difference. Every touch of his tongue made her feel a shudder between her legs, a flare of heat.

"North," she whispered. "Does this mean that you will make love to me again?" His hand flattened and slid up to her shoulder, then down her back. "I want you," she said, telling him the truth. "I want you more than a bath."

He tipped up her chin, and his lips came back to hers. "Just so you know, I am kissing the *you* whom I know. The woman who hates wigs, wears no lip rouge, and knows nothing of peafowl. Who reeks of ale."

Her heart was breaking from the sweetness of it. She kissed him, rather than the other way around: licked his lips and welcomed his tongue, and wrapped her arms around his neck.

"You know what I wondered after you kissed me goodbye at the door of my chamber?" she whispered into his ear, a while later.

"What?" His voice had fallen to a growl, a hungry, male growl.

"Whether making love could be . . . . Can you do it standing up?"

He made a hoarse sound, and twirled around. He put an arm over her head, leaning against the wall. "The answer is yes."

"You just said I smelled of ale. I must have a bath first," Diana decided. "What's so funny?"

"You," North said, kissing her nose.

"I've just realized something."

"That you and Godfrey and I will travel to Rome, where we will conceive a little girl covered with freckles?"

"That there is one time in life when it is entirely acceptable to be spontaneous!"

Much later, Diana lay on her back, her head nestled

on North's shoulder. "It was shockingly difficult to be a barmaid."

"Harder than being a governess?"

"I am not fond of changing nappies," Diana said, considering it. "But managing whining children is easier than lustful men."

North rolled on top of her. "What about this lustful man?"

Diana looked up at him. North's warrior face was tired; he probably hadn't slept the night before. There were wrinkles at the corners of his eyes and a darkness in him that would lighten, but never leave.

He wasn't the perfect future duke, the fashionable gentleman in powder and patches, but he was so much more.

"I love you," she said, wrestling with a swell of emotion that made the words catch in her throat. "I love you enough to become a duchess, or a barmaid, or a governess. I would live with you in a hovel or a castle. There is one thing I do well: love you and Godfrey, so I might as well do that."

His eyes were dark and rawly possessive. "I won't let you be crushed by the title," he said, the words growling from his chest. She wound her arms around his neck. "You're perfect as you are, and you're mine," he whispered. "My wife, my love. I have a present for you."

North rose and went to a battered traveling bag the innkeeper had put in the chamber earlier that evening. Diana watched as he pulled it open and tossed a few nappies and a change of clothing for Godfrey onto the bed.

"How did you know to bring nappies?" she asked, her heart full. Most fathers wouldn't think of it.

He looked up at her, astonished. "Is Godfrey still in nappies? I asked Prism to make sure Godfrey had whatever he needed for the night."

"Only in case of accidents," Diana said, nodding.

North reached the bottom of the bag and carefully maneuvered out a box wrapped in a length of silvery blue fabric. He brought it back to her, his eyes wary. And hopeful. He put it in her lap.

Diana looked up, loving him so much it hurt. "A present?"

"From myself and Joan."

Joan? A present from his sixteen-year-old sister was unexpected. She stared down at it, instinctively stroking the lustrous silk "I've seen this fabric before," she whispered.

"I bought it from Mr. Calico," North said. "I tried to give it to my aunt, but she laughed at me. She knew it was meant for you."

Diana carefully unwrapped the silk and stared down

at the box. At one point it had been a plain wooden box designed for snuff; a slight scent of tobacco still clung to it. But now its lid was covered with arrogant paper aristocrats with slashing paper eyebrows and tall paper wigs.

All of them male.

All of them North, by the looks of it, and cut from the prints that made him notorious.

Diana laughed. At the very center of this array was the most amusing depiction of all: North, rising from a small trunk, his muscular, hard chest lovingly detailed.

"You look like a genie coming forth at a lady's command," she said, tracing the depiction of his chest with her finger. "A *very* nicely shaped genie, I must say."

"I prefer that idea to being likened to Shakespeare's rapist," North said. There was something guarded in his voice, a hint of vulnerability. He was not certain of her, Diana thought. Because she had refused him so many times.

"Is there another present inside?" She looked up, loving the angular shape of his jaw, the darkness of his blue eyes, the way he looked back at her. As if she mattered. As if she was the center of his world.

He nodded.

She opened the lid and saw a nest of blush silk, in the center of which lay a ring. Not the ring he'd offered her the first time: that one had been ostentatious, a duchess's ring.

This ring was plainer and, to Diana's mind, more beautiful: one simple ruby surrounded by diamonds. North sank to his knees in front of Diana and picked up the ring. "The color reminds me of your hair."

She looked at him, a smile wobbling on her lips.

"Will you marry me, Diana Belgrave? For better, for worse? In the face of illegitimate relatives and sleepless nights? I love you. I fell in love with you at first sight. I never stopped loving you, and I never shall."

Diana held out her left hand. He slid the ring on her finger. It fit perfectly. "The only thing I'm not afraid of failing at is loving you," she said, wrapping her arms around his shoulders. "Loving you is like breathing."

North arrowed his fingers into her hair and it spilled over his hands. "We needn't ever attend balls or pay morning calls."

Diana smiled, peaceful joy in her eyes. "You promised Italy and babies."

"You're mine, now," North said. "No running away, Diana."

She shook her head. "I will never leave you again. I was so angry at Rose for dying that it made me afraid to love so deeply again. But I trust you."

"You trust me to stay alive?" He kissed her gently.

"I can't promise to die after you, Diana. But I will love you until the moment I take my final breath. And if I go before you, I pray that your face is the last thing I see before I close my eyes. That sight will hold me until we meet again."

Blinding joy swirled through Diana, mixing with desire, and trust, and love. An hour later, she came back to herself, sweaty, pleasure-drenched. Her mind was foggy, but one question wouldn't go away. She rolled on her side and propped herself up on her elbow.

North was lying on his back, looking like a man who had everything he wanted in life. One arm was behind his head and the other hand was absently caressing the curve of Diana's hip.

"We'll go to Rome first," he said.

"North," she asked, "how did you manage to arrive at the Beetle & Cheese just when I needed you?"

Her fiancé's smile was still rare, and the sight of it lifted Diana's heart. "I thought I timed it perfectly."

"You were waiting outside, weren't you!" she cried.

"It's possible." He stole another kiss. "You're mine, Diana. I shall be ruthless in protecting you. But I will never crush you."

"You waited outside to see if I got in trouble?" Laughter poured out of her.

"If you had struck that drunk in the eye, I would

have waited longer," he said. "I must teach you how to fell a man with a tankard."

Diana leaned over, and his large hands lifted her onto his body. She shivered, enjoying the way her senses sparked to life. "May I request another demonstration of your concern for my happiness?"

"Yes," he said, keeping it simple.

Chapter Twenty-seven

Lindow Castle
June 4, 1780
The following day

"Mother, I have some terrible news," Lavinia said, once she had greeted Lady Gray and given her a pretty hat from Manchester.

Her mother put down the hat and dropped into her chair. "I know it already."

"You *do*?"

"Diana Belgrave has stolen Lord Roland from under your very nose. At this rate, you will be nothing more than an old maid, and my horrid cousin will have a duchess as a daughter!"

"I was not referring to Diana," Lavinia said.

Her mother put a drop of Dr. Robert's Robust Formula on her tongue. "What could be more important than the fact my daughter has bungled yet another chance to become a duchess?" She sighed and tipped her head back, closing her eyes. "What I would do without these drops for my poor nerves, I really don't know."

"My pearls have been stolen," Lavinia said bluntly. "The string I have are made of paste. My ruby earrings are worthless glass."

Her mother didn't respond or open her eyes. Lavinia picked up her hand. "Do you understand, Mother? I'm almost certain that your jewelry will be found to be counterfeit as well."

"Oh, they're long gone," her mother said, still not opening her eyes.

Lavinia's mouth opened in a silent gasp.

"I'll not forgive you for many a month for allowing Lord Roland to slip back into Diana's clutches," her mother said fretfully. "I thought the emeralds would give us time, but you were too selfish to choose one of those Frenchmen."

"Emeralds? What do you mean by that?" Lavinia asked. Neither of them had emeralds, to the best of her—

A terrible thought occurred to her. "Diana's emerald necklace," she breathed, feeling as if someone had struck her hard. "You took it? You—you *sold it*?"

Lady Gray sniffed, opened her eyes, and blinked at Lavinia. "How do you think we survived? It was only because we lived in France that I was able to keep the country house and the townhouse. We have no money."

She said it as casually as one might remark on the lack of good weather.

"What do you mean, we have no money?" Lavinia cried, springing to her feet.

Lady Gray waved her vinaigrette. "I mean just that," she said, in a familiar, tragic tone. Except this time, she wasn't complaining about coddled eggs or a chilly breeze. "We have no money. We are *destitute*."

"What happened? Did you—did someone persuade you into an improvident investment?"

"What on earth do you mean?" Lady Gray cried. "I hate it when you use large words, and you know it. We haven't had money for years."

"That's impossible."

"I took Willa in," her mother said. "An orphaned child."

Lavinia felt a sudden wave of sickness. "Please tell me that you didn't use Willa's inheritance."

"Use? I took care of her, as her parents asked me to do."

"Do you mean to say that Willa's inheritance paid for our servants, our clothing, our travel . . . everything? School? Carriages?"

"No one can say that I didn't do my duty by her, because she married the son of a duke. If you were a better daughter to me, and less selfish, you'd be engaged to the heir to the dukedom now, and none of this would matter. Why do you think I allowed you to leave Paris, where we were so comfortable, and come to Lindow Castle? You were supposed to marry the heir!"

"Oh, no," Lavinia whispered. Willa had no idea; she was certain of that. Lavinia had to tell her. Repay her, somehow. And she had to tell Diana, obviously. How on earth could she ever repay the emeralds? They had to be worth a king's ransom.

"After Willa married, Lord Alaric's solicitors wouldn't pay any more bills." There was a shrewish note in Lady Gray's voice, as if she believed Willa's estate should have kept sending money.

Lavinia looked numbly around her mother's bedchamber in Lindow Castle. The pretty, festive hat she'd purchased for her mother was one of three. The duke had paid for them, and she'd told him that Lady Gray would repay him.

"The question is, what are we going to do now?" her mother said. "If you hadn't been such a ninny, turning down those marriage proposals, you could be married by now and no one would know the difference!"

"My dowry," Lavinia said dully. "Do I still have one?"

Her mother hesitated.

Epilogue

Palazzo Wilde
Florence, Italy
July 3, 1784
Four years later

Diana walked out into the large enclosed garden behind the palazzo, and shaded her eyes against the bright Italian sun. North was supervising the completion of an octagonal wrought-iron pergola designed from his own sketch; a pair of workmen were presently perched atop of it, putting into place its crowning detail, a magnificent twisting finial.

For a jarring moment, she had a memory of years earlier: North in his wig, powder, and heels, versus the man who stood before her now. It wasn't just that

North's skin was golden from the sun, or the thin linen shirt hastily tucked into his breeches. Or that he wore a wig only if she made him.

Or even the bundle tucked in his left elbow, a bundle with a small fist waving in the air.

No, the difference was written plainly on North's face, and it was *happiness*. Happiness, it seems, isn't elusive. Not when you have a partner to laugh with, eat with, travel with, and sleep with.

A partner to love.

Her husband came toward her. "She's fine," he said. "Doesn't mind the banging at all. Rose is a true Wilde, as stouthearted as can be."

Diana took their baby, kissing her on a button-sized nose graced with three adorable freckles. Rose had her father's blue eyes, and her mother's hair, and a temperament so sweet that Diana swore she'd inherited it from her namesake, Diana's sister. The baby cooed in greeting before smiling so widely that dimples appeared on both plump cheeks.

Diana looked up from Rose and surveyed the pergola. "It's marvelous, North."

"It's almost complete," he said, pointing to the exuberant finial at the top. "This afternoon, they'll stretch the canvas roof, hang the curtains, and bring in the furniture."

"I still wonder if we should have chosen diaphanous silk, so the sunlight would filter through," Diana said. "I suppose we still might, if the curtains seem heavy."

She remembered why she'd come out to the garden. "Where's Godfrey?" she asked. "We've had a letter from Aunt Knowe, and Artie included an excellent watercolor depicting a fight between Fitzy and Floyd watched by the new finch family. Apparently the pair nested in the ivy outside the Prussian Dining Room again, and there are three baby finches this time."

North tipped his head back and called, "Godfrey!"

A pair of dirty legs descended through the thick foliage of a nearby plum tree, followed by the rest of their owner, and Godfrey dropped lightly to the ground.

"Artie sent you a painting," Diana told him.

He put a sun-warmed plum in her hand in exchange for the watercolor, then trotted away down one of the paths that wove through their garden.

"When he becomes the laird," North muttered, "he'll be a welcome change from all the chattering ninnyhammers leading the English government."

Their honeymoon trip to Italy had never ended. Now the family—larger by Rose and her three-year-old brother—lived in a graceful mansion near Florence's Piazza Strozzi that North had designed and built. Assorted Wildes were always presenting themselves; the duke and duchess had fallen into the habit of scooping up Artie and any other available offspring, and sailing to Italy every August. Naturally, North had foreseen this, and designed their home to be airy, beautiful, and large enough for any number of guests.

"Ophelia sent along three new prints," Diana said, leaning sideways to kiss her husband. "Poor Betsy! The gossipmongers simply will not leave her alone. I'm sure she doesn't do half the reckless things they claim."

"She probably does twice as many," North said, and returned her kiss.

Much later that night, Diana lay in the pergola, on a daybed covered with fine linen, a bottle of champagne within reach. A single lantern provided just enough light, and heavy silk curtains swayed in the midsummer breeze.

She now understood why the diaphanous curtains would have been inadvisable.

North still slept best outdoors, or at the least, with the windows wide open.

But this chamber was not designed for sleep.

A Note about Battles and Books

Too Wilde to Wed is my twenty-seventh novel. As that number has climbed, I've often been asked if I'm growing tired of writing historical novels. I'm happy to report that my answer is invariably no, because each novel brings so many firsts along with it, and because research is so engrossing. In the case of *Too Wilde to Wed*, I knew nothing of the Revolutionary War (having forgotten everything I'd learned about it in high school) until I decided that North would call up a regiment and embark for America, or the colonies, as a duke might refer to America at the time. The Battle of Stony Point proved a fascinating history lesson. I benefited from an illuminating e-mail exchange with Jim Piecuch, a scholar of the war, who explained how the prisoner exchange that took place after Stony Point would have been managed.

The young man who dove into the Hudson River and swam all the way to HMS *Vulture* in an attempt to save the British garrison was one Lieutenant Roberts; I gave his valor to North, but I want to celebrate him here. I also took inspiration from the commander whom General George Washington had chosen to lead the American attack, Major General Anthony Wayne, who sent a dispatch to Washington announcing that he'd taken the fort and garrison: "Our officers and men behaved like men who are determined to be free."

As well as being my twenty-seventh novel, *Too Wilde to Wed* is my first in which the heroine works as a governess. (*Seven Minutes in Heaven* doesn't count, as its heroine owns a governess agency.) I've had a weakness for this sub-genre ever since reading Mary Stewart's *Nine Coaches Waiting*, first published in 1958. Diana and North's midnight feast was inspired by a similar one in Ms. Stewart's novel, as those of you familiar with it might have suspected.

Last but not least, I must credit another mid-century novel for inspiring certain details of Lindow Castle and its grounds—although my homage was unconscious: T. H. White's delightful *Mistress Masham's Repose*. While writing the first book in this series, *Wilde in*

Love, I invented Lindow's ornamental lake, and island rotunda folly. At some point I decided that the rowboat I was describing should become a punt. During the revising of *Too Wilde to Wed*, my brilliant line editor, Anne Connell, sent me a description of White's "artificial emerald" island and its "plastered temple in the shape of a cupola, or rather, to give its proper name, of a monopteron." The island was accessed by a punt, not a rowboat. I realized that the many, many times I read that book during my childhood had sunk into the recesses of my imagination. I promptly reread it with my daughter Anna, and I urge you to seek it out. You're in for a treat!

HARPER LUXE

THE NEW LUXURY IN READING

We hope you enjoyed reading
our new, comfortable print size and found it
an experience you would like to repeat.

Well – you're in luck!

HarperLuxe offers the finest in fiction and
nonfiction books in this same larger print size and
paperback format. Light and easy to read, HarperLuxe
paperbacks are for book lovers who want to see
what they are reading without the strain.

For a full listing of titles and
new releases to come, please visit our website:

www.HarperLuxe.com

SEEING IS BELIEVING!

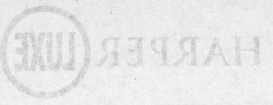